GOD HELP YOU . . .

"Did my father ever talk about any of us?" Jack asked.

The nurse's expression softened. "Yes. Sometimes, when things were slow. Sometimes he talked about your mother being gone. And of course, about your brother . . . how it worried him. How he wished he could give the boy a shot at a real life."

Jack couldn't look at her.

"He was proud of you, Dr. Harris. He said so, more than once."

Her comment loosened something inside him. "Why would someone kill my father, then make it look like suicide?"

"I don't know." The lie was in her eyes.

"But you met me here, where you knew we couldn't be seen together. There's something you're afraid of. What is it?"

"There are others." She lowered her voice. "That inmate you saw, the one with headaches . . ."

Jack's mind raced. "Havard?"

She nodded. "He wasn't the first."

"I don't understand."

It broke her nerve. She stood abruptly and stared at the door. She immediately began to collect the plates.

"I know why you came to Elrice. I knew it the minute I saw you. And I've been worried sick ever since." She walked a few steps, then turned back. "God help you if you find the answer."

MORTAL STRAIN

W. H. WATFORD

PINNACLE BOOKS
Kensington Publishing Corp.
http://www.kensingtonbooks.com

PINNACLE BOOKS are published by

Kensington Publishing Corp.
850 Third Avenue
New York, NY 10022

All Kensington Titles, Imprints, and Distributed Lines are available at special quantity discounts for bulk purchases for sales promotions, premiums, fund-raising, and educational or institutional use. Special book excerpts or customized printings can also be created to fit specific needs. For details, write or phone the office of the Kensington special sales manager: Kensington Publishing Corp., 850 Third Avenue, New York, NY 10022, attn: Special Sales Department, Phone: 1-800-221-2647.

Pinnacle and the P logo Reg. U.S. Pat. & TM Off.

First Pinnacle Books Printing: October 2002

10 9 8 7 6 5 4 3 2 1

Printed in the United States of America

For Jeannette—
the best thing that ever happened to me.

ACKNOWLEDGMENTS

I want to thank Frances and Eddie Pollock, who were cheerleaders from the beginning. I am indebted to Marlo Faulkner, Kathie Antrim, and Steven Hellman—good writers whose support and suggestions have meant much, to John Bretz and Tom Wooley for their keen reading skills, and to J. Claude Bennett, M.D., Ph.D.—teacher, researcher, and friend. Thanks also to Barnaby Conrad, Sol Stein, Walter H. Davis, Sid Stebel, Yvonne Nelson Perry, and Laura Taylor—gifted teachers who helped me become a better writer. And a special note of gratitude to Fred Klein, an accomplished man of books whose endorsement and encouragement have made all the difference.

I owe much of my understanding of prison life and the business realities of privately managed prisons to research done with the Florida Department of Corrections, the Georgia Department of Corrections, the Federal Bureau of Prisons, and Joseph T. Hallinan's excellent book, *Going Up the River, Travels in a Prison Nation*. However, my fictionalized account has taken liberties with both the prison world and the City of Atlanta, something I trust the reader will understand.

I'm also grateful to my editor, Ann LaFarge, for her insight and good suggestions that have made this a better book.

Lastly, to my agent, Elly Sidel, for her constant support, encouragement, advocacy, and friendship. No better match has ever been made between an agent and an author.

ONE

The metal door slammed behind him, effectively sealing Dr. Jack Harris in a secure compartment, the final checkpoint and last zone of guaranteed protection before he entered Elrice Prison. He took a hard breath and nearly choked on the sour taste. A pair of folding chairs had come to rest near a metal desk as if they'd been shoved back in anger, but no other clues remained to tell Jack what had happened before he arrived. He appraised the two guards, one male, one female, but there was little to be read from their expressions.

There were no windows or vents in the long gray room, and layers of old paint peeled from the effects of the oppressive Georgia heat. It was here that countless inmates had their introduction to the hellhole beyond the next door. In a place like this you did what you were told, but Jack tensed when the male guard began a strip search for concealed weapons.

The guard moved with the street attitude of a young thug, palming the gun in his holster and making no effort to wipe the sweat from his shaved head.

Jack stripped to his boxers, aware that his body was nothing to be ashamed of. He was just over six feet tall with blue eyes that women had talked about even when he was a boy. His jaw had strong angles like the other men in his family and his shoulders were broad from the years of working oil rigs before he entered med school. He kept his brown hair just long enough to bring out the waves in the back, and at moments like this—when he felt self-conscious—he could feel his mother quickly running her hands through his hair for good luck, the way some people touch a pregnant woman's belly.

He tried to ignore the female guard by the desk but there was something about the raw humiliation of the strip search that made him look at her. A part of him expected her to care, but she had dull eyes that didn't give a damn about him or any luck she might need some day. She just moved a little to get a better view. He braced himself for the inevitable questions about the scar on his back, but none came.

The skinhead finished most of the search, then pointed to the boxers. "Either I see 'em, or I feel around in there."

Jack glanced quickly at the woman, but she didn't flinch. When the man reached for some latex gloves, Jack stepped out of the boxers.

After the guard made him turn and part his cheeks for a visual inspection, Jack had to remind himself that he'd pursued this job on purpose. Two weeks ago he'd walked out of Garity Hospital in Atlanta, finishing his residency and leaving behind what the chairman of internal medicine felt would be a promising academic career. He'd been warned that taking this prison job would be a serious mistake, something that would mar his curriculum vitae for the rest of his life.

But this place had a claim on him. A claim that had changed his family forever, leaving him with nothing but questions—questions that had cut so deep they'd disturbed something in his core. Questions about his father, and how he had died. There were things opening in him since his father's death, things he didn't want to deal with. Things that wouldn't stay silent anymore.

They finished the body search and Jack got dressed. As he put on his shirt, the male guard held out his hand. "No pens."

Jack handed it over, upset at his mistake.

The guard checked off a list that confirmed he'd completed a thorough search, then looked up. "You'll write only in secure areas. They're in cages for a reason—the sooner you learn that, the better. They'll cut you with anything."

The lecture had its desired effect. He had been warned not to wear a tie, stethoscope, or any piece of clothing that a prisoner could use to choke him. He'd chosen his clothes carefully—khaki pants, blue blazer, and a new white shirt. The kind of clothes he'd never had until he was old enough to buy them for himself.

Jack had grown up in the wrong part of small towns, moving to wherever his father could find work. When his old man eventually landed the prison job here, the moving stopped. He had hoped that staying in one place would make things better, but trailer parks were about the same in Louisiana or Georgia, places where no one ever had the kind of clothes that needed to be dry-cleaned.

He'd grown up with people of the hard life. And as he watched the female guard unlock the door across the room, he realized he'd come full circle to the low end of society. Scholarships may have been his ticket out, but he'd still spent his summers working derricks in the Gulf of Mexico with the kind of people he was raised with—the kind who conquered each day with the force of their own labor. Looking back he knew it was only the thin line of fate that had kept him from landing in a cage like the ones on the other side of that door.

The woman guard relocked the door after they passed into a caged tunnel that spanned the indoor courtyard of cell block A. It reminded him of the style of zookeeping where the animals had free range and the people walked through paths encased in steel bars. But these animals stalked with sweat-carved muscles and were anything but tame.

Jack scanned the layout as the inmates were being corralled. The walkway ran perpendicular to the two walls of cells, each four stories high with forty cages to each row. The noise was deafening from men screaming their hate across the brick floor that separated the two high-rise battlements.

Just as Jack noticed that the guards had slowed down, the cell block chilled quiet and an inmate yelled, "Lookie, white boy. That cop check your ass in there? Gonna make some fine lovin'." He pumped his hips and the cell block erupted.

Jack stared straight ahead and kept walking. By the time they reached the end of the walkway, the entire cell block was whistling and jeering, some inmates grabbing their crotch, others pumping their granite arms through the bars with the threat of what they'd like to do to him.

The guard suppressed a smile and opened the next door, but Jack wasn't about to give him any satisfaction. He stared in the man's face until the guard spoke.

"We mostly get docs who've been pushed out of practice for one reason or another—coming out of rehab, stuff like that. Never had a young doctor work here."

Jack didn't lower his gaze. "What time are they expecting me?"

The guard looked him over and gripped the keys with his beefy hand. "Everybody's got a story."

Jack didn't move. "That doesn't mean everybody's got to know it."

The man's face hardened as if he wanted to make something of it, but knew he couldn't. Jack watched closely for any sign that the guard might have actually known his father, or might know the truth about his death. There was the official line, of course—a good man gone bad. But truth was a cheap commodity in prison.

The guard walked ahead and finally started talking. "We've got two clinics just off the cell blocks, and a small infirmary in a separate building. I was told to show you the infirmary first. Dr. Scalacey should meet us in about an hour."

Jack recognized the name from the list of medical personnel he'd been given. Scalacey was the doctor in charge of the clinic. Jack had asked around, but no one at Garity Memorial knew anything about him.

"Scalacey's an odd one. Not like any doctor I ever saw. Wears a ponytail and clogs. Comes and goes at all hours of the night. The physician's assistants never know when he'll show up for clinic. You ask me, the PAs do all the work and he just signs charts whenever he gets around to it."

Jack knew better than to rise to that kind of bait. They left the cell block and had to cross a hundred yards of dusty dead grass before they reached the infirmary. It was one of only three structures that remained from the original prison, most of which had been torn down to make room for the modern facility that now held over two thousand prisoners. The old buildings looked like a medieval fortress, made of stone the color of dried blood. The building ahead was close to the front gate and was familiar from his childhood, a distant memory of picking up his father.

Jack noted the fine detail of the crenelated masonry at the top where the stones crowned the building in a series of cubes, places where a child could imagine archers positioning themselves to attack would-be intruders.

Suddenly, a piercing alarm broke him from his memories. He stopped, almost by reflex, unsure if he'd done something wrong. The alarm was so loud he pressed his hands against his ears.

The guard stiffened, then looked at the guard tower. "Shit." The air telegraphed fear: the sound of men running, chains, the smell of dogs. The guard quickly checked his watch. "Come with me, and do what you're told."

The guard jogged ahead and opened the infirmary door. Inside, Jack could see men moving to what looked like a small but standard ER trauma room. Letters on their white jumpsuits identified them as trusties. One of them positioned the emergency "crash cart" near the head of the trauma table, then connected an Ambu bag to one of the oxygen tanks. Another man quickly grabbed a bag of sterile saline from a mesh basket and began to connect it to the IV tubing.

The guard moved directly toward a man who was in an intense phone conversation across the room. He appeared to be in his early forties, with a few gray hairs in his neatly trimmed beard. Jack read his nameplate and recognized the senior physician's assistant from the list he'd been given.

The man put the phone down and extended his hand. "I'm Bill Latham. Looks like we've got a baptism for you, Doc. There's one man down in the yard, maybe with a seizure, maybe with something worse.

The guard in the tower has already called an ambulance, but the count is down by two, so we can't open the gates for anything—ambulance included."

Jack's stomach hadn't been this tight since his first day as a student on his surgery rotation. "The count?"

"The guards count every camper four times a day, plus some extra counts at random. They came up short, so nothing comes in or out of this place until they prove there's no breakout."

Jack took off his jacket. "You got any scrubs?"

"Bathroom's over there." The PA pointed to the door close to the lounge. "They're in a cabinet, marked by size."

Jack grabbed a pair of scrubs, and couldn't help but notice the trusties had finished preparing the trauma area and were now standing at attention against the wall. The look in their eyes conveyed something that would stay with Jack for a long time—a sense of abject resignation. They had forgotten long ago what it meant to be men in the broad sense of the word. Right now they were numbers, and the count was down.

The noise outside the building came before Jack could change clothes. Seconds later two guards burst into the trauma room with a black inmate on a gurney. The man appeared to be in his midforties. His arms were tightly contracted against his chest with subtle twitching, but one leg jerked with violent repetitive spasms. His pants were stained where he'd lost bladder control, his facial muscles were in a constant tight grimace, and his eyes—which appeared to be jaundiced—were locked up and to the right. A fine layer of sweat covered his body. Jack recognized the classic signs of a grand mal seizure, and started barking orders.

"I need an IV with an eighteen-gauge needle, one

amp of D-50, and a gram of Dilantin. In the meantime, I want lab work for serum glucose, electrolytes, liver functions, and drug levels of any seizure meds he might be on."

Jack looked at the nameplates of the crew he hadn't met, and noted there was a second PA and an RN to help out.

The RN worked on the blood work and IV. Bill Latham turned on the wall suction and attached a hollow trochar to the tubing in case the man began to vomit.

Jack pointed at the junior PA. "Get me a list of his meds."

The PA got on the phone, then put the receiver to his chest. "No one's picking up at West Clinic. They're probably tied up redoing the count. I may have to go check the med list myself. Give me his number."

Latham looked up. "It's Otis Burke—a lifer. He's one of Dr. Scalacey's regulars."

The junior PA wrote down the name and left with one of the guards to get the records.

Latham suctioned some frothy saliva from the man's mouth. "All our blood work gets sent out. The results won't be back until tomorrow."

Jack accepted the news, then handed the thick premixed syringe of concentrated dextrose to the nurse. "Push that D-50 in case he's hypoglycemic, then give the Dilantin over a couple of minutes. We also need an EKG or some way to monitor his heart rhythm."

The other guard who'd brought the prisoner left, explaining that he had to help with the count. It cleared the way for Jack to move to the right of the man's body, the side from which all doctors are trained to examine their patients. Jack quickly unbuttoned the inmate's shirt. The man was all muscle and dirt, with a menacing cobra tattoo on his chest. The fangs were dripping blood.

The nurse finished the first injection and confirmed that the IV fluid was running well in the inmate's left arm.

Jack then bent closer and delicately ran his fingers behind the man's head and neck to check for blood or any other sign of trauma. Just as both of his hands were behind Burke's head, the man's right arm jerked up, catching Jack under the chin. In a split second that seemed like slow motion, Jack saw that the inmate's eyes were focused on his, and the facial contortions were gone.

A sharp metal point dug under Jack's chin and a burning stream of blood slipped down his neck. The inmate's other hand swiftly pulled the hair on the back of Jack's head. "Get the fuck out the way or he's dead."

Jack's neck felt like it was going to snap as he stared into the bright surgical light above. The inmate's arms were too strong for him to resist the pressure pulling his head back.

"I said *move.*"

Jack sensed that the others were backing away.

The only remaining guard was the one who'd performed the strip search. Burke told him, "Put your gun on the floor and kick it over here."

Nothing happened, and Jack's head was jerked back even farther. "I'll break this mothafucka's neck."

Jack heard the metal scrape across the tile floor, but Burke didn't reach for it.

The inmate's hot breath was on his neck. "Get me a car."

Jack heard Bill Latham's voice. "The count's off. No vehicles go in or out."

"Bring me a car or I'll drain this fucker right here."

The sharp point sliced harder, digging close to the base of Jack's tongue. He felt the blood soaking his shirt and chest. He tried to speak but couldn't.

Someone apparently made a fast break at the inmate, but Burke cracked Jack's head against the metal frame of the table, bringing a shattering pain to the base of his skull. His vision grew hazy for a few seconds but he could tell that the others backed off.

"I said car. Right now."

Bill Latham got on the phone and argued with someone on the other end until they finally got the message. He put down the receiver and spoke in measured tones. "It's coming."

"Bring it to the back of the infirmary, and I want both gates open out the front of this place. Tell those bastards in the towers that if they shoot I'll still have enough in me to cut this chickenshit to the bone."

Latham relayed the message, and argued into the phone. "Damn it, just do what I say."

Jack could imagine the guards rushing with rifles to whatever position they needed to take this prisoner out. He tried to reconstruct the layout of the prison from the minor tour he'd gotten this morning, but all he could think about was getting his carotid slit or being killed by a sharpshooter.

Jack lost all perception of time. He tried to ignore the pain, but the sharp blade continued to move ever so slightly with each breath, just enough to pierce a new wave of agony through his jaw. After what seemed an eternity, Latham indicated the car was in position.

Burke ripped out the IV but didn't bother to stop the blood from oozing down his arm. He pressed his teeth against Jack's ear. "I'm gonna get this gun. You move with me, but if you even jerk an inch I'll slit your fuckin' neck."

White-hot pain shot through the base of Jack's tongue as they moved together. For the first time he could see the other men who had backed against the cabinet wall.

"Now everybody in the back room."

After the others moved away Burke inched Jack back to the table and brought the revolver to his head. "Try anything and you'll be dead before you hit the floor."

The inmate removed the metal blade, making Jack bleed more, but he didn't dare touch the wound.

Burke shouted at the guard. *"You . . .* come out but lock everybody else in that room. I figure all the snipers will be on top of block C just waiting for me to come out back. But I ain't that stupid. Stick your shiny-ass head out there and tell them to bring the car to the front . . . doors open on our side. Then I want the driver to get the hell away. We going through that door, and you gonna be my shield."

Jack could see the resignation in the guard's face, but he followed the instructions to the letter. In less than a minute the car was at the front door.

Burke cocked the pistol. "The guard gets in the backseat and we get in the front. Now move."

Jack shuffled his feet sideways until they were at the front entrance. A concrete overhang protected them from any rooftop snipers. The inmate motioned for the guard to go out the door, and they moved with him. He could see that the officer's back blocked their only exposed flank.

Burke shoved Jack in the car and then crouched down on the floor of the passenger side. The guard dove into the backseat.

Burke kept aiming the gun at Jack's head. "Drive."

He put the car in gear, hesitating just long enough to see his way to the inner gate. There were no guards in sight. The gate was wide open, as directed, but he could hardly concentrate well enough to drive. His chest pounded with the certainty that bullets would rain down on them any minute. He floored it and drove as if he were possessed, believing that the snipers were a greater threat than the maniac next to him.

The inmate barked more orders. "Go left outside the front gate and drive straight till I tell you different."

Jack turned hard to the left after clearing the inner gate and sped through the more massive outer iron gates, turning left again onto the paved road. The large open fields outside the prison gave way to thick pine forest land. After a few minutes the woods thinned out and they began to pass an occasional shanty built on cinder blocks. He drove through a stop sign, praying that this little community had a speed trap. They flew past a corner Laundromat and small grocery store, speeding through a run-down neighborhood of narrow old shotgun houses with weak front porches and loose siding. Sirens could be heard in the distance, but they weren't close enough to be of help.

The guard sat up in the backseat. "You know they'll track us down. Give me the gun and they'll go easy on—"

The blast rang in Jack's ear. His heart raced and his fists tightened on the wheel before he could consciously interpret what had happened. In the mirror he saw the guard's blood hit the back window.

Burke was up in the seat screaming over the back, "You shut the fuck up, hear me, shut the fuck up. *You* did this to me. Just shut the fuck up."

Jack saw the gun shaking in Burke's hand, but it was from rage, not fear. They sped down the oak-covered street, past parked cars and bikes dropped in front yards. He stole a glance in the mirror and saw the guard had inched his way back into a seated position, his left hand pressing the bloody right shoulder. After a succession of quick glances Jack was satisfied that the bullet hadn't dropped a lung or severed an artery. But that was about all he could assume.

Burke sat with his back to the passenger door and pointed with the gun. "Turn here."

Jack turned right at a dirt path between the faded blue row houses. He had to slow down to navigate the trash cans and stair landings that emptied onto the shaded alley. The car whipped clouds of dust in their wake, coating the towels and sheets that draped from laundry lines strung between poles and back porches.

At the end of the long alley, two black men stood in front of a red Pontiac GTO that was blocking the road. They both wore sunglasses and dark muscle shirts. One quickly got in the driver's seat of the GTO and pointed a sawed-off shotgun through the open window. The other man was much larger, his arms covered with tattoos. He opened the back door of his car as a shield, then pointed a .357 magnum.

Burke glanced at the guard, then pressed the gun in Jack's side. "Stop here."

The dust caught up with them. Burke jumped out, then aimed at the guard. "Get out."

The guard struggled but got out of the car on his own. Jack went for his door handle, but Burke motioned with his gun. "Not you. Just him."

Jack could see about a half inch inside the steel barrel of the gun staring at him through the passenger window. He sensed the guard moving closer to the GTO, but he couldn't take his eyes off the small raised sight on the end of the gun. Burke slid into the backseat. "Gimme the keys."

Jack saw the guard being shoved into the back of the GTO. Blood from his arm trailed him like dirty coins in the alley. Jack knew this was it. He became hyperaware of everything . . . the coolness of the keys in the hot car, the white dust thinning in the air. Matted cords of dried blood caked under his jaw and pain burned to the base of his tongue. He held the key ring over his shoulder, but kept his eyes on the drooping elephant ear plant that touched the front edge of the car.

Burke eased close enough to grab the keys. The driver of the GTO yelled, "Do it. We gotta go."

Jack turned toward Burke, but the inmate shoved his shoulders, forcing him to look ahead. The blow was a cracking pain at the back of his head. The world went black before his face hit the steering wheel.

TWO

Before he even opened his eyes Jack felt the tape that strapped his head in place. The tight space was a haze of dark metal that curved around him like a drum. His eyes could only make out a few inches above and below his face, and it seemed that the silo was closing in on him. He tried to reach his hand up to pull free of the tape, but his wrists were tied down. His body moved an inch and a loud banging noise pounded from all sides.

"Just one more minute and we'll be done." The distant voice was sterile but efficient.

It was a girl's voice. His mind drifted to a childhood image. He could see her as she ran around the back of her house. She was gone by the time he got there.

A hand touched his right leg and his body moved out of the dark tube into the bright lights of the X-ray room. Someone untied his hands and pulled him to another bed. He heard metal creak and lock in place before they began to move.

The light burned, so he closed his eyes and slipped back into his bed at home, when he was a boy with pictures of the Apollo rocket taped to the bottom of the bunk above his. His younger brother jumped down from the top bunk and ran down the length of the mobile home. Ed was out the door with Jack's best pocketknife before he could catch up.

The gurney bounced over the floor gap and seconds later he could feel the bed dropping in space. Jack tried to focus on the picture ID of the fat girl standing next to him. They stopped twice before he felt the stretcher bump off the elevator. Large red rectangular signs drifted overhead, but he couldn't seem to keep focused on much of anything.

The light became brighter and the noise picked up as the gurney returned to the emergency room. He heard metal rings slide as someone pulled the curtain around his cubicle, but soon a hand pulled the curtain open again. Jack knew the face.

Dr. Daniel Linh slid onto the metal stool by Jack's gurney. He had jet-black hair, a tan complexion, and intelligent eyes. His parents had escaped from Vietnam near the end of the war only to spend the next two years in a relocation camp. They wanted their five sons to grow up as respected Americans, so they named each after traditional American heroes. Daniel Boone Linh and Jack Harris had known each other in med school and later shared a rental house during their residencies—Jack in internal medicine, and Dan in pathology. Dan was one of the smartest people Jack had ever known, and now was on the faculty at Garity Memorial. Shortly after they met Jack gave him a coonskin cap, which now hung inside the door of Dr. Linh's small office.

He felt Dan's hand tapping his face. He struggled for a minute and finally began to focus. He looked around the cubicle and saw the IV bag above his right shoulder. The tubing was buried under gauze wrapped around his wrist. Someone had yet to clean up the mess from a surgical tray on a stand near the

foot of the gurney. Discarded sponges soaked with or-
ange-brown Betadyne were piled next to the stainless
steel pan. A used pair of sterile gloves was clumped on
top of the instruments.

Jack tried to sit up on his elbows but the room
started to spin. He lay back too fast and felt something
hard against the back of his neck. He ran his left hand
over his face, then felt the bandage that ran under his
numb jaw. Most of it was protected by a hard plastic
cover. He closed his eyes and finally conjured the
words—*neck brace.*

"You better take it easy, man." Dan was putting a
cold compress on his forehead. "It's a good thing
these nurses liked you on your ER rotations. It's
busier than hell today, but they took you right in.
They got Wiggins to sew you up."

Jack heard the words slip through his ears but
couldn't retain them. His brain was sputtering to regain consciousness, and different signals from his
body were starting to fire. The back of his head felt as
if a horse had kicked him, and his mouth had the
taste of old blood. He'd had his share of fights on the
oil rigs, and knew what a punch in the teeth felt like
the next day. But he didn't remember any fights. He
looked at Dan and the IV bottle, and for a moment
wasn't sure if he was in Louisiana or Georgia.

"There are some police officers who want to talk to
you when you're awake. Just tell them you don't remember anything. You don't need any hassle right
now. You can talk later."

He remembered the red GTO a few feet in front
of the car. He was behind the wheel. The black guy
was pointing a shotgun. Then he woke up here. He
looked at Dan and tried to talk but his tongue was
numb and felt about five sizes too big.

"You're gonna be OK. The MRI looks fine. No neck fracture. Just a concussion."

There was a tug on the IV and a nurse moved away from the gurney. Jack tried to open his eyes but all he could see was two suns on the back of his eyelids. The suns moved together and became one. One surgical light. Then nothing.

Jack woke in a semiprivate room with his head pounding. The other bed was neatly made up and Dan Linh was resting on top of the covers. Through the blinds it appeared to be nearing nightfall, but his watch and the rest of his clothes were missing. He sat up and Dan came to his bedside.

"You've never looked better."

He felt the bandages. The neck brace was gone but his chin and tongue were still numb from the local anesthetic. "What time is it?"

"Seven-thirty. You've been in here since about noon."

He pointed. "Help me with this thing." Dan lowered the rail and Jack put his legs off the side of the bed. "I've got to get Ed."

"He's taken care of." He took a note from his pocket and checked a name. "Elaine somebody, from St. Michael's Episcopal Church, came by and said she was taking him to her place for the night. She obviously knew all about him, so I figured it was OK. Cute girl—I should be so lucky."

"Elaine Thomas. She runs a reentry mission to help ex-cons stay out of prison. Ed's occupational therapist got him a job washing dishes in their kitchen."

"She was real worried about you, but you couldn't have visitors."

"She's great with him, but he can't stay at her place."

"If I didn't know better, I'd say you're jealous."

"I see her when I drop Ed off, and when I pick him up. We've talked some."

Dan stared him down.

"What?"

"She shows up worried about you and knows Ed well enough to take him home and all you say is 'we've *talked* some'? You been holding out on me?"

"So I've been waiting for the right time to ask her out. No big deal." He struggled to stand.

"Look, tough guy, this isn't one of your rugby games. You better lie down. You don't look so good."

Jack leaned against the bed. "I don't think it's a good idea for Elaine to be alone with him. He doesn't have a lot of control. Plus, he's a lot stronger than she knows."

"Tell me about it."

Jack knew that he understood. He had Dan had shared a house until Dan started on staff in the pathology department, but neither of them had bargained on Ed's arrival. Ed had suffered a closed head injury at age eighteen that left him with the mind of a child. It was like having an autistic teenager around the house, but there wasn't much Jack could do—Ed had no one else.

Jack said, "You know how important routine is for Ed. Elaine won't be able to handle him if he gets scared. And it's not like his hormones quit after the accident. I better go."

Jack dragged the IV pole and opened the closet. What little strength he had seemed to drain out once he stood. He leaned on the door a few seconds, then threw his clothes on the bed. Once he was sure of his balance he unsnapped the hospital gown.

Dan was in his face. "Are you nuts? You've lost a lot

of blood . . . your crit's down to thirty. And there's no way you're going to drive on all those meds."

Jack put on his pants.

"Even if we got Ed home, you couldn't watch him."

He worked on his socks and shoes. "That's where you come in."

"No way. You're not checking out of here."

Jack opened the door. There was an empty chair in the hall just outside his room. The nursing desk down the corridor to his left was a hive of activity. To his right the overhead light was burned out between his door and a small waiting area at the end of the hall. The elevators were by the nursing desk, but the stairwell was almost directly across from his room. He noticed two muscular men in suits get up from the cushioned bench in the waiting area.

Dan peered out behind him. "There was a cop in that chair. We told him you wouldn't be available to talk until the morning." He pointed at the two men. "They're probably press. The administrator told them to wait in the lobby, but you know how they are."

"Why all the attention?"

"You better come back in." Dan locked the dead bolt and helped him to the edge of the bed. "Do you remember much about the escape?"

Jack told him the highlights, up to the point of being knocked unconscious in the car.

Dan paced. "I don't know the details . . . I've been with you most of the day. But it's all over the news. They killed that cop. I'm sure that's what they want to talk to you about."

Jack looked away and a sick feeling welled up. There was a firm knock at the door.

Dan moved closer. "This is Dr. Linh. What do you need?"

"I work for Mr. C.W. Richardson. He asked us to stay here until we found out about Dr. Harris."

Dan looked to Jack for an explanation. "*You* know C.W. Richardson?"

Jack just stared at the closed door. Richardson was a self-made billionaire and one of the most recognizable men in the country. He was an icon in the financial community, with business interests all over the globe. The fact that he preferred to do business from his sprawling estate south of Atlanta was but one of the quirks that often made its way into the press.

"The prison is privately managed," Jack said. "He owns the company that runs the prison and the clinic. In a sense, he's my boss." He eased back on the bed. "I guess we ought to let them in."

Dan unlocked the door and stepped back far enough for the two bodybuilders to fill up the room.

One of the men shook their hands and said, "I'm Vic Caster. Mr. Richardson sends his best wishes for your recovery." He had a tendency to twitch his massive neck as if his collar was too tight. "He was hoping to meet with you as soon as possible."

Dan stepped closer. "Dr. Harris isn't up to a meeting."

"You made it to the door OK. Besides, we figure you've got to do something about your brother. Maybe we can help."

Jack shot a glance at Dan, then to the two suits. "What's my brother got to do with this?"

Caster lifted his hand. "Mr. Richardson takes pride in knowing about his employees. He only wants to be sure that you are all right. We've been sent to help out. But he would like to see you this afternoon." He paused, then added, "Mr. Richardson isn't used to being told no."

Jack didn't like the thought of Ed being mixed up with these people. "How do you know about my brother?"

"Elaine Thomas at St. Michael's. You used her as a reference. Mr. Richardson always checks references."

He looked at Richardson's men. If they knew about Ed, he wondered how much they actually knew about his father. He didn't like these people knowing so much about his private life, but there wasn't much he could do about it. "Take me to get my brother; then I'll go with you."

Dan shot closer to the bed. "You are *not* leaving this hospital."

"Well then, you take me to Ed."

"I can't do that."

"Then I'm going with them. Square things for me here. I promise I'll come back after I get Ed taken care of."

Before Dan could say anything Jack ripped the tape off his right arm and pulled the IV catheter out. He slid his shirt on and held pressure to stop the bleeding. "Let's go."

Jack and Richardson's men walked down one flight to avoid a scene with the nurses, then took the elevator the rest of the way. The lobby of Garity Memorial was dingy and poorly lit. There was a permanent aura, as if dirt had long ago been waxed into every visible surface. Old people sat in chairs along the periphery of the lobby, waiting for their name to be called, or pretending to wait so they could get out of the heat. A teenager wandered about in baggy jeans that hung on his thin, bony hips. In the corner a bag lady stared at the floor and combed her long hair with her fingers. Jack had walked the lobby more times than he could count, and it always had the same atmosphere—different people filled the slots but the essence never changed.

He could hear the deep rumble of the interstate as they approached the doors of the city hospital. The thick humidity coated them as soon as they got outside. A homeless man in dirt-brown clothes slept on the concrete walk with his body rolled against the hospital. He was only a few feet from a black stretch limousine that was guarded by a tough-looking teenager leaning against the hood. Caster ignored the homeless man and handed the boy a torn fifty-dollar bill. The teenager matched it to the other half from his pocket, and stepped away, saying, "Any time, gentle-men. Any time."

Jack eased into the back of the limo. The other men sat up front and the car made a U-turn and headed south under the maze of concrete interstate bridges.

Jack suppressed a wave of nausea and looked through the glass partition that separated him from his escorts. After the limo cleared the edge of the downtown business district, it appeared to be headed for Turner Field, the new stadium that had been built for the Olympics, and which was now the Braves' home ballpark. Traffic was still heavy on most streets, but the stadium was only five minutes away and was easily seen from this side of town. Jack knew the Braves were in Chicago for three days before returning for a home stint with LA on the weekend. The stadium would be deserted.

The driver picked up a cell phone, and the conversation was over in ten seconds. Caster pointed from the passenger seat. Jack followed the direction of his outstretched arm and saw the black helicopter at the far edge of the stadium parking lot. The helicopter rotors were turning by the time the car reached the entrance of the empty lot.

Once the limo parked within safe distance, Caster got out and opened the back door.

Jack didn't budge. "I thought we were getting my brother first."

Caster twitched his neck again. "Mr. Richardson has a very tight schedule tonight. We'll get your brother after your meeting."

Jack watched the rotors blur. They had him. His car was still at the prison. Without them he didn't have a chance of getting to his brother. "I want some kind of guarantee."

"We're gonna be late."

Jack shook his head.

"I don't know how to give you no guarantee. Two hours, max. Then we take you wherever you want."

Jack could tell it was as good a deal as he would get. He nodded to Caster, who in turn nodded to the black helicopter. "Keep your head down, please."

Jack was careful not to stand too fast, but he still had to brace against the car to keep from collapsing. The muggy heat penetrated the thick bandage under his jaw and he began to perspire almost immediately. The helicopter's turbine engine had a high-pitched whine and the rotors were just a blur. Jack reached for Caster's arm, and they walked together against the hot wind that whipped off the concrete.

Caster helped Jack into the seat belt harness, then sat in the cockpit with the pilot, who wore a headset on top of a black baseball cap with a Richardson Enterprises logo. The pilot's only acknowledgment was a quick glance, apparently to confirm that everyone was buckled. The walls of the passenger section were tufted white with a few dozen examples of the same logo, which consisted of the initials CWR embossed in gold over a globe. Thick ropes reached out to encircle the earth, an obvious reference to the scope of Richardson's domain. The words *Richardson Enterprises* were written in handsome lettering under the globe, as if the man had renamed the planet.

On the far wall was a handsome burlwood box holding cut-glass decanters. A small color TV in the upper left corner was picking up a program on the stock market. The sound was off but he could read the list of today's winners and losers.

Just before the helicopter lifted with a smooth swoop, nose down, the TV was automatically changed to a closed-circuit view of the parking lot taken from under the nose of the cockpit. Jack could see the limo for just a moment as they quickly ascended in an arc. In seconds they were moving eastward, crossing another interstate, flying parallel to the airborne lanes of jets coming in and out of Hartsfield International Airport several miles to their right. Jack found himself alternating between the TV image of the streets below and the panoramic view of city lights out his window. Most of downtown Atlanta was new enough to have a crisp look to its skyline. It was a vista that highlighted the pulse of this new city of the South, one that masked the world of cons and ex-cons who seemed destined to flow through his life.

Once they cleared the city, the TV image changed to a blue screen with the temperature, their altitude, speed, and global positioning coordinates. Out the window were miles of dense pine trees interrupted by subdivisions that became less and less frequent the farther they flew. Then the screen and passenger cabin went black.

The darkness unnerved him. All he could sense was

the rhythmic pounding of the rotors, just as it had been three years ago, when he and Ed were strapped side by side in gurneys. He'd been sedated, but could still hear the blades and feel the air ambulance being tossed about by the turbulence. The accident on the derrick had taken a chunk of muscle off Jack's back, but Ed's skull had careened off a lateral pylon. In that helicopter, even sedated, Jack had feared that his brother was dying on the gurney next to him.

He found a switch and turned on a small overhead light. Jack thought about the decanters. A shot of bourbon would calm his nerves, but he worried that it would knock him out, and he had to stay awake long enough to find Ed. The thought of getting to Ed became the rope he held on to during the flight. He was doing this for him.

It was a long twenty minutes until a clearing of several thousand acres appeared in what seemed to be the middle of timberland.

A stone estate rose from accent lights on the crest of the compound. It reminded him of an old English manor house. Jack counted eight chimneys. Behind the house, a broad stone landing surrounded a swimming pool big enough for a country club. The long driveway opened onto a cobblestone circle at the front.

As soon as they touched down, Caster got out and opened the passenger door. The turbines were so loud he just motioned for Jack to get out and keep his head low.

A tuxedoed man was waiting in an extended golf cart at the edge of the helipad. Jack followed Caster, and sat in the second row. As he expected, the Richardson Industries logo was on the seats and steering wheel.

From here he could see a garage and two smaller houses to the left. Farther down the road were horse stables next to a large dark field. They drove along a path next to the main house and stopped at the foot of wide steps that led to a balustrade porch. Jack's legs felt like wet paper as he tried to keep up.

Just as he reached the others, a butler opened the door. The foyer was a massive open space of polished marble. In its center, a glistening chandelier was suspended over a round walnut table. Jack couldn't help but notice the letters CWR engraved on the silver vase holding cut flowers.

Jack leaned against the table to collect his strength while the butler disappeared down the long hall to their left. The man soon returned and nodded.

Caster checked his tie. "Mr. Richardson will see you now."

Caster opened double mahogany doors that had the deep luster that comes from years of daily care. They crossed the long room and waited in front of a large antique desk. They faced the back of Richardson's leather chair, but no one said a word.

Jack heard the keystrokes of a computer coming from the other side of the chair, so he edged around just enough to see that the screen was filled with streaming quotes from the Tokyo Stock Exchange. He smiled, recognizing the classic power play—*let them dangle awhile.*

Before he signed on at Elrice, Jack had the hospital library run a search for articles on Richardson, and came away with three pages of references in the last five years alone. He tracked down every one and devoured the articles so he could size up the man who would be pulling his strings.

The oldest write-ups could be best characterized as blatant hero worship, the kind that might have been produced by one of Richardson's media holdings.

One even featured a picture of Richardson riding with the president of the United States in the presidential golf cart. But more recently a few articles showed up that were highly critical of Richardson's tactics. A lengthy feature in the *New York Times* was laced with stinging criticism of the working conditions of his "paid slaves" in sweatshops in India and Central America. His empire cast a long shadow, but it was obvious that he hadn't gotten where he was without making some fierce enemies.

The typing stopped and the chair spun around. Richardson had a big man's frame and looked overweight in spite of it. He had the tan of affluence, with neatly cut graying hair, which was combed straight back. He wore a dark three-piece suit with a key chain across his vest. No sooner had he turned around than his expression changed to a relaxed smile. He held both French-cuffed arms out, but didn't stand. "Thank God you're all right."

Jack was expecting a number of possible introductions, but that definitely wasn't one of them. He noticed that Caster and the butler had slipped away.

"Please, Dr. Harris, have a seat."

Jack sat down in a chair that faced the desk.

"Would you care for a drink?" Richardson waved a hand toward a table with a row of decanters.

"No, thank you. I'm a little weak as it is."

Richardson's eyes scanned something on the desk, and his countenance changed. He turned the memo over, then looked up as if the document were nothing more than a transient interruption that was now far from his mind. "Thank you for coming. This has been a black day—for both of us. Two of my employees taken hostage, one murdered and the other assaulted with the intent of murder . . ." He rested his wet brown eyes on Jack. "I believe in loyalty, Dr. Harris. I am loyal to my employees." He controlled the silence, then spoke. "Tell me, are you a loyal man?"

Jack could feel the seduction of a practiced deal maker. Richardson was one of the richest men in the world, but in that second Jack knew him for what he was. He'd seen enough tough guys on the oil derricks to know the price of loyalty. "That depends."

Richardson sat up. "On what?"

"On you."

After several seconds of silence Richardson gave a faint smile. "Quite right, Doctor. Quite right."

Jack sensed movement behind him.

Richardson looked up. "I have some people I'd like you to meet."

Three well-dressed men joined them as Jack stood. "This is Dr. Hugo Voss, the director of medical services of Richardson Enterprises."

They shook hands. Voss was tall and trim, with thinning blond hair and northern European features. The round lenses of his glasses were suspended by thin gold frames. Jack guessed that he was probably in his late fifties.

"Behind him . . ." Richardson waited for the congestion around the chairs to clear. ". . . is Harold Mason, our director of security." Mason's handshake was firm and he held it longer than necessary. He was average height with a thick neck and muscular shoulders. His nose had the broad spread of an old fracture. His suit was well cut, but Jack figured he'd be more comfortable drinking a cold one and watching the fights. Mason handed him a business card with the phone number 1-800-RICHARD.

"And Dr. Felix Scalacey, the senior physician at Elrice."

Scalacey was probably in his late forties, too old to get away with the ponytail. He had a drawn face with a frame too thin for a man in good health. He looked more like a burned-out roadie than a doctor. Jack couldn't help noticing that he wasn't in clogs.

Scalacey held out his veined hand. "Sorry we weren't able to meet at the clinic."

Jack said, "I got detained."

The others smiled awkwardly, but no one laughed.

Mason put a folder on Richardson's desk. The others sat while Richardson lifted a series of eight-by-ten glossies from the file. Richardson nodded; then Mason brought the folder to Jack.

"Mr. Mason has extensive contacts. These are police photos taken earlier today."

Jack hesitated, but it was obvious that the show was for him. He opened the folder then immediately closed it.

"I apologize. I should have warned you."

Jack opened the folder again. The first photo was taken in what appeared to be the inside of a barn. Tied with his hands behind his back, around a center post, was the bald guard who'd taken him on the prison tour that morning. A rope around his ankles and another around his bare chest kept the body partially upright against the post. The bullet entry wound in the right shoulder was close to the arm, and a wide stream of dried blood ran down his arm and chest.

The second photo was a close-up. The guard's head was down, with the number 2 carved on the left chest. The next was a detail of the number. The laceration didn't appear to be excessively deep, but, oddly, had caused a lot of blood loss. On the first picture the lines of dried blood fell well beyond his belt.

The next few glossies were close-up views of whip

marks on the guard's back with extensive bruising, something Jack wouldn't expect to show up right away. The last was a detail of what appeared to be a small puncture wound in the man's left forearm.

Mason spoke from behind Jack's chair. "The police found an elastic tourniquet near the body. The initial assumption is that the guard was killed by an overdose. We don't know any further details yet. I'm sure the toxicology reports will be expedited."

Mason picked up the folder and offered it to Hugo Voss, who shook his head. Mason returned to his seat with the file.

There was a stunned silence until Richardson finally stood and walked to the tall window that overlooked the pool. "As I said before, I am a loyal man, Dr. Harris." He turned to face them again. "That could have been you in those pictures."

Richardson paced a moment, then stood behind his chair, with hands framing the top edges. "You signed on to help one of my companies, and it nearly cost you your life. What I'm about to say to you is for your peace of mind only. If it is repeated, I'll deny that this conversation ever took place. My colleagues will deny that this meeting ever occurred."

Jack shifted in his chair, more aware of a dull throbbing under his tongue.

Richardson sat behind his desk. "Suffice it to say that I have resources that far outreach the capabilities of the police. They are encumbered by the rules. I am not."

Richardson glanced at Mason. "We will find the prisoner who did these things. I wanted you to know that you will be protected by my people until that man gets what he deserves."

The room felt like a tomb. Jack's mouth had gone

dry and the pain was spreading into his neck as the effects of his earlier medications wore off.

Mason leaned in his chair. "We need to know everything you can remember about the prison escape. The more we know, the better. Little details, the works."

Jack looked around the room and at the men before him. What was it they were willing to do? He *had* been attacked today while surrounded by a few hundred armed prison guards, and look what good that had done. He thought of the pictures in the file. Richardson was right. The real world didn't work like the civics books. Those men had killed the guard. Just because the prisoner chose to knock him out instead of killing him in the car today didn't mean that the other two wouldn't come after him later. He was a witness, and could tie these men to the guard's murder.

Dr. Voss brought a glass of bourbon on the rocks and put it in Jack's hand. "I would like to suggest that anything you say to the press will help the fugitives more than it will help you." He patted Jack's shoulder twice. "Take your time, and tell us whatever you remember."

Richardson watched the helicopter's lights lift as it flew Jack Harris over his mansion. He turned from the window and looked at his well-paid employees, who stood like dutiful soldiers on the other side of his desk. Richardson walked to the bar and poured himself a finger of hundred-year-old scotch, but didn't offer it to the others, then walked around his office with slow, deliberate steps and sipped from his glass.

He looked at Harold Mason. "Tell me what we know about him."

"I have our best contact working on his background. Of course we only learned about the need for information a few hours—"

"Don't give me any excuses, Mason. What do you have?"

Mason glanced at Voss but there was no help offered. "He's industrious and exceptionally smart. National Merit Scholarship paid for college, worked summers on some oil rigs to pay for medical school. He did an extra year of internal medicine as chief resident. The chairman of his department at Emory wrote a letter of recommendation noting that his National Board scores were in the top one percent in the country."

Mason cleared his throat. "We expect to learn more about—"

"Damn it, I'm not a fool. I read his application *and* the letters." Richardson flipped pages in a rage, then threw them on his desk and jabbed his finger in Mason's chest. "I don't want a résumé, I want to know where he's vulnerable. And you're going to find out, or I'll find someone who will."

Richardson stalked the floor and spun a globe, watching the blur of the continents for nearly a minute before speaking in a calmer voice. "Dr. Voss, what's your opinion?"

Voss touched the edge of his wire-rimmed glasses. "I'm quite impressed. We've been waiting for a breakthrough, and perhaps this is it. He could be very useful."

Richardson stopped the globe with his palms. "He's perfect."

THREE

It was nearly nine-thirty by the time the helicopter returned Jack to the deserted stadium lot. The effects of the bourbon at Richardson's house had made it difficult for him to stay awake until a summer storm tossed the helicopter during their approach to the unlit landing site beside Turner Field.

The limousine driver met them with an open umbrella and escorted Jack to the back of the waiting limo. The gusts from the chopper blew sheets of rain on Jack's pants as he hurried to the car. Just after everyone was inside, the blades picked up speed and the whole car rocked from the force of the helicopter's lift.

Jack looked for an intercom, then tapped on the glass divider that separated him from the others.

Caster cut off his conversation and turned with a surprised look on his face. He caught on and lowered the glass.

"I need you to take me somewhere. It's in Virginia Highlands."

The driver glanced at Caster and seemed to be waiting for orders.

Caster must have given a sign, but Jack couldn't see it. The driver turned a little. "You gotta help me with that one." The accent was pure Brooklyn.

"Double back and get on Peachtree. Head toward Lenox Square in Buckhead. You know the area?"

"Mrs. Richardson is at Neiman's all the time."

"I'll show you where to turn." Jack sat back and gently touched the bandage under his throbbing chin. The gauze felt moist.

Caster turned to show his profile. "The button's on the front of your armrest."

"What?"

"Press the button, I can hear you talk. Finger off and I can't hear." The glass went back up.

They drove past the elegant downtown high-rise hotels and followed Peachtree Street as it weaved through the rest of the maze of reflecting glass office buildings. Jack had been to a few major cities, mainly for medical meetings, but he thought Atlanta must be one of the only cities in the U.S. that combined the best of new and old, with glistening architectural wonders built around the landscape, rather than the other way around.

He'd only been to Elaine Thomas's once, and that was with Ed at her Christmas party six months ago. Virginia Highlands was one of those tree-lined older neighborhoods that was making an expensive comeback since real estate prices in Atlanta went through the roof. It wasn't long before the area's trendy small restaurants had patrons waiting in line for tables. Small houses that cost seventy thousand in 1980 were being renovated for over a half million dollars, bought for outrageous sums and then torn down to make way for two-story places made of Dryvit and peaked roofs.

Elaine's apartment was in an antebellum house that an elderly woman couldn't afford to keep on her own, so she rented the upstairs. Jack thought he could pick out the house but without directions he figured they'd have to drive down a few streets to get it right.

Jack pressed the intercom button and told the driver where to make turns. The rain slacked off, leaving a haze among the huge oaks and pines that grew in front of the houses. The lawns were modest and close together, but well manicured. He imagined the ghosts of Fords and Plymouths in the driveways that now sported Saabs and BMWs.

As he expected, they had to try a few streets but he hadn't missed it by much. The old house was in need of repair, with ominous cracks in the four columns. Brown pine straw had fallen like cobwebs onto the wet azaleas lining the porch, and small green weeds grew in spaces on the uneven brick walk. The second-story balcony ran the full length of the main porch, which was made of thick gray planks that gave a little with each step.

A hard yellow light glowed from the fixture by the door. Jack opened the screen door, thinking that it would be the first thing to go when someone else finally got his hands on this place. The front door was ajar, one of the dangerous consequences of dividing up a home into apartments. He knocked anyway.

When no one came, he eased inside. The stairs were the focal point of the long entry hall and were a work of art. To the left was a grand room with a long antique dining table displaying fresh flowers in a cut-glass bowl. Against the wall was a tall breakfront cabinet with silver serving pieces and stacks of fine plates. There was a row of silver goblets and demitasse cups on the top shelf.

Jack started for the steps just as a downstairs door cracked open wide enough for an old woman to peer at him. Her hair was in curlers and her open robe revealed a thin cotton nightgown that didn't quite cover her bony knees. He'd be willing to lay even odds that the lady had enough money in silverware to buy a new house, but that wasn't the way things were done around here. The silver had probably been her grandmother's. It was her heritage, not her dowry.

He smiled gently, then followed the worn carpet runner up the staircase. He had to stop and regain some strength before he was able to continue to the top.

He'd learned at his previous visit that the upstairs had been converted to a couple of apartments, each with a small kitchen and living area. He studied the doors on opposite sides of the landing, neither of which had a name or number. They had both been open at the Christmas party, and the hall had been full of people. He wasn't sure which was Elaine's, but there was a ribbon of light underneath the door to his right. He knocked gently.

Elaine cracked the door open and her face relaxed when she saw him. "Hey." The door closed on her words, then opened wide after she unlatched the chain. "Are you all right? You're supposed to be at the hospital."

Jack had never seen her like this before. Her shoulder-length brown hair was pulled back into a ponytail. She had light green eyes, soft high cheekbones, and her skin had the healthy look of a runner. She was wearing a wrinkled white oxford-cloth shirt that partially covered her faded blue gym shorts.

"I'm sorry it's so late. I came about Ed."

"Come on in." She backed away from the door. "He's asleep in the guest room. I was about to make supper. Have you eaten?"

"Not yet."

He watched her walk to the kitchen . . . watched her in a way he'd never watched anyone before. He knew he would look back and remember this moment, but he had only the vaguest understanding of why. She smiled back at him, and he realized he'd not yet followed her into the room.

The living area was small and eclectically furnished with two overstuffed chairs and a love seat that held a stack of newspapers bound in twine. A floor-to-ceiling bookshelf was filled with paperbacks and a few small plates on easels. There was a healthy ficus tree in the corner by the front window.

Elaine cleared a stack of mail from the counter that separated the kitchen from the living area, moved a colander off the bar stool, and said, "Have a seat." A pot of water was beginning to boil and she dropped in enough spaghetti for the two of them.

He watched her add the rest of a jar of sauce to a simmering pot, then dip her finger in for a quick taste. She left her finger in her mouth a second longer than he expected, then said, "Needs onion. Can you chop?"

Jack glanced around for the guest room door. "Ed's asleep already?"

She reached down into a cabinet for a chopping board. "He was worried for a while, especially about leaving St. Michael's without you. But we get along pretty good, and Mr. B settled him down—that's my cat." She handed him a knife. "Onion's in the fridge."

One look in the refrigerator, and he knew she had to be sharing the last of her food.

She brushed against him for some butter. "Slim pickin's, I'm afraid. A girlfriend of mine camped out here after her husband got a little rough. She just found a place yesterday. I haven't had a chance to stock up yet." She put the butter on a small dish.

"Mom told me I was always picking up strays. Some things don't change, I guess."

"Where is she now? Your mother, I mean."

From the way her body stood still, Jack knew the answer.

"She died when I was sixteen."

"I'm sorry . . . I didn't mean to—"

"It's OK. It was a long time ago."

"I'm still sorry." He brought the onion to the counter, but put the knife back down, wondering how time would change the way he felt about losing his own parents—and the way he'd lost them.

"Thank you for bringing Ed here. I was just worried that . . . He can be difficult when he gets out of his routine."

"I think he feels at ease with me. But I didn't tell him about what happened to you—I figured it would be better for you to explain it once he could see you were OK. I just said that you asked me to bring him to my place because you were running later than expected on your first day at work."

She sliced an inch of butter into a saucepan, then passed him a red pepper. "Don't be stingy. I like food with a kick."

He cut the pepper into little crescents, then scraped it and the onion into the melting butter.

"Is it safe for you to have wine?"

"Maybe a little, once we eat."

She gave him a quick smile and put two wineglasses on the counter.

The room filled with the aroma of the sautéed pepper and onions. When they were ready he mixed them into the simmering sauce, then checked the taste with his finger, if only to recall the way she'd done it. His tongue felt like a piece of wood stuck in a bed of dull pain.

She drained the spaghetti and put some bread in the toaster. "There's a bottle of merlot in the closet."

He opened the wine, then carried the glasses to a wicker chest in front of the love seat. While she made a salad, he perused her books. Her collection was an odd mix of political nonfiction and romance novels peppered with some works by Fitzgerald, Hemingway, Tolstoy—books that most people seemed to keep after college. He picked out *T.S. Eliot's Complete Poems and Plays*. It had a good smell, the kind that permeated any used bookstore worth its stripes. A torn edge of napkin served to mark one of the "Four Quartets." She'd underlined a passage in pencil.

He read the passage again, then looked up. He could tell she'd been watching with interest.

She wiped her hands on a towel. "I was an English major at UNC."

He closed the book but held it with a sense of respect. It had a handsome cover and a good weight. "Biology major, myself. Sometimes I wish I'd gone your route."

She came over and put the plates of spaghetti on the table. He handed her the book and she studied the author's picture—three-piece suit, wrinkled face behind round black glasses, an arm cocked in defiant understanding. For an instant before she put the book away he could see a trace of loss in her face.

He sat on the chair and she sat on the floor, crossing her legs. She raised her glass. "Well . . . here's to your new job."

He smiled and raised his. "Here's to living through it."

He cut the pasta into small pieces and ate slowly, trying to chew as little as possible. In spite of the difficulty it seemed to be the best meal he'd ever had. A few hours earlier he'd been cut and left for dead, and now he'd never been more glad to see something as simple as the sauce stain on the edge of his toast. Neither one of them felt the need to say anything for most of the meal, but it didn't feel awkward. In fact, it felt good.

"Are you going back?"

"I'm sorry?" He didn't know how long he'd been looking at her, but she didn't seem to mind.

"To the prison."

He wiped his mouth. "Tomorrow."

"Surely they don't expect you back right away."

"It's not a matter of what they expect. It's a matter of whether I can cut it. If I don't show up tomorrow, I'm vulnerable every day I work there."

"You don't seriously mean to go in the morning."

"There's blood in the water if I don't."

She stood with her plate and leaned over for his. "At least wait and see how you feel."

Right then he'd have done anything she asked.

"Stay there. Your bandage needs to be changed." She disappeared down the hall and a light came on in the bathroom.

He leaned back into the deep cushion.

"All I've got is peroxide and a roll of gauze."

He watched as she carefully assembled what she'd need—some cotton balls next to the peroxide, then a clean washcloth, then the gauze wrapped in cobalt-blue paper, and finally the tape.

She edged closer to him and gently tilted his head back. Her face was only inches from his as she slowly peeled the tape off his saturated bandage. He watched her face as she worked, the subtle motion of her lips, the moisture of her eyes. Then he saw the pain in them when the wound was exposed. He hadn't seen it himself, and had to resist the urge to walk to a mirror. There was something about the moment that he didn't want to ruin.

"You're not supposed to be here, are you?" It was more a statement of fact than a question.

"I told them I'd come back to the hospital after I got Ed home."

She was still next to him, but lower on the floor. "You don't think the peroxide will hurt it, I mean, it's safe . . ."

"Peroxide is fine." He leaned for the washcloth, but she gently grasped his arm and he relented.

The pain was unbelievable, but he didn't flinch. Elaine held the washcloth at the base of his neck to dry the excess. He kept his head tilted and heard her unwrap the paper around the gauze, then felt her tender touch as she taped the bandage in place.

She sat back on the floor with the tape in her hand. "I can tell you really love him."

"He's my brother."

"Yeah, but you're giving up a lot for him. His therapy takes a lot of your time. Is there anybody else in the family—"

"No, there's just me." He averted his eyes, then stood. "Listen, it's late. I better check on Ed."

Jack felt that nervous fear again, triggered when someone wanted him to talk about his family—a fear he didn't understand, but had lived with all his life. It was as if Elaine had uncovered this raw kid. He just couldn't seem to say the right thing, and he couldn't deal with it, especially now. His legs were weak but he was able to make it down the hall without showing it.

He opened the first door without asking which was the guest room, and there sleeping on the bed was his younger brother, curled on his side, holding a pillow to his chest with one hand. Ed had a big frame and was starting to look muscular again, something that had taken over a year to rebuild after the long hospitalization. His hair was thick brown but neatly cut. It had filled in well enough that no one could see the surgical scars. Jack quietly closed the door after a cat and two kittens slid against his leg.

Elaine was standing by the love seat when Jack came back out. "You can stay here tonight. The sofa folds out."

He wanted to give her an explanation for the way he'd reacted to her questions, but it was just beyond his grasp. "I've got Richardson's men downstairs waiting for me. I nearly forgot."

She pulled the fine white curtain aside to look in front of the house. "That's Richardson's limousine?"

He was at the door. "I don't know how to thank you for what you've done for my brother . . . tonight and at the church."

"Promise me you'll go to the hospital."

"Those guys downstairs are on loan as some kind of protection until they find the prisoner who cut me. Maybe they can bring some of Ed's clothes in the morning."

She leaned into the partially opened door and searched his eyes. "I didn't mean to pry."

There was more that he wanted to say, so much more, but instead he said, "I'll call you in the morning about Ed's things." He smiled, and wanted to hold her. He looked down before turning. As he reached the bottom of the stairs he heard her door gently close.

* * *

Otis Burke drove the GTO deep into the woods, the pines reflecting their silver-green brushes in the headlights. He turned at breaks in the trees that were almost imperceptible to anyone who hadn't grown up here. He figured they had about three hours before the sun rose, and he still had a lot to do before he could sleep. Getting food was the biggest problem, but that might not happen until tomorrow night, when it was safer to move.

Neon and JT slept in the backseat. It was JT's car. Neon had brought the guns for the prison break. Burke knew that neither man had counted on him killing that cop, and neither wanted to ride shotgun anymore. But neither had the guts to cross him or tell him.

The air rushing over his arm began to cool, so he slowed the car. He could smell the mix of damp moss and sweet water grass and knew he was near the river. Burke pulled over and turned off the engine, careful to take the keys. Frogs and crickets echoed from all sides. He left the headlights on so he could make his way to the pine shack near the river's edge.

Inside the shack were two frayed cots and a stained mattress bent over on itself in the corner. There was no sink, no mirror, no plumbing. He tore some of the cobwebs and righted the table in the center of the room.

Burke turned as the other two men came onto the porch. They'd grown up in the same area, and had gone to the same school as long as the state could force them to show up. After that, they'd been left to fend for themselves, and had spent almost as many years in jail as they had on the street.

Neon was all muscle, taller than Burke by couple of inches, and meaner than most men his size found a need to be. The name didn't match him. Even his momma called him a slow thinker, but Burke could trust him to do as he was told.

It was JT he worried about. JT was lanky and tended to let his mouth get him into trouble. He'd been cut deep on his face, chest, and back, but still liked the risk of a body fight instead of the certainty of a gun. The blade he kept strapped to his leg had left every serious enemy dead or close to it.

Each one of them had killed before. Most had it coming. Still, killing a cop was different, and Burke knew what they were thinking. But he didn't care. Not anymore.

JT stopped on the dirt path, but wouldn't enter the shack. "The fuck is this?"

Burke didn't like that mouth. "Where we're stayin'. Like I told you."

"That was before. They ain't gonna stop lookin' for a cop killer just 'cause it's dark."

"So what the hell you want to do?"

"Keep drivin'. Get the shit outta here."

"It'll be light soon and we gotta lay low. Nobody knows this place. They'll check where we used to hang and won't find nothin'. By tomorrow they'll figure we two states away."

Neon crossed his arms, but didn't say anything.

JT kicked the edge of the porch. "I owed you, so I did this, but I didn't agree to kill no cop. And I sure as hell ain't sittin' on my ass around here while they send them dogs."

"You're in it now."

"The fuck I am."

Burke grabbed JT's shirt and shoved him. "So what you gonna do, huh? Walk your skinny ass out the woods? Then what?"

JT backed off the porch but hardened his expression. "You shoulda killed that white guy. He saw me and Neon."

Burke said, "He wasn't the right one. Scalacey was s'posed to be there."

"The fuck I care? He's a witness."

"He ain't shit, and he don't know shit."

"He oughta be a dead man and we wouldn't have to worry. I say we keep driving. What you say, Neon?"

Neon could only manage a glance at Burke. "You been sayin' there's money in all this. I don't see it make sense to leave the money."

Burke squared himself in the door frame. "There's money all right. I know what they looking for, and they'll pay big for it. But those bastards used me, and I owe 'em. That cop was just the down payment. We ain't going nowhere till I'm done."

He spat and stepped closer to JT. "You got a problem with that, then you got a problem with me."

JT turned and said, "Fuck this place. I'm stayin' in the car."

Burke knew by JT's look that he'd be coming at him before this was over.

FOUR

Jack shook awake in his bed. The rain was beating the heavy branches of an elm against his window. He made an unsteady path to the bathroom and turned on the shower light to limit the harsh transition from the dark. His reflection stared back while he tried to wake up. He looked as bad as he felt.

He ran cold water over the end of a towel and washed his face, taking care to keep the bandage dry. After he started to make sense of things he got his watch from the bedside table. Almost 5:00 A.M.—too early to call about his brother.

The hall led past Ed's empty room, then down the dark mahogany steps to the kitchen where he relied on the dim light from the microwave to make his coffee.

The undulations of the coffeemaker were like a mantra he used to clear the muck out of his head. When enough had brewed he got a cup and took it out to the porch swing, where he listened to the rain and tried to forget the dream. He'd had the same one before, and woke with the image of holding his father's head, recoiling when he felt the clotted blood. Mercifully, the thought of the last twenty-four hours helped to bury the demons of his sleep.

The heat and fear of the past day swarmed past him

like a movie. He relived the sharp cut under his jaw and the crack on his skull. The visit to Richardson's mansion seemed months old.

There was something about the assault in the prison that kept prying at him, but he couldn't get his hands around it. It had more to do with *why* he survived than why it happened in the first place.

He rocked the swing slowly and tried to enjoy the trace of coolness in the rain. His rental house had wood siding with a brick porch and a long series of steps that led down a small hill to the street. This area was a few blocks away from an upscale part of midtown, but the money hadn't made its way here yet. Most of the neighbors were older retired types who weren't interested in selling. But, like all things, it was just a matter of time.

All he could hear from the porch was the rain and the window air-conditioning unit that hummed from the house next door. The street and yard had a wet purple tint as the last of the night gave up on what it could do to him.

Down the hill he could see that the limo had been replaced by a black Cadillac parked next to a fire hydrant in front of his neighbor's house. The ride back from Elaine's was hazy at best, but he remembered them telling him to expect a new car. He wasn't too upset, since he needed some way to get back to his pickup truck at the prison. After that he didn't want Richardson's men hanging around. Threat or no threat, he could take care of himself.

He went back upstairs to dress. He decided against shaving and had to brush his teeth carefully because the floor of his mouth felt as if it had bamboo shards in it.

After dressing in a white shirt and blue pants he

went to Ed's room and packed new underwear and a fresh shirt into a backpack. Downstairs he poured coffee into two Styrofoam cups, and headed down his front steps in the light rain.

He tapped on the driver's side of the Caddy and the window eased down. The driver was a new man and had obviously been sleeping with his head against the window.

Jack reached in with the coffee. "I'm Dr. Harris. Time to go."

The man took the coffee and unlocked the doors. Jack climbed in back while the driver smoothed his hair.

The driver looked back. "Where to?" He had a thick neck like Richardson's other two men, but this one sounded more like Macon than Brooklyn.

"Go straight and take a right at the stop sign."

Jack tried to work out all he had to do. They began to pass a few more cars and he leaned forward. "Pull over at the next light."

They pulled up next to a small building that had once been a filling station. The work bays had been converted to a baker's kitchen and the metal awning, which once protected motorists, was now painted white and blue and covered a half dozen square tables with chairs. The store was designed so that passersby could see the bakers at work through the large windows, and it turned out to be great advertising. It was locally owned, and Jack liked this place better than the coffeehouse chains that seemed to be on every other corner in the nicer parts of Atlanta. The fact that the whole block smelled like cinnamon didn't hurt.

Jack stood in front of the curved glass display case and ordered some pastries for Elaine and Ed, then chose two cream cheese croissants and more coffee for himself. While the driver ordered, Jack stepped outside and bought a copy of the *Atlanta Journal-Constitution* from the box, then got back in the car.

A file photo of officer W.E. "Billy" Howard was on the bottom half of the front page next to the small headline GUARD KILLED IN BREAKOUT AT PRIVATELY RUN PRISON. Jack scanned the article. It referred to two hostages but he was relieved that he wasn't mentioned by name. The reporter hadn't come up with much detail to speak of, especially compared to what he'd learned in Richardson's office. There was no mention of the signs of torture, the injection site, or the number 2 carved in the man's chest.

Much of the front page space was about the dead officer's personal history—thirty-six years old, unmarried, survived by his parents and a sister, had worked in the prison for eight years after leaving the Atlanta police force. The Fraternal Order of Police was going to participate in the funeral services tomorrow. There was no comment about an autopsy.

The article was continued on page eight under an old mug shot of Otis Burke and some details about an earlier conviction on drug trafficking, specifically the packages of heroin that were found under the floorboard of his room in one of the project houses. Burke was a prior two-time narcotics offender but got a life sentence for a murder conviction in 1995. He was considered armed and dangerous and there was an appeal to the public not to approach Burke but to contact the police if he was sighted. The article went on to point out that this was the first successful breakout at Elrice since it had come under private management, then ended up with a pie chart of the breakout statistics at other penitentiaries and at the city and county jails.

Jack looked up when the driver returned. He had new coffee and a bag that smelled of warm yeast.

"I want you to let me out at the prison, then take this food and the backpack to the address I've written on the card," Jack said. He leaned forward to hand Elaine's address to the man.

He eased back into the seat and became aware of a slight chill and the sensation of fever. The chill passed, but he knew he had an infection. He carefully felt his wound and couldn't detect any significant drainage. The lymph nodes were slightly enlarged as expected, but nothing felt like an abscess. It wasn't the same as a visual inspection, but as long as the chills didn't build he reasoned that a megadose of oral antibiotics would be enough to kill any systemic spread of the bacteria. He reached into his pocket for the two acetaminophen tablets he'd taken from his bathroom, then swallowed them with a gulp of coffee. He tucked his arms across his chest and wedged himself against the seat and the door, opening his eyes only at the sound of another car's horn or a rapid change of speed.

The car had come to a complete halt but Jack didn't really wake up until he heard the driver talking to a guard at the prison gate. He sat up and checked his watch. The ride through the city and out to the more secluded region of the prison had taken nearly forty minutes, almost a half hour less than it took during a more reasonable hour. He'd had no further chills and the brief sleep had made him feel better. He pressed a button and the window rolled down.

"Officer, I'm Dr. Harris, the new man in the medical clinic." He handed his prison ID to the guard.

The guard was coming off the night shift. Jack knew

that look and guessed that the man was nearing retirement. His eyes went back and forth between Jack and the picture ID. "You're the one they took hostage." It was less a question than recognition of Jack's rising status. "If you don't mind my saying, you've got a lot of guts to come back in this cage, sir."

"Thank you, officer." He accepted his ID and the man stepped into a booth and made a call to the inner gatehouse. The guard then opened the outer gate and waved them through. Jack wasn't certain but he thought the guard saluted once they passed.

They arrived at the inner gate, which remained closed. Jack put his hand on the door handle. "This is as far as they'll let you go," he told the driver. "Tell Mr. Richardson I appreciate the help but I've got my own transportation, and I won't need any bodyguards. Don't forget the delivery."

Jack walked to the gatehouse and produced his ID. The lock on an inner steel door clicked open and he walked into a holding cage. The steel door closed and the door at the far end of the cage opened, allowing him to enter the prison grounds. He could hear the driver's voice insisting that he had strict instructions to stay with Dr. Harris. Jack walked across the wet dirt field, fully aware that Richardson's man didn't have a ghost of a chance at getting in. At least not for now.

As he headed straight for the old brick infirmary, he became keenly aware that he could have been brought this way yesterday without the strip search and parade in front of the prisoners. But there wasn't much to be gained from holding a grudge against a dead man.

The infirmary's heavy wood door was locked. He knocked and was about to knock again when the door was opened by one of the trusties. The old, thin inmate smiled as if he'd just seen a long-lost brother.

"The line was five to one we'd never see you again. But I told 'em, they shoulda seen your eyes. You one tough motha. I knew you'd be back. Had a pack of cigarettes on it." The black man gave a little dance as he pulled the door open. "One hundert Camels. Come on in, Doc."

Jack started to enter, but the man was in the way and eager to talk.

"They call me Taps. You know, like on your shoes? I used to work the clubs." His expression dimmed. "But that was some time ago."

He shook the man's hand. "Maybe we can talk about those cigarettes later."

"Health don't make no difference when you in here forever, Doc. No difference. But I can tell—you my good luck charm. You need something, just ask."

Jack thanked him, then walked into the trauma area where he'd been stabbed. He half expected to see it roped off with police tape, but the room had been straightened as if nothing had happened. The only change was that the door to the ward was closed, but through its glass window he could see that there were now a few patients in the iron beds. A guard was working to stay awake in a chair just inside the door.

A female nurse with her back to him was writing at the foot of one of the beds. All he saw was a white uniform and an RN nursing cap, something Jack always admired but which nurses rarely wore nowadays. She put down the vital-signs clipboard and started toward him. She was thin with caramel-colored skin and that old-school nurse's look that radiated no-nonsense compassion. He guessed she was in her fifties but could pass for mid-forties. He liked her before he even heard her voice.

She closed the door behind her and smoothed her

dress with her palms. She stood with noticeably good posture. "I'm Geneva Lott."

Jack extended his hand. "Jack Harris."

"I'm glad you're safe, Dr. Harris. We usually don't see the doctors on my shift." She glanced through the window at the beds. "As you can see we had three admissions."

"Tell me, Mrs. Lott, do we have a drug cabinet back here?"

She leveled her gaze but didn't answer. She reminded him of an English teacher he had had in the eighth grade.

"I think this wound is infected." He touched the bandage.

She regarding him for several seconds, obviously displeased with what she saw. "Sit on the table. That dressing needs to be changed."

She turned and opened some drawers and he did as he was told.

"We stock some antibiotics and a few other things, but most of the medications are locked in the pharmacy and delivered to the two clinics on a strict schedule." She turned back with a handful of sterile packets.

Jack sat stoically and let her change the bandage. The old one had a brownish green exudate staining the center of the gauze. She gently scrubbed the suture line with Betadyne, then used a disposable razor to shave the surrounding area. She dabbed on an antiseptic ointment, then opened a clear adhesive bandage that she used to cover the entire wound.

She then unlocked the double doors of a tall closet across the room and stood back for him to get what he needed. There were a dozen shelves with boxes of antihistamines, decongestants, antacids, and antibiotics. Most of the products were of the over-the-counter variety, but he searched through a box and found a package of Azithromycin that one of the drug reps had left. It had a full course of therapy, equivalent to ten days of IV antibiotics. He took two pills, downing them with a cup of water.

"I need a gram of gentamycin and one-point-two million units of Bicillin, IM." The combination of all three would cover a broad spectrum of gram-positive and gram-negative bacteria. He'd only gotten a brief look at the strip of metal Burke had used to cut him. God only knew what he'd been exposed to.

She unlocked another cabinet, wiped two vials with alcohol, then pulled the medication into separate syringes. "We treat a lot of venereal disease here, as you might imagine."

"I figured you might have the Bicillin on hand."

She turned. "It makes no sense, but we don't have tetanus boosters."

"I don't remember much about being in the Garity ER, but I bet they covered me." Jack rolled up his sleeve, but she shook her head, so he unbuttoned his pants and curled his body on the table. The shots in each cheek were quick, but felt like hot marbles.

He pulled up his pants and rubbed the injection sites. "Some introduction."

"Your introduction was yesterday, Doctor." She carefully disposed of the needles in a red plastic box, then turned to face him. "I'm glad to be working with you."

He nodded his appreciation. "How can I get the medical records on Otis Burke?"

She gave him that look again. Propriety went with the old school. She'd want a good reason before she gave someone's private records.

"There's still a lot I don't know about how things are done."

"If they are admitted here, one of the staff should automatically call for them. Otherwise they are kept in the records office along with the prisoner's legal documents. We can request anything you want, provided there's a legitimate reason." She walked into the ward and Jack followed. She leaned against a tan filing cabinet. "We keep them here."

"I want to know if Burke was HIV-positive."

She gave a knowing look. "I'll call, but you aren't the first to ask for them. I heard that the police were all over us yesterday."

Jack was surprised. It hadn't occurred to him to ask who had jurisdiction over a breakout from a privately managed prison. Then he realized that the police were probably looking for him. He'd be easy enough to find today.

While Mrs. Lott called the records office, Jack went to the cabinet and pulled the old charts of the three patients who'd been admitted overnight.

He took the thick brown folders to the only desk in the room. Next to him was a rack of inpatient charts with stainless steel covers. He matched the old charts with the current ones, then started to review each. The first inmate was a twenty-three-year-old white male admitted with complaints of abdominal pain and hematechesia, or bright red blood per rectum. Jack reviewed what the physician's assistant had ordered last night, then looked at Mrs. Lott as if he'd misjudged her entirely.

After she got off the phone he stood with the chart in hand. "This inmate came in with abdominal pain and bleeding. No one ordered serial blood work or a flat plate and lateral X-ray series, and from what I can tell he's not on antibiotics or even getting IV fluids." He opened the door to the ward. "Suppose he's got appendicitis or a perforated viscus—he could have died."

Mrs. Lott crossed her arms and took a deep breath. "Close the door."

Jack clenched his teeth. If she wanted a turf battle she'd get it. He wasn't a slug like Dr. Scalacey and the sooner they learned it, the better.

"I've been working this ward for nearly twenty years. Things go on in a prison that don't get written down, things they know and I know, but that's as far as it goes."

"I don't know how things have been run before, but—"

She interrupted. "That boy was raped."

Jack felt as if he'd been slapped in the face.

"No telling how many got him. Probably a territory thing between gangs—he's somebody's property and somebody else is sending a message. Or maybe it's a payback for something he did. Maybe for something he won't do. He's in here so they can't kill him."

Jack looked into the ward through the glass pane, then back at the nurse. "What happens when he goes back?"

"Depends on who needed to get the message, and whether they got it."

Jack sat with his arm on the charts and stared at the young prisoner in the far bed.

She walked over and leaned against the desk. After a tense moment she broke the silence. "Burke's chart isn't in the record room. The police must have taken it."

Jack felt a slight chill and he crossed his arms.

"You're wondering if you made the right decision coming here."

"No. I know about prisons."

Her voice was soft. "It took me a few minutes to be sure, but I can see the resemblance. Your father was assigned here before. . . ."

Jack rocked himself to shake the chill. He looked at his knees and then felt her hand on his shoulder.

"I came to the funeral."

He felt the rush of shame that he couldn't prevent no matter how much he tried. She knew. He waited for her to ask the way he expected everyone to ask— about the way he had died. That fear had simmered at the cusp of every chance encounter for months after the funeral.

"Not all the answers will be here." Her warm hand left his shoulder.

He didn't know what to say to her, and she was good enough to let it drop. Only another damaged soul would be so sensitive. In that one act he knew she'd had to deal with her own pain and understood that he wasn't yet ready. And he wasn't. Yet, something compelled him to be here, to find answers. Answers to questions he couldn't even express.

She stood by the file cabinet. "We have a logbook for the blood work we send on the prisoners. Burke's prison number and date of birth will be there. With that I can find his HIV result on the computer." She walked back to the trauma area and started looking through a ledger.

Jack watched her for a minute, and before he could think too much about his father working in the same room, he turned his attention back to the patient chart. Burying himself in work had become such an important analgesic that he hardly even noticed the transition anymore.

The second man was fifty years old, admitted with complaints of a headache and diplopia, or blurred vision. It started three days prior and had been coming off and on. There was no history of head trauma and he wasn't hypertensive. He denied nausea or vomiting or photophobia, signs that might indicate severely increased intracranial pressure or meningitis. When the PA asked about dizziness the man "wasn't sure." He'd been admitted to the infirmary for observation. Jack knew the man probably needed to be sent to Garity for a head CT, but he would examine him before writing any orders.

The third man was fifty-eight and had complained of substernal chest pressure and rapid heart rate. It started after supper, while he was walking up a flight of stairs to return to his cell. The exertional component was suggestive of angina, but he also noted increased belching, which helped relieve the pressure, a sign that pointed more to a GI cause. An EKG was on the chart, and Jack agreed with the computer interpretation that there was no evidence of acute ischemia or infarction at that time, but it had missed the abnormal P-wave. It was taller and wider than normal and had looked like two small humps pushed together. Jack wrote *Left atrial enlargement* on the interpretation and closed the chart.

The man was in for observation. At the university they'd be drawing a series of cardiac enzymes to look for any signs of myocardial cell injury that would cause more of the enzymes to leak into the bloodstream. If those were negative the man would probably have a stress test and either a cardiology or GI consult, depending on the results. But here the man would probably be sent back to his cell if the symptoms settled. There simply wasn't enough money to check cardiac enzymes here. He knew the drill: prisoners got shipped when the heart attack occurred, not before. Otherwise there would be three hundred chest pain complaints a day.

Jack then reviewed the old charts on all three men. The young guy had only been seen for minor things like a sinus infection and a rash. The man with the vision disturbance had a series of visits to the medicine clinic over the years. One of the PA notes referred to him as a "lifer." Eventually the man started seeing Dr. Scalacey exclusively, which was unusual because he'd been told that most of the prisoners saw PAs, and were referred to the MD only when specific changes in medication were being contemplated. Then they were turned back over to the PA clinic.

Scalacey had seen the man regularly every two weeks for about three months last year. The handwriting was difficult to interpret, and there were a series of abbreviations that weren't familiar to Jack. They certainly weren't part of the standard shorthand doctors used routinely.

The old chart on the guy with chest pain was quite thin, especially given his age. He, too, was a lifer. Cardiac risk factors were hypertension, a heavy smoking history, and his gender. He was already on Atenolol, a beta-blocker—an antihypertensive that was also cardioprotective. Jack noted that there wasn't a cholesterol level on the chart, so he ordered a fasting level for the morning.

Mrs. Lott called out from the front room. "Dr. Harris, it looks like you're safe."

Jack met her by the computer and was able to scroll through Otis Burke's blood work for the last two years. He was HIV-negative three months ago. A hepatitis profile one year prior had been negative for types A, B, and C. It was done along with a whole battery of tests of the liver, kidney, pancreas, prostate, plus an extensive connective tissue profile.

His total protein count was normal, but oddly, this was followed up with a very expensive radioimmuno assay, which quantified his serum immunoglobulin proteins by class. This more detailed test could break down abnormalities in these specialized proteins in the immune system. Different shifts could point to one of many diseases, but the graph of each class was normal.

This more detailed test was usually ordered only when the screening numbers showed an abnormal spike—indicating an unusual production of part of the immune system. But his screening numbers had clearly been within normal range.

Burke's T lymphocyte count was also normal, as was his ratio of T4 to T3 cells. Although the latter was usually followed in AIDS patients; it was unusual to check them in a patient who was HIV-negative. Jack had never seen it ordered as a screening test. He looked up from the screen. "Do prisoners get routine T lymphocyte screenings?"

Her expression said it all. "Are you kidding? We've got nothing but budget cuts around here."

Jack had the sudden fear that Burke might have been HIV-positive at some point in the past and later turned up HIV-negative during intense therapy. There were known reports in the literature of this phenomenon with the AIDS virus and other viruses as well. It was still unclear whether this represented true eradication of virus versus some dormancy period that could later reactivate.

Jack clicked the mouse to review older lab data,

which came up at a painfully slow pace. There were two other HIV tests in the last two years, both of which were negative. Records prior to that weren't on the system, but he knew they were probably on the old chart.

Why, Jack wondered, would Scalacey order a battery of extremely expensive tests on Burke when everything looked so normal? How had those tests been approved? From what he'd heard, privately managed prisons got that way for one reason—money. The less they spent, the more the company and its investors made. Most of the upper-level personnel on the staff had bonuses tied to cost savings, with premiums paid for divisions that came in under budget. It didn't take a genius to know how to pull that off when the money was being spent on prisoners. Who'd give a rat's ass if a convicted murderer complained about his rough life in prison? So why all the tests?

Mrs. Lott walked back in. "Doctor, shift change is at seven, but I've got to leave a few minutes early to babysit my grandchild so her mother can get to work. The day people will be here soon." She collected her purse and an umbrella. "Don't you worry about Burke. He sees Dr. Scalacey all the time and there's never anything wrong."

Jack raised his hand to wish her well as she left, then turned back to the computer. He clicked through the data again, but all he saw were normal lab values— pages of them. He had an odd feeling, as if he was missing something. Something that would explain a couple thousand dollars' worth of tests that essentially came out of Dr. Scalacey's bonus.

He went through them again, but instead of just looking for an asterisk that indicated an abnormal value, he read each and every result, item by item. The only thing that seemed even remotely abnormal had shown up two months earlier. He clicked through the pages and again found it on subsequent visits.

Although the total white blood count was normal, the percentage of one of its components, the eosinophils, was notably elevated. This could mean anything from an allergic sensitivity to cancer, but for the most part only serious ailments would produce profound elevations in their absolute number. Although the percentage of Burke's eosinophils remained elevated for three subsequent dates, the absolute count wasn't impressive. Certainly not enough to trigger an expensive battery of tests on the T lymphocytes or serum immunoglobulins.

He paced around the room, then sat at the desk, opening drawers, wondering if he'd find a protocol that would explain the odd selection of lab tests. In the bottom drawer he found a phone book, which made him think it probably would be wise to contact the police before they showed up. In a sense, the guard had been one of their own. No need to piss them off more than they already were.

He turned to the blue section of government listings. An operator at police headquarters answered right away. It wasn't quite 7:00 A.M., but he was surprised to learn that the people working the Burke case were already in.

"This is Lieutenant Lankford. May I help you?"

"I'm Jack Harris, the doctor who was held hostage by Otis Burke at Elrice Prison yesterday."

"Could you hold on a minute please?"

Thirty seconds later a new voice came on the line. "Doctor, this is Detective Ed Tarkington. We've been looking for you."

"I'm at the prison infirmary."

"If you can stay right there we'll meet you in about an hour."

"I know this might be unorthodox, but I would like to check some things in Otis Burke's medical records, and I understand it was checked out to your people. I thought maybe you could bring it. If need be, I'll look through the records in your presence."

There was a muffled conversation; then Tarkington came back on. "Doctor, we don't know anything about Burke's records. Please stay where you are. We'll be right there."

FIVE

Jack finished reviewing the inmates' medical charts, then retrieved a stethoscope he'd seen in the filing cabinet. The three new patients were still sleeping when he entered the ward. The place reminded him of pictures he'd seen of the polio hospital at Warm Springs. The old tongue-in-groove wood-paneled walls were white, as were the rows of iron beds. The light gray floor just emphasized the whiteness of the rest of the room. He picked the clipboard off the end of the far bed.

The vital signs belonged to Mac Rayfield, the twenty-three-year-old with abdominal pain and rectal bleeding. The graph paper revealed that Rayfield had no fever, and his blood pressure and heart rate were fine. Jack returned the clipboard and shifted his attention to the prisoner. His blond hair poked from under the covers, and as Jack moved closer he could see the waves of restless tension behind the closed eyelids. Jack studied the young man for almost a minute, fighting to suppress the impulse to imagine the horror of the assault.

He touched the man's shoulder, causing him to jerk awake. The young man pulled himself into a fetal position.

"I'm Dr. Harris. No one's going to hurt you."

Rayfield's gaze rested on Jack's chest.

"Try to lie flat on your back. I need to examine your abdomen." Try as he could, Jack couldn't get the man to make eye contact.

"Do you hurt anywhere?"

The man looked at the sheets, retreating deeper.

Jack moved to within a few inches of Rayfield's face, and spoke quietly. "I can't help you if you won't let me."

Slowly, the prisoner unballed himself, and Jack realized he was naked under the sheets. He pulled the covers just below the man's navel. At the same time he also observed the normal pink tone of the man's fingernail beds, and the red rim just inside his lower eyelids. He didn't appear to be anemic.

Jack began to palpate each quadrant of Rayfield's abdomen. The skin was dry and didn't feel feverish. There were no rashes or abrasions. The liver felt normal, and he was able to gently press deeply into all areas of the man's belly without producing any involuntary resistance that might have indicated a diffuse infection such as peritonitis. Ordinarily he would perform a rectal exam, but decided to wait until he could figure out if there were any private exam rooms. This guy had had enough humiliation.

"Are you still bleeding?"

Rayfield pulled the covers back and turned on his side, staring into space.

Jack studied the young man, then decided to leave him alone. "I'll make sure they bring you some clothes. You tell me if you develop any new pain or if there's more blood. It's important. So get some rest."

He wanted to say that the man would be OK in a few days, that there'd be no more trouble. But they both knew otherwise.

He moved to the next patient who was two rows up and on the other side of the room. He lifted the clipboard and checked the name. The prisoner was Emmet Havard, the fifty-year-old with double vision and headaches. He was awake, but lying flat on his back.

His blood pressure and heart rate had remained normal since admission, findings that lessened the likelihood of hypertensive stroke. Jack sat on the adjoining bed and introduced himself.

The man remained flat in bed. "Where's Doc Scalacey?"

Jack uncrossed his legs. "I'm sure he'll be in later. Do you mind if I examine you?"

"It's not like I've got much choice."

"I want to see you walk to the door and back."

The man stared back a few seconds, then tugged the covers off. He wore striped prison pants and a T-shirt that was more gray than white. He was slow to stand, taking care to hold on to the iron headboard. Jack noticed that he drifted slightly to the left on his trek, but he made it without assistance, provided he kept his feet wide apart. Once he returned to the edge of the bed, Jack held up his forefinger and told him follow it with his eyes. Jack repeated the test to confirm the subtle nystagmus, a rhythmical beating of the eyes when the man looked all the way to the left. Havard's reflexes were normal, but on further testing he had slight incoordination when he tried to follow Jack's finger through the air with his own.

He wanted to examine the back of the man's eyes to rule out papiledema, a change in the appearance of the optic nerve seen with elevations of intracerebral pressure. But there was no telling where the opthalmoscope was hidden. He made a mental note to finish this part of the exam later. "Does your headache ever wake you up?"

"Couple a times."

Jack knew more than he was willing to reveal without definitive proof. He spoke calmly. "I'd like to arrange a CT scan. You'll need to stay here until we get the results."

The prisoner nodded and lay back under the covers.

Jack wrote the order to schedule the CT of the head and for an ambulance to take the prisoner to Garity Memorial at the appropriate time. He'd have to check about how to arrange security. Whatever it took to pull this off, Jack was certain it wouldn't be easy.

The last patient was Jackson Tillis, a fifty-eight-year-old with chest pain. Jack was about to introduce himself when he heard the phone ring. Seconds later someone called his name.

He looked up to see Bill Latham, the senior PA, standing in the doorway. "Dr. Harris, there's a call for you."

"Can you get the number? I was about to examine this patient."

"It's the warden. They need you in his office PDQ."

Jack glanced at Mr. Tillis and was about to speak when Latham insisted. "Things are mighty tense around here. It would be best if you went now."

Jack walked over to Latham and handed him the clipboard. "From what I read this might be unstable angina. Better put him on a heparin drip until we sort it out."

"How much?"

"Ten-thousand-unit bolus, then a maintenance drip of a thousand cc's an hour. Have you got a heparin protocol?"

"There's one somewhere. Pharmacy has it if we can't dig one up."

"Just be sure to adjust it by the protocol. We don't

want to over-anticoagulate him. And let me know if he's still having chest pain."

"I'll handle it." Latham pointed though the window at the next building. "The warden's office is on the second floor after you enter that door."

Jack handed him the stethoscope. "I left some orders for a head CT on Havard's chart. I think he's got a tumor. And the other patient needs some clothes."

"I'll take care of it."

"One more thing. I called the police. They will expect me to be here."

"I wouldn't keep the warden waiting. Conners isn't the easiest guy in the world to get along with."

Jack opened the door.

"And, Doc, I wouldn't tell him about the police. It wouldn't exactly get you two off on the right foot. "

The lettering on the door identified the office as belonging to Horace T. Conners, Warden, Elrice Prison. Jack heard voices on the other side and waited for a lull before knocking.

"Come."

He expected the office to be standard government issue, with a gray metal desk and half a dozen filing cabinets. Instead, it looked as if the CEO of a Fortune 500 company worked here. The plush carpet seemed new. The desk looked hand-carved, and had only a few thin folders neatly lined up. There were a few pictures of politicians shaking hands with the stubby fingered fat man who was now sitting behind the desk. He didn't look like the kind of guy who could pick a suit that looked that good. The warden's chair squeaked but he didn't get up. Two uniformed officers stepped aside to make room. They all looked at Jack as if he'd dumped a dead animal on the floor.

"I'm Dr. Harris."

The warden slapped his hands on top of the desk. "I know who you are. Just where the hell you been?"

"My neck should heal in a few weeks and I think the infection will clear up with antibiotics. It was nice of you to ask."

"Don't get smart with me, son. I've got a breakout to deal with."

Jack started to speak his mind, then thought better of it. "I was told you wanted to see me."

Conners gestured to the corner. "This is Dr. Scalacey. You should have met yesterday in the infirmary."

Scalacey nodded, but didn't get up. He crossed his legs, causing his clog to swing free of his heel.

Jack noted with interest that Scalacey seemed to pretend they'd never met. In the subdued light of Richardson's office last night, Jack hadn't noticed the cigarette stains on his fingernails.

Conners shifted his weight and smiled as if he were reading Jack's thoughts. "Not exactly the kind of place you were expecting, was it?"

Jack had read how the top staff of certain private prisons had become millionaires by making a commission from selling everything from phone access rights to food contracts for the inmates and guards. He decided not to answer.

Conners said, "I don't like problems. Especially ones that tarnish my record. Right now I've got a problem. And it's you. I want to know how you're going to fix it."

"I'm the one who was cut."

"I got a dead guard and a prisoner on the loose. You know more about this than anyone, but so far we don't have a damn thing to go on. We've lost precious hours already. I want to know everything you can think of that happened. If the guy coughed I want to hear about it."

Jack struggled to keep his cool. He'd survived worse than this during his clerkships in medical school. There was a time, before med school, when he would have snapped back. His volatile sense of self-preservation was a product of living on the wrong side of the tracks in too many towns. Traces of that pain lingered despite his best efforts.

Jack snuffed his rising anger. "I'd like to sit."

He noticed that the other officers were captains. Conners moved his hand and one of the men cleared some papers from the only available seat.

For the next forty-five minutes Jack relived everything he could recall about the day—the tour in front of the prisoners, the inmate's fake seizure, the two men who met them in the dirt alley, waking up in the ER. They interrupted him just before he was going to tell them about the trip to Richardson's estate. They kept pressing him for more details about the reaction of the others in the infirmary, and then about the accomplices in the alley. By the time they had hashed and rehashed the story, something told him to keep his meeting with Richardson to himself. Richardson had been clear that he would deny any meeting if Jack was stupid enough to tell about it. Richardson had also said how much he prized loyalty, and from the way things were adding up, Jack was beginning to wonder who his real friends would be. So there was no mention of the photographs he'd seen in Richardson's office, or of the man's plan to take care of the escaped convict with his considerable means.

Conners became visibly angry. "Is that all you have to add?"

Jack didn't like the tone. "That's it."

Conners looked at the other officers, then stood.

He paced in a small arc, then leaned across his desk. "Do you deny sending not one, but two guards out of the infirmary shortly before the breakout occurred?"

Now he understood Conners for what he was. "I didn't send anyone anywhere."

The warden picked up a typed report. "Officer Kidd states in his report that he was sent to the dispensary in West Wing to look up the list of medications that prisoner Burke was taking. Do you dispute this statement?"

"I don't know Officer Kidd. I gave a number of orders to the medical personnel. He was in *status epilepticus.* A seizure that won't break is a life-threatening condition. I was running a code and asked for a list of the inmate's medications so I could administer the proper treatment."

"So you agree that the prisoner was brought under your supervision with an adequate contingency of guards, and that they remained until you dismissed them."

Jack shot an angry glance at Dr. Scalacey, but it was obvious he wasn't going to go to bat for him.

Conners planted a finger on the file. "I know my men followed the prisoner transfer procedures to the letter. If you hadn't interfered, there would have been no breakout, no dead guard, and no fugitive at large."

Jack leveled his gaze at Conners. The man wasn't interested in his side of the story. The fake one covered his own ass just fine. Jack stood and opened the door.

"One other thing."

Jack stopped.

"I understand you have a meeting with the police this morning. I suggest you postpone it long enough to get yourself an attorney." Conners sat down and picked up the report from his desk. "You haven't heard the end of this, Doctor."

SIX

Jack left the warden's office and crossed the wet field to the infirmary. He didn't work for Conners, but he knew the man hadn't risen to his position without knowing how to use the system or how to divert blame to others. And Scalacey wasn't going to be any help. There was going to be trouble over this, and it pissed him off. He then realized that someone had to have tipped the warden about his meeting with the police. The PA had advised him not to tell Conners about the meeting, so who else knew, other than the police and the PA? Someone was undercutting him.

His muscles grew tense as adrenaline shunted blood to his arms and legs, a primal defense that prepared the body to fight. He picked up his pace, but it didn't help. He needed to run a couple of miles or spend an hour punching the sandbag in the gym. He'd learned the value of the sandbag on the oil rigs—it drained a man's anger and had kept more than a few from killing each other.

Jack was about to jog when he saw a navy Ford with black sidewall tires outside the infirmary. He stopped close enough to see his reflection in the driver's window. Jack knew Conners was just slinging bullshit, but the story was too good and too well thought out to be a bluff. He had no way of knowing whether it started with the guards or whether Conners had seen an opening and ordered the guards to lie. He had a sinking feeling as he thought about what the police would believe.

Maybe he did need a lawyer, but there was no way he could afford one now. He wouldn't get his first paycheck until the end of the month, and almost all of it was already spent on rent and therapy for his brother. He thought of Richardson's offer and wondered how far it would extend. As much as he might need it, Jack couldn't see himself asking Richardson for legal help.

Part of him wanted to leave. He could go home and have time to sort things out before the cops tracked him down, but that would just make Conners's story more believable. Besides, he'd never been one to run from a fight. He walked around the car and entered the infirmary.

The investigator was talking to the senior PA, but turned at the sound of the door closing. He had thick black hair with some gray along the temples. He appeared to be in his mid-forties and in good physical condition. The man produced an ID from his khaki suit. "Ed Tarkington, I'm a detective with the Atlanta PD."

"Jack Harris. But I guess you knew that already." They shook hands.

"Is there someplace we can talk?"

Jack looked at his PA for a sign that he'd ratted to Conners, but if he was guilty, the guy was all ice. "Bill, give us a few minutes alone."

Latham picked up his coffee. "I need to check the clinic schedule anyway. You can use the trusty lounge. They'll be in the laundry for another hour."

After Latham left they entered the lounge and grabbed a couple of chairs.

"I hear you took a shiv up your neck."

"It will heal."

Tarkington pulled out a small tape recorder and put it on the card table close to Jack. "I got jumped a few years ago. My partner killed the guy. Another second and I'd have been history."

"The warden seems to think I need a lawyer."

"Why?"

"I was hoping you could tell me."

The detective studied him for several seconds before he spoke. "You got some reason to need a lawyer, then get a lawyer."

"I don't think I need one."

"Then tell me what happened."

Tarkington identified the two of them for the sake of the tape, then recorded Jack's consent for the interview, including another admonition that he had the right to talk to his attorney.

Jack spent the next hour going over everything he could remember up to the time he regained consciousness in the hospital. He was careful to mention the circumstances of the guards leaving without giving it too much emphasis.

They went through a couple of cups of coffee each as Tarkington asked many of the same questions more than once, and from different angles. But the story remained the same, and Jack could sense that the interview was coming to an end.

Tarkington threw his paper cup in the trash. "Tell me about the guards."

Jack tensed. "What about them?"

"The warden says Burke didn't make his move until you sent the guards away."

"He tried to slit my throat."

"But you've got to admit it looks bad . . . the timing and all."

Jack just stared at the detective. Conners knew about this interview because Tarkington had already talked to the warden. Maybe he did need a lawyer. "I didn't tell them to leave. They informed me when they left. There's a difference. Ask the guards, they'll tell you."

"I have."

Jack wondered what the guards might do to cover themselves. He wanted to say that it would be suicide for the guards to contradict Conners, but he knew it wouldn't mean much coming from him. "I've told you what happened."

"The way I heard it, Officer Howard made you undergo an unauthorized strip search in front of a female officer yesterday."

Jack began to boil inside, but he kept silent. *That sick bastard had probably enjoyed every minute of it.*

"The female guard is on unpaid leave and is facing dismissal, if it makes you feel any better."

Jack didn't say a word.

"A suspicious person might wonder if your coming onto the scene just before a breakout was more than just coincidence. That maybe you were supposed to be the only hostage, but Officer Howard was taken along because of what he did to you." He paused, eyeing Jack for his reaction. "You see, there's something that doesn't make sense. Why kill one hostage and let the other one go free?"

Jack stood. "You have my statement."

"I just want the truth, Doctor."

"You just heard the truth."

Tarkington regarded him in silence, seeming to decide what he believed. "I want you to come look at mug shots. Maybe you can ID the two men who helped Burke escape."

"I have patients to care for."

Tarkington stopped the tape recorder and put it in his coat pocket. "I've taken care of that. Dr. Scalacey will be here soon. That means you're free to help me with the investigation."

"It doesn't look like I've got much choice."

"Not unless you have something to hide."

They left the infirmary together, but before they could reach their cars they were swarmed by a mass of reporters, some reaching out with microphones. Lights glared above cameramen and several of the group nearly fell because of the crush.

The first to get in his face was a woman with short hair and stark yet attractive features. "Warden Conners says you dismissed the security guards just before the breakout. He says you're responsible for the officer's death. Do you have any comment?"

The sound of motor drives from still photographers surrounded him as Jack pushed against the group.

Someone shouted from the back, "Are you being taken into custody?" A cameraman turned to tape Detective Tarkington getting into the driver's seat of his car.

"Is he being charged?"

Jack kept his head down. Two other photographers aimed at Tarkington, making a hole in the throng. Jack walked between them and worked his way around to the other side of his truck.

"We hear you just finished your residency. Have you passed your boards?"

"Did you know Otis Burke before the breakout?"

"Do you know Burke's location?"

"Do you have any *other* criminal record?"

Jack looked back at the last voice, but regained his composure before he said the wrong thing. He got in the truck but they stuck like flies after he closed the door. Two TV cameramen were aiming at him from the front grill. Jack started the engine, but they didn't move. The reporters pressed against the truck, shouting a barrage of questions, often at the same time. He just looked ahead, trying to imagine what an innocent person should look like.

Finally Tarkington was able to move his car, and Jack began to drive slowly. The ring of reporters and cameras gradually opened, but they moved with him until his truck reached the outer gate of the prison. The fact that they remained probably meant Warden Conners was going to have a press conference. His face would be on CNN in less than an hour.

Jack caught up with Tarkington's car and followed him downtown, grateful for the silence.

They kept him looking at mug shots until just after 3:00 P.M. He told them that he'd been too far away from the GTO to identify the two other men, but Tarkington insisted. Every once in a while another officer would bring a thick book of pictures and would ask some of the same questions Jack had already answered a half dozen times, but he went along with the game. He'd have enough trouble handling Conners—he didn't need to piss off the police, too.

When they finally let him go, he was told to stay in the city in case they had more questions. He made what he thought looked like a dignified exit, but didn't breathe easy until he felt the sun on his chest. He walked down the granite steps of the downtown police station and went to a row of pay phones on the corner. After twenty rings he got the paging operator at Garity Memorial Hospital.

"This is Dr. Harris. Could you page Dr. Daniel Linh? I'll hold."

He didn't have to wait long. Pathologists didn't get many pages, and they often came as a welcomed break in the routine. "I have him, Doctor."

"Where the hell have you been?" Dan's voice was strained.

"Look, I'm sorry about leaving the hospital. A lot's happened and—"

"I'll say it has. Have you seen the TV lately?"

"I haven't exactly had time."

"Well, you better make time. Channel eleven is running promo commercials for the local news tonight and you're the poster boy responsible for the breakout."

Jack instinctively looked around for reporters. "How bad is it?"

"I don't know. Gotta watch tonight. But it doesn't look good."

"The warden's trying to make it look like the breakout was my fault. He wants to cover his own ass."

"Jack, it's the press you've got to worry about now. If they come after you, I'd show off that neck wound. How is it, by the way?"

"I'll live."

"I can meet you at the house if you need help."

"No, thanks, but I could use a couple of favors."

"Shoot."

"See if the ER cultured my wound and check the sensitivity against Azythromycin."

"No problem. What else?"

"Are you alone?"

"Yeah. I'm in my office."

"I need you to check the medical examiner's autopsy findings on the guard who was killed. His name was W.E. Howard."

"How'd you know it was done here?"

"I just assumed—"

"Most criminal autopsies are done in the ME facility downtown, but they brought the body to our ER like he still had a chance or something. From what I hear the guy was DOA."

"He was a cop before he became a guard. One of their own. Maybe they were hoping that something could be done."

"Maybe, but things seemed pretty organized to me. You know Dr. Edelman's still the medical examiner for Fulton County. . . . He was all over this case. The room was off-limits during the post. I don't think they'll tell me anything."

Jack wondered if Richardson's people had put the clamps on the records—not an easy thing to do. He thought of the pictures he'd seen in Richardson's mansion. "My butt's on the line here. I'm not asking you to steal anything, I just want you to check a few things out."

"Such as?"

"Toxicology reports, any unusual blood work, cause of death."

"Tox won't be ready for another day or so."

"He may have been tortured before he died, maybe even injected with something. There was a bullet wound but I don't think it was enough to kill him. I'd like to know what the official examiner's report says about it."

"How do you know all this?"

"Can't tell you that, Dan."

"I'm not sure I like the sound of that."

"For now you've just got to trust me."

There was a brief silence while Linh apparently weighed his options; then he spoke. "I can get the blood work off the computer, but I can't promise anything about the ME's report."

"Just do what you can, and call me tonight at home."

"You better keep an eye out for reporters."

"There's not much I can do about that. If I get into a shouting match with the warden, I may lose my access to the prison. And then I'll never find out about my father."

"Look, Jack . . . as a friend. I still don't think this is a good idea. You can't bring him back."

"It's something I've got to do. Thanks for your help. I'll talk to you tonight."

Jack hung up and looked around again. Maybe he couldn't bring his father back, but he could bring him some justice. And it didn't matter what it cost him in the process.

Things were spinning out of control much faster than he ever dreamed. He could just imagine a mob of reporters hanging out in front of his house, interviewing neighbors, stalking him as the fresh meat of the day. Maybe he did need a lawyer, but he knew whom he wanted to talk to.

He dug more change from his pocket and called Elaine at St. Michael's Episcopal Church to check on Ed. A lady volunteer connected him, and after a few rings Elaine finally picked up.

"Outreach office."

"It's Jack. I wanted to thank you for all you did last night. For me *and* Ed."

"We got the croissants. They were great. And Ed's been fine. How's that hole in your neck?"

"You get an A in battlefield bandages."

"We run on a shoestring budget around here . . .

I've gotten good at patching Sheetrock, so if the thing doesn't heal, just give me a call."

"I'll keep that in mind." He imagined how she must be holding her head as she cradled the receiver. "Ed's been through a lot. I was hoping I could pick him up a little early today."

"He's been fine all morning. I don't think he knows about what happened."

"If you can manage without him, I think we need to spend some time together. It's more for me than him."

"I'm sure he'll be glad to hear it. I'll get him ready."

Jack got in his truck and drove across town to Enterprise Gardens, a world of apartments and concrete that everyone except the chamber of commerce called the Projects. The brick apartments were dark red but the whole area was overwhelmed by gray— gray fences, gray concrete, gray walls. Even the graffiti were sprayed on a canvas of gray. He knew that Elaine felt a calling to work where hope was in short supply. How she did it was beyond him. Each time he came down here he feared for his own safety.

He found a place to park a block away from the brownstone church and walked along a chain-link fence that framed a few dozen boys playing basketball. The courts were divided up on a concrete slab and none of the goals had nets, but it didn't seem to matter.

Jack took the worn steps to the side entrance of the old church. The caulking peeled around the tall windows of the sanctuary. The windows were opaque, having been painted with broad strokes of white mixed with light blue.

Once inside he could sense the heart of Elaine's ministry. The building had a familiar smell of old mahogany. He heard voices to his right, and he followed the sound into a large open room housing about twenty rows of rectangular tables. A black woman in a nursing uniform was filling cups with Gatorade and lining them up in rows. She looked out a window and counted the kids playing basketball, then added two more drinks to the table.

He walked over to her. "Excuse me. I'm Jack Harris. I'm looking for Elaine."

She put down the pitcher and wiped her hands. "Henrietta Franklin. I think she's still in the kitchen."

"Looks like you've got your hands full."

"Those boys will drink the well dry. But this is where they need to be."

He smiled and walked across the large room, where the door to the kitchen was propped open. Midway along the wall was a pass-through window where people could pick up food. Closer to the corner was another window where the dirty utensils and glasses were dropped off. Signs instructed that paper plates and drink cans were to be put into the appropriate recycling bin, and each bin had a drawing that indicated its role.

Elaine had told him that nearly sixty percent of the people they served were functionally illiterate. The drawings helped, but she was pushing the church to start an adult reading program. So far, the parish had neither the money nor enough qualified volunteer teachers to get the program off the ground. But it was a project she'd have to leave to someone else. She had her hands full trying to run both the soup kitchen and the prison outreach program.

He walked into the spacious kitchen and found Ed and Elaine peeling potatoes next to a huge aluminum pot. His brother was just over six feet tall and built like a linebacker, but still struggled with fine motor skills. He'd made remarkable progress in therapy with his hand, but the left foot still turned in a little when he walked. As Jack got closer to the pot he could see several mangled potatoes with strips of unpeeled skin. They meant so many things at once . . . Ed's problems and his progress. Jack knew it was good practice for him, and to Elaine's credit she never reached in to fix Ed's mistakes.

Ed beamed when he saw Jack. "Hey, my brother." Ed dropped his knife and a half-peeled potato and gave him a bear hug.

"Not so hard, Ed. I gotta breathe."

"Sorry. Too hard." Ed let go but kept his face within an inch of Jack's.

"So I hear you did all right at Elaine's." Jack gently eased his brother's big frame back a step and whispered, "Remember to give people a little room."

Ed's eyes sparkled and he whispered back, "OK, Jack. I remember. Just like you said."

"You had a good time last night?"

"Can we have a cat?"

Elaine put down a potato and smiled.

"Well, you'll have to help feed him. Can you do that, Ed?"

Ed hugged him tight and lifted him a few inches off the ground. "I'll feed him every day."

Jack hugged him back and was let down to earth. He looked at Elaine. "Could you help us find a good cat? I'm a dog man, myself."

He watched her stand and the way she rubbed her hands on the paper towel. She had on a light yellow blouse and jeans, and looked about perfect.

"They practically take care of themselves."

"So you'll help us?"

"I know a lady at the Humane Society. I help her place three or four every month. I keep them at my apartment once we know they don't have AIDS or any feline viruses. He can have one of the kittens he saw last night."

Ed picked up a potato and rubbed it nervously. "Will that man come again?"

Jack looked at Elaine. "What man?"

Her expression grew serious. "A police officer came to the church earlier today and wanted to ask Ed some questions."

"What kind of questions?"

"When I realized what was going on, I told him to leave."

"What kind of questions?"

"He had a photo of that prisoner . . . I can't remember the name."

"Burke?"

"That's it. He asked Ed if he'd ever seen Burke before. Then he asked if he'd seen you talking to any black men in the last few days. That's when I told him to leave."

"You get his name?"

"Yeah." She walked to a bulletin board by the phone and removed a pushpin from a card. "Here it is. Lieutenant Paul Lankford."

Jack reached for the card. "Mind if I use your phone?"

"There's one by the door."

"Is there one with some privacy?"

"My office, if you want to call it that, is straight down the same hall you came through. It's the second room on the right after you pass the side entrance to the parish house."

"Thanks" He took the card and found her office easily. On the wall behind her small desk was a poster about the United Thank Offering for World Hunger. There were over a dozen pictures of happy young men and women, mostly black, taped to the wall. To the left was a case packed with books. The titles varied in subject. The top row alone had books about theology, economics, social work, and federal grants. Above the case was her diploma from the University of North Carolina. Two metal folding chairs had piles of notebooks and manuals, and her desk looked as if someone had dropped a bunch of papers from the roof. He checked the lieutenant's card and dialed the number.

Behind her chair was another thin table with pictures of Elaine and some friends in the snow. They were all bundled up in down coats and had probably just finished a snowball fight. Another picture was of Elaine and a young man, their arms around each other's back. In the center of the picture arrangement was a polished stone cross with blue and silver hues. Jack studied the picture of the guy with his arm around Elaine and wondered if he still meant anything to her.

An automated voice on the other end of the phone told him to punch in the extension of the party he wanted, or to press one for more options. He punched zero and waited for a human being.

"How may I direct your call?"

"Detective Tarkington." Jack paced in the small room, concentrating on the floor while he waited for a response.

"Tarkington here."

"You kept me down there so you could send some goon to harass my brother."

"Excuse me?"

"We both know what's going on, so let's cut the 'I don't know what you're talking about' crap. My brother's got the mind of a child, and you people scared him to death. Not to mention that somebody leaked my involvement to the press."

"You finished?"

"Leave my brother alone."

The line was silent, and Jack felt like hanging up, but he didn't. "I'm finished."

"We've got a job to do, Doctor, and we're going to do it. But we didn't know about your brother's condition. I sent Lankford when you were tied up with us, but the lieutenant left as soon as he realized the score with your brother."

"He left when one of the staff people at the church told him to."

"He didn't have to leave. And he could have dragged your brother downtown."

"So you think I owe you an apology?"

"No apology. Just some respect."

"What about the press?"

"That's not from us. We got some calls, but we refuse to comment about ongoing homicide investigations. I'd suggest you do the same."

Jack realized it was the second time he'd received that advice in the last twenty-four hours. "I'll do that." He hung up the phone and noticed Elaine leaning against the doorway.

He felt a rush of embarrassment. "I probably said some things . . . this being a church."

"We're in the middle of the Projects. It's nothing I haven't heard before. Besides, you sounded pretty tame to me."

"It's just something that needed to be said."

"I wasn't trying to eavesdrop." She touched her neck. "Listen, I've been invited to this reception, and I was wondering if you might want to come as my date."

He followed the fine line of her neck and shoulder, somehow drawn to every tiny detail of how she carried herself.

"Well, you don't have to act so eager," she said.

He felt his cheeks flush. "I'd love to go. When is it?"

"Night after tomorrow. Mr. Richardson's being honored by the Service League."

"C.W. Richardson?"

"He's their Man of the Year, in honor of his history of supporting several Atlanta charities."

"The same leverage buyout guy who's gutted a half dozen companies just to make a buck?"

"Amazing, isn't it? He's our biggest benefactor. Members of our congregation live in unbelievable poverty—without him we'd have no outreach program at the church. But it's not just us. He gives to many worthy causes, and he doesn't ask for any recognition. I don't think I've ever seen anything about his donations in the press."

"So how much does it cost to get named Man of the Year?"

"I've got no idea, but I don't think he does it for that reason. From talking to some of my contacts, I'm sure he gives well over a million dollars a year to local charities, and that doesn't include building funds and endowments that he's started."

Jack had a hard time imagining Richardson as a secret philanthropist.

Her smile seemed to touch him from across the room. "It's formal—I even bought a dress." She found the engraved invitation under a book on her desk. "The gala starts at six P.M., at the Richardson Enterprises headquarters. It's usually at the Omni Arena, but I hear he wouldn't accept the honor if they spent any money on a facility. It's usually quite a party. All the proceeds from ticket sales and a silent auction go to charity."

"I should probably rent a tux."

She put the invitation back on the desk but stayed close enough for him to smell the scent of her hair. She seemed to understand about the cost of a tux. "I'm sure a dark suit is fine. We're an indigent charity, after all."

He thought of his first roommate in college. The guy came from one of those old trust-fund families. His wardrobe included a tux, which he kept in a special suit bag. Why in the world he'd need a tux was beyond Jack. But, sure enough, the guy wore it to a private reception at the college president's mansion, and gave Jack his first lesson in shirt studs and cummerbunds. It was just one of a number of ways that Jack discovered there was a whole other layer of people out there.

"Listen, there's going to be some press people after me. If this gala is a big deal they might cause some trouble. I just thought you might ought to know."

"Did you do anything wrong?"

"No."

"Then just make sure they get a picture of my new dress. I'm going to look fabulous."

He wanted to hold her but all he dared was a smile. "I wouldn't miss it."

SEVEN

Jack put the litter box he'd bought on the flatbed of his truck, while Elaine and Ed remained in the cab with the new kitten. He hadn't seen his brother this happy in two years. Ed had already changed the cat's name six times since they got the adoption papers from the Humane Society.

Jack was startled by the harsh tone of his new beeper. He checked the number and motioned for Elaine to roll down her window.

"I've got to answer a page. It shouldn't be but a minute."

"We're fine." She smiled and turned to help Ed get the kitten off the back of his neck.

Jack crossed the hot parking lot of the strip mall to a pay phone outside a drugstore. He double-checked the number as he dialed.

"Infirmary."

"This is Dr. Harris."

"John Samson, we met yesterday."

"I remember. You went to check on Burke's other meds."

"Listen, I'm sorry about how things are turning out. Conners has our backs against the wall—"

"You gotta do what you think's right."

The physician's assistant took a breath.

Jack let him stew a little, then said, "I didn't know I was on call."

"It's about Jackson Tillis. He was admitted last night with chest pain."

"I saw his chart."

"He doesn't look so good, Doc. The nurse called me in about a half hour ago."

"I was called to the warden's office before I saw him. What did Dr. Scalacey think about him?"

Jack heard Samson flipping pages in the chart. "He didn't see him."

Jack's jaw tightened. "I told Latham to start IV heparin. I was told that Scalacey would see him when he got in this morning."

"I called Latham. He said Scalacey was unwilling to take responsibility for the patient after you'd reviewed the chart and given orders. At the time Tillis was stable and Latham didn't think he'd go bad before you could see him in the morning. Tell you the truth, it's not that unusual. There are times when a couple of days go by before Scalacey has seen the patients we admit."

Jack couldn't believe what he was hearing. He'd never have left the patient if he had any hint that Scalacey was such a weasel, or that the police would tie him up all afternoon. But it was his own mistake, and he knew it. Legally Jack was responsible the minute he gave the verbal orders to the PA. Never mind that the early administration of heparin could prevent a heart attack in someone with unstable angina. "Where's Scalacey? Isn't he on call?"

"You were listed on the original schedule. I guess we forgot to change it."

Jack's head began to pound. He knew better than to lose his cool, especially with someone who worked under him. "We'll have to deal with that in the morning. What's Tillis look like?"

"Sitting up in bed, real short of breath."

"Vitals?"

"BP's 102 over sixty, heart rate's 120, respiration twenty-four to twenty-eight."

"Is he still having chest pain?"

"It got worse about two hours ago."

"*Two hours?* What was done for him?"

"The only orders we had were for the heparin drip, but the nurse used the standard admission orders and gave him sublingual nitroglycerine. When he got worse she called me. I started him on two liters of oxygen and gave him two of morphine, then four more when I knew he could tolerate it."

"Good. How about an EKG?"

"We're getting one now."

"He needs to be shipped to Garity."

"We got a problem there, sir. The warden won't let us move anyone without an MD on-site."

Jack checked his watch. "It will take me forever to get there in rush-hour traffic. How do we override this stupid rule?"

"The rule took effect today. The warden was all over us. No exceptions."

Jack looked back at his truck across the parking lot. "At least order the ambulance so they can be there when I arrive. In the meantime I've got to walk you through some things."

"Shoot."

"Do his lungs sound wet?"

"No, sir."

"How about a blood gas?"

"I sent one as soon as I got here. The pH is seven-point-five, pCO_2 is thirty-four, pO_2 ninety-two, with an oxygen saturation of ninety-one percent."

"Is that on room air?"

"Yes."

"He's hyperventilating, blowing off CO_2. But the oxygenation is normal. He's not in heart failure."

"But he looks rough."

"Are his pulses equal?"

"Radial and femoral felt strong bilaterally."

"That lessens the chance of an aortic dissection, but he could still have a small rip that's walled itself off."

"Now that you mention it, the pain is pretty sharp."

"Did you get that EKG yet?"

"I've got it right here. The computer interpretation says it's normal."

"Anything make the pain better or worse?"

"He said it was worse when he sat forward, but his breathing was so labored that I made him sit up anyway."

"Jesus, if he has pericarditis the heparin might have made him bleed into the pericardium. He could have tamponade. Does he have a pericardial rub?"

"I'm not sure. I'm not too good at hearing rubs."

"It can be hard to hear, especially if he's breathing loud. Do you know how to check a *pulsus paradoxicus*?"

"I've heard of it, but—"

"Check the BP again, but you've got to be very specific and slow. Pump the cuff until the mercury is real high, like 200. Then slowly let it down. There are two parts to the systolic pressure. The first time you hear the beat is actually very soft—a lot of people miss it, but you've got to listen carefully. You'll hear that soft beat when he breathes out, but it disappears when he breathes in. Write it down, then let the cuff down slowly again. When you can hear the beat in both inspiration and expiration, that's the second systolic number to write down. The difference between the two numbers is what I need to know. If the difference is over about ten to twelve the pericardium may be full of so much fluid that it's choking the heart."

"I'll check right now."

"I'll hold on. And listen, cut off the heparin drip."

"Yes, sir."

Jack sorted the possibilities while he waited. If Tillis had an aortic dissection, the heparin would have prevented any clotting, and the man would probably be dead by now. If it was an MI, the heparin might have saved his life. But if the MI extended, the heart wall could actually rupture and fill the pericardium with blood. But the lungs would be congested with blood that had backed up from the failing heart. And none of the data fit that diagnosis.

He knew an inflammation in the pericardium could mimic a heart attack and was notoriously difficult to diagnose in the first day because the EKG changes and physical findings could lag behind the onset of symptoms. But the pain was usually worse when the patient leaned forward. The lifesaving benefit of heparin he'd given for unstable angina could be quite dangerous if the sac around the heart was raw from inflammation.

Samson picked up on the other end. "It's thirty-eight millimeters of mercury."

"He's probably got pericardial tamponade."

"What do we do?"

"We've got to drain it. Do you have a pericardiocentesis needle there?"

"No chance."

"If I have to I could use a spinal needle. Surely we have spinal tap trays."

"We've got that."

"But he could go down the tubes while I'm stuck in traffic. This is what I want you to do—call the ambulance and call the ER at Garity. Let them know what to expect. But first I want the warden's home number. Maybe I can get him to change his orders and you can get Tillis to the hospital without having to wait for me."

"Hold on." Samson came back on after a few seconds and gave him the warden's number. "But I don't know how he's gonna like being called at home."

"You let me handle it. We're old friends."

"So I hear."

"Call Garity and the ambulance. I'll let you know what the warden says."

Jack hung up and looked back over to his truck. It would waste too much time to walk over and explain what was going on . . . time that Jackson Tillis couldn't afford. He put his last quarter in the phone and dialed Horace T. Conners.

It rang eight times before it was answered. "Yeah."

"Warden, this is Dr. Harris. I know I'm the last person you want to hear from, but we've got an emergency at the infirmary."

"You trying for another breakout?"

Jack ignored the slap. "I'm on my way to the prison, but I can tell from the PA's evaluation that we've got an inmate in critical condition. He could die in the time it will take me to get across town. I'm calling to ask if you'd direct the guards to take him in an ambulance and let me meet them at Garity."

"In all my years in the field of corrections I've never once had anyone make this kind of request."

Jack could imagine Conners's fat fingers clutching the receiver. "I'm still asking for your intervention."

"Your word doesn't mean diddly to me, son."

Jack turned toward the brick wall as a woman walked by. "I'm making an official request. If that man dies, I'm not the only one who's going down." He caught himself before saying anything about a press conference.

"I'm going to eat you alive."

"You just might, but tonight you're going to call the infirmary and send that inmate to Garity or risk being the only one who stood in the way of a lifesaving procedure. Who do you think channel eleven will believe then?"

"You little bastard. Nobody talks to me like that."

"What's it going to be?"

He could hear Conners's breath. "I'll make the call. But you better have your butt in my office at ten A.M. You understand me, son?"

"We understand each other just fine." The line went dead before Jack could hang up on him.

Jack ran his hand through his hair and stared at the mortar and bricks above the phone. How the hell did he get into this? Conners was out for him, and Scalacey was either incompetent or was setting him up for a fall. He had the sinking feeling that Scalacey and the warden had a long history of covering for each other.

He scanned the parking lot. Traffic was thick on the street and the lot was filling with cars as people stopped for errands. He focused on the two silhouettes in his truck, their heads bobbing as they enjoyed the kitten's playfulness. Sweat traced its way down his back. He could swear that it was hotter than it had been at noon. He worked out a plan while he walked back to his truck.

He opened the door and heard Ed's laughter. His brother had the kitten buttoned up inside his shirt, and the little black and brown head was poking out from the top, licking Ed's chin, then darting back inside.

Elaine touched Ed's chin with catnip, then pulled back to watch the kitten pop back out for another treat. The innocence and joy warmed a part of Jack that nothing could take away, no matter what they did to him.

He leaned over to Elaine while Ed was laughing. "There's an emergency at the prison with one of the inmates. I've got to meet them at Garity." He hesitated just long enough to know it was OK to ask. "You could drop me off, and I could get a ride back to the church to pick up Ed."

She leaned closer and slipped her hair behind her ear. "One of the volunteers is closing up tonight, so I'm free. Give me directions to your house and I'll get everybody settled. Our little friend will do better if we take her to her new home. . . . Anywhere else will just confuse her. You can take me home after they're asleep." She looked at Ed. "We're a team, aren't we?"

Ed nodded. "You and me, and Whiskers."

Jack reached over and gently rubbed under the kitten's jaw and felt the purring vibration of approval. "Whiskers really likes you." He tapped Ed's knee.

"This is the best thing you ever did for me."

Jack felt the pain of Ed's words. He stared ahead and tried to fight the shame that if it weren't for him, Ed would still be normal. It was something he could never forget, something for which he could never be forgiven.

Someone finally let him into the line of traffic, but none of the lanes were moving. He stared blankly at the sea of cars. No matter what he did, there was no way he could ever make it up to his brother. Just when he thought he'd locked his guilt away, here it came again to kick him in the gut. And there wasn't a damn thing he could do about it.

He'd been inching along the road for nearly five

minutes when he realized he hadn't said a word to either of them since they left the parking lot. He heard Ed playing with the kitten, but Elaine was quiet, and had probably noticed his awkward silence. He looked over at her. "What do you know about Warden Conners?"

"I've dealt with him for about two years. Without the support of the wardens we don't stand a chance with our prison outreach programs. His first and second answers are always no. I don't think he's ever seen an idea he liked unless it would get him somewhere."

"I understand there's a lot of money to be made from privately run prisons."

"I don't know much about it. We deal with several prisons—state and federal. Conners is a lot different from the other wardens."

"He's setting me up to be the fall guy over the breakout."

"So that explains your concern about the press."

"Word is that I'm on the six o'clock news. With this traffic it looks like I won't even catch my fifteen minutes of fame."

She turned to look out her window. He sensed that they both knew it would last more than fifteen minutes, but neither wanted to say it right now. He concentrated on driving and Elaine eventually turned her attention back to Ed and the kitten.

The drive to Garity was forty-five minutes of short-cuts around deadstill traffic. At times the only things moving were vapors of shimmering heat off the cars and pavement. He turned off Peachtree Street and cut behind the main artery of traffic to navigate the narrow tree-lined streets, crossing zoning lines every few blocks. Clusters of small wood houses changed with each turn from boutiques to a neighborhood of

wealthy young families, then back to bungalows selling antiques. Even in his anxiety he couldn't help but
notice the arching trees that most big cities could
claim only in trophy areas. Shade from the oaks and
pines was already covering large sections along their
drive, but the beauty of nature seemed out of sync
with what had happened in the last twenty-four hours.

They got closer to downtown and turned back onto
Peachtree. Traffic moved faster once they got within visual range of the gold dome of the state capitol. Not so
many blocks away, Garity Memorial stood out between
the interstate and towering hotels, a twelve-story chunk
of light brown brick that looked like the only architectural mistake in the Atlanta skyline. Jack knew it as a
scrappy, tenacious mother of medical wars, a fortress
where he'd cut his teeth as a doctor, somehow surviving
the grinding hours he'd worked to salvage whatever he
could of someone's piss-poor protoplasm.

He drove up to the emergency room entrance.
Three ambulances were parked in reverse, each with
the back doors open. One still had its emergency
lights flashing. Jack stepped out of his car and
scanned the area but saw no evidence of extra police
cars, which would have accompanied an ambulance
from the prison. An Atlanta policeman was slowly pac-
ing inside the glass double doors.

Jack leaned back into the truck. "They're not here
yet. I'll draw you a map to my place."

Elaine came around by Jack and reviewed the directions. "Technically, Conners works for Richardson.
I've worked with both of them a long time. Perhaps I
could get Richardson to convince Conners to call off
the dogs."

"How did you get mixed up with Richardson?"

"Through his involvement with our outreach program. I guess a cynic would say it makes him look good when a prison run by his company has a low recidivism rate. Less than ten percent of the inmates who participate in programs like ours return to prison. The return rate without our program is between fifty and sixty percent."

"Is this the point where I get the fund-raising talk?"

"I've made 'the talk' so many times I guess it's hard to turn off. But that's why we're connected. Those kinds of statistics can help his company land new contracts with other prisons. Personally, I don't really care what his motives are. We're making a difference, a real difference, in the lives of these prisoners. That's all that matters to me."

Approaching sirens pierced the air. Two police cars flanked the cement drive and an ambulance rushed into a blind corner, then backed up to the ER doors. A third police car pulled in behind the ambulance and a half dozen officers quickly secured the area.

"I've got to go. There's some leftover lasagna in the fridge. Sometimes all he'll eat is Eggo waffles."

"We'll be fine."

He was torn about leaving, but voices from the ambulance decided his fate. He looked back and saw them wheel the stretcher through the glass door. "I'll call if it looks like I'm going to be late." He leaned inside. "Ed, I'll be home in a couple of hours. Elaine is going to help you get the kitten settled into her new house."

"Can Whiskers sleep in my room?"

"Sure."

Ed smiled and looked back down to play with the kitten.

Jack moved aside and let Elaine get behind the wheel. "Thanks." He closed the door and jogged to the ER as she drove off.

* * *

The glass doors slid aside when he stepped on the black rubber mat. The ER was affectionately known among the residents as the Saturday Night Knife and Gun Club, a trauma center like any major inner-city hospital that caught the debris from the combustion of hot summer nights, poor angry men, and crack.

Jack took the ambulance entrance, effectively bypassing the triage desk and the congested waiting room. The ER was awash with motion . . . residents and med students crisscrossing the main hall, some with clip boards, others with tubes of blood, others bringing computer printouts of lab work from the central desk. The ER had a noise of its own—always loud, with bursts of someone shouting orders, and almost always someone crying hysterically behind a ring of curtains.

To an outsider the area seemed chaotic, but Jack navigated the human traffic without having to think about it. There was no sight of the troops from the prison, but he knew they would be either in the trauma room or one of the three beds reserved for cardiac emergencies.

As he got closer he saw a tech maneuver the portable X-ray machine into one of the cardiac cubicles. The curtains were still open and there were nurses on each side of the prisoner working in concert to get vital signs and start an IV. A med student in his short white coat connected the oxygen tubing to the wall unit, and a tired resident in scrubs was near the foot of the gurney. Four armed officers lined the perimeter of the cubicle.

Jack reached over the counter and waved to Erlene,

a black unit clerk who'd run the ER since even the old-timers could remember. "Hey, beautiful."

"Doc, I thought they got rid of you." Her huge body assaulted her creaking chair.

"Can't stay away. Do me a favor and call Cardiology stat, then see if Dr. Linh is still in-house. They've got a pathology conference until seven . . . Ask him to come on down if he's still here."

"Damn, you're bossy." She tugged the blue jacket across her breast.

"You miss me?"

"Hell, no." Her smile was easy.

"Gotta go save a life. Tell Raymond hello."

"That man don't deserve me."

Jack was ten feet beyond her. "You ever kick him out, give me a call."

She laughed and pushed the air at him. "Lawd, what you white boys don't know."

He came up behind Jason Ulrich, the third-year resident in charge of the shift. Jack knew him well from the last two years. He put a hand on his shoulder. "Long day?"

Ulrich looked back, then gave a relaxed smile. "Hey, man. Glad to see you." They shook hands. "It's been a bitch."

Jack gestured to the patient. "I sent this guy over from the prison." He could tell the inmate was in distress, breathing thirty times a minute, gasping for air, fighting to sit up. He was almost combative, so much so that the nurse lost the IV site she was working on. With a look of disgust she undid the tourniquet and moved to the other arm.

The resident crossed his arms. "I see you can't stay away from this place."

"It grows on you. My new job even comes with staff privileges."

"You gotta get a life, man. When I'm done I'm never setting foot in this hole again."

The X-ray technician pulled the machine away from the inmate's chest just as a nurse shouted, "I've lost his pulse."

Jack instinctively looked at the heart monitor, which showed a sinus tachycardia of 120 beats a minute.

Ulrich checked a carotid pulse and barked, "Call a code. He's in EMD."

In rapid succession an aide rolled the inmate on his side and a nurse slid a rigid plastic board under the man. They rolled him back and the aide started compressions on his chest.

Jack knew the end stage of cardiac tamponade was playing out before their eyes. Electrical mechanical dissociation occurred when the pressure of the fluid surrounding the heart got so great that the blood couldn't get pumped out, regardless of the electrical signals that were trying to coax the heart muscle to contract.

Ulrich shouted to the charge nurse, "I need a central line setup."

Jack rolled up his sleeves. "And a pericardiocentesis tray."

Ulrich was trying to get to the head of the bed. "I need some room here." The team pulled the gurney out three feet. "Suction and an ET tube."

A nurse quickly opened a sterile endotracheal tube and held it out in one hand while she turned on the suction canister with the other.

Ulrich extended the man's neck and slid a curved metal blade on his tongue, then lifted gently to expose the vocal cords. His eyes never left the target as he reached his free hand in front of the patient just as the nurse handed him the ET tube. Ulrich got the tube in place on the first pass, then blew up the tiny balloon inside for stabilization. He stepped aside as an aide tied the tube in place.

Jack was opening the sterile drapes of the central line tray. "He's in tamponade. I called for cardiology."

"They just took a sick one to the cath lab. I don't think we've got time for the backup to get here from home." Ulrich put on sterile gloves and wiped Betadyne antiseptic on the man's chest and shoulder in quick, broad strokes. "I'll get this IV. You know how to do a tap?"

"I did a couple with the cardiology attendings when I was chief resident."

"This guy won't live long enough to get to the cath lab. You're going to have to do it without fluoroscopy."

Jack knew he was right. The man was unconscious and unarousable. His chest and abdomen pulsed with each chest compression, and an aide forced air into his lungs with an Ambu bag attached to the ET tube. Despite CPR, he was turning blue from his chest to his head.

A breathless nurse ran up with the tray, interrupting his thoughts. "I got it!"

The bed was surrounded, and Jack had to ask a few people to step back to make room. The guards moved to the nurse's desk, but not out of view.

Jack swiftly opened the tray, leaving the innermost layer of sterile towels untouched. He looked at a nurse and with his hand motioned at a defined area. "Wipe his chest and belly with Betadyne."

He put on a surgical mask and a blue paper surgical gown. After gloving, he unfolded the final barrier of sterile towels. In the stainless steel tray were two syringes, sterile drapes, a six-inch needle, a valve, and a bag with tubing. He spread the drapes over the patient's chest and abdomen, leaving open a diamond-shaped field of skin still wet with Betadyne. His target was where the ribs joined just above the stomach.

He connected the long needle to a syringe, then waited for Ulrich to finish obtaining central access for IV fluid and medication. Jack had known Ulrich since he was an intern, and was impressed at how his skills had grown in the last two years.

Ulrich slid a needle under the patient's left collarbone and almost instantly a rush of dark blood flooded the syringe. Removing the syringe, he then slid a small flexible guide wire through the needle and into the subclavian vein. The needle was removed and a long floppy central IV catheter was threaded over the wire. The wire was then removed, and the catheter connected to a line of IV fluid.

Ulrich immediately looked up. "I need an amp of epinephrine and normal saline wide open." He reached for a packet of sutures. "It's all yours."

Jack held the syringe and needle while he reviewed the landmarks and technique in his mind.

"Still no pulse, Doctor."

Jack heard Ulrich's voice. "Resume compressions. We're ready, Jack."

He looked at the monitor. The heart rate was now dropping below fifty beats a minute, and the tracing of the QRS complex was beginning to widen, a sign of impending death. Jack glanced around quickly, and was now certain that the cardiology fellow hadn't arrived.

He carefully placed his gloved left hand on the inmate's lower chest, feeling the manubrium—the small bone at the inferior border of the sternum. The spot moved a little with each compression of the man's chest. With his other hand he placed the syringe and long needle just under the bone. Steadying his hand at the base of the syringe, he pushed with just enough force to puncture the skin, then quickly felt the hard rib on the end of the needle.

Having made this landmark, he pulled back slightly and redirected the needle deeper, but on an angle toward the left nipple. "Hold compressions." The needle was harder to push as he passed through more and more layers.

A nurse yelled, "PVCs on the monitor."

He knew he'd brushed against the pericardium, creating electrical irritability. If he pushed too hard, the sharp needle could pass through the sac of fluid and puncture the heart or lacerate a coronary artery.

Jack's heart pounded in his ears. He took a quiet deep breath and pushed the needle a half centimeter deeper. Dark blood started pushing back the plunger in the fifty-cc syringe.

"PVCs, couplets, short run of V-tach, PVCs." The nurse was shouting louder than he liked.

"It's OK. Pull the tray closer." He carefully balanced the syringe, aware that it would only take a twitch of his hand to drive the needle too far.

Dr. Ulrich had put on a new set of sterile gloves and was handing a guide wire off the tray. "Nice work."

Jack knew the next step held another land mine. He grasped the hub of the needle and meticulously removed the syringe, being careful not to let the needle dive deeper in reaction. Blood continued to pour out of the large-bore needle until he slid the flexible wire through the hub. Without fluoroscopy there was no way to direct the wire away from the heart, but his only consolation was that the amount of fluid in the pericardium was probably so great that the wire's action wouldn't be as traumatic as the needle.

"PVCs increasing, three beat, now six beat run of V-tach."

Jack pulled the wire back slightly, and carefully pulled the needle out of the body, and back over the wire. He had a death grip on the wire where it entered the skin. The other end bobbed in the air.

Ulrich handed the catheter, a flexible hollow tube with a soft pigtail curve on its end. Jack didn't move his eyes from the wire. "Help me thread this thing on."

Ulrich carefully inched the catheter down the wire until it met the skin. Jack had no choice but to let go, but was able to grab the exterior end of the wire. "Scalpel."

Ulrich handed him the surgical knife, and Jack made an incision wide enough to let the catheter pass through the man's thick skin. It was another step where fluoroscopy was key, since it was very easy to pull the wire out of the pericardial space while one gave enough resistance for the catheter to move into place. But there wasn't much he could do about that now.

He advanced the catheter in small increments as he tried to judge the position of the exposed wire—hoping to pull back with the same increment that he used to push the catheter. In less than thirty seconds he felt the resistance ease up. Blood was tracking its way out the hub of the catheter, dripping off the wire.

Jack glanced at Ulrich, "That's about as close as I can get it."

"Agreed."

Jack carefully pulled the wire out.

The nurse called out, "PVCs"

Jack watched as the PVCs danced across the monitor, then disappeared. He then connected a two-way valve to the catheter, and hooked one end to the syringe, and the other to flexible tubing that emptied into a sterile bag.

He began to draw off the bloody fluid. When the syringe was full, he'd move a small lever on the valve and discard the contents into the bag fifty cc's at a time. After about a hundred cc's were off, the heart rate was up to ninety.

"I've got a faint pulse." The nurse smiled and began to check the blood pressure.

Three hundred cc's later the pulse was eighty-eight, normal sinus rhythm.

"BP's one-ten over seventy-four."

Ulrich took off his gloves. "Way to go, man."

The tension in the alcove evaporated. A few in the crowd added their own congratulations as they peeled off to their other work. Jack carefully sewed the catheter in place, then watched for signs of neurological recovery as he continued to remove the fluid.

Within a minute the prisoner opened his eyes and was breathing spontaneously.

Ulrich sent a third-year med student to work the syringe, and Jack moved to the man's head. "You're OK. You had some fluid choking your heart, but we've got it drained off."

The man's eyes jumped to each of the people around him, and he started biting the ET tube.

Jack leaned down to the man's face. "I know it's hard to relax, but it will be easier if you can hold still. We'll get that tube out of your mouth in just a minute."

The inmate's eyes settled on Jack's face for a few seconds; then he calmed down.

"What's this guy's name?" Ulrich tossed his gown into a tall trash bin.

Jack looked back from the head of the bed. "Jackson Tillis."

"Mr. Tillis is lucky to be alive."

Jack moved away from the bed and spoke quietly. "Mr. Tillis is doing a life sentence." He glanced back at the man. "If you call that luck."

"Why are you working with these people?"

Jack knew the implication of what wasn't said—*when you could be in some first-rate group anywhere you chose*. "It's a long story. We'll get a beer sometime and I'll tell you about it."

"If you're buying."

"Deal."

"I'll handle the orders. You want him admitted to you or to cardiology?"

"Better ask Cards. My staff privileges are mainly for show. They allow me to check on how my patients are doing, but I won't have time for rounds over here. Listen, don't forget to send that fluid—"

"For gram stain, bacterial and viral cultures, AFB, TB culture, cystospin, CBC, protein—"

"Maybe I owe you two beers."

Ulrich gave him a friendly salute and walked to the nurse's desk to begin the paperwork.

Jack sat on a swivel stool at the foot of the gurney. This had been a close one. Too close. Had he not insisted on them bringing the prisoner directly, the man wouldn't have made it. And if he himself had examined Mr. Tillis this morning, maybe he would have heard the pericardial friction rub that the PA missed. But maybe it would have been too faint to hear. Maybe.

Erlene called from behind him. "Dr. Harris, there's a call for you."

Jack checked the bag. Over 400 cc's out. He gave

some instructions to the med student, then went over to the nurse's desk.

He punched line three. "Dr. Harris here."

"Are you psychic or something?"

"Dan?"

"I got some news on your prison guard."

"Where are you?"

"My office. We just got out of the med-surg conference."

"Are you going to keep me in suspense?"

"Your man died of acute leukemia."

"What?"

"Blast crisis. Probably bled to death from that bullet wound."

His mind raced with the pictures he'd seen in Richardson's mansion. "You're not serious."

"I've got the slides in my office."

EIGHT

"See for yourself." Dan Linh eased back from the microscope in his office.

Jack stepped across a pile of medical charts on the floor and made his way to the workbench that ran almost the entire length of the small office. Dan's desk was shoved under the only window at the end of the narrow room. Aside from six diplomas and certificates, the metal venetian blinds and an aging computer were the main contributions to the room's décor. The desk, like much of the floor, was covered with stacks of paper, most torn by Dan from medical journals with the good intention of one day creating a neat filing system. The anemic ceiling light seemed pitiful in comparison to the powerful halogen bulb at the base of the binocular Zeiss microscope.

The workbench was lower than most tables to compensate for the height of the instrument. On either side of the jet-black microscope were stacks of elongated cardboard tablets designed to hold a row of pathology slides. Jack leaned over the scope and noted that the open tablet to his left had *Howard, W.E.* written in black Magic Marker next to a sticker with a coding number.

Jack made subtle adjustments in the fine-focus knob, bringing the vivid red and purple hues into sharp definition. He carefully moved the microscope's platform and scanned the entire slide. There was no doubt about it. Saturating the background of normal red blood cells were numerous blast cells. These rapidly dividing cells were the early precursors of the white blood cell line. The cells shouldn't have been present in the circulation, and clearly represented a form of leukemia. If present in great enough numbers they essentially overtook the normally differentiated immune cells, creating a massive number of immature and improperly functioning cells of the body's defense system, rendering the patient unable to ward off even the normal bacteria that populated the human skin. This so-called *blast crisis* set up the leukemic patient for an overwhelming and life-threatening infection.

Jack pulled back from the microscope, briefly shutting his eyes after looking into the intense light shining through the slide. "What about the other slides?"

"Eosinophils all over the place."

Jack studied his friend. An elevated eosinophil count could mean anything from an allergic reaction to rare inflammatory diseases to cancer. "Did they do a bone marrow biopsy?"

"I looked, but I couldn't find any slides. And the gross tissue reports are locked up."

"What's the platelet count?"

"Forty thousand . . . low enough to bleed to death."

"Did he have a hemothorax?"

"The autopsy is under wraps. I don't know whether they found blood in his chest or not."

"Then why'd you tell me on the phone that he bled to death?"

"It's an assumption, but after a bullet wound how

could he stop bleeding with only forty thousand platelets?"

Jack leaned against a filing cabinet. "I need to see the postmortem report."

"Fat chance. Dr. Edelman's not the top dog in the department, but he's still the medical examiner for Fulton County. And he sealed all access. I don't think we've got a prayer of getting to it."

"You've been here five years. You ever hear of an autopsy being locked up?"

Dan started throwing a small rubber ball against the floor, catching it as it bounced off the wall by his desk. "No."

"I think some important people don't want anyone to know how Howard died."

Dan stopped tossing the ball. "Why?"

"I don't know, but I think the answer may be in that report."

"What's going on at Elrice Prison, Jack?"

"I don't know that either. But something's not right. I don't think Howard was taken at random by that prisoner. That's why they killed him, but left me alone."

"Did you catch the news?"

"No."

"I skipped the first part of the conference to see it. The warden said you dismissed the guards just before the escape."

"He said that on the air?"

"It gets worse. They had pictures of your house and the reporter went out of her way to emphasize that this was your first day on the job. Made you sound like an intern. They're doing a real number on you. Man, you've got to make a statement of some kind. People will take your silence as a sign that the charges are correct. You can tell by the tone of the reports that it's already happening."

Jack ran his hand through his hair. "Anybody around here say anything?"

"Not yet."

Jack knew what that meant. Any thoughts he'd had about cutting out for private practice were dead after this kind of news broke. No one would ever say it to his face, but prospective groups wouldn't want to take the risk of hiring him with this on his record. He'd worked years for a reputation that was being ruined by strangers in a single day. But if he challenged the warden publicly, Richardson might lock him out, and what he needed more than anything was access.

He also knew his chances of getting information about his father would be worse tomorrow after everyone had a chance to see the news or read the paper. "I can't issue a statement."

"Why the hell not?"

"I've already told you."

"It's a dead-end street, Jack. You've got to let it go."

"I need some more help."

"There's got to be a damn good reason. You're asking me to help you trash your professional reputation."

"There's something I'm not supposed to know," Jack said.

Dan watched him with keen eyes but didn't say anything.

"There's a mark on the officer's left forearm, near the anticubital fossa. It looks like a needle injection site."

"I'm not following you."

"It wasn't there before he died."

"How'd you—"

"I saw some police photos of the body where they

found him. There was a close-up, so the police know about it. And that means the medical examiner knows."

"How can you be so sure it wasn't there before?"

"This guy gave me a strip search an hour before the escape. I was looking at his arm when he tried to check the family jewels."

"No needle marks?"

"I'm certain of it."

"So that's why you asked about the tox reports. You think they killed him by injecting something lethal."

"Maybe, maybe not. But I don't think this break-out was as simple as we're being led to believe. If they injected this cop, then they had to have been planning on it. They had to have the stuff ready. It would have been a lot easier just to shoot him in the head."

"In his statement, the warden made a big deal of the fact that the guard was killed, and you weren't even harmed. When they cut to the reporter, she said a lot of questions were being raised about the fact that you were released and not even held hostage. They essentially accused you of having something to do with it. Now if word gets out about a lethal injection, who do you think they'll suspect as the source of the drugs?"

Jack slowly rubbed his eyes. He felt the ache under his tongue for the first time in hours. "Can you get me in to see the body?"

Daniel squeezed the ball in his hand. "I'll check on the tox reports, but I think the body's already gone."

"What about the dictated autopsy report?"

"I nosed around earlier. Usually one of the secretaries transcribes them, but none of them got it."

"Meaning?"

"Meaning it's being handled by the ME's office downtown. We're out of the loop."

Jack stared at the microscope. "Why are they hiding all this?"

"Because it's none of your business."

"That's where you're wrong. I think this guard did something, or knew something about Elrice. Something that some powerful people don't want anyone to know about. And I think my father may have discovered the same thing. That's why they're both dead."

Dan drove him home in his blue MG convertible. It spent more time in a repair shop than it did in Dan's driveway, but Jack thought it was one of the best-looking cars ever made. He had tried to buy it more than once, but Dan wouldn't budge.

The streets were wet from an evening shower, and with the top down the night air seemed almost cool as it beat against the back of their heads. The day had taken its toll, and Jack felt a heaviness he'd never experienced before. It was as if his arms and legs were in concrete. Pain shot under his tongue with the slightest turn of his head.

When they drove up to his house, Jack half expected to be confronted by a reporter when he got out of the car. He looked around, but the only thing out of the ordinary was Richardson's man parked half a block away in the black Cadillac.

Jack leaned over the car door. "Thanks for the ride."

"I'll call you if I find out about the autopsy. In the meantime, you think about what I said. At least fax your side of the story to the newspaper."

Jack watched a car drive by. "I'll think about it."

"Later." Dan checked his mirror and drove off.

Jack turned in the dark and climbed the steep concrete steps to his house. Only a little of the moonlight filtered though the dense trees onto the ivy slopes to either side, their wet onyx leaves merging into the blackness of the neighbor's yard.

He reached a landing of grass that passed for a front yard. Three more steps and he was on his porch. Through the beveled glass door he could tell that the only light downstairs was from the kitchen, in the back of the house. He heard the porch swing creak before he reached for his keys.

Elaine rocked slowly. "It's nice out here."

As she rocked back he could only see her bare feet and the legs of her jeans in the moon's soft light. "Sorry I'm so late."

"Ed fell asleep an hour ago. I've been enjoying your swing." She stopped the rocking motion and slid over a little.

Jack sat with her and the swing creaked in rhythm as they matched each other's stride. "And the cat?"

"We cut the top off a nice box and made a little bed. She's sleeping in his room."

Their knees touched but neither one moved away. "Thank you for what you've done for Ed."

They rocked the swing together for almost a minute before she said anything.

"I like this place."

"I'd like to buy it, but Ed's therapy takes most of my cash. Someday I'm going to own my own home. That's something my family never had."

"Ed told me about your mother leaving."

He looked down and tried to put it into words. He stopped rocking, causing the swing to sway. It came still, and he felt her calm patience. An eternity of memories, of pain, leaked from cellars closed long ago.

Elaine waited silently, allowing him to discover how much he could say, how much he could face himself.

"My parents had a hard life even before . . . before Ed's accident. My father never went to college—I don't even know if he finished high school. But he worked hard. He was a two-fisted kind of man who believed it was his role to provide for his family and to make sure things ran. When jobs dried up, we didn't go on welfare, we moved. He always found work somehow, but it was never easy.

"I think it must have been too much for my mother. She cried a lot. Sometimes he'd come home and she hadn't even fed Ed or me. Even then, Dad couldn't come right out and do anything about it. The only thing he did was teach me to make a peanut butter sandwich in case we got hungry and Mom didn't cook.

"Sometimes Momma seemed normal, and things were great. I remember how my body would roll toward hers when she sat on my bed to read me a story. But there were other times . . . once or twice she even left for a few days. I wasn't even two years old the first time. I don't really remember it—who could at that age—but I think she must have left me by myself. I still wake up sometimes scared to death that I'm alone."

He felt her hand on his arm. "Even when she was home there were plenty of days she didn't get out of bed, plenty of days we didn't have breakfast. I remember a long period when my father worked double shifts. He was gone before six in the morning, and didn't get home until after ten. I'd get Ed up and make sure we got to the school bus on time. Most nights I made sandwiches for supper. But I loved school. I felt safe there. We both did."

"You must have been so scared."

"Nobody ever hurt us. We just did what we had to do.

The worst part was this constant fear that one of my friends would find out. And I mean constant. It permeated everything in my life. We grew up playing these mind games, like nothing was really wrong. You learn real fast how to deny pain. But I knew it wasn't right."

"Did he ever try to get her professional help?"

Jack looked at her. "She wouldn't have gone. She was convinced that the doctors would tell everyone she knew that she was crazy. Just telling you this makes me nervous."

"Oh, Jack . . ." Elaine reached her hand into his, and he held it tightly.

"I can hear her now, stroking my hair while she'd tell me that you can't trust people with family secrets. How they'd use it to hurt us, to take her away."

"My God, you've kept this inside all your life."

Jack could only look at her, the deep fear welling up as overpowering as it was when he was six.

Elaine touched his face, closing his eyes with the light touch of her finger, kissed him on the cheek, then on the lips. She held him until he could find the strength to open his eyes.

"It's like if I tell you, then she'll never come back."

"It's not true, Jack. I won't hurt you. I won't hurt her."

They rocked in silence for a long time. He wanted to trust her. It was such a risk for him to speak about his family, but he wanted desperately to open up, even if only a step at a time.

Finally Elaine said, "Your father stayed with her all those years."

"Sometimes I wondered if his working multiple jobs came from a dread of having to be at home with her. I can't blame him if that's the case, but he still stayed with her. We went through some pretty lean times, and he did what he had to do to make ends meet.

Things got a little better when he found steady work as a prison guard at Elrice."

"Elrice?"

"Like father, like son." They began to swing slowly. "I'd just finished med school when Ed fell." He looked ahead to the dark bushes on the other side of the porch and rocked until he could say it.

"Ed had a long two years of therapy; then the physical therapists said Mom and Dad could do the rest of the work on him at home." He closed his eyes. "They had no idea what kind of pressure that put on them. One day Mom just left. We don't know if she's in an institution as some Jane Doe . . . we don't even know if she's alive. We checked all the hospitals, every ER you can imagine. The police got involved but they didn't do any better than we did. And we were limited—I couldn't leave my residency program, and if my father took off much from work, he'd be fired. Then there'd be no insurance to help Ed. We tried everything we knew to do. She's just gone."

"Where would you want to search?"

"There were places on the bayou where she was happy. I called everyone I could think of, tried medical facilities, even the state mental institution, and got nowhere. If I had even the slightest clue of where to start, I'd go. But there's no trace of her—anywhere."

"I don't see how you keep all this inside."

"Denial—sometimes I think it's what I do best. So I finally decided to pretend she's in Louisiana and somebody's taking care of her. Sometimes that's enough. Sometimes it isn't."

"You could go look for her now. I can help with Ed."

"Not yet. It's not that simple. I've got something else to settle first."

They rocked a while in silence. Eventually she said, "Tell me about your father."

"He was a good man—just didn't have a lot of education. Seeing Ed the way he was . . . eighteen and unable to feed himself or clean himself after going to the bathroom. My father, the man who could fix anything, couldn't do anything to help his son. How could a man like that even begin to understand brain injury?

"Ed had been a standout athlete in high school, and now he had to use a walker, and that was on good days. I know Dad did what he could, but losing Mom and losing Ed was just too much, I guess."

Jack eased out of the swing and looked down at the slope of his yard. "When I was a resident at Emory, I got a page to come to the chief's office. When I got there I learned that my father had gone in his room and had taken his own gun . . ."

He shut his eyes. It was as if everything were back. A stinging stillness that no one can comprehend, even if you've gone through it. The eternal questions of why. A thousand questions but all were about knowing why. "I just can't believe that he could kill himself. There's got to be another answer."

He felt her hand on his shoulder, and he turned to face the silent tears on her face.

He could hardly get the words out. "I've got this hole inside that nothing fits into."

Her arms held him tight. The two of them held each other, his eyes on the prism of light in the leaded glass door.

He wanted her to stay, but he didn't dare ask. It was too soon. In this moment he knew for certain that he couldn't bear to lose her.

"I better take you home."

* * *

Even after the rain, the heat from the concrete basketball courts went straight to his bones. But Burke didn't care. At least there was an occasional gust of wind. He never got a breeze in prison.

Everything was gray and chain-link except the brownstone of the old church he'd been watching for an hour. His eyes were on the side door at the top of a dozen brick steps that were framed with iron railing, loose from years of hand traffic. The children had come out already, so she wouldn't be much longer. And she'd be alone.

Neon was on the other side of the church and JT was across the street, in case she took another exit.

Burke crouched behind a Dumpster and watched through the glare of pole lights. The streets were deserted. Anybody hanging out late in this neighborhood wouldn't want to be doing their thing in full view of all these lights. The lights worked against him, too, but he wanted to take her here, by the church. It would say it all—there *was* no forgiveness for what she'd done.

The nausea returned, as it had for several weeks now. He lurched behind the Dumpster just in time to vomit the chili dogs. After he wiped the traces away from his mouth, he looked around, satisfied that Neon and JT couldn't have seen it. They'd have taken it for fear, and the one thing he couldn't show around JT was any loss of nerve.

He got back in position to see the side door. He knew her, like he knew the others on the list. She knew him too, but mainly as a number. It didn't matter. It had been almost a year, but he could still feel her skin and those strong hands . . . and what they had done. She was going to pay.

His body quickened when the side door opened. When she paused to lock it, his disgust rose at the sight of her white nursing dress. He hated the way the white stockings looked over her hot black skin. They were coming off—he'd make certain.

She didn't walk outside the fence to the sidewalk, but turned instead and walked right toward the Dumpster. She might have been thirty, but he couldn't tell. Years take on different meaning when you've been in prison.

He knew she had a good body under that dress. She'd brushed it against him when he couldn't act on it. But this time he was free, and could do whatever he wanted . . . whatever he needed. And he needed her.

He checked the small tubes and tourniquet in his pocket. Once he'd made up his mind about what he needed to do, it had been easy to steal some things from the prison clinic whenever Dr. Scalacey kept him waiting. He'd been sure to get the right ones with the little white powder that kept the blood from clotting—a distinction he'd learned from one of the trusties. The syringe was easy. He'd been using them since he was nine.

She came closer, and Burke saw JT crossing the street. He'd want in on some of that fine body. Maybe it would settle JT down to get a piece of her. The more he thought about it, the more sense it made. He'd let the other two take their turn when he was done.

The others on the list were white, and Burke was content to leave them alone after watching the life drain away—like he'd done with that guard. But she was one of his own kind, and he wanted a taste of her before she died. Like dessert.

NINE

Jack braced his arms against the mattress, waking to his racing heart. He sat up in the dark room and felt the sweat that soaked the front of his T-shirt. His head cleared enough for him to realize that the phone was ringing.

He sat on the side of the bed and fumbled for the receiver. "Hello."

Elaine's voice trembled. "Jack, you've got to come down here. It's terrible."

"What time is it?"

"Almost four-thirty. The police called. It's Henrietta. The sanitation crew found her body."

He turned on a lamp and immediately averted his eyes from the glare. "Where are you?"

"The church. The police have taped off the area by the Dumpster. She closed up for me last night while I was with you. Oh God, this is awful."

"I'll be right down. Ed won't wake up until seven." His mind raced. "I'll stay as long as I can."

He put the phone back and stood by the bed. Years of being on call had taught him to stand immediately or he'd fall asleep in seconds. His stomach burned. He'd been awakened enough times in this part of his sleep cycle to know that no matter what he did, he wouldn't feel right all day.

He pulled on some jeans and changed into a clean shirt. Downstairs he started the coffee and made two pieces of toast, chasing them with a full glass of milk, the best acid remedy he could muster for now. He walked out the back door to his neighbor's as the coffee began to drip.

The light was on in Mrs. Logan's kitchen and through a window he could see her working at the sink. She always rose before the sun—farm girls never changed their sleeping habits, she once told him. She was in her seventies and had been widowed long before Jack moved into the neighborhood. He helped her when she needed the strength of a young back to move a couch or put up the Christmas tree, and she watched out for Ed every afternoon. Whenever Jack was on call she'd stay overnight, or Ed would go to her place. She said she'd do it for free, and Jack believed her, but insisted on paying her anyway.

He knocked on the screen door and let himself onto her small back porch. He waited by her kitchen door next to several crates of returnable Coke bottles stacked one on top of the other. She parted the flowery curtain and then unlocked the door and kept talking as she walked back to the stove. "Come on in. The water's just boiling. All I've got is Sanka." He was always struck by her kind blue eyes. Her hair was chalk white and she was wearing a faded pink dress with a yellow sweater.

"No, thanks, Mrs. Logan. I can't stay long." His gut was burning with the news of the murder.

She uncovered her parakeet's cage and waved a finger between the bars. "Morning, love."

Jack closed the door behind him and stood by her Formica table. "I just got an emergency call, and I may be gone all day. I was hoping you could check on Ed when he wakes up."

She stirred her Sanka and sat down. "I'd love to. Gets lonely in this old house."

"He won't be going to work at the church today."

"Jack, I told those awful people from the TV station what a fine boy you are. But they were hateful on the news. I called and told them that, too."

"They were out here?"

"Some mouse of a man with his camera people poked their nose in my front door. But I told 'em to leave me alone."

"I'm sorry about all that. What they're saying about me isn't true, Mrs. Logan."

"I know that. They're just hateful, that's all." The parakeet pecked at a small jingle bell in its cage. She gently rose to feed the bird with her arthritic hand.

Jack said, "Some people tried to bother Ed yesterday. They may come back."

"Don't you worry about me. I'll shoo 'em away. Give me a minute. I'll change and cook breakfast at your house. You sure I can't make you some eggs?"

"Some other time, Mrs. Logan. Right now I'm in a hurry."

"Well, run along. I'll be over in a few minutes." She walked down her unlit hall and he let himself out.

Jack paused long enough at his house to pour some coffee in a travel cup, then jumped into his truck. It was still dark and he noticed the headlights of the black Cadillac behind him before he made the first turn on his way downtown to St. Michael's. Once they finally reached the Projects, the trailing car dropped back several blocks, but was still within sight.

He rounded the corner and had to brake suddenly to keep from ramming a police car. Three patrol cars and a blue and white police truck funneled onto the sidewalk next to the church. Spotlights focused on the back corner of the building, making everything in the foreground that much darker. Jack parked and jogged the rest of the way.

Yellow and black police tape sealed off the area between the side entrance and a large green Dumpster. He looked for Elaine, but all he could see were the officers moving around in the harsh light. A few people looked out windows from their subsidized apartments, but except for one woman standing in the street in a nightgown, the neighbors were either sleeping or chose not to get involved with anything that brought the police out.

Jack ducked under the tape and walked to the Dumpster, amazed that no one stopped him.

A man with his back to him threw a clipboard on the ground. "Take the damn cover off until the coroner gets here. You're gonna delay the body's cooling. Didn't they teach you anything ?"

The tarp looked as if it were covering a piece of furniture, but as a uniformed officer pulled it away, Jack could see the rope from the Dumpster leading down to the thick wrists of a black woman. Her arms were pulled back over her head like she'd been dragged down the street on her back. Her white dress was shoved above her hips and one leg was bent flat on the ground. The other was straight, and still had a wad of panty hose bunched at the ankle. Hair partially covered her face, but Jack could tell this was the woman who'd been setting up drinks when he visited the church yesterday.

"Who the hell are you?"

Jack turned just as the officer bumped his chest against him. "Dr. Harris. I was called down."

"Yeah, by who?"

"Someone who works at the church."

The officer pointed to the police tape. "Can't you read? Now move it."

He was about to leave when he saw Detective Tarkington in a circle of men near the body. The detective was obviously giving instructions, but stopped abruptly as their eyes met. He pointed a finger and walked briskly in Jack's direction.

Tarkington's eyes were bloodshot. "What are you doing here?"

Jack positioned his hand to block the glare of the lights. "Elaine Thomas asked me to come."

Tarkington flipped his notepad back a few pages, obviously looking for her name.

"She runs community outreach for the church."

"And why, exactly, would she have called you?"

"I'm surprised you're out on this. I'd have thought Officer Howard's murder would keep you too busy."

The detective's eyes hardened. "And you seem to be the common thread."

The two men stared at each other. Tarkington had crossed the line when he sent his man to interrogate Ed. There was a time Jack would have slugged him. On the derricks an affront didn't pass without payback. But that was then. He felt the blood pumping in his arms, but he kept his control. "She helps my brother, but I think you knew that already." He watched to be sure the detective got the message. "And we know each other socially—so she called. Anything else, you'll just have to ask her."

Tarkington worked his jaw muscles, then closed his notepad. "I've got a lot of work here. There's coffee in the church. Don't leave without checking with me."

* * *

The only light in the narrow brown hall was coming from her office. He walked past the pictures of former rectors of St. Michael's, then stood by her open door. Elaine was on the floor staring at some pictures that had fallen from a scrapbook in her lap.

She looked up but was unable to speak. Jack got down on his knees and held her against his chest and felt her whole body tremble. He pulled her tight and whispered, "I'm sorry."

He wanted to say that it would be OK, but it wouldn't, and they both knew it. There was nothing he could do but be there.

Elaine eventually spoke. "What kind of monster . . ." Her tears overwhelmed her.

He held her until she relaxed. She took a deep breath and picked up a picture from the pile. It showed a woman at a graduation ceremony.

Elaine struggled to compose herself. "When I first met Henrietta, she was about to come out of the Mc-Kensey Women's Prison. We helped her . . . she had so far to come, but you wouldn't believe how much she changed. Three years later she was going to night school and working as a volunteer here. She said she found a new life at St. Michael's." She dropped the picture on others in the stack. "Why?"

He picked up the picture of Henrietta in a white robe and mortarboard. She and Elaine were arm in arm in front of a large fake plant. Elaine looked like the proud parent.

"Prison to nursing school. You made a real difference in her life."

"She was a nursing assistant. And she wanted to change. She did it, not me." Elaine looked over the pictures before her. "We work with so many . . . so many that never seem to put their lives back together. God knows we try. We talk, we teach, we train in basic skills—we even teach manners. And we try to knit them into a spiritual community that will keep them on the right track. But I swear the basketball goals draw more people than I do."

She touched the skin around her eyes. She looked like she hadn't slept all night. She lifted a few pictures and found a tissue. "I was so idealistic when I started doing this work, but that was a long time ago. I meet them in the prison, I follow up when they get out, I go door to door in this neighborhood trying to catch the kids at risk. I've done it for almost six years, and the truth is I'm not sure I'm making any difference at all." Her eyes widened as if she'd finally said out loud what she'd been afraid to face.

"More than once I've been ready to pack up and leave. All my friends are married and having babies." She swept her hair away from her face. "But then someone like Henrietta rises out of all this muck and makes it." She slowly shook her head. "And now this."

"Does Father Dawson know?"

"He's in the narthex with Henrietta's mother. She lived with her in the Projects about two blocks from here."

There was a knock on the open door. They looked up to see Detective Tarkington. "Miss Thomas, I need to ask you some more questions."

Jack stood.

Tarkington gestured with his hand. "You can stay, Doctor."

Jack squared this shoulders. "I wasn't going anywhere."

Elaine cleared the pictures to make room but remained on the floor.

Tarkington kept staring at Jack while he entered the office. He put his Styrofoam cup on the desk. "I appreciate the coffee, by the way." He thumbed to a blank page in his notebook. "You said the victim had recently changed jobs."

Jack saw Elaine's body react to the word *victim*. "She works . . . worked at Comfort Heart nursing home."

"That's the one out by the airport?"

"She could take MARTA from downtown, and it would drop her off within a couple of blocks. We try to find employment in areas that are served by the transit system. Very few of our people have cars."

"And before that?"

"She had an externship in a medical clinic."

"At Elrice," Tarkington said, and looked directly at Jack.

Elaine stood. "Mr. C.W. Richardson is one of our principal sponsors. He's arranged for over a dozen of our people to work in one of his companies, including Elrice."

"Did you know the victim, Dr. Harris?"

"I saw her yesterday at the church when I came to pick up my brother. But we didn't know each other."

"I mean at the prison."

Jack watched the man's eyes. They were dark blue, and steady. Not malicious. He decided that Tarkington was just being thorough. "No. I've never seen her at the prison."

Elaine said, "She hadn't worked at Elrice for nearly a year."

Tarkington seemed to ignore her. "Now I want you to think hard about this, Doctor. Was she in the alley or in the car that met Otis Burke after the breakout?"

It was then that he realized the odd thing about the woman's body. He'd noticed it but it just hadn't registered. One sleeve had been ripped apart. With her wrists tied to the Dumpster, the strips of nurse's uniform dangled down onto her shoulder, and there was a yellow rubber tourniquet on the ground directly below her arm.

"You saw her, didn't you? I could see it in your eyes."

Jack focused on the detective. "The breakout was more than just a news story to me. That's what you saw in my eyes. The only time I ever saw her was at the church."

Tarkington stared directly at him and let the silence become awkward. "There was something there, all right. You know something that you're not telling me."

Jack reached for the detective's cup. "Don't forget your coffee."

Tarkington worked his jaw and was about to say something when a woman's wailing voice shouted from the hall.

"*You* did this to my baby." Father Dawson, a frail and aging man, tried to block the black woman, but she was too big for him to keep in the hall. She forced an arm over his shoulder and thrust it toward Elaine. "You brought her here, you made her do this work. That should be you out there."

The shock seemed to propel Elaine back against her desk.

The woman was screaming and crying at the same time. "I hope you rot in hell." Her arm sliced wildly through the air.

Tarkington pushed his body against the priest's to help control the woman. "That's enough, ma'am."

Father Dawson shot a panicked glance at Elaine, but she didn't see it. She was in tears, looking at the floor.

Tarkington had a lock on the woman and helped marshal her into the priest's office. Jack turned and faced Elaine from the doorway. She was crumpled in the corner with her knees to her chest and her face down.

He knelt in front of her and after a few seconds of not knowing what to do or say, he slowly touched her shoulders, then nestled his face against the side of her head. "You didn't do this. She would have had no hope at all without you. It's not your fault."

She trembled like she had a chill. "God help me. What have I done?"

TEN

Tarkington spoke from the doorway. "Mrs. Franklin says you left her daughter here by herself last night."

Jack's body was still hunched over Elaine, shielding her in the corner of her office. Whatever tolerance he had for Detective Tarkington was evaporating fast.

"Father Dawson says you two left the church together."

Jack gently released his arms from Elaine. He turned his head toward Tarkington. "This isn't the time."

"I'm afraid you're wrong there, Doctor."

Jack stood and faced him. A base instinct sized up their differences. He was a good two inches taller and was clearly stronger than the detective. He stepped closer. It was all he could do to control himself. "Not now."

He heard Elaine behind him. "Jack."

Blood pumped so hard he could feel it around his eyes. His shoulders contracted, ready to fight. He focused on the annoying way Tarkington tightened his jaw muscles—the target he'd hit first.

"Jack . . ." He felt her hand on his back.

He forced a breath and broke his gaze. He turned and saw the look of impotent fear in her eyes, her cheeks still wet. The heat of his own rage made him sick.

He looked at her face for what seemed like minutes, his arms growing heavy with unspent adrenaline. She touched his face, with one finger gently resting on his lip. Her eyes softened despite their pain. "It's OK."

She moved her hand to Jack's arm and looked over his shoulder at the detective. "Maybe we should go to the kitchen. I could use some ice water."

Jack turned and Tarkington put the notepad in his coat. He seemed to be assessing what he'd just seen in Jack. Finally he nodded in agreement with her suggestion, but didn't say a word.

They followed Elaine down the dark passageway. Only one of the ceiling lights was on in the parish hall, and their footsteps echoed off the dark wood floors. School cafeteria tables were neatly lined up in preparation for the homeless who depended on them for breakfast, which usually started at six-thirty. Jack wondered if they'd even try to pull it off today.

Elaine switched on the fluorescent kitchen lights. Deep pots dangled together over a long stainless steel worktable in the center of the room. The floor was dark red tile, and like the rest of the place, was spotless. A small light glowed at the base of a coffee urn just inside the door. Tarkington filled his Styrofoam cup while Elaine filled a glass with ice from a large bin.

Jack took a mug down from a shelf near the urn. Tarkington pressed the toggle to fill Jack's mug, but still hadn't spoken to him.

Jack tapped some sugar from a jar into his coffee and offered it to the detective.

"I take mine black."

Jack used an iced tea spoon to stir his coffee. "I was out of line back there. I'm sorry."

Tarkington regarded him a few seconds. "People

are always ticked off in my business. Nerves on end."
He swallowed some coffee. "I don't take it wrong."

Jack thought the words seemed carefully chosen.
"And just how *did* you take it?"

He leaned against the counter. "It's my business to
notice things. You know, it's usually not the facts that
nail a case. I mean the facts gotta be there, but it's the
other stuff that pulls it together."

Elaine eased next to Jack and he reached his arm
behind her shoulder. "For example."

Tarkington put the cup down. "You know, you're a
different person every time I meet you. Different in
every room, like one of those . . . whata you call 'em
. . . those lizards that change colors."

"Chameleon."

Tarkington nodded slightly but held eye contact
long enough to make a point of it. "But maybe not.
Maybe I just expected a certain kind of guy, you being
a doctor and all."

"Not smooth. Not refined. Is that what you mean?"

"I saw what Burke did to that guard. I also asked
about how you reacted that morning in the prison.
With that shiv in your neck, you could have bled to
death—but you didn't even flinch."

Jack touched the bandage under his chin, wondering if the detective was paying him a compliment or
insinuating that the threat had been a sham. "What's
your point?"

"Maybe there is no point. I'm just trying to figure
you out."

Elaine interrupted. "You said there were more
questions."

"Yes, ma'am." Tarkington reached for the notepad
and flipped to a blank page. "The victim—she was an

ex-con, and I take it there are others she would be in contact with here."

"We don't like to refer to them as ex-cons, Detective."

"It may not be politically correct, but I'm trying to find her killer. If she's around people with a history of violent behavior, I gotta know about it."

"I understand."

"Have you got a master list of some kind I could copy? I'd like to cross-check it downtown."

Patches of red flushed on her neck. "I don't see how I could do that. It's taken me years to establish credibility; it could ruin everything I've worked for."

"Look—"

"I'm not trying to hurt your investigation, but I can't turn over that list. You'll just have to get it another way."

"Such as?"

"I want to cooperate, but you'll have to work on that yourself."

"We can get a subpoena."

She drank the rest of her ice water. "Maybe you have other questions I can answer."

Tarkington shook his head as he made a note. "You guys feed a lot of street people. Anybody give you trouble lately?"

"A lot of these men and women are regulars. Many of them try to get day-labor work but depend on us for the only warm food they get all day—"

He held up a hand. "We're on the same side here."

Elaine seemed to accept this. "No one's made a scene."

"Did she ever mention anyone trying to hit on her?"

"No." She glanced at the clock over the door and a visible sense of urgency came over her face. "We have several transients each day. We may see them once and never again. But even the regulars tend to keep to themselves. It's very demeaning for most of these adults to have to depend on us." She seemed to catch herself. "I don't mean to preach. If she had a run-in with anyone, I'm not aware of it."

"I'm gonna need you to come downtown and look over the books."

"I've got a kitchen to run. This room will be full of people expecting breakfast in an hour."

"Not today, they're not. Forensics won't be through for several hours."

"These people can't just change plans and go somewhere else for food."

"I understand, and I'm sorry. But that's the way it is."

She started into the Parish Hall. "I'll have Father Dawson call the bishop."

Tarkington called to her from the kitchen door. "I wouldn't go in there if I were you."

Jack watched as Elaine stopped with the realization that Mrs. Franklin was probably still in the priest's office. She looked back at him, obviously hoping he could come up with an answer.

Jack stepped close to her. "We've got to do what he says."

She looked out the window, and Jack followed her lead, the way he might when coming on a group of people staring into the sky. Buildings and housing units blocked the glow of the morning sun, leaving the Projects with only the gray tint of light in the first few minutes of sunrise. From where they stood they could see the empty concrete basketball courts in the distance, and more closely the yellow and black police tape that snapped in the wind. A white van with the seal of the City of Atlanta maneuvered around a squad car, then pulled up to the tape.

"No offense, Miss Thomas, but I don't think people will want to eat here today." Tarkington was still in the kitchen doorway. He seemed to wait long enough for his comment to sink in. "Why don't you come with me downtown? At least this time of day we won't have the traffic."

Jack moved closer, gently touching her shoulder. "I can come with you for a while."

Tarkington had moved within a few feet. "I'd like to have her interviewed alone, if you don't mind."

Jack shot a glance at the detective and felt Elaine's head bow onto his chest. When he looked back he could see that Elaine's eyes were closed, but there were no more tears. The color was gone from her face, the way families looked after a few days' vigil in the ICU waiting room. He touched the back of her head, and only then realized that she was praying.

Jack stood on the corner and watched Elaine drive off in Tarkington's unmarked car. The acid in his stomach was working overtime from too much coffee and too little food. He scanned the streets that came together at the church corner, but knew before he even looked that there wasn't any place to eat in this part of town. There used to be a fried chicken place that had good biscuits, but it closed after the night manager was robbed and murdered about a year ago. No one else was willing to take the risk, and he could hardly blame them.

Across the street, a smattering of people on the top two floors of the housing project were watching from their porches, but his view of the protected zone around Henrietta's body was obscured by the thicket of official vehicles. FORENSICS was written in small black letters on the double doors of the white van he'd noticed earlier. Two uniformed officers were extending the police tape to block off the side entrance to the church, in case anyone had any doubts that the kitchen wasn't open today.

It was five-fifty, but Jack thought it odd that none of the street people had even come close enough to be turned away. Often the lines started before sunup. But he knew from his years of working as a resident in Garity Hospital's indigent clinic that the street had a culture of its own, and to survive you had to know about trouble without stumbling onto it.

It made him think of Leroy Molton. He was known by all the Internal Medicine residents because he'd be admitted every few weeks near death in a coma. Over the years he'd probably taught half a generation of doctors in Atlanta how to manage diabetic ketoacidosis. His name had become a slang reference—even the ER docs would say they had a *Molton* when they called to admit someone with DKA. He'd hit the unit and the residents would work slave away for days to keep him alive. But discharge meant a return to the street where there was no such thing as a regular meal or routine insulin dose. He'd be sick in a week, and readmitted before a month would pass.

At the suggestion of one of the attending physicians, Jack and another resident followed Molton, living and surviving like him for a Friday and Saturday night. Jack lost his frustration and anger with his indigent patients that weekend. It was a desperate, hard life lived among the rare but unannounced person who'd cut your throat to steal your coat while you slept. But most people didn't bother anyone else, and they all depended on strangers to help them survive the night. It was a day-to-day struggle, but in a world where no one had anything, there wasn't much to lose by sharing.

By the end of Jack's first night sleeping in half a box under a bridge, he'd already been told where food could be found, and what corner to hang out on for day-labor jobs. Word got around—word of help, and word of trouble.

As he now looked at the police cars near the church, Jack knew the word was out about St. Michael's.

He drove back the way he'd come, then took the interstate south out of the city, moving in and out of the maze of eighteen-wheelers that were on the road early to beat the rush-hour traffic. He passed Turner Field on his left, and checked his rearview mirror. The black Cadillac was two cars back.

He took an exit eight miles outside of downtown. Coming off the interstate was like dropping into another world compared to the glitz of the city. At the intersection just off the ramp were two truck stops with rows of gas and diesel pumps. The Texaco place was new and had its pumps covered by well-lit wings, but they had only about half the business of the Bulldog Truck Stop. Tractor-trailer rigs covered the Bulldog's expansive asphalt parking lot, so he parked with other vehicles on an abandoned field where cracked red clay squeezed the life from patches of scrub grass.

The plate-glass windows of the Bulldog were covered with aged advertisements for Evinrude motors, Snap-On Tools, and old Georgia football calendars with schedules as far back as 1962. Crowded tables were on either side of a center meal counter and a half dozen swivel stools gleamed with the sun's reflection from the open door. A sign designated the tables to his left as the no-smoking area, but it didn't seem to carry much influence. Jack took an empty stool close to the cash register.

He gave his order and unfolded a newspaper that someone had left. He'd been coming here for years, even when it meant driving well out of his way to avoid the trendy places where young couples showed up for breakfast in matching designer jogging suits. Here he could still get breakfast for under five dollars, and the truth was he felt more at home eating with people who made a living with their hands.

His fried eggs and grits arrived as he finished the sports page. The pile of newspaper had obviously been read by several others, so he tried to put the loose sheets back in order. Page three of the metro section was folded in half, then folded again down the middle, where someone had held the article in one hand while he ate. He started to unfold it, and then it hit him. His first instinct was to look up as if others might have been waiting for him to spot his picture at the bottom corner. He quickly scanned the room but no one was paying him any attention.

They had somehow gotten the picture from the composite poster of all the residents in the department of medicine. The composites were posted at almost every nursing station in the hospitals served by the house staff, but still weren't out where the public could see them. The ones with his picture would have been replaced a few weeks ago when the new academic year started in July. That meant the only remaining composites were probably on the wall in the waiting area of the department chairman's office. Someone had obviously done his homework.

The headline read DOCTOR'S ROLE IN BREAKOUT QUESTIONED. Jack looked up nervously and tilted the paper against his chest when the waitress refilled his coffee.

He ate the eggs, then turned the paper so he could read it.

In a new development in the investigation of Monday's breakout at Elrice Prison, Warden Horace Conners openly questioned the possible role played by Dr. Jack Harris, a physician in the prison clinic. At a hastily called news conference Conners said, "Dr. Harris broke long-standing policy when he directed two armed guards to leave the prison infirmary just minutes before inmate Burke took his hostages. The timing of this action is so peculiar that it clearly calls for further investigation."

Officer W.E. Howard and Harris were both taken hostage by Otis Burke, who was serving a life sentence under the Repeat Offender Statute. Officer Howard was later found dead in an abandoned barn, approximately 45 miles southwest of Elrice. Harris was found alive, but unconscious behind the wheel of the getaway car just 15 miles from the prison.

The warden, who himself has been criticized for comments last year in which he described a group of inmates as "apes," outlined his case against the young physician. "Less than an hour after Doctor Harris first appeared on the prison grounds, a breakout occurred. This man dismissed the guards, eluded police as he drove the inmate to a remote location, and walked away with only a few cuts. Yet Officer Howard, a veteran policeman and guard with several years' experience, was brutally executed. Under the circumstances we are investigating to see if Dr. Harris may have had any prior links to Otis Burke."

Harris, age 31, was unavailable for comment.

In response to our questions the following statement was issued from Emory University Department of Med-

icine. "Dr.Harris recently completed a year as Chief Medical Resident, and served with distinction throughout his residency. The position of Chief Resident is chosen on the basis of superior performance and medical knowledge."

When asked about the warden's statement, a spokesperson for the Atlanta Police declined comment about whether Harris is under investigation. The escaped prisoner remains at large.

Jack read the article again, this time reacting out loud. "Eluded police, my ass." He looked up and realized several people were staring. He left enough money on the counter to cover the bill plus a tip, then took the metro section with him.

ELEVEN

The drive home only gave him more time to fume as he reran the lies from the morning newspaper. The reporter wouldn't have known how to get that picture from his residency composite. Someone was leaking the information, someone who knew his way around Garity and the medical center.

Jack figured no one at the prison expected him today, so showing up late would still look like an achievement. On an ordinary day his street wasn't easy to navigate because everyone had to park in front of their house. But this morning it was all but impossible because of the TV news vans choking the flow of traffic. Jack tightened his grip on the steering wheel, and thought about turning around, but his brother needed his morning physical therapy. If he missed another day, he'd lose ground that might take a week to recover.

Jack parked a few houses away and walked briskly down the sidewalk. He heard a van's door shut. The sound of other doors followed like dominos. Jack thought of jogging to his steps, but the image of that on the TV made him think twice.

The first reporter was shouting and running with her microphone extended. "Dr. Harris, can I have a word with you? We'd like your reaction to Warden Conners's accusations."

He kept walking, keeping his face straight ahead.

A woman reporter had caught up with him. "What can you tell us about the escape?"

He got the morning paper from his yard. It felt heavy, as though the words were made of lead.

He was on the steps to his porch when the next question came. "Silence won't help you, Dr. Harris. We're trying to be fair here. If you won't give us your side, we'll have to run only one side of the story."

He turned and was about to say it. He was being screwed over. He was just trying to do his job, and was in the wrong place at the wrong time. Conners was a bureaucrat who now had a chance for a sweet retirement package if he kept his record clean with Richardson's company, and the easiest way to do that was to paint someone else as the scapegoat. Instead, he waited until the other reporters caught up, and said, "Sorry, no comment."

The burst of questions jackhammered his back. He unlocked the front door, then locked it behind him. He watched as one of them started to come up the steep steps, then apparently changed his mind. The reporters began to talk among themselves. It was plain from their faces—he was guilty.

He stepped back far enough to glimpse their presence without any of them being able to take his picture. In their place he would come to the same conclusion, and it meant that most of the people in Atlanta would do the same. But Richardson had been clear—no talking to the press. Just one mistake and Jack could blow his access to the prison, and lose any chance he had to uncover the truth about his father.

He heard Ed coming from the kitchen. "Hey, my brother."

Jack returned the hug. "Sorry I wasn't here when you woke up, big guy. You ready for some PT?"

Ed's smile faded. Since the accident, his emotions were mercurial and his facial expressions telegraphed the changes. His moods tended to jump to extremes—he laughed in excess, often too long and too loud, or cried over little things that a normal person might not even notice. He didn't cry now, but the message was the same every morning. His physical therapy was like going through hell.

Mrs. Logan came in from the kitchen wiping her hands on a dish towel. "You're back early."

"I've got to go back, but I just needed to check on Ed."

"I guess you saw all those reporters," she said.

"Like a pack of wild dogs."

"Vultures is more like it."

"They bother you?"

"Can't say as I like them hanging out in front of the house, but I'll get by." Her expression lightened. "You hungry? Got fresh biscuits and gravy."

"I'd love one. Maybe just butter." He wasn't hungry, but had long since learned how her feelings got hurt if he turned down her cooking.

"Ed, let's get to it."

Jack pulled a mat from the closet and put it on the living room floor. Ed got on his back and Jack started with the hamstrings. The muscles on the affected side were smaller than the other, but they were so tight they required a series of mild stretches followed by relaxation, with each subsequent round gaining a little more stretch. The benefit only lasted a few hours, but without the routine Ed would have permanent contractures in his leg, arm, hand, and neck. The most painful was when Jack had to work through the cords in his calf. Ed turned his head, trying to choke back the tears that left marks on the rug after they finished.

He helped Ed up after the routine. The kitten eased past the door frame then rubbed herself around Ed's good leg.

Jack rubbed Ed's shoulder. "Your little friend loves you."

"Every day hurts so bad. It's not any better," Ed said.

Jack answered the same question several times a month. "You're making good progress. It takes a long time, big guy. You're better than you were two months ago, and lots better than you were at Christmas."

Ed's face brightened. "You know what I want for Christmas?"

"No idea."

He picked up the kitten. "Two cats."

They ate the warm biscuits with butter and honey while the sunshine pierced the kitchen window, reflecting off the refrigerator like new snow. Jack licked the dripping honey from his fingers. "I'm going to be busier than usual the next few days, Ed. It will get better in a little while, but I've asked Mrs. Logan to stay over here with us this week."

Ed glanced quickly at Mrs. Logan.

Jack touched Ed's arm "The good news is that today is sort of like a weekend day. You won't have to go to work at the church."

Mrs. Logan had a concerned look on her face. Jack got up to clear the plates and mouthed to her, "I'll explain later."

She winked and stood. "Ed, let's see if this kitty likes to play with yarn."

Ed smiled, then moved so fast that the kitten scampered into the next room.

Jack pulled Mrs. Logan aside. "A woman was murdered outside St. Michael's early this morning. The police shut the place down. Try to keep him away from local news on TV if you can."

"Who'd murder a churchwoman?"

"I don't know, but that's where I was this morning. The police think it might be related to that prisoner who took me hostage."

She clutched a dish towel to her chest. "Are they after you?"

"I don't think so. They had their chance already."

"Let me change that bandage."

"It's OK, Mrs. Logan. I'll work on it at the infirmary. I just wanted you to be prepared if those reporters say anything."

"I'm not going near them."

"Maybe they'll take off when they see me leave."

"Don't go back to that prison. It's a bad place, with bad people."

"I've got to go back."

"No good can come of it, Jack."

The drive to Elrice was slow. Today was going to be another scorcher. The traffic delay just gave him time to relive the newspaper article. The details they had on him could have come from a number of sources—Conners, Dr. Scalacey, the physician's assistants trying to save their jobs, even the police. The press had been little more than rude so far, but if the police leaked his name in connection to Henrietta Franklin's murder, all hell would break loose.

He was seething by the time he arrived at the prison, but something about the place made him slow to a standstill in the outer parking lot. He got an odd feeling as he studied the dark central building with its medieval masonry. It had fascinated him as a boy, but it was different now, as if the stone blocks themselves were giving off an aura of cold deceit. He watched them for nearly a minute, then pulled up to the guardhouse by the outer gate.

He held his ID out the window and was waved through by the same guard he'd seen yesterday morning. It was after eight, almost two hours before he had to face Warden Conners over how he forced him to transfer Jackson Tillis to Garity Hospital last night. He was tired and his jaw hurt like hell, and if things went as he hoped, he'd finish rounding in the infirmary with time to kill before he had it out with the warden.

He decided to park in the small lot just inside the outer fence and was quickly cleared through the gatehouse of the inner wall. He then waited in the holding cage as they locked the door behind him before opening the one in front. He started onto the dirt courtyard, then noticed two armed guards with German shepherds coming from opposite directions on their patrol of the perimeter. Each dog stared at him. Jack was a foreign scent, so he waited for them to clear before he crossed to the infirmary.

He knocked and waited at the door. Under the concrete overhang, a security camera turned and the lens zoomed in on him. He was certain it hadn't been there yesterday, and was surprised that a place with so much paperwork could make such quick adjustments. He stared without smiling.

The trusty he'd met earlier opened the door. "Mornin', Doc."

"Good morning, Taps." He looked through the glass partition into the ward. The beds were empty. He walked over to Bill Latham, the head PA.

"Where are the patients?"

"Sir?"

"My patients. What happened to them?"

He glanced at the redheaded guard in the far corner. "Dr. Scalacey discharged them."

"Tell me Havard got his head CT."

"He's back in his cell."

"So he can die when that brain tumor gets big enough?"

"He was gone before my shift started. There's nothing I could do."

Jack was furious. "The guy can't balance. He's got a cerebellar mass." He looked around the room. "I'm going to see Conners about this. Right now."

The guard stood in front of the door. "He wants you in his office at ten, but not one minute before."

Jack turned and walked to the ward with the empty beds, trying to think of some way to get the prisoner a CT scan.

Taps stripped the sheets off the only bed that had not yet been made. He turned his back to the others and spoke softly to Jack while he worked. "The press will be there. He's setting you up."

Jack could tell that Taps had betrayed something that could cost them both if he didn't handle things discreetly. His nod to Taps was almost imperceptible.

Jack looked around, then walked back into the small office. He sat at the physician's desk and addressed Latham. "So, I'm just supposed to sit here until ten?"

Latham handed him some files. "There are a few things that need your signature."

He lifted a few thin charts and flipped to some pages, signing by the stick-on arrows. Thirty seconds later he was done. He'd deliberately sat by Latham when the guard wasn't close by. If Latham knew about the warden's setup, then he didn't take the opportunity to give Jack the same warning that Taps had given. He studied the senior PA, wondering just what he knew.

Jack paced the room then entered the trusty quarters. "Taps, I want to see the other medical stations in the cell blocks." He looked at the guard. "If that's OK with you."

The guard said, "I'll call ahead. You'll need a guard escort."

"You mean a watchdog."

"It's policy."

"You do some calling, because I'm not cooling my jets in here for two hours."

With a new guard in tow, Jack followed Taps across the dying grass to cell block A. The new guard had a faded red and green tattoo on the back of his hand. It showed a sword piercing the middle of a rat. The inscription read *Law Makes Order*.

They were met by another officer at the cage door entrance. Each guard put a key in the lock on his respective side.

The drill was repeated at two other doors. It seemed odd to Jack that he and the guard had to produce their employee badges before they were allowed to pass while Taps was just waved through. No one even questioned the trusty's presence. The last checkpoint was a centralized station like the center of a wheel that had a clear view of three corridors of cells. Behind a cage within the station, a guard drank coffee while he watched a bank of TV monitors.

The final door was made of soundproof, bullet-resistant glass. Once they got into the actual cell block, the most obvious change was the noise. Some prisoners screamed, others sang. There were at least three different radio stations blaring out, reverberating off the cement floor, walls, and ceiling. Some voices were clearly Hispanic, some black, others just sounded nuts.

From their position, Jack could see guards patrolling the four floors that opened onto a central cement courtyard, but there was no sunlight inside the cell block. Jack asked their guard, "Why don't any of you have guns?"

"If a guard gets compromised, he's the first one who'll get a bullet. There's armed guards in each turret—that was the last checkpoint we went through. They've got video and audio on us at all times. And we've all got these remote alarm sensors." He pointed to the one on his belt. "Something goes down, we hit the button, and men from the turret will be here in seconds. They carry pepper spray. And if they can't handle it, the KA squad is just a few minutes away from any point in the prison."

"What's KA stand for?"

"Kick Ass."

Taps said, "Kill Ass, is more like it."

For an instant, the guard started to react, but instead he just smirked, seemingly proud of the name. "It's a special group. They carry live ammo, and every son of a bitch in this place knows they'll use it."

They walked past cement tables with benches that grew out of the floor, then stopped at a door at the other end of the enclosed courtyard. The guard on the other side let them through, and they quickly found themselves in what looked like a dispensary of some sort.

Taps said, "This is West Clinic, where the PAs usually work. Inmates who got to have routine medicines for high blood, or the sugar—things like that—they come here for their pills."

Jack said, "I hear that Dr. Scalacey has a special clinic."

Taps pointed to a door. "In there."

The guard unlocked the door. The long room was dark and damp. Jack flipped the light switch. The two bare bulbs were spaced poorly enough to cast more shadows than light. Long tables with charts and manila envelopes lined both sides of the room. At the far end was a rolltop desk. Jack opened the top, surprised that it wasn't locked. There wasn't much there—a few notepads from pharmacy reps, paper clips, and a stethoscope in one drawer.

Near the desk was an exam table that looked like it was manufactured in the early 1900s. Against the wall, however, was a stainless steel cupboard and desk. Inside the glass cabinets were vials for blood samples. Clean glass jars held white cotton balls and a collection of alcohol swipe pads. A dozen or more dark yellow tourniquets were draped over a crook at the edge of the cupboard.

He thumbed through the manila envelopes and the loose stacks of paper, until he'd seen them all. There was no mention of special attention to any prisoners. And no reference to his father.

Jack looked at the guard. "Could you give us a minute alone?"

The guard looked at Taps, then back at Jack. "I'll be right outside the door. Call if you need me."

The guard left, and Jack sat on the exam table. "Taps, tell me something."

"Shoot, Doc."

"That young man who was in the infirmary yesterday."

"The one got it up the ass?"

"Why'd they do that?"

Taps shook his head. "Lots of reasons. No womens around here. Somethin's gotta give eventually."

"But about him, specifically. Do you know what's going to happen ?"

The trusty looked at him warily.

"Look, I need you more than you'll ever need me. I'm just trying to figure my way around. Whatever you say is strictly between us."

Taps checked the door, and lowered his voice. "I heard some things."

"Such as . . ."

"It's the gangs. The blacks got two gangs. This was set up by the 'Cutters'—they the worst. See, there's this thing between the Cutters and this spic group, the Latin Cobras.

"This white guy, he's caught in the middle. For some reason, he can't get protection from none of the white gangs. So he approaches the spics for protection. But he's got nothing they want, so they gang-rape him and leave him in the shower. But before they through, they tell him he can get protection if he'll kill one of the Cutters."

"And if he doesn't do what they say?"

"He got only two choices. Be somebody's fuck puppy, or kill the guy they want killed."

"But if he kills another prisoner, he'd risk execution or a life sentence."

"Life's a bitch, ain't it, Doc?"

"I want to see him."

"Talking ain't goin' change nothin'."

"I'd still like to talk to him. Can you arrange it?"

"Just ask the man with the keys."

They walked to the door. Jack motioned for the guard, who then locked Scalacey's office behind them.

Jack checked his watch, then spoke to the guard. "I had a prisoner as a patient yesterday. I'd like to see him. Can you help me do that?"

"What's the name?"

"Mac Rayfield."

"I'll make a call." The guard used the phone in the dispensary, and soon had the information. "He's eaten already. Should be in the field cage right outside."

They passed through another series of locked gates, and finally found themselves outside in the central outdoor field of the prison complex. There were about fifty men spread out mainly in groups . . . some walked the perimeter fence, but most were either playing basketball, or standing in line for their turn at lifting weights.

They found Rayfield by himself, doing chin-ups. His biceps looked massive compared to his trim frame. Jack had the guard and Taps wait by the basketball court.

Rayfield saw him, but didn't stop his routine.

Finally Jack said, "Thought I'd see how you felt this morning."

The prisoner did three more chin-ups, muttered "fifty," then dropped from the crossbar. "How'd you feel the day after a bunch of queers fucked you in the shower?"

He wiped down, then threw the towel on the ground. "The towels are too damn small to wipe a dog's ass. Everybody's so afraid one of us is going to hang themselves. There're easier ways to get killed in here if you don't want to keep on living."

Jack said, "Is that what you're about to do? Set yourself up for a death sentence?"

"I don't know you, and you don't know me. You walk

out of here whenever you want. I'm here for seven more years. Twenty-four hours a day. Damn radios and queer parties all night long. And now they think my ass is their new target. They got another thing coming."

"What if I could get you transferred?"

Rayfield stopped cold. "I'm listening."

Jack suddenly realized he'd offered something he couldn't take back; offered it even before he knew whether he could follow through. "I don't want to mislead you. I can't make any promises except that I'll try. I'm meeting the warden this morning. I can ask around. We could contact your lawyer."

"Shit. My court-appointed lawyer must have flunked night school. What an idiot. And the warden doesn't give a flying crap about me or anybody else in this shit house."

"You're only twenty-three. Seven more years and you're out. If you do something foolish, it could mean a life sentence. Or worse."

"Or better."

Jack didn't know what to say to that. He couldn't bring himself to imagining being gang-raped in the shower week after week for seven years. "Just give me a chance. What do you have to lose?"

"So what's in it for you?"

"Nothing."

"Bullshit. There's no such thing. You think I'm going to put out for you, just because you're white and they're not?"

"It's not like that. I'm a doctor—"

"Yeah, I know about prison doctors. Thanks, but no thanks." Rayfield started walking toward the weights.

Jack followed him. "Give me a couple of days."

"Man, I don't know who you think you are, dropping in here like some fuckin' white liberal who's going to save me. You go home and sleep in your nice bed and watch whatever you want on TV. In here, it's me, or them. And it ain't going to change. So fuck off."

Jack just stood there, aware that most of the other inmates had quit pumping iron and were just staring at them. He couldn't help but notice that all the blacks were playing basketball, and only Hispanics were lifting weights. The whites were walking. Two of the lifters crossed their arms and started laughing.

Jack turned, and was met by the trusty. Then the guard came up and said, "Nice neighborhood, huh?"

Jack followed the guard and Taps across the field. Cell block B looked and sounded just like A, but Jack hardly noticed the noise this time. He gave only a cursory inspection of the East Clinic. His mind was on Mac Rayfield, and what he might do, and when he might do it.

The guard interrupted him from his thoughts. "Sir . . ."

"I'm sorry. What were you saying?"

"There's not much time before your appointment with the warden. I suggest we cross over on the second floor. But it means we'll be walking right in front of the cells."

"Fine."

"Just try to ignore them, Doc."

Another guard opened a door to the stairwell, then locked it behind them. The ritual was repeated at the next landing, where the noise banged off every wall. Jack noticed that the guard immediately moved to the outer rail to be out of arm's reach from the cells. He did the same, but was just far enough behind the guard to miss the brown liquid that flew from the third cell, landing on the guard's chest.

The guard immediately hit the sensor on his belt.

The alarm siren pierced so loud that Jack and the trusty bent to their knees with their hands covering their ears. From the far end of the second floor, the door to the turret burst open. Before the guards arrived with pepper spray, the stench of the brown liquid registered with Jack: rancid feces and urine.

He heard a crazed laugh coming from the cell to his left, but before he could even see the inmate, one of the onrushing guards grabbed Jack by the back of his collar, then forced him back to the stairwell he'd just left. Someone had already opened the door by the time they arrived. He was practically shoved down the stairs, then hustled out of the cell block.

Jack could see other guards racing into the cell block. He looked at the guard who'd shoved him to safety. "There's a trusty still in there."

"You can't go in, sir. You might see something you later wish you hadn't."

Jack looked at the man with the odd sense that he'd just been warned. Or threatened. "Can you get to him?"

"He knows the drill. If he keeps out of the way, he shouldn't get hurt."

"Shouldn't?"

The man stepped back to get a full look at him. "We have eight or ten of these emergency response codes a week. We have to resort to firearms about five times a month. If we don't shut them down fast, those assholes would kill us."

Jack straightened his shirt. "That liquid . . . it smelled like . . ."

"They call it 'the brew.' You got to be a crazy-ass to keep your own shit and piss under your bed. Some actually spit the stuff."

"So what's next."

"They clean up, maybe teach that guy a lesson."

"How so?"

"One of those things better left unsaid, Doc."

Jack could tell he wasn't going to get much more from the guard. "Can I go to the warden's office on my own, or do I need an escort?"

"The rules say that nobody moves during a code. The guys in the towers get nervous. I wouldn't recommend stirring them up."

"So what do I do?"

"I'm just shittin' you, Doc. They've probably got that ass hole clamped by now. You can go. Just realize that some of the codes can be serious. I've seen some close calls."

"I guess I should thank you for getting me away from that prisoner."

"I was getting you away from the guards. See ya around, Doc."

TWELVE

There was a guard in front of Warden Conners's office who braced a twelve-gauge shotgun across his chest. He didn't seem interested in Jack's appointment time. Jack finally used a phone in the outer office to get through to the warden's secretary. A few seconds later, she peeked through a crack in the door, then opened it enough to let Jack inside.

She looked embarrassed, but quickly secured the dead bolt. "We have to lock up in here whenever there's an alarm. They figure the warden's office is target number one if the prisoners can manage to overpower a guard."

Jack was expecting a roomful of reporters, but the place was empty. Before he could sit down, the warden came through a side door, and sat behind his desk. He nodded for the secretary to leave them.

The warden waited until she was gone, then spoke. "Son, you've been nothing but trouble since you signed on here. Let's get something straight. Don't you ever, and I mean *ever*, call me at home again. We've got protocols around here. You need something, you call the watch chief. If he can't handle it, then he calls me—if he's got the balls, that is. I've been in the prison business for twenty years, and I don't need some pissant calling me in the middle of the night whenever his pacifier needs to be rinsed. Got the drift?"

"I want to know why someone discharged two of my patients from the infirmary without my authorization."

"Let me spell it out for you. You aren't in charge here. You don't give orders. This is day two for your little college boy's ass, and you've got no idea about the hell that goes on in this place. We don't run things like the Junior League, because we've got over two thousand prisoners who'd kill you or me for the sport of it, and never give it a second thought. I've survived all these years because I don't take shit off of anybody—no prisoners, no guards, and least of all somebody like you."

"The first one was raped by a gang right under the nose of your guards. The second is probably dying from a brain tumor, which may well be resectable if you don't prevent me from giving him proper care."

"I'm not preventing you from doing anything."

"Then you won't object if I transfer these men back to the infirmary and arrange a CT scan at Garity?"

"I've got enough to worry about. Take it up with Scalacey. He's your boss, if you haven't noticed."

"He wasn't in either clinic. I just checked."

"He'll be in the infirmary."

"I've already been in the infirmary."

"Look, son. We're not going to get along, and I don't give a damn. I put in a complaint with Mr. Richardson's people. Scalacey will be in the infirmary today because I've recommended that you be transferred."

Jack knew that was the one thing he couldn't allow. "I don't work for you, and I've not done anything wrong."

"The way I hear it, that man you had to transfer last

night wouldn't have been an emergency case if you hadn't screwed up and given him blood thinners."

"I was told that Dr. Scalacey would take over his care."

"*Who* told you, Doctor?"

Jack had to think a moment. He'd spoken to the PA about giving the heparin just before he'd been summoned to Conners's office yesterday. But had Latham actually said that Scalacey would cover? Then he realized the answer. Inspector Tarkington had told him that Scalacey would watch the infirmary while they went to review mug shots.

"You didn't even bother to check out to Dr. Scalacey."

"They told me he would—"

"Nobody with an MD behind his name told you anything, now, did he?"

"No. But I was clearly led to believe that—"

"That man is in Garity with a tube draining blood from around his heart because you didn't follow standard procedures. One of my guards is dead and one of my prisoners is at large for the same reason. I don't need somebody like you around here."

"I don't work for you."

"We both work for the same man. Different companies, but Mr. C.W. Richardson owns both of them. And my guess is that by tomorrow, you won't be around to cause me any more trouble. You're dismissed."

"Suppose I tell those reporters outside your office that your guards deliberately avoided the showers while the Latin Cobras raped Mac Rayfield? Word is that some of the guards take bribes from gang members to look the other way when they need to enforce some of their rules."

Conners's face flushed crimson. "Who told you about the reporters?"

"Gang rules demand that a potential new member

must murder some target as an initiation rite, or an unsuspecting inmate may be forced to kill just to gain protection from being murdered or repeatedly raped. And all this goes on under your watch. I suspect the *Journal-Constitution* could do an entire section in the Sunday paper on the subculture you allow in this place."

"You'll be cutting your own throat. Richardson doesn't like bad publicity. You couldn't pick a worse move if you tried."

"This isn't between me and Richardson. It's between me and you."

"Play your cards, Doctor. It's your funeral. Now get out of my office."

Jack was met in the outer office by glaring lights hovering over a dozen reporters and their camera crews. A woman shouted, "We understand a prisoner you treated was rushed to the hospital because of a complication of your care. What do you have to say?"

Jack made the effort not to use his hand as a shield against the lights. "No comment."

"You've just met with the warden. What can you tell us about that meeting?"

Jack waded through the fence of people. "No comment."

"Have you been fired?"

He turned toward that questioner. "I have not been fired."

His response opened the floodgates. Questions came at once. "Do you know anything about the escaped prisoners' whereabouts?" "What is the condition of the prisoner you sent to Garity?" "Are you suspended?" "Are you going to Officer Howard's funeral?" "Are you being brought before the State Medical Licensing Commission?" "Some are saying you may be charged as an accessory to Officer Howard's murder; do you expect to be charged?"

Jack knew his face had colored with that last comment. *Accessory to murder.* How far was Conners willing to go? How long could he keep silent before he'd be tried and convicted by the media?

He kept walking, sure that they would follow him across the grounds to the infirmary, but to his amazement, Warden Connors appeared from his office with some forms, and said to the reporters, "I have a release for you."

They turned their attention to the warden, and Jack got out the door and jogged to the infirmary before anyone had a chance to catch up. He wanted to see that press release, but needed to get away from those people. He figured he'd hear about the contents soon enough.

He stopped to compose himself in front of the infirmary before knocking. Taps let him in. Jack realized how much he owed that man for the heads-up about the press.

Dr. Scalacey was leaning back in a chair with his bare feet on the desk. His coat was off-white and wrinkled. He was tapping a pencil and laughing with Latham.

Jack waited for the next joke to run its course, then said, "I'd like to speak with you, if I could." He looked at Latham. "Alone."

Scalacey tightened his ponytail, then said to Latham, "Give us a minute?"

Latham put on his coat, and seemed to deliberately avoid eye contact with Jack. "I've got some work in the East Clinic anyway."

Scalacey pointed to the empty chair, but Jack said, "I'd rather stand."

"What's on your mind?"

"You moved my patients."

"So?"

"Yesterday you wouldn't touch Jackson Tillis because I'd given heparin orders, but you turn around and discharge two men before their workup is done. I don't seem to understand the rules."

"This isn't about the rules, now, is it?"

"Havard needs a head CT. I think he has a cerebellar mass."

"I've known Emmet Havard for years. He hasn't got a tumor. He's got alcoholic neuropathy."

"It doesn't fit."

"He's got poor balance and foot drop."

"He's got headaches and double vision."

"You know how many prisoners say they have headaches? Belly pain? Anything you can imagine that we can't independently verify?"

"He's got nystagmus. Alcoholic neuropathy won't give that, and you can't fake it."

"Oh yeah?" Scalacey mimicked the rhythmic beating of his eyes to the right. "He's got alcoholic neuropathy and access to the library where he can look up medical signs and symptoms. He's had these same complaints for years and hasn't lost one inch of ground."

Jack suddenly felt like a fool. Perhaps he'd been taken. But the signs were perfect. Havard didn't seem to be faking the balance problem . . . he was too good. Not overplayed, as he'd expect a scam artist to do. He decided to examine him again later, and not push things for the moment.

"I need your advice about that other patient."

"Prisoner, you mean."

No, he thought, *that's not what I mean at all.* "I hear he's been tapped to kill one of the Cutters, or he can look forward to being raped routinely for the rest of his sentence."

"There's more anal sex here than in San Francisco. Nothing we can do about it, either."

"Can we contact his lawyer or try to get him transferred to a different cell block?" Jack realized that a request for transfer to a different prison was too ridiculous to bring up.

"Not a prayer." Scalacey stood and put on his clogs. "So this guy's admitted that he's going to kill one of the Cutters?"

"No. I just heard some talk."

Scalacey looked over Jack's shoulder and into the trusty room and smiled. "Take my advice. This place is full of con men. Even a snake will snuggle up and wait for you to drop your guard so it can bite."

"You mind if I examine Havard again?"

"Be my guest, but we aren't spending the money on a CT unless he's in a coma. For now, you need to lie low and stay out of the warden's hair. I've got the infirmary covered, and I'm due in clinic. You look like you could use some rest after all you've been through. I'll see you tomorrow."

Before Jack could object, Scalacey was out the door, headed for the West Clinic. But no sooner had he entered cell block A than the door to the cell block burst open to reveal a half dozen guards dragging a prisoner across the dusty field. Scalacey didn't follow them.

Jack ran out to meet them halfway. "What's wrong?"

The men kept their awkward but brisk pace. They held the prisoner by both arms, facedown, just a foot above the ground. His face was already swollen, and fresh blood dripped from his nose, lips, and from one eye. The man seemed unconscious, but was breathing.

Jack ran alongside. "What happened?"

Only the front guard answered. "He fell."

"On what, a reaper?"

The guards smiled, some suppressing their laughter. The first guard said, "Don't know. We weren't there. Just got a report from some of the other campers."

When they entered the infirmary, Jack looked back in time to see the guard who'd escorted him this morning come out of cell block A. He was bare-chested, revealing strong shoulders and a tight muscular abdomen. The stench of the rancid urine and feces rushed back to Jack's memory.

He got into the infirmary just as the guards dropped the prisoner on the floor next to a bed. Jack said, "He's the one who threw the brew on the guard, isn't he?"

The guards stepped back. The one who'd been doing all the talking said, "Not sure about that, Doc. We just found him like this."

"Put him in the bed."

The guards didn't move.

"I said, put him in the bed. He's been beaten unconscious."

"This one took a bad fall, Doc."

Jack leaned down to the man and felt his head. There were several areas that had already begun to swell. The pattern was long and narrow, like a nightstick might make. He stood. "Help me get him into the bed."

Most of the guards stepped back. The one who'd been talking helped Jack get the prisoner in bed; then they turned him onto his back.

Jack held the man's eyelids open and watched for

papillary reaction to his penlight. The right eye was so swollen that the lid wouldn't close on its own. He checked inside the man's mouth, and palpated his neck and the outside of his trachea.

He pushed through the guards and returned with a stethoscope from the desk. Air was moving quietly through the trachea without stridor, and both lungs were clear. Jack lifted the man's shirt. Bruises were already forming on the chest and abdomen. He pulled up the trouser legs, and saw purple streaks swelling on each leg.

Jack moved the pillow away, to ensure that the man's airway wasn't cut off. He noticed that one of the guards was using the phone. Jack looked at the only man who'd been willing to talk. "You men beat this prisoner after he threw that brew on that guard this morning. I was there."

Another guard said, "This guy has a streak of bad luck. It's a rough place in there. Things happen."

"He's got a concussion, and could be bleeding internally. He may need to go to the hospital."

The first guard said, "This one ain't going nowhere, Doc."

Jack stepped right up to the guard. "That's not going to work."

Before the guard could respond, Dr. Scalacey walked in. "What seems to be the problem?"

Jack realized that they hadn't expected him to be here still. The guard had called Scalacey when they discovered that Jack hadn't left.

Jack said, "A first-month medical student can figure this one out."

Scalacey took Jack by the elbow, and walked him aside. "Let me handle this."

"They tried to kill him. It's retaliation."

"I got past my first month, Jack."

"OK, so what do we do? We can't just—"

"I can handle this. Why don't you get that rest we were talking about?"

Jack straightened, ready for the fight.

Scalacey leaned close, speaking softly. "I've been here for years, and know how to handle these guys. They'll leave in a few minutes, and I'll do all that's necessary to help this prisoner. But you're a lightning rod right now. Don't make this harder for me than it already is."

Jack looked at the guards. They were probably the ones who had rushed from the turret with the pepper spray. He wondered if they even bothered with the spray. The batons seemed to be pretty effective.

Jack looked back at Scalacey. "I'm going to Garity. I can arrange a transfer if you think this one needs it."

He walked past the guards, men his father had worked with. He tried hard to suppress the implications of what his father's actual day-to-day actions must have been, and what that said about the kind of man he really was.

Jack left the infirmary alone, the heat burning its way from the dry field up his legs, settling in his chest like hot coal.

THIRTEEN

Jack got off the elevator on the fourteenth floor of Garity Hospital and walked to the end of the hall. The guard attack on the prisoner had left him shaken, raising questions about the kind of man his father may have been. His father had been a member of the fraternity of guards, and Jack had just seen firsthand what that meant.

He hit the metal plate on the wall, opening the double doors of the CCU. As with so many other painful times in his life, he found comfort in throwing himself into work or his studies, into anything that would help him forget—or avoid—the pain. This hospital was a thriving example of a place where a person could engulf his personal life with an unending supply of needs to be met. Just being here now helped him focus on the work that needed to be done. It was like passing through a veil that pushed his pain aside.

He'd spent countless hours working in the unit, and was proud that he had a good relationship with the nurses. He knew they trusted his medical judgment, but he still wasn't sure of the reception he'd get now that Warden Conners had used the press to slaughter his reputation.

The floor plan was U-shaped, with patient rooms behind glass partitions on the periphery, and a nursing station in the middle. The lights were always bright in this unit, and most of the patients kept their curtains drawn. He knew he'd timed things well, since the house staff would be in the medical education auditorium at the weekly Cardiology catheterization conference.

The patients' names were written in blue marker on a white board behind the unit clerk. Most of the nurses were doing their paperwork. It was a rare time for them to get things done without having to worry about the flurry of med students, then interns, then residents who'd been coming in sequence since about 5:30 A.M. to prepare for rounds. Jack figured he had about fifteen minutes before the teams returned from their conference, and he wanted to be gone before they appeared. He wasn't up to being a spectacle on his home turf.

Jackson Tillis was in room fourteen, on the other side of the nurse's desk, and on the opposite end of the U from the conference room. An armed guard was sitting in a folding chair just outside the door.

Jack nodded to the officer, tapped on the glass, and slid it open. He parted his way through the curtain and saw that the nurse had her back to him, busily adjusting one of the output parameters on the cardiac monitor above the patient's bed. Tillis was asleep, with covers pulled up over his stomach. His chest had a maze of wires and EKG pads and was still stained brown-orange from the Betadyne. The drain Jack had placed in his pericardial sac was still in place, but now the syringe had been replaced with a Heme-Evac reservoir, which kept up a gentle but constant suction to keep the fluid draining.

The nurse turned and smiled. "Hey, Dr. Harris, didn't expect to see you here."

"Hi, Jennifer." He didn't know if her question had a deeper meaning, but was glad she was the nurse.

They got along fine, and she wouldn't make a big deal of things. "Mr. Tillis is my patient, or rather was my patient before he got admitted to Cardiology."

She came over to Jack's side of the bed and assessed the amount of urine in the Foley catheter bag, and then the amount from the pericardial drain. "He's still draining a lot." She wrote down the numbers.

Jack scanned the IV bottles. One with D5W with a gram of magnesium sulfate added was going at seventy-five cc's an hour. He also had a lidocaine drip hanging, but it wasn't running anymore, serving only as a precaution in case he developed any serious ventricular arrhythmias from the irritation of the drain.

Tillis opened his eyes and took a moment to focus. He moved his legs and only then did Jack realize that one was handcuffed to the rail.

Jack sat on the end of the bed. "I'm Dr. Harris. . . . "

"I remember you, Doc."

Jack noted the man had calm and regular respirations. The monitor was showing his last BP as 134/82. "Do you remember last night?"

Tillis looked down at the wires and tubes. "Not much."

"I'm afraid I'm the one you've got to blame for that tube in your chest."

He started to sit up, a natural reaction that quickly halted when he felt the irritation from the catheter around his heart. "Yeah, they told me all about it. Said you saved my life."

"To be honest, I was worried you were trying to have a heart attack in the infirmary. I gave you the blood thinner to stop any new clots from forming in the arteries to your heart. Unfortunately, your pain was from an irritation in the sac around your heart, and you bled into it because of the blood thinner. I came by to tell you I'm sorry."

"Nobody's told me they were 'sorry' since I was a kid."

"It's going to hurt a little worse when the fluid stops draining."

"Why?'

"Your heart is surrounded by two membranes that ordinarily have only a trivial amount of fluid between them. But if you make too much fluid, it collects between these membranes and the outer one stretches like a water balloon until it can't compensate any more. The pressure can get so high that it chokes the heart. What we did last night was stick that drain tube in to release the fluid. You got better almost immediately. But the membranes are raw and when they come back together it's going to hurt."

Jennifer slipped out and Jack knew he wouldn't have much time to talk to Tillis alone.

"You know, I'm new at the clinic."

"Yes, sir."

"But you used to see Dr. Scalacey."

"He saw me any time I had a problem. I can't say enough about him. I mean most of the people, they wait a week and then they only see one of the PAs. Me, I'm lucky. Doc Scalacey arranged it so all I had to do was say the word, and he'd see me."

Jack wondered why the prisoners had such high regard for Scalacey. Tillis's critical deterioration was a prime example of Scalacey's not pulling his own weight.

"Anybody else get that special treatment?"

"I don't know. It's not the kind of thing you brag about. People on the inside don't like it when you start getting special treatment. Either they want it for themselves, or they figure you're a snitch. Either way ain't good."

"What kind of health problems have you been having?"

"You know, colds, headaches, that sort of thing."

"Anything else—night sweats, fever, chills, rash, bad cough?"

"I had a rash."

"When?"

"Two, three months ago."

"Was it around your eyes, like a short mask?" Jack wondered about lupus as a cause of the pericarditis.

"No, it was all over, especially on my chest and in the crease of my leg." He pointed to his inguinal area.

"So you think a lot of Dr. Scalacey."

"Yes, sir. He cares a lot, takes blood, does X rays. He checks everything until he's sure you're OK."

"You know about me and the breakout."

His eyes seemed to focus on the sutures of Jack's wound. "I heard."

"Did you know about it before it happened?"

Tillis seemed to withdraw, clearly uncomfortable with answering.

"Look, I'm not asking to get you in trouble. Truth is, *I'm* in trouble over the breakout. I thought maybe under the circumstances you might help me out. You know, point me in the right direction."

Tillis looked nervously at the silhouette of the guard against the curtain. Jack moved close enough for Tillis to whisper.

"I know some things."

"Like . . ."

"Things. Things about Burke, maybe some others, maybe just Burke. Just rumors, you never know."

Jack was unsure of what to ask next. So far it wasn't making any sense. "What about Dr. Scalacey?"

"He was one."

"What do you mean?"

He picked at the EKG cable for several seconds and didn't answer.

"One what?"

"Burke had the privileges with Scalacey, just like me. Only he didn't like him. He'd be mouthin' off in the yard about Doc."

"Why?"

"Who knows, man? Burke's crazy and he got crazier the last few months. The *time* will do that to you. I didn't mess with him."

"How'd you know about Burke and Scalacey? You said people keep that sort of thing secret."

"We crossed paths in Scalacey's clinic a couple of times. He always saw me in the West Clinic. Me and Burke, we were in cell block B and were supposed to go to the East Clinic. In that cell block, most people have to wait for the PAs to refer them to the doc, and that don't happen much. One day I saw Burke leaving West Clinic just as I was walking in. It happened maybe three other times. So I figure he had the same kind of deal as me."

The nurse came back in and Tillis changed his expression. Jack knew the conversation was over.

"I better go. I'll try to come back tomorrow. Maybe we can talk some more."

"Thanks for the drain, Doc."

Jack slipped out of the room and left the CCU. He checked his watch. He'd missed lunch, but the antibiotics were starting to mess with his stomach, and he didn't feel much like tackling hospital food. He hit the down button, then stared back at the CCU doors. Tillis had nearly told him something back there, but something stopped him.

Jack tried to rerun the conversation in his mind, trying his best to remember the details. It was hard to piece together but there was something wrong. He knew it was in the words. How had he said it, exactly?

He said the words out loud, as if to test his doubts. "He was one." *One what? One of them?*

Jack heard the elevator struggling to the top floor long before the door opened. He got in and pressed B. The car jerked each time it stopped to let someone on. After a few stops there were about six people in the elevator and Jack was in the rear. Then he remembered.

Tillis wasn't answering about Burke. Jack had just asked him about Scalacey. *He was one. Scalacey was one.* Tillis had almost divulged something, but caught himself and covered up by changing the subject back to Burke. He'd already said that he didn't know if anybody else had the special privileges, then not a minute later said Burke got the same treatment. The smooth con had almost worked. He was protecting Scalacey, but why?

The door opened on the bottom floor. The morgue was in the basement in most old hospitals in an effort to keep the public from accidentally stumbling in on an autopsy. How anyone could do that was beyond him, but stories abounded. All it took for some people to open a door was a sign that said NO ADMITTANCE.

The walls and floor of the poorly lit hall were of white tile and the place smelled like Formalin. After his first week of gross anatomy, everything Jack owned smelled like it. Despite disposable gloves and half-hour showers, he could never get rid of it. He smelled it in class, when he ate, and when he slept. Some of his textbooks still had traces of the odor eight years later. A couple of students always washed out of med school over gross anatomy. Most people thought it was because of having to work on cadavers. Jack thought it was because of the smell.

Dan Linh's office was in the pathology department

on the third floor, but he was assigned to do autopsies every Wednesday. Everyone on staff had his or her turn in rotation, but criminal cases were almost all handled by Dr. Carl Edelman, the medical examiner.

Jack followed the hall until he came to the morgue. It was one of those horse-stall doors, cut in half, with the bottom lined with a metal sheet. There was nothing that identified the room, only a button on the wall with a sign on the door that said RING TO BE LET IN. The only people who rang the buzzer were people who had no business being there. The alarm gave the personnel time to cover the bodies.

He opened the heavy door and saw Dan in the far end on the other side of a ghost-white corpse. He was gowned and gloved and his surgical mask had a clear plastic shield that protected his eyes from accidental contamination.

There were two other autopsy tables closer to the door, and both held bodies that were being attended to by technicians. The closest body had obviously been the first case, since the tech had sewn the abdominal cavity almost completely closed. The tech working the middle table was spraying a water hose on two long stainless steel trays that had held the heart, liver, spleen, and pancreas. Those organs were still in large bowls, having been weighed on a scale suspended from the ceiling. The stench of old blood and gastric contents almost overtook the smell of Formalin and other preservatives in the room.

Jack walked over to the third table and waited for Dan to look up. He never came to a postmortem exam without recalling the first time he'd ever seen one performed on a patient he'd tried to save, someone he'd actually known. He'd awakened with nightmares several times the following week. Even now, he doubted that he'd ever get used to it. Some people could only deal with it by making crude jokes, and others, particularly the pathologists, even got so jaded they could eat in the same room. But he never liked that. These bodies were still someone's patient, someone's mother, father, wife, lover. Maybe that's why he hated being here.

Dan Linh finished his detailed gross description of the body and shut off the recorder. "How's your neck?"

Jack touched the stitches through the clear bandage. "It'll be OK."

"I'm surprised you're not at the prison, or did you decide to quit?"

"One of the inmates is a patient upstairs." He gestured at the woman's body on the table. The abdominal sutures looked so new there wasn't any evidence of the early healing granulation tissue. "She die on the operating table? Looks like a fresh wound."

Dan looked at the suture line. "Organ donor. They harvested the liver, kidneys, and pancreas just before they took her off life support." He started to touch the towel covering her head, then apparently thought better of it. "A drunk crossed the median and hit her car head-on."

Jack looked away. His father's casket had been kept closed.

"This isn't a casual visit, is it?" Ed removed his mask. Hearing no protest, he took off the gown and gloves, then washed his hands.

Jack waited for him to walk into the next room, which was little more than a closet-sized alcove with a desk and dictaphone. The trash can by the desk had a Styrofoam plate with the remains of someone's fried chicken from the hospital cafeteria. The other wall had a large open door that led to the morgue itself, where bodies were stored in refrigerated cells.

Dan sat on the desk. "Did you look for me in my office?"

"No, I remembered your schedule."

"Just as well. You're on a lot of minds today."

"You saw the paper."

"Two people came by the office to be sure I hadn't missed it."

Jack rubbed his eyes with one hand. There'd be more for them to gossip about after tonight's news. "It's probably not too smart for me to show up. I don't want to put you in a bad light."

"Cut the crap. I don't care about that, and you know it."

"Yeah, I know. But I haven't asked you yet."

"Asked me what?"

He checked to be sure the technicians were still preoccupied. "A body was found this morning outside St. Michael's. I'd like to know what the post shows."

"Ed's church?"

"And Elaine's."

Dan propped a foot on the chair. "And?"

"Her name was Henrietta Franklin. She was beaten up, probably raped."

"I don't get it."

Jack checked the technicians again. "There was a tourniquet on the ground by her arm. Just like that guard."

Dan stood. "Like I told you yesterday, those cases don't come here, Jack. Edelman does the posts at the ME's office, down by the police station."

"But you guys rotate down there."

"Sometimes. We're all paid by the county, and everybody's got to pull time."

"So, you could get in."

"We're talking police, the DA—these guys are serious. And Edelman has to sign off on everything done by anyone on the staff."

"They're trying to pin that guard's murder on me. The two murders are related. I need to know as much as I can."

"What you need is a lawyer."

"And what am I going to pay him with?"

Dan looked at the floor, then back at Jack. "Look, I can front you whatever it takes."

"It may take more than you've got. Thanks, but I'm probably better off getting the court to assign me one that I don't have to pay."

"You have to get arrested before they give you an attorney. Your career will be ruined by then."

"That's why you're going to help me."

Dan held up a hand. "I'm the low man on the totem pole. They don't rearrange the schedule just because I say so."

"Then I'm going to Edelman." Jack started for the door.

Dan shouted across the cutting room. "You're radioactive right now. He won't help you."

Jack was headed for the elevator and didn't look back. Even after he read the morning paper and the press attack in Conners's office, the sting of what was happening to his reputation hadn't gotten deep enough to be real. Until now. *Radioactive*.

He walked on, trying to act as if it didn't matter. Just wait until the local evening news ran the video of his so-called press conference at the prison. He could hear his steps reverberate—the sound was hollow and seemed to mock him. He knew that the prison guard and the woman at Elaine's church had been killed in the same way, but the very fact that he knew it would make him more suspect. Asking the police about the tourniquets and puncture wounds would be to admit he knew something about the prisoner's death that only the killer could know.

A needle prick would be easy to miss, especially in a black person. And even if they were noticed, the bruises could be written off to the trauma of having been beaten and raped. If the person performing the autopsy missed the evidence of an injection, he wouldn't order the right blood work and would miss the true cause of death—something Jack might need for his own defense.

If Dan didn't make it happen, he didn't know what else to do. He pressed the elevator button, then heard Dan's voice from down the hall.

"It won't work."

Jack glanced back, then punched the button twice.

"He's not there."

"Who?"

"Edelman. He's giving a talk in New York."

The elevator door opened but Jack stood in the hall looking at his friend. "So you'll do it."

"It could get me fired."

"And . . ."

Dan stared back, his shoulders lowered. He shook his head and seemed to say something under his breath before speaking louder. "Allen Carter's assigned to the examiner's office today. He hates it down there. Maybe . . . *maybe* . . . we can trade off."

"I owe you one."

Dan was already headed back to the morgue. "You got that right."

FOURTEEN

They took Dan's MG to the medical examiner's office. Jack had parked his truck in the residents' lot on the other side of the hospital, and after a few blocks was satisfied that they'd given the slip to Richardson's man. The ride only took five minutes. Dan shut off the ignition and pointed with the key as he spoke. "If anybody raises even a minor question about your presence, you come sit in the car."

"I already told you—"

"I want to hear it again," Dan demanded.

"I'll leave without blinking an eye."

The two-story building looked out of place given the backdrop of office towers that surrounded it. Rather than go in the front entrance, Dan walked to the side of the building and down the small incline where the parking lot dropped to the basement level. The white van that Jack had seen at St. Michael's was parked in front of a wide metal garage door big enough for a small plane to fit through.

Dan pulled a card from his wallet. "Somebody gets murdered in a car, the police can bring the whole thing into the lab for special forensic testing before they even remove the body." He swiped the card and the lock released on a door marked AUTHORIZED PERSONNEL ONLY.

The hall was narrow but well lit. To Jack's surprise there wasn't a policeman or even a secretary guarding the access. Dan stopped in front of another door and pressed an entry code on a keypad. The inner hall was lined with plate glass on each side. To the left was a break room with two vending machines and a coffeepot. There was a sofa with worn cushions and the floor was littered with wrappers and loose paper. At the end of the hall was another door with MEDICAL EXAMINER written on a black nameplate. Through the windows on the right he could see a massive room with four stainless steel autopsy tables, each gleaming in the bright lights that somehow emphasized the pattern of perforations that drained into large collecting vessels suspended underneath. The tables seemed oddly out of place in the huge, empty expanse that looked like the cleanest garage he'd ever seen. The massive metal door was on the far wall.

Jack tapped the glass. "They even painted the floors."

"It's a special surface. The glossy gray makes it easier to locate fibers that might fall, and it's resistant to pressure or temperature extremes so it won't flake off and contaminate the samples. It's a hell of a lot easier than trying to vacuum the woods."

"You really get into this, don't you?"

"It's interesting, and I've learned a lot from Dr. Edelman—he's quite an expert, and the forensic technicians that work in the field do incredible work. But I wouldn't want to make a career of it."

The ME's door opened and a young man in surgical scrubs waved as he walked toward them. "I appreciate this, Dan. You sure it's all right?"

Dan introduced them and they shook hands. "Allen Carter, this is Jack Harris."

Jack waited for the man to recoil when he heard the

name, but his infamy obviously hadn't made its way into the halls of the dead.

"There's only one post so far. Greg can fill you in. This will help me a lot. I've got to gather some slides for a talk this week."

Dan lowered his voice. "Do whatever you have to do. I'll cover things here. We'll just not make a big deal about it."

"Right. And thanks again." He continued down the hall and closed the door behind him.

The ME's area had an outer room with four desks, each stacked with folders and several loose forms. On one, a bone was serving as a paperweight. The back of the room had dark gray curtains suspended by a metal rod. They were pushed aside far enough for Jack to see a long row of doors that obviously sealed dead bodies in the refrigerated cells.

Dan had described the routine on their way over from Garity. The refrigerated compartments held bodies for the few hours before and after a postmortem exam, and then they were released to the funeral home. The only ones that remained for any length of time were those awaiting identification. The backlog of unclaimed John and Jane Does at times got so severe that there were no empty cells for new bodies. One of the reasons they still did some criminal autopsies at Garity was to accommodate the overflow.

Jack survived the next round of introductions to the forensic technicians without incident. Dan said he was a colleague from Garity who'd be visiting today, and they seemed to accept it without question.

Dan reviewed some forms with Greg, the senior technician, asked him to bring the body out, then turned to Jack and pointed to a dressing room. "We've got to change. No one goes in or out of the exam area without new scrubs, booties, hair net, and surgical masks to prevent cross-contaminating the case."

They were left to themselves in the locker room. Jack found an open locker, and said, "I tried to find the medical records on Otis Burke at the prison, but they're missing. The police claim they didn't take them. Would there be any reason for them to be down here?"

"I doubt it."

"So somebody made them disappear before the police could get to them."

"Or maybe somebody misfiled them."

Jack put on the shoe covers. "I checked his recent lab on the prison computer. His eosinophil count was high."

"So he's got allergies."

"Remember that slide you showed me of Officer Howard's blood?"

"What's your point?"

"If this nurse's eosinophils are high, then there's a common thread."

"Yeah, like pollen and cut grass. Howard's smear looked like a blast crisis, not an allergy. You've got nothing here, Jack."

"Just check it, OK?"

"This isn't the county fair. We won't miss anything."

When they entered the autopsy room, Henrietta Franklin's body was already waiting on the exam table, covered from the neck down with an opaque plastic sheet. The senior technician was rinsing a basin, but stopped when Dan got his gloves on.

Dan looked over the body. "What do we have, Greg?"

The technician read from a brown folder. "Thirty-year-old black female found behind a church downtown early this morning. Her arms were tied and outstretched over her head, with one end of the rope tied to a Dumpster. She was wearing a dress, which I've got in the clear bag on the counter behind you. Her undergarments and panty hose were ripped . . . all that's in the report when you need it.

"Detailed collection revealed some skin and fibers under the nails of both hands except for the nail of digit two on the right, which was torn, as you can see. The samples are in these containers." He held up one of six small plastic bottles. "The number on the container refers to the location on the body diagram in the file."

He placed his hand on top of a medium-sized box on the counter. "There's no question about rape. We have more than adequate sperm samples for DNA identification, and we cataloged several loose hairs on the victim's pubic area that are grossly different than her own. They appear to be from the assailant."

Dan waited until it seemed that the report was over. "Thank you."

"There's also a deep cut on her breast. Just thought I'd warn you."

No one seemed to know what to say.

"It's a *two*."

"What?" Dan was tying on a surgical mask.

"Like the number." Greg pulled the sheet back and pointed. "You'd know better than me, Doc, but from the deep bruising it looks like she was still alive when she got cut."

Jack had to turn around and shut his eyes. How could someone be so sadistic? The murder scene had been bad enough, but to see the body displayed under bright lights was more than he was prepared to deal with. The pictures he'd seen in Richardson's home hadn't been much different, but a picture still allowed the psyche a thread of doubt that it wasn't real. But there was no escaping this moment.

"You need to sit down, Doc?" Greg asked.

Jack heard the rollers of a chair coming his way. He eased into it. The carving was obviously a calling card, or a clue, but he had no idea what it could mean.

Greg said, "I'm sorry about that. I forget sometimes. You get sorta nuts working around here."

Jack took several deep breaths then swiveled around to face the body. The carving explained why Inspector Tarkington was involved.

He looked at Dan. "What about the arm?"

Dan eased the arm around and ran his finger carefully from the inner aspect of the forearm up to the crook of the arm. "There's some bruising and a punctate entry site just below the left antecubital fossa."

The technician moved over with interest. "I shouldn't have missed that."

"It's subtle. The bruising and complexion of her skin make it more difficult."

"I still shouldn't have missed it."

Dan's eyes studied the technician. "What do you make of the *two*?"

"At first I thought it was a gang sign. But it's the same as that prison guard the other day."

Jack looked at Dan, then quickly covered his reaction.

Dan asked, "Did you work that case?"

"No, it was done over at Garity. But I heard about it. And when I saw this carved on her this morning, I figured they had to be related."

Jack wanted to ask about the toxicology report on the officer, but knew he'd have to depend on Dan to get it somehow.

Dan pressed down on a transmitter that looked like

a beeper clipped to his pants, turning on the wireless voice-activated recorder. He dictated his name with the date, case number, and victim's name, then shut off the recorder.

He held the woman's hand up. "Look at these, Jack. The cuts on the ventral aspect of the hand and palm are classic defense wounds. The perp had a knife . . . the cuts vary in length and depth because of the slashing motion, but my preliminary guess is that it was a small blade." He gently put the hand back on the table. "Greg's right about the breast wound. I'm afraid she was alive . . . or at least her heart was still beating."

He moved closer to her head. "See these marks on the neck? The pattern is consistent with bare-handed strangulation. The cross-sectional cuts through the trachea will tell us for sure." He backed away a few steps, taking it all in. "The puncture wound in the arm could be for blood withdrawal rather than an injection site. But I can't figure why would anybody want to take a blood sample. An injection is more likely. We'll run a broad tox screen, and maybe hold a couple of tubes out in case we think of something later."

Jack was startled by a loud banging on the glass partition. He turned and saw Detective Tarkington jabbing his finger in his direction. He was furious and obviously shouting, but they couldn't hear anything through the thick glass. Jack shot Dan a look, but there wasn't much either of them could do, and they both knew it.

They saw the detective look up as the medical examiner's door opened. One of the other technicians obviously had come to check on the banging. Tarkington ran through the door and in a few seconds appeared in the autopsy area.

He was breathing hard. "What the hell is *he* doing here?" He jabbed a finger in Jack's direction.

Dan remained calm under the mask. "You're contaminating the forensic field."

Tarkington glanced down, as if he'd find the boundary line painted on the floor. "I don't give a rat's ass. That guy's a suspect in my investigation and I want to know how he gets off influencing the autopsy."

"He's not influencing anything." Dan flattened his hands on the table behind the body. "I suppose you've got some identification."

Tarkington reached into his coat and flipped open his badge at the same time that Greg spoke up. "He's with homicide."

"I'm Dr. Linh. You need to change if you're planning to watch."

Jack knew Dan was bluffing. By bringing him here, Dan had risked his job. Jack stood. "I asked Dr. Linh if I could come. He did it as a favor. If there's a problem, it's between you and me, not him."

"I'll bet." He pointed again. "You're coming with me."

"On what grounds?"

Tarkington looked as if he'd swallowed steam. "Obstruction of justice, accessory to murder, and anything else I can think of."

Jack sensed that Dan was about to get involved, so he moved over to Tarkington. "I know this looks bad, but it's not what you think."

"I've been listening to that voice for two days. Now I'm looking at the facts. You're coming with me and I'm gonna have a talk with the DA." He grasped Jack's arm, and looked sternly at Dan. "I want this noted on the record."

Jack decided not to look back. The more Dan appeared to be out of the loop, the better. But it was inevitable that the word would get back to his department. Jack had made him take the risk, and now there wasn't a thing he could do to protect him.

As they got to the edge of the room, Tarkington turned and thrust his finger at Dan. "I'll be back."

FIFTEEN

Tarkington kept a tight grip on Jack's arm, all but shoving him out of the ME facility and across the street. The forced march continued on the hot sidewalk to police headquarters, several blocks uptown. The area was thick with people on their lunch break; several had to step aside when Tarkington plowed ahead with no intention of letting go of his prisoner.

It was the look on their faces that sobered Jack to the reality of being painted as an accomplice to murder. He slowed a little after realizing the press were bound to have people hanging around the police building. By the end of this day he'd be crucified in the media. He saw his future compressed before him—a promising career lost and his record forever tarnished even if a jury finally saw the folly of what was crashing down on him. He should have listened to his department chairman's advice and taken that job in Philadelphia. He would probably have been married in a couple of years with a handsome house in the suburbs. Now he was on the brink of losing it all.

Tarkington flashed his badge and whisked him through the checkpoint in the spacious marbled entrance of police headquarters. When he'd been brought in to look at mug shots, they'd entered through the back where the detectives parked, but now he wasn't a "friendly," and he wasn't being treated like one.

Tarkington hadn't said a word to him on the way over, or in the elevator that opened on the sixth floor. The detective moved him halfway down the hall and opened a door. "Wait here."

The room was small and rectangular. There was a modest table in the center with four chairs around it. Jack noticed there were no windows or mirrors. "I want to make a phone call."

"To who?"

"I've got a right to a call."

"That's if you get booked."

"You're either going to arrest me or not. Either way I can make a call to whomever I want."

Tarkington looked like he was trying to keep from saying something he'd regret.

"You got some reason I can't know who this *whomever* is?"

Jack stared at him in silence.

Finally Tarkington slapped the outside of the doorjamb a couple of times. "Pay phone's in a room at the end of the hall. But you're not leaving my sight."

"I don't have any change."

Tarkington seemed to be reading him. Jack could sense the detective's radar as it looked for clues from his words and body language. Ever since he was a kid that kind of scrutiny made Jack want to fight. He knew the tension in his voice wasn't going to help his cause, but he couldn't change the gut reaction that had been formed long ago when he heard whispers, calling him trailer park trash.

The two looked at each other for half a minute before Tarkington put a finger in the air. "One call."

Jack walked with the detective to an open room

with a dozen cluttered desks lined up in three rows. They were unoccupied except for one in the far corner where a detective was on the phone with his back turned to them.

Tarkington handed him the phone. "Dial nine." He made a point of not moving away.

"I'd like to speak in private."

From the detective's expression it was going to be a real hardship, but he gave in. "I'll move, but I'm not leaving."

Jack nodded, and after the detective moved to the other side of the room he dialed the number he'd been given at Richardson's estate. An electronic voice prompted him to make several choices and he finally got an operator. "I need to talk to Mr. Richardson. Tell him it's Dr. Harris."

"I'm sorry, Mr. Richardson is unavailable at this time. Would you like to leave a message?"

"Let me talk to the security chief."

"Hold while I connect you to Mr. Mason's office."

After a few seconds a voice came on the line. "Mason here."

"This is Dr. Harris. I've been brought in to police headquarters downtown."

"I don't appreciate you giving my driver the slip. You're either with us or against us. You get my drift?"

"Loud and clear. But it wasn't my idea." Jack didn't want to get into how he got Dan to take him to the ME's office because he didn't want Richardson's people to know. At this point he was beginning to wonder whom he should trust more—Tarkington or Mason.

"What have the police said?"

He eyed Tarkington, then turned his back to him. "It looks serious. I've done my best about questions from the press, but even that is a losing battle. I need some serious help and right now, if I'm to keep our meeting from the police."

"You got a lawyer?"

"I suspect that Mr. Richardson has someone he could spare."

Mason took a deep breath. "I'll make some calls. I think we can get things handled. Until then, don't say a word. But don't misunderstand me. The call I'm going to make will stir up a lot of attention. You're going to have to square this with Mr. Richardson."

"Maybe we'll have a chance at the gala."

"There'll be a lot of press."

"Just do your part. I'll do mine." Jack hung up and collected himself before he walked over to Tarkington. The detective was leaning on a desk.

"When are you going to tell me why I'm here?"

Tarkington stood. "Why'd you take the prison job?"

"Like I told you before. The working hours fit my brother's schedule. He needs me right now."

"I've been thinking about that. Seems to me you aren't spending a whole lot of time with him. It wouldn't have been much different if you'd gone into private practice. I'm sure a bright doctor like you would have had a lot of offers."

How could he tell Tarkington the truth? It would sound ridiculous to say that he suspected his father was murdered. He needed more evidence, and his only chance was to preserve his access to Richardson and the infirmary.

Still, some of Tarkington's comments hit the mark. Jack had gone out of his way to coordinate transporting Ed so he could run into Elaine and lately they'd spent more time talking about each other, and less about Ed. In reality, if he didn't count the time he and Ed slept in the same house, he was only with his brother about three hours a day. And that was on a good day.

"Doctor . . ."

"I'm sorry, I've got a lot on my mind."

"I bet you do." The detective directed him across the hall to the sparse room he'd first opened. "Wait here. I've got some calls to make."

Jack hesitated, then stepped inside. The door closed before he sat at the table. He looked at the door as if he could see through it, and wondered what Tarkington really thought. It was absurd to be considered an accomplice to murder, but being in this room brought him face-to-face with the possibility that the authorities could squint hard enough to actually make a case against him.

He studied the pattern on the floor, counted the rings in the wood door, and inspected every inch of the table, top and bottom, but Tarkington still didn't show. The fatigue of the last few days began to weigh on him. He'd hardly slept in two days, and this was the only time of quiet solitude he'd had since he started at the prison. He rested an arm like a pillow on the table and laid his head down.

He was startled awake by Tarkington's hand. He jerked his head up and quickly shut his eyes against the harsh light. It took him a moment to regain his orientation. When he did, he realized he'd been asleep for over two hours. His brain pounded behind his eyes and he felt a ridge where the table had pressed against the side of his face. Tarkington put a cup of black coffee and two bags of sugar in front of him. Despite the gesture, the detective now had a

harsher edge about him as he sat and turned on a
pocket-sized tape recorder.

"What were you doing at that autopsy?"

Jack drank some coffee and waited for his head to
clear. "I did it for Elaine. I wanted to see if I could find
out something . . . anything . . . that might help her
put the pieces back together."

Tarkington started to write something down, but
instead kept his eyes on Jack, probing with an uncomfortable silence.

"So she knows you were at the medical examiner's?"

"No."

"But you just said—"

"I was hoping to discover something that would be
a comfort. There was no need to mention the autopsy.
That would have made her feel worse."

"So that's your story?"

"It's not a story."

"I called the examiner's office. The technician said
you wanted to know about the needle marks on the
woman's arm."

Jack felt the rush of panic, but fought to keep his
cool. "Dr. Linh pointed out some things to me."

"That's not the way I hear it."

Jack just looked at him. He knew the more he said,
the more they could use against him.

"How'd you know about the injection site?"

"You'll have to ask Dr. Linh."

"I don't think so. I think you know something
you're not telling me."

Jack touched the suture line under his chin. The
swelling had receded but the thick dull pain was still
there. He took another sip of coffee.

"What did they inject, Doctor?"

"I don't know what you're talking about."

Tarkington tapped on his notepad. "You said that Elaine Thomas called you this morning."

"That's right."

"What did you do with your brother?"

"The lady next door helps out each day. I can call on her if I'm in a jam."

"I'd say this definitely qualifies." He looked through his notebook. "You knew the Franklin woman?"

"I saw her once at the church. Yesterday afternoon. We've been through this already."

Tarkington looked up from his notes. "Hasn't been your best week, has it? Wherever you show up, people start dropping like flies."

Jack somehow found the wisdom to keep his mouth shut long enough to regain his composure. "How long do you intend to keep me here?"

"Did you know Otis Burke before you started working at the prison?"

"No."

"Ever hear of him?"

"No."

"Meet any of his relatives?"

"No."

"Friends?"

"No."

"We've got men going door-to-door in Burke's old neighborhood with your picture. If I find out you're lying, you'll be charged with obstructing justice, and accessory to murder."

Jack began to boil at the thought of his residency picture. "You're the one who leaked to the paper."

"Not my style."

"You jerk me around like a convict in front of my colleagues, and expect me to believe you're above feeding me to the press?"

"Believe what you want. I don't like the press nosing around my investigations—"

A knock interrupted the detective, and he stared at the door a few seconds before he opened it. In the hall stood a well-dressed man who looked to be in his fifties. He had a deep tan and his hair was impeccably groomed. "I understand you are holding my client."

Tarkington looked back at Jack. "You must have some important friends, Doctor."

Jack studied the attorney, but tried not to look surprised.

The man held out his hand to the detective. "Nathan Carruthers."

"I know who you are." Tarkington didn't shake hands.

Carruthers walked past the detective and placed a handsome leather document case on the table. Jack thought the exchange was a clever method of telling Jack his name before it became obvious that they'd never met. But the way the detective reacted made him worried about the kind of people who were coming to his rescue.

"I suppose you read my client his rights."

Tarkington braced. "We haven't brought any charges. At least not yet."

"I'll take that as a *no*." He sat next to Jack at the table.

"Dr. Harris showed up early this morning at a homicide scene I was working. I'm just asking some routine questions."

"From what I read in the newspapers you seem to be the only one who doesn't consider my client responsible for the prison escape. It doesn't take a law degree to know you'd like to make him an accomplice to that unfortunate guard's murder." He adjusted the way his tie draped in front of his shirt. "You know as well as I that any information obtained before my client was Mirandized can't be used in court."

"In my experience, innocent people don't jump to a high-powered lawyer so fast."

"I don't know how long it's been since you read the Bill of Rights, but my client enjoys the presumption of innocence. So unless you have some compelling evidence that merits his incarceration, I'd say this meeting is over."

Carruthers and Tarkington rose at the same time. Carruthers lifted his leather case. "Doctor, I think it's time for us to leave."

Jack followed the lawyer to the elevator, and did his best to ignore the detective staring from the end of the hall. Jack spoke as soon as the elevator doors closed. "Richardson called you?"

"Some of his people." Carruthers gave a half smile. "I was in court when I got beeped by my secretary. Mr. Richardson is our firm's biggest client, and all his dealings go through me. He doesn't like a lot of people knowing about his business. And he doesn't ask twice. If he says 'jump,' I ask, 'How long should I stay up?' It's been quite profitable for both of us."

Jack assessed the attorney. He looked more like the kind of man who bought thoroughbreds than the kind who'd jump when someone called. But he also knew that we all have our price.

They were outside the building before Carruthers spoke again. He stopped on the bottom landing of the marble steps. "You'd do well to listen to Richardson's advice. Things could get nasty." He looked around as if he expected to see someone. "Mr. Mason tells me you're planning to come to the gala tomorrow."

"Do you have a problem with that?"

Carruthers checked his Rolex. "You will be a magnet for the press. A least have the good sense to blend in." He looked Jack over as if seeing him for the first time. There was a trace of condescension in his expression as he took a wallet from his coat and produced five hundred dollars.

Jack held up a hand to refuse the money.

"Take it. You don't know what the next few days might bring. If you need more, I'm sure Richardson will cover it."

"I don't need your money."

Carruthers put the bills back in his wallet. "They're sending a car. It would be best for you to stay away from your usual routine for a while." He looked around again and pointed to the street. "There he is now."

They walked to the black Cadillac that had just pulled up to the curb. The chauffeur got out to open the back door and Jack recognized him as the same man who'd driven him to Richardson's helicopter. Jack slid in and Carruthers followed.

"I'm told there's a pack of reporters in front of your house. We've seen enough pictures of you in the paper and on TV. You can't stay there."

"I could stay at a friend's." As he said the words he realized his presence at Dan Linh's would only cause more trouble for his friend.

"I understand you have a brother who needs special attention."

"Leave my brother out of this. That goes for Richardson, too."

"I'm not trying to intrude."

"The hell you're not."

Carruthers moved his hand to the front of his coat, pretending a crease needed attention. "Since you're not going home, I assumed you needed to make arrangements for him."

Jack's emotions were raw. The man was right—he did need to talk to Mrs. Logan about Ed. Unfortunately, he didn't have many options right at the moment. "He's with a lady who lives next door."

Carruthers pulled a cell phone from the armrest between them. "She's going to have to make do until the reporters leave. It won't take more than a day or two. Eventually some new scandal will get their attention and you can go home again. But not today." He held the phone up between them. "Tell her that the driver will be by to pick up your things. Perhaps you could tell her what you need."

Jack reluctantly took the phone and after a few seconds decided Carruthers was right. He let it ring a long time—Mrs. Logan didn't get across the house easily, but she finally picked up.

"Mrs. Logan, this is Jack."

"Reporters have been asking questions about you."

"What did you tell them?"

"To mind their own business."

Jack smiled at the memory of this white-haired woman chasing people off her porch with a broom. Even the Mormons knew not to ring her doorbell. "It's best for me to avoid the house for a few days. It sounds like the reporters are getting more aggressive. They could make a scene—there's no telling what that would do to Ed."

"He's been awful nervous today."

"Can you handle it?"

"I was raised on a farm—you probably didn't know that. I can handle him."

She'd told him about the farm at least a dozen times, but he didn't mind. "Can I talk to him?"

"It's better if you don't. Time doesn't mean anything to that boy. I'll tell him you'll be back soon. That'll hold him."

Sometimes she was the only one who could calm him. Much as he wanted to talk to his brother, she was probably right. "Someone is going to come by my place to pick up some clothes. I'll tell him to walk up the back alley. I didn't want you to worry if you saw him."

"I cleaned up a bit after you left."

"You didn't have to do that, but thank you."

"Call and let me know how you're doing."

"I promise. The man will be there before dark."

"OK, honey. I'll see you."

"Bye, Mrs. Logan." The car stopped in front of a towering office building just before Jack put the phone back in its cradle.

Carruthers opened his door. "Mr. Richardson keeps a house nearby for out-of-town business guests, but Dr. Scalacey's using it for now. There should be room for the two of you. Not my first choice, mind you, but it wasn't my decision. Tell the driver what you need from your house and he'll bring it."

The attorney got out of the car and leaned an arm on the open door. "We'll talk more tomorrow. If we cross paths at the gala, just keep walking and act as if you've never seen me." He closed the door without waiting for an answer, then walked toward the building.

Jack knew the score even if he didn't know the game: Carruthers's job was to protect Richardson, not him. And Richardson wanted something. They could easily have taken him to a hotel right away, but they wanted him at the guest house—and with Scalacey. Why?

He watched Carruthers cross the concrete walkway, and for a brief moment mistook the heat vapors for slime.

* * *

It was after four by the time they navigated their way out of the midtown traffic and into a quaint neighborhood of three-bedroom houses with postage-stamp lawns that sold, the day they went on the market, for just under a million dollars. In return you could jog less than ten minutes to a coffeehouse and read papers from all over the world and be seen by enough beautiful people to make you feel that your seventy-hour workweek was worth it.

The driver stopped in front of a one-story house with a wraparound porch shaded by oaks. Jack gave him a list of things he needed from his house, and the driver gave him a card with his number on it. The car pulled away and Jack walked up the steps to the front door. Through the glass panes it looked like there was a party going on.

He rang twice before a strikingly beautiful girl in a bikini opened the door. In the process, she managed to spill her drink, and licked the traces of orange juice off her finger before she spoke. "Drinks are out by the pool."

Someone called her name, and she joined a trio of laughing girls who looked like they modeled lingerie for a living. Jack closed the door and stood there, trying to take it all in.

The living room was decorated in soft brown leather chairs and tables with sleek Scandinavian lines. There were at least twenty people between him and the sliding glass doors that led to the backyard. Grateful Dead music was loud enough to make any normal person want to call the police. Hoping to avoid the crowd, he made his way down the hall. The bedroom door was ajar, allowing him to see two girls on either side of a teenage boy who was leaning over doing a line of cocaine.

Jack closed his eyes and backed away. He could see the headlines now. This was the last place he needed to be.

He made his way back through the living room and onto the patio out back. The same music was playing through speakers under palm trees. The only one besides himself with a shirt on was the bartender who poured margaritas and occasionally flipped fajita skirt steak on a stainless grill. A twelve-foot-high stone fence enclosed the backyard, which was much bigger than the others in the neighborhood. Two young women were sunbathing topless by the pool, and no one seemed to take notice.

Scalacey slid his arm onto Jack's shoulder. "Hail the conquering hero."

A few people parted and smiled politely, but the music and party didn't skip a beat. Scalacey's breath was laced with beer and his eyes revealed a fatalistic sadness. "Can't believe those bastards had the nerve to send you here."

Jack pulled himself away. "Believe me, it wasn't my idea."

"Never is. Never is." Scalacey lit a cigarette, then waved his hand toward the backyard. "What do you think of the place?"

"Why aren't you at the infirmary?"

"Hell, it's late. They don't need a doctor twenty-four hours a day."

"Why here?"

"Got a call. Mason said something about this concern for my welfare, some risk that the escapee might be targeting people from the prison, including me."

"Where'd they get that kind of information?"

"Come now. You saw how Mason operates."

"They haven't told me anything."

"Welcome to the club. All I know is that I'm not to return to my house. I'm to camp out here for a few days, and if I read the tea leaves correctly, I'm history after that."

"You're quitting?"

He laughed. "Hardly. I live at the pleasure of C.W. Richardson." He gave an exaggerated bow. "This whole place will be yours soon."

"What do you mean?"

"Don't play dumb with me, son."

"I think I better leave."

Scalacey put his arm back around him. "No, no. Can't have that. I'm to show you a good time. You're the new fair-haired boy." He took a swig of Budweiser. "How did the devil put it? All this can be yours, if you just fall down and worship me." He laughed but the coughing stopped him. He stepped on his cigarette.

"Look, this wasn't my idea. Just let me call a cab, " Jack said.

"It's not your fault. It's just Richardson's way of showing me the door."

"None of this makes sense. I'm not interested in your job. And after today, I'm not sure I'm interested in *my* job. I don't think you've got much to worry about."

"Don't count on it, kid." He stood more erect, like he was about to make an announcement. "If not you, it will be someone else. They must have lost my invitation to the big gala event tomorrow night, so I decided to throw myself a party. A last hurrah."

The teenage boy he'd seen in the bedroom brushed past with a girl hanging on. They jumped into the pool, sprinkling water on one of the topless girls whose only reaction was to briefly lift her sunglasses. The couple surfaced in an animalistic kiss. In seconds their bathing suits were drifting to the bottom of the pool and a dozen people watched as they began to have sex.

Scalacey watched them, but didn't leave Jack's side. "Ever try coke?"

"Not my style."

"There was a time I would have agreed with you." He started walking to the pool. "Make yourself at home. Find somebody you like, and enjoy yourself."

He watched Scalacey say something to the girl who'd been splashed. She took his hand and they disappeared inside the house.

Jack made his way back through the house to the front door, and scanned the street before he was sure there weren't any photographers. Getting caught in this place would be the last nail in his coffin.

He walked to the next block and waited at the corner for nearly an hour until the chauffeur returned with his clothes and shaving kit. Before the driver could get out, Jack got in the backseat. "Call that attorney or anybody else you've got to, but I'm not staying here. Have them make a reservation at the Ritz in Buckhead, and put it on Richardson's tab."

To his surprise, the driver did just that. Jack sat back and tried to make sense of all that had happened today. The turn of events was too bizarre to believe. Scalacey was the one he couldn't figure out, but he was becoming more and more certain that Scalacey was part of his father's story.

The more he thought it through, the more Jack understood that somebody wanted him off-balance. Maybe they wanted him to think Scalacey was on the outs, in hopes that Jack would drop his guard and perhaps even confide in him.

If anyone was on thin ice over the breakout, it was Jack, not Scalacey. Warden Conners clearly backed Scalacey while pulling the rug out from under Jack. It made no sense for Scalacey to see Jack as a rising star. There had to be more to it . . . something Jack couldn't see.

Yet one thing was clear: Jack was getting more attention than he deserved, which he took as a sign that they knew why he'd actually come to Elrice.

The car stopped at a red light. At the corner, the smooth sidewalk was disrupted by the gnarled roots of a red oak whose subtle but persistent need to take over had heaved and canyoned the concrete.

Almost imperceptibly, he nodded, as if the earth were confirming the odds against him.

SIXTEEN

It was just after 10:00 P.M. when Otis Burke pulled the GTO alongside a rusted toolshed. JT had been bitching about some beer, and was out of the car before the engine was off. Neon walked next to Burke, but didn't seem to be in the mood for talking. The only light came from a bare fixture jutting out from a tree overhead. The rutted dirt clearing was nearly full—mostly old cars, a handful of pickups, and one faded red motorcycle with a scratched green tank that likely came from the junkyard next door.

"Armless" Jackson owned both the junkyard and the bar with no sign and no official name. By word of mouth it was called the Ice House. Burke had been here off and on over the years, and knew they could slip in, do their business, and leave without any big deal. It was a place where people with things to hide could get something cold to drink, and maybe find a woman, yet no one would remember having seen them if the question ever came up.

The inside was only about the size of two double-wide trailers, with corrugated metal walls and uneven plank flooring, but it was dark and divided with worn curtains to separate the bar from the back, where men shot craps and poker games were going every night.

Burke's eyes adjusted to the dim light about the time JT took his beer through the curtain in the back. The main room had no circulation to speak of, and smelled of cigarettes, old beer, and the musky sweat of black laborers. Except for the beer, the odor wasn't much different from the prison.

A heavy black girl in a green floral dress was leaning into the red haze coming from the jukebox at the other end of the bar. She began to sway her hips and pulse her beer bottle as James Brown's voice began to rock the room.

Most of the tables were upturned cable spools with mismatched chairs. There didn't seem to be any open seats, but that didn't bother Burke, since he preferred the bar, where he could keep an eye on the door and make a quick move if he had to.

He stood at an angle behind a man who was working hard on the girl seated on the next bar stool.

Finally the bartender noticed him. "Armless" was what everybody called him, but never to his face. He was in his fifties, had a shaved head, and except for the nub where his left forearm used to be, was a solid mountain of muscle. He'd lost his arm in Vietnam, had done time for attempted murder, and had a seething anger that periodically needed to erupt.

The place attracted a rough crowd. For anybody who tried to test him, Armless had a machete stuck in a carving block behind the bar. People who had the means to find this place knew that troublemakers could wind up chopped, and nobody would breathe a word about it.

Burke had gotten money from Neon before they left the river shack. He paid for two beers, and handed one to Neon, who then made his way over to the girl by the jukebox. Armless motioned for Burke to meet him at the other end of the bar, where they could speak in private.

The bartender dried a stack of mismatched glasses with a towel, and was careful not to look at him directly. "I'm surprised you showed up."

"Any problems?" Burke drank his beer and looked out at the couples who'd cleared a place to dance.

"Some talk. No trouble."

Burke didn't say anything, but listened to the music. He saw JT buy two more beers, then disappear behind the curtain again.

"What's the matter with your eyes?" Armless asked.

"What you mean?"

"They almost orange."

"Nothin' wrong with my eyes." But he knew the truth. In daylight his fingernails looked as if he'd been scraping the inside of a pumpkin. It started soon after the nausea and vomiting. Scalacey had told him that jaundice often looked that way in blacks . . . as if that was enough to make up for what they'd done to him. "Get me another beer."

Armless lifted the cooler hatch and put the bottle in front of him, then went to help another customer. Burke watched as a small piece of ice slid down the side. He hadn't had a beer in nearly ten years, and the cold splash in his throat tasted like freedom. He finished the first one, then peeled the label, like he used to when he and his buddies sat on the hood of a car and talked bullshit.

When Armless finally came back, Burke put a ten-dollar bill on the bar. "What's the word on us?" Burke asked.

Armless pocketed the bill. "Most been sayin' you three probably in Mexico by now. Cops been all over your neighborhood, hasslin' folks. Most people clammed up after some guys got the serious treatment from a group of plainclothes cops. But it might have scared some others. No tellin' what they might do."

"Plainclothes?"

"Real rough on a couple of the brothers who played ball with you in high school. Messed them up pretty good."

"They sure it was cops?"

"Who else do that kinda shit?"

Burke put a five on the bar to cover the beer. "Thanks, man." He found Neon dancing with the big girl, and shouted in his ear, "Meet me outside in a minute." Neon stopped dancing and the girl shoved her hands on her hips.

Burke parted the maroon curtain and saw JT on his knees shooting craps against the side wall. He had a fistful of bills. Burke leaned over and said, "We got trouble. Better clear out."

JT was up as if he'd been stuck by a hot poker. "The trouble is you, motherfucker. Leavin' that white guy alive." He turned to a young man against the wall. "Tell him what you told me."

The man squeezed his money. "The news tonight showed that white doctor trying to run away from the reporters. They say he had something to do with the breakout. Police been interviewing him for clues— shit like that."

Burke eased his muscled chest against JT's trim shoulder. "Time to go, JT. And quit talking to these people."

JT didn't turn, so Burke grabbed his arm, but in a way that the others couldn't see. "There's a problem, and we need to go."

"Yeah, well, fuck you." He drank some beer.

"Now—before there's trouble." He gave JT a subtle shove.

JT bashed the top of his beer bottle and brought the jagged glass swinging at Burke's face. Burke jerked back just in time, then chopped his foot against the side of JT's knee. His body crumpled as he screamed, his hands around his knee.

Before anyone could react, Burke was on top of him, stripping the knife from the sheath above his ankle.

Armless pushed the curtain aside, the machete reflecting the low light.

Burke picked JT up by his collar and shoved him against the wall. He spoke to the owner. "We're leaving right now. Won't be any more trouble."

Armless pointed with the blade. "Out the back way."

Burke marshaled JT out the back door, half holding him up, half pushing him along. They stopped next to a row of beat-up garbage cans. Bugs swarmed around their heads.

Neon came around the side by the cars. "Why we got to go?"

Burke didn't move his gaze from JT. "We got trouble."

"I want that girl," Neon said.

"People say there's been plainclothes police roughing people up in our old neighborhood."

"So what you expect, dumb fuck?" JT said. "You killed a cop."

"It ain't police. It's people from the prison." Burke was certain that it was some of the men he'd seen before with Scalacey—the kind that meant business. They'd want to get to him before the police did, but he wasn't about to tell JT and Neon the true stakes they were playing for.

JT winced as he tried to bend his right knee. "I

been sayin' we should get the hell outta here, but you had to get that nurse, and you still won't move on. I'm cuttin' now. It's my car."

Burke pointed with the knife he'd lifted. "You ain't goin' nowhere. Your knee's busted good. Who you gonna get to drive?"

"You and your fuckin' payback. You don't care if it gets you killed. But me and Neon, we didn't kill no cop, and we don't owe nobody no payback. We gonna get the hell out. What you say, Neon?"

"That girl, Shanta, she likes the way I dance. She wants me to take her home. You got a piece of that nurse, but I haven't got any in a long time. She wants me, and I'm not leavin'."

Burke was beginning to realize that JT might be right—leaving that doctor had been a mistake, one he might need to fix. But right now his mind was on Scalacey. There wasn't anything on earth that would keep him from killing that son of a bitch.

Bugs were biting his face, and a few people had come out to the parking lot and were staring at them through the shadows. He needed to resolve this now. If Neon linked up with JT, they'd take the car, and what little money they had.

Burke looked back at Neon and said, "Go get her. We can drive down the road a ways. Me and JT will take a walk and you can have her in the car."

JT said, "Walk? I can't stand, you motherfucker."

"You can walk with help. If I wanted that knee dead, it would be dead."

"Why not take her to the shack? Just leave us awhile, she won't say nothin'," Neon said.

"If they beatin' up people, it won't be long before they find our scent. I don't know who they got to.

Somebody might have told about the shack. We can't go there no more."

Neon looked at both of them, then seemed to make up his mind. "I'll go get her. You guys get in the backseat, but then you leave us by ourselves, like you promised." Neon looked down and worked the dirt with his shoe. "She's mine. You don't get none of her, and that's it. You two leave us be. Give us a half hour. But if we still at it, you keep walking."

Burke was getting anxious. Time was closing in, and he'd learned his lesson—they couldn't afford any more witnesses. "Just get her." He stopped short of saying that they'd have to kill her when Neon was done.

Harold Mason walked back to the Humvee and punched the speed dial on his cell phone. The high beams over the windshield illuminated the shack as if it were a movie set. Six of his men were searching the immediate area—some by the river, others in the woods—for evidence that could tell them anything about Burke. In the bright lights, the grass was still splayed like twin silver trails where the GTO had driven, but there was no way to tell how long he'd been gone. From the bed count, Mason reasoned that Burke had at least one accomplice still with him.

A black man was hunched over in the front seat, holding his ribs. His jaw was grotesquely swollen on the left, and was most likely broken in more than one place. One swing of the bat, and the guy had spilled his guts about the shack where he and Burke used to take girls. His lower lip was so swollen he couldn't close his mouth adequately to keep the blood from dripping out. Mason handed him a rag with some ice from a cooler in the back, but he just ignored him, preferring to study the floorboard.

After being put on hold twice, Mason finally heard Mr. Richardson's voice through the phone. "Got the bastard?"

"No, sir, but we've found his hideout. It's about an hour and a half south of Atlanta, deep in the woods. I don't think he's been gone long."

"So you were late."

"It's a safe bet that he camped here while he waited to attack the nurse at St. Michael's."

"You think he's coming back there?"

"Hard to say, but he left some food and a couple of Sterno cans. Could have taken them if he was gone for good. My guess is that he goes out at night, and comes back here before daylight."

"You'll need more men."

"I've already arranged for them. But we can't stay too close or he might smell the trap. I'm going to leave the men I've got here in the woods, and I'll meet the others at a crossroads a few miles back."

"I want this bastard before the police find him. You damn well better find out everything he knows, and who he's blabbed to. After that, make sure he never turns up. The last thing we need is a damn autopsy."

SEVENTEEN

Jack gave up hope for any meaningful sleep, and pulled back the heavy curtains of his hotel window. It was just before 5:00 A.M., and he could see the headlights of several cars on the streets. Through the fine haze of humid air he watched a lit American flag whip from the end of a high-rise crane, and for a moment wished that he once again had a simple life, with defined work to be done—real work—work that demanded the strain of sweating muscles. Work with a beginning and an end. Work that made his body so tired that past sins couldn't override the need for rest.

He cleaned up the miniatures of Jack Daniels's he'd drunk from the minibar last night, put some water in the coffeemaker, then showered and shaved. The wound was looking better, but the bluish yellow bruising was working its way down onto his neck.

The lobby of the Ritz Carlton was small but well appointed with dark wood paneling and a vase of flowers on a center table just inside the entrance. He was preparing to ask for a cab when he recognized one of Richardson's drivers in a chair just to the right of the front doors. The young man stood immediately and put on his black hat. Jack realized he had probably given them the slip for the last time.

He picked up a *Wall Street Journal* from the table and walked over to the driver. "Have you had coffee?"

"Enough to float this place. Mr. Mason said I'd lose my job if you got out of here without me."

"I'd like to get an early start to Elrice."

The driver looked uncomfortable, like he'd memorized his words. "I've been instructed to extend an invitation for breakfast with Mr. Richardson at his club." He quickly added, "Sir."

"I've got patients to see. I don't see how . . ."

The driver held up his hand, and shifted his weight to the other leg. "They told me you'd say that. There's another doctor who's going to work for you today. Sir."

"Scalacey?"

"I wouldn't know, sir. I just know that Mr. Richardson wanted your schedule cleared."

Jack folded the paper. "What time?"

"Mr. Richardson works out early at the City Club if he's in this part of town for business. Usually takes his breakfast between six-thirty and seven. I was just about to call your room."

Jack ran his hand over his white shirt and khaki pants. "I'm not dressed for that kind of place. I don't even have a tie." The only tie he had with him upstairs would be needed for the gala.

"They have coats for gentlemen who have come off the tennis courts. I'm sure they can fit you."

"Short pants, but coats for breakfast?"

"Yes, sir."

"This, I've got to see."

They drove into the residential section of Buckhead, the most exclusive and expensive area of Atlanta. Even the quality of the road seemed better. Many of the houses were behind tall walls, but through the gates he could see stately mansions with long brick drives and perfect hedges. Hundred-year-old oaks seemed to be the norm. Traffic slowed when they passed the governor's mansion. Just four blocks farther and they turned into the drive of the City Club, whose only demarcation was a discreet brass sign embedded in a stone column.

A security guard came out of his air-conditioned house with a clipboard. After a few words from the driver, the electronic gates slowly parted, and they were waved through.

On either side of the drive were lush green lawns set apart by hand-cut cedar fences that had aged to a natural gray. Through the pines, Jack could see several tennis courts off to the right, and large umbrellas around the outdoor pool to the left of the main building, which itself was an understated white clapboard structure with a black roof and black shutters. It appeared to have been added on to over the years, with at least two wings that he could make out from his vantage in the circular driveway.

A trim black man in a dark suit opened Jack's door. "Mr. Richardson is expecting you in the men's grill, sir. I'd be happy to show you the way."

The inside was honey-colored tongue-in-groove pine, with pictures of former club presidents lining the hall. Without any condescension, his guide stopped at the coatroom and brought him a blue blazer that was better in quality than anything he'd ever owned.

"Forty-four regular," the man said as he helped him with the jacket. It fit perfectly.

The men's grill was off the back hall, with a view of a putting green. The room was small and had the noisy competition of bravado conversations. Jack was the youngest patron by twenty years, but he noted that several men had the same style coat from the front room.

C.W. Richardson rose from a corner table flanked by ceiling-high windows. He met Jack halfway across the room, showing surprising grace for such a wide man. Richardson's hair was brushed back tight on the scalp, still wet from his shower, and he was wearing pleated white pants with a dark navy jacket.

Richardson put his arm around Jack. "I'm so glad you could make it. Sorry to spring this on you at the last minute. I'm afraid my life's full of quick changes."

They shook hands and a waiter with a silver name badge picked a cloth napkin from Jack's plate, then pulled back his chair. "Can I bring you some coffee, sir?"

"Please." Someone poured from a silver pot and placed sugar and cream next to his cup.

Richardson said, "There are no menus, but the chef can make anything you want." He turned to the waiter. "I'd like salmon and capers over poached eggs."

"I'll have the same," Jack said.

Someone brought water and orange juice.

Richardson got a concerned look, and leaned forward. "How's that stab wound coming?"

"Better, thanks."

"Looks like bloody hell. It's got to hurt."

"A little, but nothing that won't heal."

Richardson nodded in approval. "I play racquetball here at least once a week. Beat the hell out of men ten years younger than me." He swept his arms toward the windows. "Just look at all these trees. And tucked in the middle of Atlanta—most people probably don't even know it exists. You stick around, I could get you in."

Jack laughed. "I don't think it's in my league."

Richardson raised his eyebrows. "That's one of the things I wanted to talk to you about."

The seduction was so smooth that Jack had to work to even be aware of it.

"I've been impressed by the way you've handled yourself. Both at work and more especially with the press."

"They sure know how to make the water boil."

"I know, I know. That's one of the reasons I thought you should take a break from the prison today. Scalacey's got things covered. Think of it as a vacation from those guttersnipes—none of them are any better than tabloids. The break is a reward. You've done a good job."

Jack couldn't help but think that the press vacation helped Richardson as much as it helped him. Jack saw another club member walking toward them, but to his amazement, one of Richardson's men got up from a nearby table and politely stopped the visitor before he could get close. Richardson's expression didn't even acknowledge the event.

"I won't beat around the bush. I want you to come work for me at corporate."

"Sir?"

"It's no secret that I built my empire from nothing. And I mean nothing. One reason is that I know talent when I see it. I've got hundreds of junior executives working for me, but in my experience the truly gifted ones shine immediately. I don't need to watch you three to five years to know that you've got what it takes. I can see that already. You're much more valuable to me at corporate than out in one of my prisons."

"I'm a doctor. I'd go crazy sitting behind a desk."

"Who said anything about a desk? I want you to spend some time with Hugo Voss . . . you met him the other night at my place. He's in charge of anything in

Richardson Enterprises that has the word 'medical' in it, including the private medical clinics like the one at Elrice, health for our employees, even medical research."

"That's a broad responsibility."

"Damn right, it is. And he needs good people to help him."

Two men brought the poached eggs with broad strips of salmon. The waiter leaned and asked, "Bearnaise?"

They both accepted the sauce, and Richardson said, "Leave it."

"I appreciate your faith in me," Jack said, "but I'm the kind of guy who likes the trenches. I've always seen myself in direct patient care."

"Well, there may be some way to make us both happy. Let me give you some facts that might change your mind." Richardson began to eat.

"In 1980 it cost each person in this country about thirty dollars a day to pay for housing prisoners. By 1992 that figure rose to a hundred and twenty-three dollars. So people started to look for ways to control costs. I had already seen the opportunity in the early eighties—you've got to be ahead of the curve if you're going to make it big in this world.

"We weren't the first, but we've become the second largest manager of private prisons in the country because we can control costs." He buttered a french roll and indicated to the waiter that he wanted more coffee.

"In the mid 1990s it cost prisons an average of fifty-five dollars per inmate, per day. Today, our prisons do the same job at a cost of forty-five dollars, but we contract at fifty dollars per prisoner. The more prisoners, the more we make. And that's where you come in."

"I don't follow you."

"The longer prisoners live, the more money my companies make."

"Rather cold, don't you think?"

"If you're not cold in business, you're not in business very long." The waiter brought a small plate of warm orange marmalade rolls, and placed them on Richardson's side of the table. "Besides, somebody's going to get paid for those prisoners. No reason it shouldn't be me. And I'm still saving the taxpayers five dollars a head per day. Good for me, good for them. That's good business."

"I don't see how I could help you."

"Just hear me out. I'm not asking you for a decision today."

"I just want you to know where I stand."

"The prisons in this country spend almost thirty-eight billion dollars a year—that's more than most industries you've ever heard of. Since we went public, the stock has split six times and the value has appreciated over nine hundred percent. And so far we've only captured about two percent of the available market of prisoners. The potential is mind-boggling.

"If you were one of my executives, you'd have stock options that would make you a millionaire many times over. Work as much as you like, but after a few years with me, you could retire. Even if you want to keep working, you sure as hell won't have to be taking night call when you're sixty years old."

The lure was obvious. Jack had understood that Warden Conners had a lot to protect, but the magnitude suddenly hit him in the gut. Conners and his top staff would probably resort to anything to have the prison breakout pinned solely on him. "I'm listening."

"On top of the day-to-day prison business, federal and state prisons spend over three billion a year on health costs from prisoners. So we also decided to get into the prison HMO business, if you will. Today just over twenty-five percent of all prisoners are under some managed-care health program, and my company has forty-five percent of the total market."

"But the less you spend on their care, the more you make. I can't be a part of that."

"Now settle down. Just because I can make money on it doesn't mean I'm Hitler. You're right about the HMO end of the equation, but the bigger money is in keeping them alive since my other company gets that five dollars per head per day profit. So I'm not squeezing the HMO side. We control costs without denying service."

Jack thought it sounded like a TV ad, but the time seemed right to test Richardson's theory. "I've got a patient named Emmett Havard in the prison who needs a head CT, but Dr. Scalacey overruled me and sent him back to the cell block. In private practice the guy would have his test, and it would have been good medicine regardless of the answer we got."

Richardson smiled. "You're good. You can't teach timing like that." He ate an orange roll. "But I make it a point not to micromanage my businesses. I hire the best I can find, and I depend on their judgment. You'll meet with Voss soon enough—make your best case. If he gives the green light, then your guy, Havard, gets his CT. Fair enough?"

"Yes, sir."

Richardson checked his watch, then stood. "Sorry, but I've got to get to work. I hear you're coming to the gala tonight."

"Elaine Thomas invited me."

They walked down the hall. "She's the one at St. Michael's. I'm on her board."

"She told me."

Richardson nodded to the valet and the young man ran to the parking area. When they were alone, he said, "I wanted you to know that we're getting closer to nailing that bastard who cut you."

"Dr. Scalacey told me that Burke might be targeting him."

Richardson's features grew hard. "When did he tell you that?"

"Yesterday. They've moved him to the house you keep in town."

Richardson grabbed some hard mints from a bowl, and crunched them like rocks in his mouth. Reflected sunlight flashed his face. "There's my car. You think about what I said."

Jack stood on the front porch and watched Richardson drive his red Mercedes convertible down the shaded drive. A dark car with the man who'd blocked the visitor in the dining room followed close behind.

Jack watched the drive long after the cars got out of view. Eventually he sensed his chauffeur by his side. Jack rattled some mints in his hand and said, "Let's go find my brother."

The row after row of tables in the parish hall at St. Michael's were littered with traces of spilled breakfast, and less than a dozen homeless men remained of what had obviously been a full room. The trash bins were overflowing, and there were no stray plates or trays, most of the diners having respected the rules.

Jack made his way into the brightly lit kitchen. Father Dawson was wiping down an industrial gas stove top, and Ed finished rinsing a tray of plates before sliding them into a steam cleaner.

They were clearly understaffed, and the reason was painfully present on Father Dawson's face. Jack hadn't thought about it until this moment, but realized that Henrietta Franklin's funeral might well be today.

Jack nodded to the priest and walked over to Ed, being careful not to surprise him. Ever since the accident, Ed overreacted to things that would startle him—sometimes he'd swing his good arm as if he were in a fight, at other times he'd almost cry. Once or twice he'd even lost control of his bladder, but that hadn't happened in several months.

"Hey, big guy," Jack said.

Ed put his good arm around Jack's shoulder. "My brother!"

Jack noticed that this was the first time since his recovery that Ed hadn't given him a bear hug. Even as he felt the dampness from his brother's arm on his back, Jack felt this gesture was another sign of improvement. They came like that—without transition.

Elaine came out of a walk-in pantry at the other side of the kitchen. She was pale and showed signs of the stress she was under.

Jack walked over and hugged her. She rested her head against his chest and said, "I don't know if I can do this anymore."

They parted enough for him to see her eyes. "You don't mean that."

"Yes, I do. It was so hard to come here this morning. I just wanted to get on the interstate and start driving. I didn't care where or which direction—I had no destination in mind, just as long as it was anywhere but here."

"But you came back."

"I came because I had to, not because I wanted to."

Jack was quiet for a moment, unsure of what he

should say. "Seeing her body was traumatic for *me*—I can't imagine what it must be like for you. This can't be a good time to make a big decision. You are needed here. Maybe you just need some rest."

Father Dawson had been listening with a degree of apparent unease. "Elaine, why don't you take the day off? We can finish here."

She stood back, taking a deep breath. "There's too much work to be done."

"The women of the church have arranged to handle the rest of the meals until after Henrietta's funeral."

"I'd like to come," Jack said.

Elaine said, "The coroner hasn't released the body. We've scheduled the service for tomorrow at two."

"I tried to call you last night. The line was busy."

"I took the phone off the hook. I just wanted to be by myself."

"We haven't talked since Tarkington took you to headquarters."

"It was awful. I looked at hundreds of pictures. I think they believe one of the people we help in our outreach program did it. They want to bring in undercover officers to eat here."

Jack thought it best not to relate what he knew of Henrietta's autopsy and the carving on her breast that linked her murder with that of the slain prison guard. "I came to see if you and Ed wanted to do something to get all our minds off this."

Father Dawson said, "Wonderful idea. Go with them, then try to get some rest."

"I didn't sleep last night," Elaine said.

"That settles it, come with us. We can go to the zoo, or maybe Underground Atlanta."

Elaine looked around at the kitchen. "I'd really like

to just finish cleaning up here and go take a nap. We've got the Service League gala tonight."

Jack tried to hide his disappointment. "Are you sure you won't let me help?"

"I didn't say that." She found a weak smile, and handed him a broom.

Jack cleaned the parish hall, taking as much time as he could without being too obvious, but he couldn't convince Elaine to spend the day with them. After she sent them off, he spent the rest of the morning distracted by her absence. It wasn't that he didn't want to be with Ed, but she was in pain and Jack couldn't understand why she didn't want him to be the one to bring her comfort.

It turned out to be a day of mixed blessings. Ed was as happy as a ten-year-old touring the Coca-Cola Museum, where he could sample drinks from all over the world. And he didn't seem to miss a single country. From there they went to Underground Atlanta. Over the years it had gone through various incarnations, but the recent Olympic Games had been sufficient reason for the city to spruce up the place and add much needed lighting and security. It housed dozens of bars and several touristy restaurants with a few shops that sold things like stained-glass lamps and turquoise rings. Jack had been a few times for beer with fellow residents, but today he mainly followed his brother through an arcade stall.

Ed was waiting in line for a video game where he could shoot masked assailants when Jack saw a flash to his right. He'd noticed the thin man as they came out of the Coke Museum, but the guy had blended in with a group off a tour bus, so Jack hadn't made much of the numerous pictures he was taking. Now he realized what was going on.

The guy saw Jack's stare and started running. Jack left in full pursuit, leaving Ed alone with Richardson's driver. The photographer tore through a small crowd that had just come out of a theater, then ran down the concrete passageway, which was wide enough for a car. Jack gained ground quickly, reached the guy on the lower steps that led to the street level, and ripped the Nikon from the man's shoulder.

"Who the hell are you?" Jack demanded.

The man reached but Jack was too quick for him. "That's private property."

Jack had the back of the camera open, and stripped the film into the sunlight on the steps. "You didn't answer my question."

The man took back his camera, but Jack wadded the exposed film.

"I'll press charges. Assault and battery."

Jack pushed him against the wall. "Then I guess there's no reason for me not to beat the shit out of you. Might as well make it worth my time."

The man's eyes darted around, but there were no witnesses.

"Give me the rest."

"There's no more."

Jack pinned the man against the wall, then frisked his pockets. There were two canisters of film in pockets on the outside of his pants. Jack opened them both, stomped on the film casings, then pulled the film out of each.

"I'm press. You won't get away with this."

Jack stood back from the guy. Back in his oil derrick days, he'd have broken the guy's nose. Instead, he just walked away, and said, "I just did."

Jack retraced his run, but deliberately took his time. Rage was pounding through him. Those bastards had no right. No right to follow Ed. He didn't care what happened to himself, or how the press would blow this story out of proportion, but they weren't going to involve his brother.

His shirt was soaked with sweat. He paced up and down in front of the arcade, then finally decided he'd calmed down enough to go back in without upsetting Ed.

The room was filled with electronic zaps and sounds of gunfire and explosions. He saw that the driver was by the snack bar, but Ed was surrounded by four teenagers who were probably skipping school. As Jack got closer, he realized that one of the boys was taunting Ed.

"Man, you stink. You can't hit nothing."

Jack held back, watching as Ed tried to shoot the figure of a man rappelling down the side of a brick wall. After a few misses, the character tossed a grenade toward the viewers, and GAME OVER flashed in red military stencil.

The boys couldn't let it go. One said, "You a freak with that hand? Man, my sister can shoot better than you."

One of the boys wanted to take over, but Ed had two more games due him, and he held his ground. The next game went as badly as the first, and the teenagers finally moved on to another game farther in the back.

Jack waited long enough to make it seem that he hadn't witnessed what had gone on. "Hey, big guy. How about some popcorn?"

Ed kept to himself, watching the video as other moving targets flashed before him, unharmed by his impotent aim. After a few more shots, Jack said, "Try some with your good hand."

Ed looked back at him. "But you said—"

"I know what I said. Just try a couple of rounds with your good hand. It won't hurt."

Ed took the gun in his right hand and started scoring with each shot. He missed only one on the next game, and made it to the sharpshooter level. Jack gave him enough money to play for the next hour.

Jack watched the colors burst as the noise clashed with other explosions and roaring car engines throughout the arcade. He noticed the good side of his brother's body come to life, and thought that if there was any justice in the world, the smart-ass kids would come back by and eat their words.

Jack checked his watch, and wandered over to tell Ed it was time to go. The driver was going to take him back to spend the night with Mrs. Logan while Jack got ready for the gala. Ed played two more rounds, then walked out with his bad arm around Jack's shoulder.

The kids never came back. Jack finished a pack of peanuts and threw the wrapper in the trash.

EIGHTEEN

Jack adjusted his tie in front of the mirror, checked the time, then put his razor and dirty clothes back in the bag the driver had brought from his house. Shaving around the stitches had been a problem, but he'd done the best he could, then covered the wound with a small bandage.

He crossed the hotel suite, swirling the melting ice in the last inch that remained of the Jack Daniel's, and lifted his coat from the walnut writing desk.

The last time he'd worn the dark suit had been at his father's funeral. The coat felt odd, as if the cold cemetery wind were still trapped in the lining. He'd kept alive the dim hope that his mother would show up at the graveside service, but in the end it had been only he and his brother in the front seats by the coffin. He still wondered if she knew about his father's death, or for that matter if she was still living herself. It was almost too hard to bear—both parents gone.

A handful of his fellow residents came to the service, and there were three or four adults standing at odd distances from the grave. He assumed they were his father's coworkers from the prison, but he never found out who they were. Geneva Lott had said she'd been one of them, but even now they were little more than shadow figures keeping their distance in an unclear memory. Death was bad enough, but with suicide no one knew what to say.

Jack finished the drink, switched off the light, and picked up his bag.

The driver was right on time, and the Ritz doorman waved the black Cadillac to the portico in front of the hotel. It was a different driver than the one who'd taken Ed home. The muscular chauffeur looked back and spoke with his Brooklyn accent. "We picking up your date?"

Jack sat back. "Change of plans. It's just me tonight."

As the driver drove out into the traffic, Jack watched the street signs and relived the phone conversation he'd had with Elaine an hour earlier. He didn't really want to go to this gala, but he desperately wanted to see her.

He had known by the tone in her voice that she was still in shock over the murder. "I've just been wandering around all afternoon . . . I can't sleep, I can't focus. I don't even remember driving home." Her silence hung in the air. "How could anyone have done this? Sometimes I think it's not real, but I was there. I saw her."

"I'm sorry." He wanted to hold her. "Let's skip this thing tonight. I could come over."

She took several slow breaths. "I've got to go. For all practical purposes, Richardson is my entire program. He's very generous, but he's easily offended. It's hard to understand how one of the richest men on the planet could be so insecure. If I weren't there, he'd notice, and he'd never forget it. I might lose the grant."

"At least let me pick you up. Richardson is sending a car."

"I'd rather meet you there."

He hadn't known what to make of her comment. Maybe she didn't need to be with him as much as he needed her. He'd nervously tried to deflect the issue. "He says he's sending the car to keep the press off my back, but I think he wants to buy my soul."

"Don't let him, Jack."

He didn't know why he'd said what he did, but the weight of her response resonated a chord of fear that had been sounding deep within him all day.

Her words still bothered him as he rode in the backseat of the Cadillac. He studied the back of the driver's head, occasionally making eye contact with him in the mirror. The man had the eyes of a predator. Jack recalled Richardson's offer to have one of his men watch out for him until they tracked down Otis Burke. Richardson had resources that the police didn't, and he wasn't encumbered by the rules. Jack met the driver's stare once more and the man looked away, revealing the fine line between being guarded and being watched.

The Cadillac paused at a gated entrance where the guard checked a list before waving them through. Beyond the gate Jack could see the manicured grass lawn and the drive lined with azaleas and dogwood trees, each with subtle accent lights. They rounded a curve and saw the Richardson headquarters building lit up on a hill. It was on the other side of a twenty-acre lake that had a magnificent central fountain, which was lit in such a way that it resembled a geyser of silver coins, something Jack suspected was no accident. The front of the headquarters was dominated by a large semicircle of glass through which he could see a staircase that wrapped around the interior, with a landing on each of the eight floors. As the car cruised along the winding drive he could see the lights from several more buildings in the thick woods.

A half dozen cars were in line ahead of him. As the row of black Mercedes and Lexus vehicles inched forward, Jack felt sorry for the lone white limo, whose owners obviously hadn't gotten the memo about what car to wear to the party. A trim woman in a black gown, with tennis arms and hair tightly coiled, stepped out of a Mercedes with a practiced smile for the doorman. As the line progressed it seemed to Jack as if the same woman got out of every car.

His driver handed him a card with a printed phone number. "The doorman can call for me when you're ready to leave. I'll be across the lot."

Jack stuffed the card in his coat. He wanted to tell the driver he might as well go home for the night, but he thought better of it. His door opened, giving him an excuse to leave without having to respond.

The landing in front of the main building was lit with soft lights that made people want to talk in small groups before they went inside. No one was paying him any attention, but Jack knew he stood out. He smoothed his hand over the front of his blue suit and entered through the revolving glass door.

Music from a string quartet flowed throughout the marble and glass lobby. Men in tuxedos and women in floor-length dresses stood bunched in small groups to either side of him. The bar, or at least one of the bars, was over to his left, so he weaved politely and ordered a Jack Daniel's on the rocks.

A few women gave him quick, disapproving looks, but most of the men gave a cordial glare, the kind they'd give if their caddy had crashed the debutante ball. He picked an appetizer from a passing tray. Traces of clarified butter laced across crab meat in a warm pastry shell. It tasted as good as it looked, and he caught up with the tray just in time to be stopped in midstep by a face across the lobby.

Standing near the violinist, basking in the apparent rapt attention of two women, was Dr. Carl Edelman, the Chief Medical Examiner. His thick black hair was more neatly combed than usual, and he seemed much more imposing in a tuxedo than in his rumpled white coat.

Jack's first instinct was to assume that Edelman's presence was somehow related to the trouble Jack had caused for Dan Linh. Jack eased behind a column, and wondered how he could get away from the party without leaving Elaine in the lurch. But the more he watched, the more he realized that the man didn't seem to be scanning the guests for him. Within a short time, the ME and a woman who was probably his wife drifted through the far doors and into the banquet hall. Jack attempted to reassure himself that Edelman, being on the faculty at Emory, and a prominent member of Atlanta society, probably attended the gala every year. And yet, he couldn't shake the uneasiness he felt at seeing him here.

He took a swig of his drink and began to look around for Elaine. He turned just in time to see C.W. Richardson lean to kiss her on the cheek. Jack started toward her, but at that very moment, a TV news crew turned bright lights on Richardson. Jack stepped back into the protection of the crowd.

Elaine was on the other side of the lobby, but she was all he could see, as if the other people were only mannequins. She was wearing a black strapless dress with a subtle black sequin design that flowed at a graceful angle to her ankle. She made small talk and smiled as if nothing in the world had happened at the church.

The TV lights went off, and Elaine touched

Richardson on the arm, and they resumed their conversation. They were no more than ten feet away, but with the chamber music and the reverberation of cocktail voices, Jack couldn't hear them.

A blond woman with a boy's haircut eased next to him. Her low-cut dress was vibrant silver and didn't leave much to the imagination. She eyed him as if they'd known each other for years. "These people are so boring. Sometimes I feel like my whole life is the same party over and over. Only the house changes."

Jack rattled the ice in his drink. "I just got here."

She reached for a new glass of champagne from a waiter's tray, then pressed her palm by the edge of his lapel and held it there until he could feel her body heat on his chest. "We're not like these people." She slid her fingers and held on to the fabric where his coat was buttoned. Light danced in her eyes as she took a sip of champagne. "You have a motorcycle?"

"Not anymore."

"Harley?"

"Right now I wish it was. A Suzuki. I was just a kid."

She moved closer. "I love to ride Harleys. Full bore with the wind in your hair and that engine between your legs. There's almost nothing like it."

A tuxedo moved in close. "Let's go, Kelly."

Jack saw that the man's hand had grabbed her arm. He had a health-club body and wore horn-rimmed glasses and one of those inch-wide bow ties. Kelly rolled her eyes in disgust, but left with him without another word.

Elaine broke away from Richardson and came over. "For a minute I thought you'd found a new date."

Jack cracked an ice cube with his teeth. "Hardly." Jack made a conscious effort to quit watching the silver dress disappear through the door.

She took him by the arm and they moved closer to an ice sculpture of the Richardson logo with its ropes around the world. "He asked about you."

"Who?"

"Richardson."

The carved logo was beginning to shine from the heat of the lights. "What did he want to know?"

"He was acting protective of me. How much do I really know about you? Things like that."

"He's a smart man."

She looked at him calmly, as if she'd made up her mind. "I was rude on the phone. I should have let you come get me. At the time . . . I just needed some space."

"And now?"

The light caught the shifting emotions in her face. He'd once dated a girl who fancied herself an actress. She and her friends were always talking about craft and inner pain and how the truly great actors could project their deepest thoughts into a space outside themselves without needing words. It had never made sense until now. In the turn of Elaine's head he knew everything about her. It was so subtle, yet so real, that he wasn't sure if it was her sensitivity or his, but he knew her answer.

It was one of those rare moments he'd remember all his life, and he didn't want it to end. He turned to her just as a strong hand grasped his shoulder from behind.

Richardson opened his arms, and the white tux shirt flashed from under his coat, showing his massive girth. "Dr. Harris. I'm so glad you could make it."

"I apologize for my suit." The two shook hands.

"Nonsense." He guided Jack easily into the circle of people behind him. "You know Elaine Thomas." They smiled at each other, and after a mutual gaze that no one else could miss, Elaine broke eye contact and looked at the floor while Richardson continued. "This is Dr. Hugo Voss. He's responsible for our worldwide medical operations. It about broke me to get him to leave Switzerland, but I think Atlanta is beginning to grow on him."

Voss smiled in agreement and the men shook hands as if they'd never met.

The rest of the introductions were lost on Jack as he smiled and nodded to several other men and their wives. The blue suit didn't register on anyone's face after Richardson's blessing.

Dr. Voss guided Jack aside. "Mr. Richardson feels we should talk." Voss had a precise crispness to his accent. His frameless glasses were as clear as the melting ice.

Jack moved to Elaine's side. "I'm not sure this is the best time. It's been a trying day."

"So I'm told." Voss seemed uncomfortable at pressing the issue. "But Mr. Richardson has been quite clear that I should show you around our facilities."

Jack looked at Elaine, trying to signal that he wanted to leave with her.

Voss was graceful in his perception. "I'd be delighted to have Miss Thomas join us." He chose two flutes of champagne from a tray and presented them as if they were gifts. "I won't keep you long."

Jack shook the ice in what remained of his Jack Daniel's and Voss kept one flute for himself as Elaine took hers.

"Then it's agreed. Please follow me." Voss led them to an elevator with chrome doors polished like mirrors. Once inside he inserted a key and an alphanumeric keypad appeared in red letters on a black screen. The regular buttons showed only floors one through eight, but Voss pressed *B-1* on the keypad and the elevator began to descend.

"Only a limited number of people have access to the lower floors. The world has become a place full of technological wonder, a fine time to be alive. Don't you agree?"

Jack was thinking about the contrast between Richardson's reputation and Voss's calm charm when he heard Elaine answer the question.

"I think technology is making people have more contact without the benefit of personal connection. We're more distant than ever. It makes us care less, which in itself creates anxiety."

The elevator opened and Voss guided them down a bright white hall with bare walls. "You have a point, Miss Thomas. But that's precisely why people with a humanitarian view should strive to be players in the new world."

Voss placed his right hand on the glass surface of a rectangular box to the side of the door. Light passed under his hand like a copy machine, and the door lock clicked open. There were several doors on either side of the inner hall. They stopped at the first and through its narrow glass pane Jack could see what looked to be a standard research lab with long, tall tables with black counters and built-in sinks, Pyrex glass beakers drying on wood racks, and a ventilation hood in the far corner.

Voss sipped his champagne. "You make a good point about technology. I am a believer in a traditional education beginning with the classics and ending with a deep contemplation of the humanities to complement the empiric sciences. I believe you still call it liberal arts in this country. At one time it was considered essential that physicians and even medical research scientists come from such backgrounds. But with the crush of scientific knowledge the pendulum has swung to the opposite extreme."

Jack tapped on the door's window. "What do you do here?"

"This section is devoted to pharmacology. We have ten of these labs on this floor alone."

"I take it there's more."

Voss smiled. "You are quite right, Doctor. Mr. Richardson believes in diversification, and like myself, is convinced that a revolution in medical therapy is at hand."

"From what I read, Richardson has contracts with prisons in eighteen states. You oversee all those sites, and still have time to run a research program?"

Voss gave him a look of respect. "You've done your homework." He put one hand in his pocket. "I knew from your résumé that you were exceptional. I am indeed stretched thin with my duties. I could use someone of your talent. If you have a few minutes, I'd like to show you more."

They started down another corridor followed by a maze of halls with labs off each and finally through another hall without doors. Jack felt they must have walked from one building to another.

"Is this a tunnel?"

"Precisely. We're headed toward the animal containment facility. Our operating suite rivals any in the world." Another sensor scanned his handprint and the white double doors unlocked.

The damp odor of animal feed and dung rushed at them. The long hall was lined with gray bars from floor to ceiling, not unlike a series of jail cells.

Elaine's face was distressed. "I don't want to go any farther."

Voss stopped. "I assure you it's quite humane." He

moved on as if his PR statement had taken care of her reservations, then pointed into a cell. "This should interest you, Dr. Harris. Tell me what you see."

Jack looked across the hay on the floor, then caught the motion near the corner. After a few seconds he could make out an animal, which had obviously tried to burrow under some hay. "Looks like a rabbit."

"Not just any rabbit, Doctor. Look carefully."

He kept staring, but it looked like a normal rabbit. He was about to give up when the animal hopped slightly, turning in the process, and revealing its right front paw. Or what should have been a paw. He only had a quick look before the view was again hidden by the hay, but he'd seen enough. It took a moment for his brain to process the abnormal association.

"You've grafted a limb."

"Details?"

"Looks like a pig hoof."

Voss gave a subtle nod of respect. "Bravo."

"What kind of research are you doing here?"

"We cover many fields, but the payoff will come from our work in genetically engineered drugs to treat autoimmune diseases ranging from rheumatoid arthritis to organ transplant rejection. A few cages up you'll see a strain of monkeys with rheumatoid arthritis. We're nearing clinical tests on a drug that has wiped out any trace of the disease. But that's just the tip of the iceberg. If this rabbit can accept a transplant from another species, just think of what it could mean to the thousands of people who die each year because of a lack of human donor organs."

"How long before the rabbit rejects that graft?"

"You have a clever way of asking how far along we are in this process. What's your best guess?"

Jack glanced back into the cage. "Two, maybe three days post-op."

Voss smiled and read a card attached to the cage door. "This one is going on eight months without any signs of rejection. He had a partner who was also on RC-130 and two controls who received only conventional treatment. The controls rejected the limbs in less than a week. The partner who received the drug was sacrificed at six months so we could document the effects on the vascular supply, tissue regeneration, and side effects of RC-130 on other organs."

Elaine turned away, ready to crumble. "I've seen enough."

Jack squeezed her hand. "It's been a bad day, Dr. Voss. We better go."

"I am aware of your recent difficulties, Dr. Harris. The work we are doing here has the potential to advance medical science into a new era. And you can be a part of it. If you agree to my proposal, I am confident that Mr. Richardson can make your problems disappear."

"I didn't *have* any problems until I signed on with Richardson." He realized he'd overstepped by the reaction on Voss's face. "It's not his fault, but he's not the one with the press and the police breathing down his neck."

"I'm not sure he'd agree." Voss paced and seemed to think out loud. "Right now you are still his employee. We both know he could send you to another prison clinic—perhaps in Montana." He paused for the threat to sink in. "I, of course, am on your side. I'd argue that no matter where he ships you, your other problems won't go away. And then there's your brother to consider."

"Leave my brother out of this."

"He's very much a part of any decision you make."

Elaine leaned her side into his, her hand touching his back, signaling it was time to go.

Jack knew he couldn't leave Voss like this. "What is it you want me to do?"

"I need someone with your kind of background and skill. There are any number of ways you could be useful. For example, we fund clinical trials of our products at several major university medical centers. I need someone who can communicate between our researchers and the academic clinicians. We've got a half dozen drugs in clinical trials with two more to come on-line before the end of the year. Quite simply, it's more than I can do."

"You mean I'm giving the Richardson name a bad image in the press and he wants me out of the prison. Out of sight."

Voss maintained an elegant stance but seemed to be controlling his expression. "I mean just what I said. Nothing more."

"And if I agree?"

"I'm confident Warden Conners can be persuaded to have an aggressive and very public change of heart."

"What about the police? There's a detective who's got it in for me."

"Once Conners backs off, there's no case. Things will die down, and then you won't have to worry about it."

Jack quickly weighed his options. "What if I don't agree?"

Voss stood rigid, the skin tightening on his face. There was a tense silence before he spoke. "Perhaps you are right. It would be best for you to leave now." He walked to the elevator.

Jack felt as if he'd dropped a glass vase. He glanced

at Elaine. She put her finger to her lips and they followed Voss to the elevator.

The shiny doors opened. Voss pressed the button for the first floor, then stepped out, leaving them alone in the car. "Mr. Richardson doesn't make offers more than once. In his eyes, you're either with him, or against him. If I were you, I'd think it over very carefully before I turned him down."

NINETEEN

They took Elaine's car from the party. Jack had considered telling his driver to take the night off, but he
knew they'd be followed anyway. And tonight, of all
nights, he wanted to be alone with her. He watched the
varying lights bathe her features as she drove. They
hardly spoke but he couldn't stop looking at her.

They walked up the stairs inside the antebellum
house with their bodies so close that she brushed
against his chest, but neither of them moved apart.

Once inside, she said, "I don't want to be alone."

He drew her close, feeling the softness of her face.
"I don't want to leave."

He slowly kissed her lips, her cheeks, and her closed
eyes as if he could heal the tears and pain of what
she'd seen. He felt her hold him with an irresistible
softness.

She said, "Everything I've taken for granted seems
so fragile now. I could be gone tomorrow. I feel so
ashamed to say this. It's unbelievable what we saw—
what Henrietta must have gone through—I feel this
empty sadness for her that I can hardly express, but I
don't want to miss any more of my life. I don't want to
wait through another lonely night."

She led him to her bedroom and dimmed the lights.
Undressing was a tender dance of having more of each

other. He caressed her face, gently massaging her back as she lay against him until her breathing deepened.

He felt the warmth of her skin against the cool sheets, and moved in the scent of her neck until she lifted against him in waves that seemed to flow through her. She pulled tight, the side of her face on his as he quickened into his own release.

He stayed in her and they lay together, his hand tracing her face, her neck, the small of her back, feeling them like a sculptor exploring the passion of his art.

He woke to the sounds of the landlady's vacuum cleaner downstairs. He reached an arm across the sunlit bed then realized he was alone. The sense of missing her was unlike anything he'd ever felt.

He'd had other girls, a few of them he'd actually called girlfriends, but not many serious relationships. In high school there was always the trailer park stigma, and people could see it like red paint. Other jocks had little trouble dating whomever they wanted, but the kind of girls who said yes to him were the kind who liked muscles and fast cars, the kind who couldn't see beyond next week. None of them stirred anything inside him. Not the way Elaine did.

He threw on his shirt, then found her in the small kitchen. He was about to invite her back to the bed, but every emotion in him changed at the sight of her eyes.

The front page was folded in front of her on the counter, and she was crying. Jack moved gently to her, fearing that the reporters had revealed the details of Henrietta's autopsy. But as he came close, she got up and moved away.

Her voice was tense and stinging. "Why didn't you tell me?"

"Tell you what?"

"It's all there." She pointed to the paper.

Jack turned it and saw the article on the bottom of page one. FATHER OF PRISON DOCTOR LINKED TO GUN SMUGGLING. He scanned the article that was continued to an inside page complete with an employment photo of his father. It read fast; he knew the details.

"You told me he killed himself. You didn't say he'd been fired for selling a gun to a prisoner."

The old anger within him surged. Push the right button and it was as if it had happened yesterday. "I didn't tell you, because he didn't do it. And I'm going to prove it."

She shook her head and started to say something, but turned away instead. She held the edge of a curtain. Her voice was soft. "Why do things always happen like this?" She watched the street as if the answer would come by. Finally she looked back at him. "I just want something to work right in my life. I want to be stable, I want to be loved. I don't want another quest. I'm tired of fighting."

"He was framed."

She was at the brink of tears, and pointed to the newspaper. "There's so much evidence there. They wouldn't just make that kind of stuff up."

"What they said in the paper is a crock. It didn't fit then, and it doesn't fit now."

"You told me yourself—your mother had left him, Ed was almost a vegetable, and he had no way to cope. The paper says he did it for money. Maybe he needed it to help Ed. It fits, Jack. It even fits your story."

"But it doesn't fit *him*." He paced, then stopped. "My father was a marine. Not just in the marines. He *was* one—and there's a difference. He wasn't well educated, but he was a man at a time when that still meant something. He got laid off a couple of jobs along the way, but it was never his fault. He was too proud to go on welfare or draw unemployment. He moved, and we moved with him. And he always found work. He didn't quit, it just wasn't in him.

"When I wanted to quit school to bring in more money for the family, he sat me down and said, 'You think I work this hard just to see you end up like me?' That's the kind of man he was." He touched the newspaper, then pulled his hand back.

"My father wouldn't have smuggled a gun in for a convict for all the money in the world. And he wouldn't have killed himself."

"You don't know what he would have done. You describe this perfect man, but you told me yourself that he left you and Ed before dawn, leaving you—a child—to fix breakfast, even when he knew your mother was incapable of caring for you. He practically abandoned you."

Jack froze, and the tense silence cut between them.

Her hand came toward her mouth, as if to catch the words. But it was too late. "Jack . . . I didn't mean that."

He stormed off to her bedroom. His pants were tossed near the corner, and his underwear was next to the bed. The bed where he'd felt like everything was beginning to come together, where it felt so right for the first time. But now the sheets felt cold and unmade. Just another place he had to get away from.

"Jack, please don't leave. Not like this."

His shoes were under his arm when he opened the front door.

Elaine was still standing where he'd left her. "How will you get home?"

"I'll walk."

* * *

He had no idea how many blocks he'd pounded before his head was clear enough to think. Of all the people whose trust he needed, it was Elaine's he needed most. How could she have said that? None of it made sense. He was beginning to love her, but suddenly the price was a choice he couldn't reconcile—the choice between his love for his father and his love for Elaine, between his need to put away the anguish that possessed his sleep, and his growing need for her.

He was almost unaware that he'd stopped. A tree across a deep lawn seemed to hold him transfixed. The anger in him welled up and he shouted at the oak, "I hate her." Then, before he knew the words were there, he heard himself scream, "I hate him."

He fell to his knees, shaking his head at the truth he'd never faced. He hated his father. He loved his father. This man who'd provided for him against tough odds, but who hadn't been there when he needed him most, when he needed protection and security, and a guide. When he needed his love. The words dribbled out. "I was just a kid. . . . "

His anguish was met almost immediately by an overpowering sense of shame. It was too much for him to handle. The more he tried to claim it, the less he sensed it, as he began to slip the pain away where it couldn't be seen or felt, a gift of denial learned in childhood. A gift that had become a curse. It was the only way he knew how to survive the pain. A way that was as much a part of him as his skin. And with equally fleeting sadness, he felt that he could no more change the one than he could the other.

He sat on the curb, and for a while he just felt numb, but eventually he became attentive to his surroundings again. He noticed the occasional jogger, and the hiss of automatic sprinklers. A man in a bathrobe came out for his morning newspaper, and Jack braced himself, fearful of being recognized.

He began to concentrate on the newspaper article, his mind quickly finding a safe path from the pain, and the truth about his father.

Somebody was feeding dirt to the newspaper. It had to be someone with lots of pull to get both his residency picture and the one his father wore on his prison ID. Jack hadn't seen the TV so he wasn't sure if the leak was going to every media outlet or just one reporter with the right connections. He made a mental note to compare the bylines of the newspaper articles.

Warden Conners had it in for him, and obviously wasn't a stranger to using the media to sing his song. But if Dr. Voss was correct, Conners was under their control. Jack remembered how Voss's countenance had hardened last night before he sent them packing. Maybe today's article was a shot across the bow, a little reminder of how influential C.W. Richardson's empire had become.

The only problem with this theory was that he couldn't imagine Voss hiring him once he found out about his father. Conners, and perhaps even Dr. Scalacey, had more to gain from leaking the story.

If Voss hadn't known about his father before, he certainly knew by now, and the deal he'd offered last night was probably history. Moreover, Jack realized that if he was going to find out anything about his father's last few days at Elrice, he'd better do it this morning, before all his access dried up.

His walk led him to a small row of mom and pop businesses with plate-glass windows and clean sidewalks. He passed two darkened restaurants and a hardware store before he realized it was only six o'-clock. Coming across a cab in this part of town would be about as easy as finding a horse.

A filling station was open two blocks up the street. Inside he found an old man who looked like he hadn't changed clothes in days. Jack got change and called Dan Linh from a pay phone outside.

"It's Jack."

"You get my ass in a crack over that autopsy, then disappear until now?"

"I'm sorry, but how was I to know that Tarkington would show up for the autopsy? What did they do to you?"

"Nothing so far. I've been lying low. But who knows what today will bring."

"I'll talk to anybody you need me to."

"I don't know if that's such a good idea. In case you haven't noticed, you've got the award for Pissing off the Most People in One Day."

"I guess you saw the paper."

"Front page news, twice in one week. How could I miss it?"

"I'm being set up."

"They're doing a damn good job of it, too. Did you really threaten their photographer?"

Jack shook his head. "He was stalking us. I just snapped."

"You've got to settle down. They'll crucify you now."

"I've got to warn Mrs. Logan."

"She called me already. Some reporters came to her door again last night. She got all worried, so she called me to see if you were OK."

"Did they harass Ed?"

"She didn't say, but knowing her, I'd bet Ed didn't know about it."

"I'm going to call her."

"Where are you?"

"At a filling station down the street from that Italian restaurant you like in Virginia Highlands. I was hoping you could give me a lift to Garity to get my truck."

"What's it doing there?"

"It's a long story. I haven't gotten it since you took me to the medical examiner's downtown."

The silence on the other end said volumes. "If your hunch wasn't right about that blood work, I'd hang up and let you fend for yourself."

"What did you find?"

"That nurse's blood smear showed elevated eosinophils, and a few blast cells."

"Like Officer Howard."

"Not as dramatic. But similar."

"You know it's not coincidence."

"That's why I'm still in the game with you."

"You're the best, Dan."

They hung up and Jack had to collect himself. Both the prison guard and the nurse at St. Michael's had a dramatic eosinophil reaction, and both had preleukemic blast cells, but there wasn't enough time between their assault and their death for any injection to have produced those changes. It meant that they had to have been exposed to something much earlier. But why did they have fresh puncture wounds? Was someone taking their blood? It just didn't add up.

Jack's second call was to Mrs. Logan. She confirmed what Dan had said about the reporters, or "pests," as she called them. Most had abandoned their stakeout, but there was still some "wire of a man" in an old car out front. Every once in a while he'd point his camera and big lens at Jack's house or her porch. She'd called the police but they said they couldn't do anything about it unless he came on her property. Ed was taking things in stride, believing her reassurances like a child. Ed's cat was causing her parakeet to jump around with new life, but Mrs. Logan thought the exercise would do him some good. She didn't ask Jack about where he'd spent the night, and he didn't offer any explanations except to thank her for watching Ed, and to say that he planned to be home tonight.

Jack went back to the old man behind the counter and bought a Coke and a pack of six little doughnuts, then waited at the corner until Dan pulled up in the MG. It was a good day for a convertible, and the noise from the wind and other cars made it hard to hear each other, which was fine with Jack. He'd had enough conversations already this morning, and needed time to think of how to convince Dan to do him another favor. A favor he wouldn't want to do.

They took back roads as long as they could, but finally had to merge into the traffic as they got closer into town. They were dead in a nest of cars two blocks from the hospital before Jack spoke.

"I want to see my father's autopsy."

Dan just looked at him, his expression changing from disbelief to pity. "You don't want to do that, Jack."

"We both know I have every right to see it. You could get it without causing attention, but I'd have to go through channels, and that takes a lot of time. A lot of time that I don't have."

Dan stared ahead, collecting his argument. "With that thing in the paper, people will have their eye on the report. It's going to cause the same attention if I ask for it."

"That's why you need to do it now, before everybody gets their ducks in a row."

"Jack, you're under a lot of pressure right now. It's not a good time to read something like that."

"There's never a good time, Dan. Don't you think I know that? I didn't want to see it even when I had the chance. He had a closed coffin, thank God. You think I want to see the forensic pictures?" Jack looked away, studying the door handle of the car in the next lane. "Maybe there's something there, something I can use."

"Use for what? It's over, Jack. He's gone."

"Suppose my father had an elevated eosinophil count or some early blasts in his blood?"

"And so what if he did? What will that change?"

"It's another piece of the puzzle."

"I was there with you when it happened . . . I saw what it did to you. You can't drag yourself through this muck again."

"I went looking for an explanation when I took that job. I didn't know things would explode. I didn't even know that I'd find any answers, but in my gut I knew I had to try. As long as there was another stone to turn over I couldn't find peace. I hoped I'd never have to read his autopsy, but the article this morning and what you've told me about the blast cells have forced my hand. Maybe somebody doesn't want me to put these clues together. In a few hours the file might even disappear."

"Now you're acting paranoid. I'm telling you, you've got to get away from all this before it kills you."

Jack looked him in the eye. "It's killing me now."

TWENTY

Jack drove from Garity and stopped his truck at the outer gate of Elrice Prison, where he was cleared by the guard. As he pulled into the employee lot, he saw Geneva Lott coming out to her car. Parking quickly, he got out and shouted her name.

She unlocked her car, then turned at the sound of his voice. She seemed tense, but spoke politely when he got to her. "Good morning, Dr. Harris."

Her aging Ford LTD was well polished and the inside was spotless. "I'm glad I caught you. I need your help about Emmett Havard."

She nodded, but didn't say anything.

"The inmate I wanted to send for a head CT."

"I remember him."

"I think he's got a tumor, but Scalacey thinks he's goldbricking. You've seen him before. What do you think?"

She stood more erect, and seemed surprised that he wanted her opinion. "About what?"

"Is he a malingerer?"

"I've seen him occasionally, but it always seemed appropriate for him to be at the infirmary. But of course Dr. Scalacey might have seen him many more times in his clinic."

"Why would Scalacey say he's making up this stuff?"

"I don't know anything about that."

Jack held out a hand as if to settle the water. "I'm not trying to put you on the spot. I'm not even trying to get any gossip about Dr. Scalacey. It's just that I think Havard has a cerebellar mass, and if I'm going to appeal Scalacey's decision, it seemed wise to do a little checking first. I might be dead wrong about Havard, and I don't want to find out after I put my neck on the line."

"If you don't mind my saying so, you ought to think of this place sort of like the navy—you don't make waves, and you won't get swamped. Do you understand what I'm trying to say?"

Jack had never been adept at reading between the lines, but he was sure there was something she wasn't telling him. Something important. "Can I ask you a personal question?"

She pulled her purse against her lower abdomen. "Perhaps."

"You said that you knew my father . . . that he worked the night shift sometimes with you."

"Yes."

"What did you think about him?"

"He was a good man," she said. "I liked him."

"There're some things I'd like to ask you about him . . . things I can't get clear in my head. I just thought that you—"

She interrupted him and opened her car door. "I don't know." She got in, and placed her purse on the passenger seat.

"Please don't run from me."

The words meant something to her. She started the engine, but looked straight ahead. "This isn't a good place."

Jack tensed, realizing her message loud and clear.

Someone was watching her. "Can you write down some place we can meet?"

She pulled a card from her purse, then revved the engine when she spoke. "You know this place?"

The card had the red outline of a pig and said *Rudy's Bar-B-Que*. He didn't know the address, but could tell that she was afraid someone could overhear their conversation. "I can find it."

She closed her door, then cracked the window two inches. "After the lunch crowd thins out. About three." She rolled up the window and backed out of the parking space before he responded.

He watched her leave, then walked into the guardhouse office next to the inner gate. At the far end of the room was an armored cage that reminded him of a holding shoot for cattle, designed so that you had to walk through one steel door, then have it electronically locked behind you before the other door at the end of the cage would be unlocked, allowing you access to the inner yard of the prison.

The guard buzzed Jack through the first door; then nothing happened. Jack turned to see that the guard was slowly rising from his chair, his gaze fixed on the TV monitor overhead. Seconds later, the guard said, "Holy shit, we've got a problem in the exercise yard." The guard hit a red button on the counter, and a siren blared overhead. It was the same one that had heralded the breakout.

"What's going on?" Jack asked.

The guard kept staring at the monitor, then spoke into his walkie-talkie. "We've got a hit on the south fence of the exercise yard. Two men down, one's not moving." He kept studying the screen. "The other's hurt, but he's standing back up. I can't see the weapon."

Jack positioned himself at the front end of the cage and could see the black and white TV monitor. It showed gray figures, poorly focused; dark hair was the only distinguishing feature of the inmates. One was on the ground, possibly facedown, but Jack couldn't tell for sure. The other man was thinner, and seemed to be staggering.

The camera moved to show an entanglement of prisoners about twenty feet away, several of them punching or stabbing one or more than one person— he simply couldn't make out enough detail. Then the camera switched to a wider angle view. He recognized the uniforms. A dozen armed guards dressed in black Kevlar jackets, pants, and combat boots descended on the group. The guards wore protective helmets with gas masks.

Several prisoners peeled away from the periphery of the fight, holding their throats or rubbing their eyes. Each was swiftly met by a guard, who disabled him in almost no time, forcing the prisoner onto his belly, handcuffing his wrists behind his back.

The scenario was repeated in rapid succession. At the top of the screen Jack could see that one prisoner was punching a guard in the gut, but suddenly two other guards sprayed the inmate, then began to beat him with billy clubs. The injured guard fell back against the fence, then slowly got back to his feet while the other guards clubbed the prisoner, who showed no evidence of moving.

Jack said, "Let me in there."

The guard behind the desk didn't take his eyes off the monitor, but said, "Nobody goes in or out during a code."

"I'm the doctor. I've got to get in there."

The guard looked at him. "No can do, Doctor. Nobody in, nobody out. We don't need any civilian hostages."

"Some of those men may be dying out there. Open this damn cage, or call your supervisor. Now."

The guard shrugged and called into his walkie-talkie. Jack watched the exercise yard fill with guards. Two were hunched over the first prisoner that he saw facedown. They moved fast, motioning for help. A few feet away the prisoner who'd staggered away from the first inmate was now surrounded by other guards, who put his head down, and raised his legs.

The supervisor's voice came on. "What?"

The guard said, "I've got the doctor in the cage. He wants to come to the exercise field. I explained about the code."

"Get him out here. And call for four ambulances. May need five."

The guard buzzed the lock and Jack pushed his way onto the dry field that lay in front of the older section of the prison. Guards were running through the large arch in such numbers that another officer just held the iron gate open. Jack ran through with the group.

He had to pass through two other checkpoints before he made his way onto the exercise field. At the last one he was handed a gas mask, which he put on without hesitation.

The sunlight was diffused by a haze of chemicals that had been sprayed to disperse the inmate fight. Guards were running across the field, blocking a clear view, but Jack quickly estimated that at least six prisoners were down, with others injured, but walking. As he ran, he tapped on several men's shoulders and spoke through a self-contained microphone. "Doctor here, let me in."

They parted and Jack could see at once that there

wasn't much he could do. The prisoner who'd gone facedown by the south fence was an obese black man, whose throat had a jagged but very effective slash from ear to ear. Several liters of blood had been pumped from his severed carotid arteries onto the ground around his head. The man probably died in less than ten seconds.

Jack turned, and jogged to the guards who were holding the other prisoner's legs, trying to maximize the blood return to his head. Jack's mask was beginning to fog, but even through the condensation what he saw made him close his eyes.

Mac Rayfield was lying before him, struggling to breathe, his shirt and pants covered with blood from the dead man who lay ten feet away.

Jack worked his way in and kneeled next to Rayfield's chest. He shook his head and asked, "Why?"

Rayfield didn't answer. He stared at him with distant eyes that would have seemed dead if it weren't for the look of terror on his face. His breathing was rapid and very shallow, and after Jack stuck his finger into a rip in Rayfield's shirt, he knew why.

Jack stood and shouted through his mask. "I need a walkie-talkie here."

A guard handed one over, but Jack didn't take it. Instead he kneeled down and pressed his palm against the bubbling wound in Rayfield's chest and said, "Get me the infirmary."

The guard looked like he didn't understand, and Jack commanded, *"Do it!"*

Seconds later, he had a response. Jack took the walkie-talkie with his free hand. "This is Dr. Harris. Get the physician's assistants out to the exercise yard, stat. I've got a man down with a sucking chest wound. I need a stethoscope, some heavy gauze or anything I can use to seal the chest. I'll need tape, a long needle, a two-way valve, and the biggest syringe you can find."

A voice on the other end repeated the list, and Jack handed the walkie-talkie back to the guard. Rayfield's face and neck were now covered with beads of sweat.

Jack put his head to Rayfield's chest and heard decent breath sounds on the right, but none on the left, the side with the chest wound. The rip was halfway up, and on the side, where the arm might brush against it. The hole was about five inches wide, but no telling how deep. Blood covered Jack's fingers, but the bubbling was decreasing—a bad sign indicating that the lung on that side had stopped inflating at all.

Jack felt the front of the inmate's neck, but couldn't tell if the trachea was being pulled to the side. But he knew an X ray would confirm the collapsed lung and shift of the midline structures associated with a tension pneumothorax. From the looks of things, Rayfield didn't have long to live unless Jack could seal the hole and suck some air out of the cavity surrounding the collapsed lung.

One of the PA's was already on the field assessing other prisoners. Jack sent the guard over there, and he soon returned with the senior PA, Bill Latham.

Jack pointed quickly and said, "The one over there is dead. This one slit his throat, but wound up with a tension pneumo with a sucking chest wound. The other guy must have gotten him with his own knife. Anybody over there worse off?"

"No, sir. Several bad cuts, but mainly blunt trauma—kicks, head butts, maybe a concussion or two. Scalacey's been called in. He'll handle those guys."

Latham shook his head. "Hell of a place, ain't it?"

"We need a needle and a big syringe. I don't imagine we've got a chest tube kit."

"No, sir. We could use about one a month, but the metal trochar is too dangerous if one of these campers ever got a hold of it."

Jack could imagine the damage a prisoner would do with the solid metal rod with a sharp, beveled point, which was used to push the chest tube into the thoracic cavity.

"I overheard you radio the infirmary," Latham said. "One of the men should be here soon with the things you asked for."

"You handle the ones you've been checking, I'll stay with this guy. The code will hold up the ambulances. How do we get them in?"

Latham smiled through his fogged face mask. "You sound like a veteran, Doc."

"Just make it happen. This guy may have more going on than just a pneumo."

A guard ran up with a clear plastic tub with the items Jack requested. Jack ripped Rayfield's shirt off the right of his chest. The prisoner looked like a dying animal, but was struggling so hard to breathe he didn't fight back. The only antiseptic was a few one-inch-square alcohol prep pads.

Jack got two guards to hold the man down, then wiped the wound with the alcohol pad as Rayfield's body jerked in pain. Then he wiped down a broad area near Rayfield's clavicle, packed the wound, and sealed the outside as well as he could with white tape. It wasn't perfect, but it was as good as he could make it.

He didn't have any anesthetic, but at this point, the man was going to die unless Jack acted soon. He punctured the skin near the clavicle with a long needle, then buried it nearly halfway into the chest cavity.

Rayfield bucked with more strength than Jack imagined he had left in him, forcing Jack to move the needle back and forth to compensate for the wide swings in his chest. Jack shouted for another guard to help hold the prisoner. After a few false starts, they had the man pinned well enough for Jack to pull air out through the syringe.

Once the syringe was full of air, he turned the valve between the syringe and the hub of the needle, and expelled the air. After about twenty discards, it looked like Rayfield was breathing slightly better, though the pain from the wound and his needle puncture must have been unbearable. Jack kept pulling the air out.

Most of the other prisoners were accounted for and taken off the field, each accompanied by two guards. All but two inmates made it on their own power.

Then Rayfield passed out. Jack feared they were losing him. He yelled to Latham, "We've got to get a chopper. He'll never make it long enough for an ambulance ride."

Latham came over and took his mask off, then helped Jack with his. "Doc, I know what you're thinking. But there's simply no way."

Jack wanted to argue, but knew the score. Latham had summed it up. "We need to intubate him, and we need a BP cuff. He probably needs dopamine and normal saline IVs. Can you get the things out here?"

"I'll make the call."

After a few minutes, a guard arrived from the clinic with the equipment.

Latham took over on the syringe evacuation, and Jack carefully intubated Rayfield, then connected the breathing tube to an oxygen tank and an Ambu bag.

He showed the trusty how to squeeze the oxygenated air into the man's lungs.

He then tried to get a blood pressure reading, and couldn't hear anything. Using his finger to get a brachial artery pulse, he determined that he had a palpable blood pressure of only eighty millimeters of mercury. His pulse was weak, but tachycardic. The breath sounds on the left were now present, but were still very poor. "Let's see if we can get his BP up on wide-open normal saline and dopamine at ten micrograms per liter, per minute."

Latham set up the IVs and they did their best to estimate the flow rate for the dopamine, since they didn't have a metered pump that could be used on the exercise field. Jack and Latham took turns on the evacuation of the air in the prisoner's chest.

Eventually they heard ambulance sirens. Other guards accompanied the ambulance crew onto the field and put the prisoner on a stretcher. Rayfield hadn't regained consciousness. Jack knew that his only chance was to get to Garity ASAP, and it didn't look like that was going to happen.

Jack stepped back to get an overview.

He'd done what he could. The knife wound must have severed an artery or at least caused more damage than he could diagnose with his eyes, ears, and hands—certainly more than he could treat without being in a hospital. Based on his vital signs, Rayfield had probably lost a lot of blood. But they didn't have any blood on hand for a transfusion. "Let's go."

Jack went with the stretcher to the ambulance and then followed behind in his truck, knowing full well that Rayfield didn't have much chance of making it to the hospital alive.

TWENTY-ONE

Jack could do little more than watch while the ER doc pronounced Mac Rayfield DOA, then waited around the ER long enough to fill the doctors in on the details. He was grateful to have colleagues who were as shocked as he when they heard the story that led Rayfield to his option of kill or be raped at will for years.

Jack felt as if he'd been kicked in the gut. He'd seen his share of people crash and burn, but it was different this time. He'd been a player in the game—he saw it coming, but couldn't do a thing to prevent Rayfield from taking the option he did. He wondered what he himself would have done in the same predicament.

Jack went to the ER loading dock for some fresh air. The noise of the city and the rhythmic pounding of cars on the interstate a half block away buffeted his senses until he couldn't think of anything else to do except to go back to work.

He looked at the ER doors, and decided to walk around the front of the hospital. He didn't want to see Rayfield's body.

Once inside the front lobby, he took the elevators to the CCU. No one but the guard even looked twice as Jack made his way into the prisoner's room.

Tillis was sitting up in bed, the covers concealing the manacle that chained his ankle to the bed rail. He was clean shaven, with an IV running into his right arm. He gave a kind of smile when he looked up—a prison smile. "Hi, Doc."

Jack shook his hand. "How do you feel?"

"You don't lie, I'll say that much."

"What do you mean?"

"About my chest. You know, after the fluid drained out. Hurts like hell."

Jack pulled the sheet back from the man's chest and examined the flexible tube and the reservoir that was taped to his belly. "Have they said when they might pull the drain?"

"That little intern said it might come out after they finished rounds this morning."

"It hurts for a second, but not much worse than what you feel now. And the pain should drop off about a day after it gets pulled."

"What's this thing they found inside me, Doc?"

Jack looked for a chart, but realized it was at the nurse's desk. "I haven't heard any reports. What did they say?"

"I can't make sense out of all them words, but they saw something on that sonar thing." He whipped his finger back and forth across his chest.

"I'll see what I can find out." He put his hand on the curtain around the bed.

"Hey, listen, Doc. You know they can't send me back until you OK it."

"What do you mean?"

"I heard 'em talkin' last night. The prison called and wanted to know why I ain't back yet."

Jack was surprised, but tried not to show it. "It's the attending physician's job to determine when it's safe for you to leave. I can't imagine you going anywhere for a few days."

"Yeah, maybe. But just remember, they can't send me back until *you* OK it. It's a rule. They give you any trouble, you tell them I'm one of Scalacey's patients. He'll set them straight."

Jack didn't know what to make of the comments. Indigent patients were notorious for last-minute ailments or conveniently remembering unusual problems that would delay their discharge, so his first reaction was to discount what he'd heard. But there was one thing about long-term inmates—they knew the system and the rules cold.

"What do you mean, until *I* OK it?"

"It's part of their contract with the hospital. The prison can't be surprised by a transfer, so nobody comes back without the OK of the prison doc who sent them."

Jack studied the man a second. "Let me check your chart."

Jack sat down at the desk and began to look through Tillis's chart. He skipped the history and physical. The chest X ray in the ER had shown a "water bottle heart," so-called because the fluid around the heart had distended the pericardium to the point that its shadow looked like a hot water bottle, wide at the base and narrow at the top. The progress notes were unremarkable except the notation about the unusual echocardiogram findings, with a further comment by the resident wondering if an MRI wouldn't be helpful.

He sorted through the lab results. The printed lab sheets on the chart were a day behind, but the preliminary values from the ER showed a normal total white count, but an elevated eosinophil count. There were no blast cells. The profile was more like the one he'd seen on Burke's old computer records—values a few months old. He wondered what Burke's numbers looked like now. He suspected that if Richardson got to him before the police, the numbers would get lost somehow. Jack copied the numbers and put them in his pocket.

He thumbed through the other pages, looking for the cell count on the pericardial fluid, but it wasn't back yet. He looked at the desk, but the unit clerk had the computer terminal tied up processing what looked like at least six charts with stat orders. He'd have to find out later.

The echo report was under a separate section. It described what remained of the pericardial effusion and made note of the drainage catheter. The size of the upper chambers, the atria, were normal, as were the size and thickness of the ventricular walls. The ejection fraction, which was an estimate of the pumping function of the left ventricle, was normal.

But the surprise was in a separate paragraph. It described what appeared to be a tumor pressing on the right side of the heart. It was small, an estimated size of three by four centimeters, with several cysts on the inside, and an echogenic bright spot having the characteristics of a calcified mass. In fact, it looked like a small tooth inside one of the cysts.

A voice came from over his shoulder. "Gross."

Jack looked up from the chart. A nurse's aide obviously had been reading without his knowing.

She was overweight and had eyebrows that squirmed as if her brain were hearing conflicting voices. "That's the kind of stuff you read in the tabloids."

Jack flinched. All he needed was more publicity, especially that kind. He tried to placate her with the truth. "Embryonic tumors are well described in the medical literature. Any tumor is rare in the heart, but this type makes up a respectable percentage. Teeth and hair are often the way the pathologic diagnosis is made."

"It's still gross."

Jack felt that the more she knew the more comfortable she'd be—and the less likely to sell the story for a wad of cash. "It's really quite understandable. Embryonic tumors are thought to arise when something goes wrong with a cell's normal signal to become a heart cell instead of a brain cell, for example. Most tumors start as a mistake when the DNA reproduces itself. Since every cell contains a full complement of DNA, theoretically any one of them can express the genes that make up any other cell type in the body. In this instance a gene sequence for a tooth was turned on.

"But in the normal development, only a specific sequence of genes should get expressed and the others are somehow inhibited. That cell then eventually develops only as the specific gene sequence directs. So one group of cells become brain tissue, another group becomes heart, and so on. It's called differentiation. When a cell finishes its path and becomes a neuron in the brain, it's said to be fully differentiated."

He watched her pained expression; he was losing the battle. "You know, this is hard enough on people like us who have the professional training to act responsibly. Can you imagine how frightened this man would be if he hears the wrong thing about this growth?"

Her features softened and she looked toward the curtain drawn around Tillis's bed. "He'd be scared to death. Poor man."

"Then I can depend on you to keep this confidential. Wrong word to someone and before you know it the cleaning lady will be in hysterics in there."

"You can count on me, Doctor."

Jack smiled at her, but wasn't at all sure he'd accomplished a thing. He kept the chart closed in his lap, now aware that some of the morning shift of nurses were milling around the nurse's station. To his relief, he saw the resident in charge of Tillis's case walking through the unit. They'd worked together on the hematology/oncology consult service last year.

Jack cornered him close to the automatic doors. "How's your service this month?"

"Full. Like always, I guess. We're on call tonight, so who knows what the chopper will bring."

"Listen, I know you've got to meet your attending, but can I ask about Mr. Tillis?"

The resident brightened. "You ought to see that echo. Un-be-lievable."

"I saw your note about the MRI. Seems like a good idea."

"I thought so. But the attending is getting heat from the prison. They won't pay for the MRI."

"You're kidding."

"It's out of my hands. That company that runs the clinic . . . I guess you know all about that. Anyway I'm trying to see if we can't get him scanned under somebody's research grant."

"Talk to the chief resident. There's money in the educational fund. They'll jump at a case like this."

"Good idea. I'll run it by the attending. I bet that will work." He started to walk off.

"How much does Mr. Tillis know?"

"Not much. But he'll have to find out soon because the CV surgeons will be involved. That is, if your company will pay to fix the guy." He hit a square sensor on the wall and the doors opened. "I've got to go."

"Thanks. And, listen, it's not my company."

The resident waved over his head but didn't look back.

Jack stood there a moment, then walked back to Tillis's room. "I talked to your resident. It does look like there's some kind of growth in there." He waited for the words to sink in, for him to ask if a growth meant tumor, or cancer. But he didn't change his expression or ask anything.

"I'm sure that's what caused the irritation of the sac around your heart. They want another test that can see it better; then they'll know what to do."

Tillis seemed to take the news as if he'd just heard the weather report. "OK, Doc. Whatever you say. And don't forget to tell Scalacey. He'll take care of me."

"I'll check on you later."

Jack closed the curtain, and stood there a second before leaving the CCU to wait at the elevator. He never was quite sure with people like that. Never sure whether they were so ignorant that they couldn't comprehend the magnitude of threat facing them, or whether they had a more simple life—one in which they had so little control that it wasn't worth getting riled up. How Tillis could have that attitude and yet live in the same hell pit that drove Mac Rayfield to kill and be killed was beyond Jack's understanding. He envied the ability to trust that your problems would somehow work themselves out, that someone would show up and take care of things.

The elevator door creaked open and Jack caught his reflection in the circular mirror in the back corner. One thing for sure. Nobody was going to come riding over the hill to pull his butt out of the fire. Nobody except himself.

Dan was waiting in his office. He stood and closed the door after a quick glance to see if anyone was eavesdropping.

Jack looked around at the stacks of charts and

cardboard pallets that held pathology slides. "Did you get it?"

Dan sat at his desk. "I put in a request. It's not here anymore. It's in the Mayfield Building."

"That could take forever."

"You forget I'm an attending now. Usually they actually respond."

"How long?"

"I wish I could say today. Realistically, it will be tomorrow. At best."

"If it's still there."

"You need to relax a little. I'll get the file."

Jack looked around the office as if he'd find answers by sheer willpower. He told Dan about what had happened to Rayfield at the prison. Dan listened with the same sense of horror that Jack had felt.

Neither of them said anything for a moment. Then Jack said, "I thought that I'd gotten myself ready . . . mentally, I mean . . . for my father's autopsy. But after what happened today . . . it's probably best that we do this tomorrow."

"Jack, I still don't think this is such a good idea. Why don't you let me look at the report, and you can ask questions? You can sit right there, and I'll check anything you want to know."

Jack leaned against a filing cabinet and considered Dan's advice. If things were reversed, he'd probably give the same logical suggestion. But logic doesn't have much impact on things that wake you in a cold sweat.

He studied his friend. Maybe he was right. "We'll try it your way first. But if I don't get what I need, I'm looking at the file."

Dan was visibly relieved. "I'll page you when I get it."

"We could talk about it at my place."

"I don't think I should take the file from the hospital. But it might be better if we met after everybody's out of the office."

"I'm not so sure this place is as safe as you might think."

"What's that supposed to mean?"

"Dr. Edelman was at Richardson's gala last night."

Dan sat forward. "What are you saying?"

"Edelman put the wraps on some of these autopsies, and then he shows up at Richardson's corporate headquarters."

"Are you crazy? You're talking about the county medical examiner. Don't say anything like that outside this office. You aren't exactly making a lot of friends out there."

"My patient in the CCU has an elevated eosinophil count."

Dan sat forward. "Blasts?"

"No."

"Any relation to the guard and that nurse?"

"They've all been in Elrice. But that's all I've got. There's something going on, Dan. I just can't seem to put it together. But I know there's a connection."

Dan seemed to be thinking over the options, and finally said, "Lay off the comments about Edelman. I'll page you tomorrow when I get your father's autopsy report."

Jack checked his watch. He had some more plates to keep balanced in the air. "I'll see you."

Jack left the pathology department. He had a call he had to make, and didn't want Dan more involved than he already was.

He took the elevator to the eighth-floor call rooms. As expected, there was no one in the residents' lounge this time of day. The room had bad fluorescent lighting with chairs and sofas that were twenty years old, and looked it. There was a strong aroma of burned coffee from the machine that someone had left on too long. The room almost never had the same arrangement, except during football season, when you could count on everything lined up to face the TV. At least they had cable.

He sat in a chair by the phone and tried to collect his thoughts. He'd never had so much happen to him in a week, much less twenty-four hours. Henrietta Franklin's murder. The fight with Elaine. Rayfield's prison rampage. On top of all that, the information about his father in this morning's newspaper might have given Richardson reason to reconsider his offer of a job at his headquarters. And without Richardson's protection, it was just a matter of time before Warden Conners forced him out. If he was going to find the truth about his father, he had to preserve his connection to Elrice.

After getting an outside line, Jack reached the operator at Richardson Enterprises, who connected him to Hugo Voss's office. Voss came on the line seconds later. "Dr. Harris. I've been expecting your call."

Jack listened for any trace of sarcasm, for some hint of an ax being sharpened, but he detected nothing. "I thought about your offer."

"Sleep often clarifies the mind."

"You've seen the paper?"

"Yes."

It felt like high-stakes poker. "Does the offer still stand?"

"As I explained last night, it's Mr. Richardson's offer, not mine. He's a very loyal man, as he told you himself. This new information has made things difficult, but we talked earlier this morning. He'd like you to meet him again tomorrow. If he gives the OK, then you'll come work for me."

Voss didn't seem pleased with the prospect, but there it was—access. It was what he'd been looking for, but now that it had appeared, he had the uneasy sense that he was making a mistake. A mistake in pursuing something he couldn't give up even if it meant losing himself. A mistake he'd already made. Sealed the day he walked into Elrice. Born the day of his brother's fall.

They knew, and yet they still wanted him. On the surface it made no sense. Maybe the connection with his father was news, possibly a leak from Warden Conners's office, and Richardson was trying to save face. But Jack found that hard to swallow.

The only alternative was that they'd known all along. If so, they must have known the truth about his father's murder, and if they knew that, they surely knew his son was poking around, asking questions. But the newspaper article gave them the perfect opportunity to push him out of the picture—so why grant him further access? What looked like the opening he needed smelled more like a trap.

"Take it or leave it, Doctor."

"Where should I meet him?"

"Come to our headquarters. Mr. Richardson will be at the archery range on the back of the property. You're to be there at seven-thirty sharp. He'll only give you a few minutes. I expect he'll do all the talking. If he gives the final OK, you'll be brought back to my office."

"How do I get there?"

"Go to the reception desk on the main floor of the building where we had the gala. Someone will be there to take you to Mr. Richardson. It would be the mistake of a lifetime to be late."

Before Jack could respond, Voss said, "Until then, Doctor," and hung up.

TWENTY-TWO

Jack left Garity Hospital, checked the card in his pocket, and referred to a city map before driving his truck out of the residents' parking lot. He'd never been to Rudy's Bar-B-Que, much less that part of town.

The drive took almost an hour, but there was no sign of Richardson's men—somebody would probably lose his job. The traffic seemed to thin the closer he got to the neighborhood he'd circled on the map. Almost half the businesses were long dead, their windows boarded up and decorated with graffiti and the occasional bullet hole. Young black men and boys leaned or sat near corners, eyeing him with a mix of apathy and hate.

A purple Oldsmobile pulled dead even with his car. At the periphery of his vision, Jack could see a muscular black forearm propped through the open window of the car, but he stared ahead rather than make eye contact.

He slowed a little, and the Olds slowed with him. Rap music pounded so loud it vibrated inside his truck. Jack gunned it as a light turned red, and the Olds gunned right beside him. He knew it would be trouble the minute he looked over, but he managed to keep his cool and concentrate on the fast-food stores, pawnshops, and the occasional beauty salon that had somehow been able to survive in this little outpost of hell.

He recognized the name of a crossing street, then saw the building on the left. The place had a square layout and a flat roof that supported a big ceramic pig with a chef's hat cocked to one side. RUDY'S was painted in red cursive on the pig, but it was nearly obscured by the hickory smoke that billowed from a central brick chimney. When Jack pulled into the gravel lot, the Olds made a U-turn and parked on the street.

He went in the front door and heard two car doors close behind him. He hadn't seen another white face for a dozen blocks, and he had the clear sense that he'd crossed onto forbidden turf.

The place had booths and tables with red-checkered cloths. Jack took a seat at the counter. The only customer this late in the day was an old black man by the window, nursing his iced tea and reading the paper.

As a waitress put a half-sized glass of ice water on the counter he heard the entrance door close behind him. He spoke before she could ask what he wanted.

"I'm looking for Mrs. Geneva Lott. I was told her husband works here."

He followed her eyes and could tell that the men had come up behind him. Jack knew there'd be a fight as soon as she left. His back was to the door—a rookie mistake. They could get a knife in his kidney before he could turn around.

At that moment a man came out from the kitchen. His face was beaded with perspiration from working near the fire. He had on a worn short-sleeve shirt, unbuttoned halfway down his thick chest. His arms looked like black logs. Jack sensed the men behind him as they moved closer.

The man wiped his hands on a stained half apron. "What you want with Geneva?"

"She told me to meet her here."

"I'm alone."

Lott motioned with his hand, and Jack heard the men behind him take seats at a table. "She'll be out back."

Jack knew he'd come close to serious trouble. He got off the stool without looking at the men who'd followed him inside and followed Mr. Lott through a storage area piled with crates of hamburger buns. Behind the building was a small grass yard framed by a wooden fence that had seen better days. Beyond the fence he could see a street with old houses and tall pines.

The man motioned for him to sit at one of the picnic tables, then left him alone in the hot Georgia sun. Alone except for the mosquitoes and swirling smoke.

A few minutes later, Geneva Lott came through another door near the kitchen. She was carrying two plates of barbecued ribs with coleslaw and baked beans. The young waitress followed her with a pitcher of iced tea and a full loaf of sliced white bread, which she put on the table. She slit open the length of the bread bag with a butcher knife, then went back inside without saying a word.

Mrs. Lott had changed out of her nurse's uniform, but still held herself with the kind of dignity and slow-motion poise his mother used to refer to as "carriage." It wasn't something Jack often saw, but there was no mistaking the precision and pride that Geneva Lott had in her life. And yet she was unashamed to meet here, where her husband cooked hog meat on a pit. Jack looked at her keen eyes, aware that there weren't many Geneva Lotts in the world.

Jack said, "There was a massacre at the prison today.

That kid who got raped the other day killed a member of the Cutters, then died a couple of hours ago en route to Garity."

She looked away. "I heard about it on the radio. I didn't know who was involved."

The news cast a pall over their meal. The ribs were the best he'd had in a long time, but after all he'd been through today, he couldn't bring himself to eat more than a few bites.

She toyed with her food, and Jack sensed that she was feeling the aftershock of what he'd told her.

They sat mainly in silence until she poured more tea. Her countenance changed, and she looked him in the eye. "Why did you come?"

"You mean here?"

"Don't play games. You know what I mean."

He looked at her brown eyes. Sharp, yet sad. "You said you came to my father's funeral."

She bowed her head. "Yes. I was there."

"You told me he sometimes worked the night shift with you at the infirmary."

"Why do you want to drag all this up? Can't you let your poor father rest?"

"Do you think . . ." The rush of emotion brought a knot to his throat. He drank some tea and looked off.

"Do I think he took his own life?"

He looked back, almost afraid to hear her answer. "Do you?"

"Let it go, son. No good can come from all this."

He grabbed her hand across the wood table. "There's something you want to tell me, or you wouldn't have agreed to meet today."

She didn't pull back. She just kept searching his face, seeming to assess what he'd do if she told him. "When you work with people, most of the time you don't know their lives, what makes them do what they do. But your father was different. He had a core to him that you could see if you took the time to notice such things."

She paused and he let go. He felt she was trying to tell him something without saying it.

"No. I don't think he took his own life. But I can't tell you why, other than to say it like I've just done."

"When was the last time you saw him?"

"A few hours before."

He didn't need to ask "before what?" They both knew. "Did he seem upset or depressed?"

She thought a minute. "Upset, maybe. But not depressed."

"I want you to think hard. Did he say anything?"

She looked over his shoulder so intently, he thought someone had come up. He glanced back, but no one was there.

He finally decided that it was her way of saying she wasn't going to answer him. "Did he ever talk about any of us?"

Her expression softened. "Yes. Sometimes, when things were slow. His shift and mine were different, but there were plenty of times he worked overtime to make extra money for your brother. But he'd always make it home to fix supper for that boy. Once his son was asleep, he sometimes would come back and work part of someone else's shift, like from midnight to six."

"What kind of things would he say?"

"Just chitchat mostly. Sometimes he talked about your mother being gone. And of course, about your brother . . . how it worried him. How he wished he could trade places, and give the boy a shot at a real life."

Jack couldn't look at her.

"He was proud of you, Dr. Harris. He said so, more than once."

Her comment loosened something inside him, but it wasn't enough. He wondered if there'd ever be enough. "If he didn't commit suicide, then someone killed him."

She sat silent, her shoulders looking frail for the first time.

"Why would someone kill my father, then make it look like suicide? Why?"

"I don't know why."

The lie was in her eyes. "But you met me here, where you knew we couldn't be seen together. There's something you're afraid of. What is it?"

She wiped her dress with her hand. She was about to say something, but didn't.

"I think there's a connection between the guard who was taken hostage with me and that nurse who was killed outside St. Michael's."

"There are others."

"What do you mean?"

She lowered her voice. "That inmate you saw, the one with headaches . . ."

Jack's mind raced. "Havard?"

She nodded. "He wasn't the first."

"I don't understand."

There was a commotion from the kitchen, someone shouting. It broke her nerve. She stood abruptly and stared at the door. She immediately began to collect the plates. "I know why you came to Elrice. I knew it the minute I saw you. And I've been worried sick ever since. But a person's got to live their own life.

"I should never have had you come here. Please leave this alone. I pray about it every night. Pray that you will give this up to the Lord, and find peace. But I can see now that you won't." She walked a few steps away, then turned back. "God help you if you find the answer."

* * *

Detective Tarkington got out of the backseat of the police car as soon as it pulled off the side of the remote road. Two county sheriff cars and the one local police car were already parked in the grass. He could see the yellow tape cordoning off an area that extended about forty feet into the woods.

He walked up to a sheriff, whose body language said he was in charge. "Thanks for calling us in."

The sheriff pointed toward the woods. "The girl's name is Shaundra Jackson. Got a broken neck. Local guy was out with his hunting dogs and came across the body."

"It's not hunting season."

"We thought we'd give him a break on that, considering what he found."

"How long's she been dead?"

"Haven't got the coroner yet, but her uncle said she left his bar last night with three men about eleven-thirty. He identified one as that escaped prisoner in your APB."

"What about the other two?"

"Didn't know them."

"Maybe we can jog his memory."

"Maybe. This guy runs a shanty bar about ten miles up the road. The local police told me they've been there before, trying to track down leads, but it seems anybody who walks into the place gets some kind of amnesia. This guy volunteered the information about Burke as soon as he got word about his niece being killed. I think he'd have said if he knew the other two."

"You did good work here, sheriff."

The man touched his hat. "You need anything, let me know."

Tarkington bent under the tape and walked into the woods. A photographer took a final shot, then began to put his equipment up.

The girl was black, and her torn green dress was held on her only by the right shoulder strap. Dried leaves and pine needles bunched up her hair, and matted dirt covered much of her back. She appeared to have been rolled out of a shallow grave, and there were streaks of dirt where the dogs had been digging.

Tarkington came back out to the highway, found the police car where they were holding "Armless" Jackson, then introduced himself.

"Tell me about Burke."

Jackson had anger in his eyes. Tarkington could tell part of it was directed at him.

"He was at my place. Him and two others."

"We'll come back to them in a minute. What kind of shape was Burke in?"

"Normal. Looked normal to me."

"No injuries?"

"He had these orange eyes. I asked him about it. He said there wasn't nuthin' wrong with them. He looked OK other than the eyes."

Tarkington took notes. "Any idea where he might be headed?"

Jackson shook his head.

"Anything you tell me can be kept secret. No one will know where the information came from."

"Like you think people are so stupid they can't see my niece is murdered and all of a sudden you cops find Burke? Well, let me tell you something, I know people will talk about me, but that was my kin, my sister's only girl, they killed in there. I don't give a damn what people say. Burke can rot in hell. If you don't find him, I will."

"Was there anyone at your bar that night that might have known the other two men?"

"If they did, they won't tell you shit after the way you people beat them folks."

Tarkington was caught off guard. He had a close team working on this case. No local police, and certainly no one who'd be involved in a shakedown. "But they might trust you, if you were the one who asked."

Jackson looked out the side window away from Tarkington, and seemed to be thinking things over. "I can ask around, but I ain't promisin' no answers."

Tarkington wondered if Warden Conners had sent a vigilante team to comb Burke's old neighborhood. "None of my people beat anybody. If what you say is true, there'll be an internal affairs investigation."

"Yeah, and like that's really gonna make them cops pay. Same old shit from you people. You do what you want, and get away with everything."

Tarkington knew there was no point in arguing. He held out his card. "I want to find the guys who did that to your niece. Call me if you learn anything. I'll do my part to keep your name out of this."

He got out of the car and looked up and down the road. No cars had driven by since he'd gotten here. There were dense woods for miles around—good enough to hide in, but he couldn't understand why Burke hadn't fled the country, much less the state. Bulletins were out for them nationwide, but the evidence still said they were in the area.

He wrote a summary of what Jackson had told him, including the information about the beatings. Then he looked at the back page of his notes where he'd made a list of the common denominators in this case: *2 carved on chest or breast; location—Atlanta.* And to that he added *surrounding area; Jack Harris.*

He closed the notebook and leaned against the police car. Burke was staying in the area for a reason, and the reason looked like Dr. Harris.

Jack could hardly remember the drive back from Rudy's Bar-B-Que, having made turns and lane changes by luck and subconscious memory. His mind was flooded. Geneva Lott knew his father had been murdered, and she knew why—Jack was sure of it. But when he'd followed her back into the restaurant, her husband told him she was gone. Jack insisted, but it became clear there was going to be trouble if he didn't leave. So he did. He had no choice.

He found himself in the parking lot of a beer joint he and other residents used to frequent, with no clear recollection of having driven there. His mind was too jumbled to let Ed see him like this. The only person he wanted to see was Elaine, and he'd stormed out of her apartment earlier in the morning acting like a damn fool.

He went inside and found a pay phone beyond the pool tables in the back. The phone rang awhile before Mrs. Logan answered.

"Things aren't going so well, Mrs. Logan. I don't know if it's a good idea for Ed to see me like this."

"What's wrong, hon?"

"A lot has happened today—there was a riot at the prison. Pretty nasty stuff. I just need some time alone."

"I saw about the riot on the news. They said the doctors tried to save the prisoners who got stabbed, but nothing could be done."

"Did they mention me?"

"No. They interviewed some guy with a ponytail.

Jack, I don't think they're suitable people for you to be working with."

Jack wasn't surprised that Conners kept his contribution out of the media. "I'm beginning to think you're right. How's Ed?"

"He's happy, playing with that cat. He's going to wear out that little fur ball."

"I may stay at a hotel tonight. I'm not up for dealing with the press at my door."

"They've settled down a little, but there's still someone camped out across the street."

"Sorry I've put you through all this."

"Tell you the truth, it's been exciting. By the way, your lady friend came by."

"What did she say?"

"She said you forgot your coat when you left her place last night. I've got it in the living room."

"Did she say anything else?"

"Just to tell you she came by."

"Thanks, Mrs. Logan."

"You ought to call that girl. Maybe you can go to a movie or something tonight."

"I'll call her. And thanks for watching Ed. I'll get by to see him tomorrow." He hung up.

Jack ate a burger at the bar and drank three beers before the tension of the day started to slack off. He could still feel his hand inside the sucking chest wound that led to Rayfield's death, and the way his hand felt in his dreams when he touched the back of his father's bloody head. There wasn't enough beer in the room to erase the raw brutality of life.

It was dark by the time he drove to Elaine's. Jack could see the light through her upstairs window in the antebellum house, but he stood by his truck like a freshman trying to summon the courage to ask for his first date. He didn't know how to begin to make up for the way he'd treated her this morning, but the weight of his problems pulled him to her like gravity. He couldn't get through another hour without her.

The front door of the house was unlocked, as before, but he stood at her apartment door for nearly a minute before he mustered two quick knocks.

Her door cracked open; then she closed it and unfastened the chain lock. Elaine was in a sleeveless silk nightgown. She stepped back into the soft music in her living room. Her eyes moistened and he reached out for her. They held each other in a tight embrace without saying a word.

Whatever he wanted to say was lost in emotion. She kissed him, and he caressed her face in his hands, kissing her soft lips, her cheeks, and the gentle tears that needed no explanation.

In her bed, he removed her nightgown, his hand gliding over her skin. She held his face in her hands and it was as if there were nothing in the world to see but her eyes. She guided him inside her, pulling her arms and legs tight against his back, her palm lingering on the jagged scar, holding on with heated strength as if life itself depended on not letting go.

They woke together. She began to stroke his hair gently. She kissed him, then said, "Don't leave me."

He pulled her against his chest and they lay together, legs partly under the sheets.

She rested her head under his chin and spoke softly. "I had no right to say those things about your father. I had no right to even ask."

Outside her window the moonlight traced the oak leaves in silver. So much of his nature called for him to bury the secret, but she had changed him, and he'd come to fear that his pain could devour them both. "There's something else you need to know."

He felt her breathing begin to slow, but she didn't risk a word.

"I took Ed with me to the rigs off Louisiana the summer before his senior year. He was sort of aimless. A good guy, good at sports, but no clue about the future. I thought maybe he'd see what life could be like without a college degree. I hoped it would change him like it did me.

"It was night and we were riding out a bad storm. The swells were so huge that the platform swayed with the rise and fall of each crest. One end of a stabilizer bar near the top of the derrick tower came loose. It stripped the power line and shorted out the lights. I climbed up to secure the bar before the thing whipped up enough momentum to damage the drill shaft. You could hear the wind moaning through the tower and it was so black you couldn't see five feet in front of you. Ed followed me up but I didn't know it."

Elaine lifted her head.

"The wrench you use on one of those things is about three feet long and weighs over forty pounds. You pull with enough force to throw you out into the gulf if you're not harnessed right. I was pulling with all my strength when the bolt on the stabilizer broke. The wrench snapped loose and struck Ed." Jack's throat tightened and he closed his eyes.

Elaine started to touch the tears at the corner of his eyes but he turned away.

"He fell about sixty feet. Hit his head on a boom; then he spiraled onto a net by the helipad. My harness broke and I fell into the gulf, but not until the edge of the platform stripped some muscle off my back. I saw him hit that boom. I was sure he was dead, and all I wanted was to keep sinking down into the dark mass of water."

"You can't blame yourself."

"I should have known he was there. Whatever I did, he did. We were always like that."

"It's not your fault."

"Tell that to my old man."

"Oh, Jack. He didn't."

"He did. And he was right. The first thing he said to me when I woke up in the hospital was, 'Why'd you do it, Jack?' How do I answer that? My whole family came unraveled because of me."

"I . . . I had no idea. The things I said this morning . . ." She sat up, suppressing more tears.

He sat up and held her. "You were right about my father. I haven't been willing to admit it. I love him, but he wasn't there.

"There's so much I had to do on my own. You're supposed to open up slowly to the world, and your parents are supposed to help you open up because there are parts of you that are too vulnerable. You've got no idea of what's coming, but it opens up whether you are ready or not.

"But they weren't there, neither one of them. And when I opened up, I was touched by fear—the threat of anyone knowing what my family was really made of. So I closed down. What else could I do? Neither one of my parents was emotionally capable of helping or protecting me. Instead I opened by myself; my only choice was to get tough or be eaten alive."

"You don't have any idea where your mother is?"

"She's not around here, that's the only thing I'm sure of. But she loved Louisiana . . . she said it was where she was always happy. I don't know if that's true or just fantasy, but if there's any way, I think she would have made it there, somehow."

"But you don't blame her."

"I *can't* hate her. Who gives you permission to resent your mother when she's mentally ill? Who fixes that one for you?"

Neither of them spoke for a moment. Then Jack said, "When I get all this settled, I'm going to look for her."

"You're not responsible for what happened to your parents."

He looked out the window. "If he really was suicidal, why didn't he call me? Didn't he love me enough to call me instead?"

"I love you, Jack. Please leave all this. Get away from Elrice. Get away from Richardson. We could go away together."

They embraced, and he held her more fully than he'd ever held another woman. He wanted to believe that she could make him whole, that leaving all this behind was actually possible. But he knew the truth.

"I've got to settle this between me and my father. My mother left, and my brother will never be the same. But someone killed my father, and I'm going to find out who did it, even if it means losing everything else. Even if I don't owe him, I owe me."

TWENTY-THREE

Jack was up by five-thirty. Elaine had told him she was taking another day off from St. Michael's, so he let her sleep. He left a note explaining that he'd be with Dan Linh tonight, and that he'd call when he got a chance. He got to his house in time to stretch Ed, shower, and explain to Mrs. Logan that Ed didn't need to go to the church today.

He got to Richardson's headquarters with a few minutes to spare. The receptionist at the front desk walked Jack to a side door where a guard was waiting with a golf cart. They took several trails through dense pine woods, occasionally entering a clearing with white buildings, only to be engulfed again in acres of forest land. After what seemed like two miles, the path opened onto a large rectangular clearing with a small house to the left and a series of archery targets at the far end.

Richardson had just let an arrow fly, and he turned, beaming at Jack as if a foreign head of state had just landed. He handed the compound bow to an underling, who took it aside and leaned it next to a matched set of crossbows.

Richardson's face looked oiled, and there were thick rings of perspiration under his light blue shirt. His khaki pants were big enough to cover most of a hammock. "Glad you could make it, Dr. Harris." He brushed the shirt with his hands. "I love these fishing shirts. Found them in the Bahamas. Ever go bone fishing?"

"No, sir. Can't say that I have."

"The king of all fly-fishing events. They're white as a bone and swim over sand that looks like sugar—damn near impossible to see. The guides take you out in flatboats, and they stand on these platforms on the stern so they can look for the fish's shadow when it forages for shrimp larvae.

"These shirtsleeves unroll for when the sun's too much, but you can roll them up and secure them with this strap, so the sleeve doesn't unfurl when you cast. Can't believe you've never been bone fishing. I keep a Chris-Craft down there. We take the jet down six or eight times a year—sleep on the boat, and fish off the skiffs. You'll have to join us for a trip sometime."

"I'd like that."

"Our next trip will be in the fall. No breeze this time of year and the damn mosquitoes will eat your skin off."

Richardson motioned to the assistant. "Let me have the crossbow."

The helper pulled the short arrow to maximum tension, then handed it over.

Richardson aimed, then pointed the bow to the ground. "I wanted to make a dove field back here, but the damn city wouldn't let me. Hell, I own three thousand acres. We could shoot elephants out here and never hurt anybody." He lifted the bow and quickly fired. The arrow just missed the inner circle.

"Packs a whollop, I'll tell you. Of course the crossbow's outlawed in some states, but I'll be damned if they can tell me what to do on my own property. We bow-hunt deer on the farm and I like to keep in practice. Plus it's good PR. Typical example, group from Indonesia will be in later this week. Never met a leader yet who doesn't enjoy the hunt. We'll wine 'em and dine 'em, but you ask me, it's the breaks we take down here that close the deals."

He picked up a compound bow and looked at his assistant. "Let's have some deer." The man walked inside the little house and pulled some levers. At the far end of the range, the padded targets turned 180 degrees, revealing a painted camouflage backdrop. Richardson pulled an arrow back just in time for a moving deer target to cross. The arrow pierced the target in the neck.

The helper smiled. "Very good, sir."

Richardson took another arrow from the man without acknowledging his compliment. "You know, some people rake me over the coals about the wages of our workers in underdeveloped countries. But it's a hundred percent more than they'd make without me . . . and it's *my* money on the line, not theirs. Every time I build a plant I'm taking the risk that some mob could burn the facility to the ground, or some damn hothead in the military could throw a coup and nationalize my factory. But I still do it.

"I can show you statistics on how the lives of hundreds and hundreds of families have been changed because of Richardson Enterprises. The only complaints I ever hear is from sissy newspaper writers with five graduate degrees and no idea how to live without electricity and running water. No idea of how to take an idea and build it from scratch. An idea so good it helps both their rich parents and those Third World countries that I'm supposedly raping for my own good." He fixed another arrow and angrily let it fly into the camouflaged wall.

Richardson's face and neck were dark crimson, with perspiration now streaming from his temples. Jack wondered if the newspaper article had convinced Richardson that he should be the next target, but instead the man presented him the bow.

"Care to try?"

"My brother and I used to hunt in Louisiana, but I've never shot a bow."

"The crossbow does half the work for you."

The assistant fixed the short arrow and showed him the trigger. He then went into the house to release the next deer target. Jack steadied the stock of the crossbow into his shoulder. Just as he squeezed the trigger, Richardson said, "I guess your father taught you how to hunt."

The arrow flew through the air, but landed ten feet shy of the target.

"You should have told me about him, son."

Jack dropped the bow by his side. "Would it have made any difference?"

Richardson now looked at him with critical eyes. Eyes that had cut a thousand deals and left others in his wake. The silence was uncomfortable.

Jack handed the bow to the assistant. "Truth is, I'd probably never have met you if I hadn't been taken hostage."

"Truth. An interesting word." Richardson kept an assessing glare; then suddenly, as quick as throwing a switch, he'd made a decision. "Took a lot of balls for you to come out here after that article about your old man in yesterday's paper. I told you I like loyalty, and I like a man who doesn't piss in his pants when he starts to take some flak." He checked his watch. The jeweled face of the Piaget glistened in the sunlight. "You've got an appointment, if I'm not mistaken."

Jack walked toward the golf cart. Before they drove away, Richardson yelled back, "Don't fuck with me, son, or I'll pin those balls of yours on my target."

Hugo Voss's office was on the top floor of the main building. The corner walls were glass from floor to ceiling. From that vantage Jack could tell that the compound included a half dozen buildings, two without windows. There were sculpted walking trails with occasional benches, and in the distance he could see a fenced field with a few horses, and another clearing with the archery targets. Despite the recreation facilities, all the employees appeared to be inside, no doubt hard at work. In the distance, downtown Atlanta seemed to rise from a sea of treetops.

The morning paper was still on Voss's desk, and he didn't rise or shake hands. "I received a visit this morning from a Detective Tarkington."

Jack sat down in front of the desk. "We've met."

"Odd that we didn't make the connection between you and your father."

"Harris is a common name."

"I'm sure that's it." Voss seemed to be toying with him.

Jack sat in silence, having learned a thing or two about its advantages.

Voss made a steeple with his fingers and touched them to his lips. "Things are getting complicated, to say the least."

Jack recalled the smooth handling he'd experienced at Richardson's estate. He had to sharpen his senses to feel the oil, but it was here, laced in a Swiss accent.

Most, if not all, employers would have cut the rope and let him drift away from the company. But

Richardson, with his glorious mantra of loyalty, was willing to stand by him no matter what. Jack didn't buy it. They wanted something.

"Mr. Richardson said the offer still stands."

"Yes."

"Even after the newspaper articles and Tarkington's visit?"

"I can sense your skepticism, so let me be blunt. As long as you are in our control, you are less dangerous. Mr. Richardson wants you, and that's all that matters."

"What about you?"

Voss seemed to be controlling his reaction. "My opinion doesn't matter at this point."

A classic nondenial denial. He suspected Voss had argued to cut their losses and move on. He'd be looking for an excuse to hang him out to dry. "Just so I know where I stand."

Voss walked to the window. "It will be up to you as to whether we make the best of this arrangement. For whatever reason, Mr. Richardson likes you—it's an enviable position, whether you know it or not. But you're not the first. It's hard to fall from his graces, but not impossible.

"If you choose to cooperate, we can offer you a great deal of protection, and you could actually contribute to the advancement of science. You might even become rich in the process." He returned to his desk. "The ball is in your court, as they say."

"Since we are being blunt, I don't have much to return to, and you know it. I came here to accept your offer."

Voss smiled as if he'd completed a huge merger. Jack saw it for what it was . . . a well-polished act.

"You will be assigned here, but there are a few other details from your time at the prison that we need to iron out." He opened a legal-sized folder and looked at some documents. "There's the matter of a Mr. Jackson Tillis, who was sent from Elrice to Garity Memorial Hospital. We need to arrange his transfer back to the prison."

Jack never took his eyes off Voss. "I saw him yesterday. He's not ready for discharge."

Voss straightened his back. "He has a tumor. Realistically, there is nothing that can be done for this man, Doctor."

"Except save his life."

"For what, the electric chair?"

"The tumor could be removed with a simple thoracotomy."

"I disagree."

"There's nothing to disagree about. It's almost definitely a benign tumor. He'll recover if it's removed."

"Perhaps God is seeking vengeance."

"What?"

"Do you know what Mr. Tillis did to land him in Elrice?"

Jack didn't have to answer. They both knew he had no idea.

Voss referred to some papers under the manila file. "He raped and murdered a thirty-three-year-old housewife in front of her daughter. He had two prior rape convictions and had been released early for good behavior. He wasn't out two weeks before he killed that young mother.

"Your patient is a monster, Dr. Harris. You may wish to make a philosophical argument about your Hippocratic oath, but facts are that in our contract with Elrice, I am the final authority about which procedures are necessary. We don't waste money on monsters."

Jack felt his gut tighten. If he'd been on the jury,

Tillis would fry. But he wasn't on the jury. He was a doctor. Tillis was no different from the scumbag who'd spit in his face after Jack saved him from an overdose of Valium. Being a doctor didn't mean he had to like everyone who got sick on his watch. But it did mean he had to do the right thing.

It dawned on him that he'd been expertly maneuvered into a trap. If he didn't sign, Voss would know he couldn't be trusted, certainly not well enough to gain access to the kind of places he needed. But if he did sign, he was telling Voss that he could be bought, and at a low price. To sign was the equivalent of agreeing that another man's life was worthless compared to protecting his own interests.

Realistically his signature wasn't critical. If he didn't sign, they'd just arrange to have Dr. Scalacey do it. He couldn't win with either option. He decided to stall.

"Why the rush? The company will come off looking cold when we pull him out of Garity. There's still the chance that the surgeons may turn him down."

"I doubt it."

"Hear me out. I know how they are. Ever since Medicare started publishing mortality data, the surgeons hate high-risk cases. He's a heavy smoker, and probably has poor pulmonary function. That alone makes him high risk. Perhaps there're other reasons to push them away . . . maybe a questionable HIV status. If the surgeons balk, then the company is off the hook."

"You're willing to plant the HIV question?"

"I can say something to the resident. Then they'll have to draw lab and get records from Elrice. That information won't come out easily. But in the process we can leak his conviction story. Enough roadblocks and it may be just too much trouble for them to go out on a limb for a guy like that."

"But if they agree to operate?"

"The way I see it, you've got me by the balls." He felt the uneasy memory of Richardson's last words to him.

"And?"

"I'm not getting squeezed for a guy like that."

Voss seemed to be considering the plan, but then he began to shake his head.

Jack felt the deal was slipping away. "Let me see what I can do. If all else fails, I'll go back to Elrice and write the transfer orders on his chart. That way there can be no question."

After a tense moment Voss said, "You have twenty-four hours."

Before Jack could say anything Voss stood, indicating the meeting was over. "My secretary will show you to the necessary people. Handle this Tillis matter as soon as she's done."

Jack walked to the door. "If I'm to be effective as your liaison I'd like to learn as much as I can about the research protocols. I'd like to talk with the researchers themselves."

"Clearance and access takes a little while."

"Perhaps you could expedite the process. I could start first thing in the morning if you agree."

Voss gave his secretary a stern look, as if this were her fault. Then his facade of charm returned. "Ms. Lock, take care of all the necessary arrangements."

Jack started to follow her out of the office, but stopped as Voss spoke. "And, Doctor, you're in the big leagues now. Twenty-four hours means just that. Any problems and you'll be on your own. Trust me, it's not a very safe place to be."

TWENTY-FOUR

It took over an hour for Voss's secretary to run him through the human resources department and the red tape Richardson demanded of his employees. He signed legal forms in which he agreed that any discovery or breakthrough significant enough for a patent would be the sole property of Richardson Enterprises. There were also agreements prohibiting employees from transferring data to competitors, another establishing a no-compete clause that prevented him from being employed by any research facility for three years after leaving this job, and a stack of papers prohibiting him from writing any medical journal articles, newspaper or magazine accounts, or books pertaining to anything he might see, or gain knowledge of, in the course of his employment. Jack had the sense that he'd traded one prison for another.

In the next room was a sterile cubicle staffed by a woman in a white uniform. There he signed another form, agreeing to random blood and urine samples to screen out substance abuse among employees, and yet another paper showing that he understood that an abnormal test would be grounds for dismissal. After he gave the woman a container half filled with his urine, she smiled, then deftly drew a blood sample.

The secretary then walked him to the security station near the back of the building. While he was filling out more forms, Harold Mason, Richardson's security chief, came out. The collar of his white shirt was loose around his thick neck, and a gun was holstered under his left arm.

"Dr. Harris. I heard you'd be coming on board."

Mason handed the papers to a girl behind a counter and said, "He's cleared. Just put those on my desk and I'll handle everything."

He slapped Jack on the back. "Voss says you need retinal and handprint ID. When I started twenty years ago, all we had was dog tags."

Jack followed him into what looked like an ophthalmologist's exam room, with black walls and a low chair in front of a box with a chin rest. Without being told, he sat there and adjusted the soft cushions around his eyes to block the ambient light.

"You had one of these before?"

Jack leaned back from the machine. "It's a retinal mapper. They do it every time I get my eyes checked."

"Not like this they don't. This thing's linked to the network server. You got to get into some of the secure rooms, there'll be a camera that scans your retina and compares it to what we have on record. There's even a camera on your computer monitor that will read your eye whenever you access certain files."

"And I suppose you keep a record of who's worked on those files."

"You bet your ass. We keep the retinal access logs forever. If some other company miraculously comes out with something close to what we've been researching, we cross-reference those logs with anyone who's left the company, and my people find out if anybody on the list went to work for the competition."

"Impressive."

"I get a printout of everyone who enters a secure area. Anybody entering at an unusual time triggers an e-mail to the central monitoring room."

"What about the handprint? I saw Voss use it to access some of the labs downstairs."

"Different level of security. Retina is the big stuff, handprint is earlier technology, and we use it in higher-volume areas, like the animal pens."

"Will this take long? Voss wanted me to clear up some things at Elrice this afternoon."

Mason sat behind the retinal mapper. "You'll be out of here in five minutes."

It was late in the day when he got out, but Jack thought there was still a slim chance he could block Voss's plans for Jackson Tillis.

He drove toward town, occasionally turning off the main streets into neighborhoods, once pulling into a driveway, until he was convinced he wasn't being followed. Just why Richardson's surveillance had dropped out was unclear. He wondered if they'd finally decided just to give up.

The wind had picked up ahead of a bank of thunderclouds coming in from the west. The farther he drove the darker the sky became.

He pulled into a Seven-Eleven and bought a Coke while he waited for a college girl in tight blue denim shorts to finish using the pay phone at the corner. He sat against the front fender of his truck, and smelled the fresh ozone from the oncoming storm. The clouds had cooled the air by the time the girl finally hung up.

He put money in the slot before she pulled away. He watched her car disappear down the road while he waited for the Garity operator to come back on-line to connect him with the resident he'd talked to earlier.

"Sorry to bother you. I called to check on Mr. Tillis. Any progress on getting that MRI?"

"It's on for late today. Your suggestion about the chief resident worked. I'm just sorry they get to take it out in Texas."

"What do you mean?"

"The company that runs the prison has got some national contract for cardiac surgery. He's going to Houston."

Jack couldn't believe what he was hearing. "Unless you can get the CV surgeons to take him to the OR tonight, he'll die with that tumor still in him."

There was a long silence on the other end before the resident spoke. "You know as well as I do that the surgeons don't like anyone calling their shots."

Jack could hear the resident's beeper through the phone.

"I gotta go."

"If anyone asks, I didn't make this call." Jack held on to the phone long after the line went dead. Voss had known this all along, even when he let Jack spin his plan about planting the HIV story. He figured he was right about the confrontation over his signature— it was just a test to see where Jack stood. They were going to move Tillis back to the prison and let him die, and there wasn't much he could do to change it.

He got back in his truck and drove it for all it could take, with the windows down, as if the rarified air could clear the dissonance in his mind.

It was raining by the time Jack reached his neighborhood. He didn't want to risk another run-in with the press in front of his house, so he parked a couple of blocks away and walked up the gravel alley that ran behind the houses on his street.

Mrs. Logan met him by the back door with her hand up. "Wait on the porch until I get you a towel." She was still talking halfway into the kitchen, and the only words he could make out were "crazy" and "pneumonia."

Ed was right behind her when she came back. "Hey, my brother." Ed almost knocked Mrs. Logan over as he rambled to give him a bear hug. Ed let go and touched his shirt, momentarily confused about why he was now wet.

"I walked through the rain, big guy."

Ed put both hands on Jack's soaked head, then began to laugh.

"What you say you put on some gym shorts and let's take a run in the rain? You know, like we used to."

Ed gave him that look—the one that always cut Jack to the core. His expression was not quite vacant, yet almost pitiful, as he tried to remember something he knew he was supposed to, but no matter how hard he tried, it wasn't there.

"You ran track in junior high. We'd run together when I was home from college. In the summer we'd wait for the afternoon rain, because it was cooler."

Ed touched his shirt again, then smiled. "Let's go."

Ed brushed past him and headed for their back door. These sudden surges of enthusiasm were happening more often now. The therapist assured Jack it was another hopeful sign.

"You all right, Jack?" Mrs. Logan asked.

"I'm OK." He handed her the towel. "Thanks for watching Ed. I don't know what I'd do without you."

She forced a smile, and draped the towel over her arm. "You're going to get sick out there."

Jack opened the screen door. "We'll take a hot

shower when we get back. The run will do us both good."

"That boy can't run with a lame leg. What if he slips?"

"We've been practicing. Besides, it's something we can do together."

"You don't look so good. Let me cook you a decent supper."

"That's tempting, but I've got to meet Dan at his office tonight."

"He's a nice boy."

"I'll tell him you said so."

"I'll rub Ed's chest with salve before bed."

"You don't need to do that. I'll be home in time for him to sleep in his own bed."

"Be sure and get him dried off after that run."

"I'll do it, Mrs. Logan. Thanks again." The spring closed the screen door as they exchanged waves.

Ed was ready by the time Jack had on his running shoes. The rain was coming down harder as they walked among the pink crepe myrtle plants lining the alley. Jack pulled wet honeysuckle off the vine and handed some to his brother. They smelled the blossoms, then pulled them apart and sucked the sweet stems like children.

At the end of the alley they picked up speed, moving together in a slow jog. Ed struggled to make his bad leg work, and Jack occasionally had to slow down to let him catch up, but neither of them mentioned it. At the corner he saw a black car pull over like it was parking, but it was too late. He recognized the driver as one of Richardson's. Jack tapped Ed's shoulder and they picked up the pace.

Six blocks later they crossed a soccer field and began

to jog on the recently resurfaced track of the Bennett School, a private academy where it was said that there was a waiting list just to get on the waiting list.

The rain thumped his face and chest, his feet now in steady rhythm as he tried to deal with the firestorm in his head. He was vaguely aware of his brother at his shoulder, but the rain was like insulation that freed his mind. Events floated like pieces of a puzzle. The man following them, the shiv up his neck, the nurse at Elaine's church, the smell of Elaine's skin, her re- action to the newspaper, Geneva Lott, Hugo Voss, the prisoner in Garity, the girl at the pay phone. What was it Nurse Lott had said? *"The prisoner who had the headaches wasn't the first."* First what? First to be denied transfer for evaluation?

Then the puzzle faded, leaving the image he'd fab- ricated of how his father's body must have looked. A safe image, the one he'd chosen to see in his imagi- nation. Not much blood, just a streak of red, his father lying back on the ottoman in his room. He never saw a wound in this image. Then, the thing that he'd never consciously put there, the thing that came only in his dreams—the back of someone's shoe walk- ing away from his father's body.

Ed slapped Jack's shoulder. "You're running too fast."

Jack leaned over, bracing his hands on his knees. "I think the rain's about to let up. Maybe we can shoot some hoop."

Ed's eyes seemed more focused. "I remember."

Jack stood and wiped the rain from his eyes. "What's that, big guy?"

Ed pulled, but the shirt seemed stuck to his flat muscles. "Running in the rain. Mom wouldn't let us run without shirts. They got soaked. It was like running with weights. I remember."

Jack put his hand around his brother's shoulder.

"I wish she'd come back."

Jack was stunned. Ed hadn't said a word about her since she left a few months after his accident. Jack's arm tightened around his brother's shoulder as he struggled to get the words out. "I do too, Ed. I do too."

The only light in the pathology department was coming from Dan Linh's office. Jack knocked on the door frame and pulled what was left of a six-pack out of a bag. "I figured we might need this."

Dan's face said it all. He didn't want to be here, at least not now, going over the suicide file. He stood and pulled one of the cans from the plastic rings. "Looks like you got a head start."

"I drank it in the parking lot of Kroger's." Jack pulled his second from the rings.

Dan sat behind his desk.

"So, you got the file."

"I just finished reading through it."

"And . . ."

"I still don't think it's wise for you to get into all of this. These kinds of things can stay with you."

Jack drank from his can. "I've got to know."

Dan watched him for several seconds, then opened the green cover. "As far as the blood work, his eosinophil count was normal. There's no real link to the other autopsies. You ask me, you don't need to get into the other details."

Jack was stunned. He'd been certain that the blood work would provide a common link. He had to brace himself for the answer to his most important question. "Did he kill himself?"

"From what I've read, the bulk of evidence supports calling this a suicide."

"But not everything."

"Admittedly, I read it looking for inconsistencies. Most things fit."

"Except . . ."

Dan shifted in his chair. "Statistically, the majority of male suicides involving a handgun have the entry wound in the roof of the mouth." He mimicked a gun with his hand, putting it between his teeth with the finger pointed up.

Jack had to look away for a moment.

"Are you sure, Jack?"

He looked back. "Go on."

"The wound was in the right temple. There was GSR on his right hand. The residue from the gunshot means his hand pulled the trigger."

"Or . . ."

"I don't think there is another explanation."

"Or someone forced his hand."

"You're working too hard. It's not plausible."

Jack broke the tab off his beer can. "Would a man who knows about guns, a marine who'd seen combat . . . would he be more likely to shoot himself in the side of the head or in the mouth?"

"I don't know how to answer that. I'm not a forensic pathologist."

"But you've worked with them. One of the best. You even took extra rotations."

"True, but—"

"What's your best guess?"

Dan studied the file before answering. "They say a direct shot through the palate and into the midbrain is almost foolproof. Perhaps someone with this kind of knowledge would choose that route. But many people miss and go straight up, some actually blow off the front of their face and only traces of frontal lobe . . . so they survive.

"It's just those kinds of oddities that fit a typical suicide. But this was almost too perfect. It's very awkward to hold a handgun exactly perpendicular to the temporal or parietal area. Several pages into the report, under the description of the brain dissection, there is a comment about the trajectory being parallel to the frontal plane of the skull. The photos of the entry and exit wounds support that conclusion. The perfection here is what doesn't fit. The bullet went straight across, as if the gun were exactly level."

Dan demonstrated with his hand like a gun at his temple. "In order to get your right hand around the trigger, it's almost impossible to prevent the barrel from pointing up or down, even if just a little. Given the nervousness that must go on, plus some degree of recoil, almost all of these suicide wounds have their exit higher, often as high as the frontal bone.

"And to be frank, if someone else did it, you've still got to explain the GSR. His hand was on the gun when it was fired. And it's hard to image some other person forcing your father's hand against his will and getting the trajectory I've described."

"Unless he was sedated first."

Dan remained silent, but didn't break his gaze.

"What is it?"

"There were no tox reports in the file."

Jack sat up. "Why not?"

"Perhaps suicide seemed so obvious."

"That's bullshit, and you know it."

"I think it's bullshit, too. But if anybody sent a drug

and alcohol screen, it's not here. And there's no mention of it."

"The kind of thing that would be overlooked unless you were looking for it."

"That's right."

Jack finished his beer. "Anything else?"

Dan turned a few pages. "He had mild coronary disease, and diverticulosis. But otherwise nothing."

"What about the pictures?"

Dan opened the flap of a small manila envelope that had been stapled to the back. "Any pictures at the site of his death are in the police files. These are the ones taken at the post, with clothes and without, before any dissection."

"Any evidence that he had an injection in his arm?"

Dan looked up. "What?"

"Like that guard that Otis Burke killed."

Dan finally broke off eye contact and sifted through the pictures. Finding the right one, he then took a magnifying glass from the top of his desk and scanned the black and white picture. "I'll be damned."

Jack stood abruptly. "Let me see."

Dan turned the picture over. "We had a deal."

"What do you see?"

"Sit down."

"I don't want to sit down."

"Sit down anyway."

Jack sat, aware of his racing heart.

"There's a good bit of venous pooling in the left antecubital fossa." He thumbed through the postmortem report. "There's no mention of it."

"Wouldn't a general description of the body include any bruises?"

"It should. Yes." He looked at the picture again. "This isn't that subtle. If someone injected something, or removed blood for that matter, it happened very close to the time of death."

"Before or after?"

"Either way, I can't tell."

"Who did the post?"

Dan put his hand on the file, and took a moment before answering. "Edelman."

Jack extended his fingers, one at a time with each name. "Officer Howard, Henrietta Franklin, and my father . . . all with needle marks, all connected to Elrice, and all the autopsies were performed by Dr. Edelman."

"You'd expect the medical examiner to perform the vast majority of all the criminal autopsies in the county. He's rather famous in forensic circles."

"If he's so good, then why are routine things left undone?"

"You're off base here, Jack. You're trying to see connections that don't exist."

Jack stood and walked toward the office door. He paced the room, then got another beer. "What's on the paper that came out with those pictures?"

Dan lifted the photographs and found three index cards. "Looks like an itemization of what was found in your father's pockets. It's routine."

"Can I see it?"

Dan took care to turn all the pictures over, then handed him the cards.

Jack looked at the list. It was in cursive, probably written by one of the policemen on the scene. He couldn't help imagining his father taking things from his dresser earlier that morning. Keys, an unopened Alka-Seltzer packet, a dime, a nickel, two pennies, some lint. On the back was a list of things found in his father's wallet, with a notation that all the contents were bagged and tagged, then deposited at police headquarters. Jack knew the contents. He'd received his father's personal effects from the police. But he read the list anyway, and this time he saw something that had held no meaning the day before his father's funeral. This time the names on the back of a cash register receipt screamed out.

Jack's finger burned as he ran it over the names.

Elroy Halsey, Otis Burke, Emmit Havard, Jackson Tillis.

TWENTY-FIVE

Jack didn't wait for the elevators. He left the pathology department and ran up the stairs, not stopping until he reached the fourteenth floor. He shoved open the stairwell door and ran down the hall, slowing only long enough for the automatic doors to the CCU to open.

The first few rooms had their glass doors closed, an oddity so early in the night. As he rounded the corner, he saw why.

The crowd of white coats was four deep outside the only room that had its glass doors flung open. Inside, the bed was surrounded by residents and nurses working furiously on a code. The chair usually occupied by a guard from the prison was empty.

Someone yelled, "Blood gas." A hand shot up over the heads of the people between Jack and the inmate's bed, and another person grabbed the syringe of blood to run it to the lab. Jack could tell by the maroon tint in the syringe that Tillis wasn't oxygenating well.

The nurse doing compressions on Tillis said she needed relief, and as in a choreographed dance, another nurse slipped in and continued the CPR without missing the next chest compression.

Jack was breathing hard as he eased closer to the

EKG machine. It was churning out a long trail of flat-line readings.

The senior resident he'd spoken to earlier was at the head of the bed next to the anesthesiologist who was bagging 100 percent oxygen into Tillis's lungs. The rest of the room looked as if a typhoon had hit. Two central line trays had been pushed to one corner leaving a trail of Betadyne solution from the sheets to the wall. The residents close to the action were in surgical scrubs and had thrown their white coats in a pile, having learned from experience about the blood, mucus, and feces that can get splattered during a code.

The view box had a chest X ray showing good place-ment of the endotracheal tube in the man's trachea. Jack knew this was a bad sign, since it meant the code had been going long enough for the technician to have taken the X ray, developed the film, and run it back up to the CCU.

Near the head of the bed, a half dozen bottles of IV medications were running. Jack checked the labels of the ones within reach. Dopamine to raise the blood pressure, Dobutamine to unload resistance from a failing heart, Isuprel to stimulate contractions and electrical activity, Levophed—used only as a last resort to raise blood pressure in spite of its propensity to clamp off blood flow to the kidneys. He recalled the admonition he'd been taught: "You can live without kidneys, but you can't live without blood pressure."

Jack leaned close enough to be heard by the senior medical resident. "What happened?"

"Flat-lined."

"What was the rhythm just before it?"

"Monitor memory showed sinus rhythm just before the QRS widened, then asystole."

"How about the pericardial drain?"

"It's working. No clots. We've all checked it. Try it yourself if you'd like. We've been coding him for over a half hour. Still nothing."

Jack glanced around at the bevy of people. "Which one of you is his nurse?"

The resident raised his eyebrows above the surgical mask. "Good question."

"What?"

"Agency nurse. His regular one didn't show up."

"She can't just have disappeared."

"One of the other nurses was walking by and saw that he was flat-lined. Could have been that way for minutes. The monitor alarms were off. His nurse wasn't in the room when the code was called. Nobody knew her, and nobody's seen her since. The head nurse is looking all over."

"Did you give him insulin?"

"He's not diabetic."

"Give him ten units of regular insulin four and an amp of D-50."

"Why knock down his potassium? It was fine at four P.M."

Jack's eyes were fixed on the resident. "Maybe somebody *gave* him some extra potassium."

"Jesus." He pointed to a nurse at the end of the bed. "Do what he said."

They continued with their efforts another five minutes, but nothing changed. Jack eased against the glass door.

Finally, the technician came back from the blood gas lab and handed the paper to the anesthesia resident.

"Oxygen is only forty-eight." The anesthesia resident looked up from the slip. "It's been going down with each blood gas we check. We save this heart, there's not going to be much brain left to go with it."

The medicine resident looked at a nurse who'd been recording the medications on a clipboard. "What's our time?"

"Thirty-eight minutes."

The residents looked at Jack. The move was in deference to his seniority and the fact that he was the referring physician. Jack looked at Tillis, stripped naked, a catheter in his bladder, four IVs—one in each arm, two in the chest, a pericardial drain with fluid that had turned bloody from the trauma of CPR. His right leg was dangling off the bed because the side rail was down, pulling the handcuffed ankle with it. His skin was pasty white on the abdomen and extremities, but dark purple from chest to face.

The medical resident spoke up. "I think we should call it."

Jack felt the index card's worn edges in his hand. "Somebody killed this guy."

The room hushed in stillness. The nurse doing CPR looked at Jack. "What do you want me to do, Dr. Harris?"

Jack looked at the flat-line tracing on the monitor above the bed, then to the faces around the room, finally resting on the senior resident. "It's your call. I'll stand by whatever you decide."

The resident put his hand on the shoulder of the nurse doing compressions. "You can stop." He looked at the team that had helped him. "Thank you, everyone."

Jack turned away but stood still as others walked around him. He was getting close to something important, obviously too close. Someone thought he knew enough to ask Tillis the right question, a question that would bust things wide open. But he had no idea what that question was.

He jumped, feeling a hand on his shoulder. The medicine resident looked tired. "We've got to get a post on that guy. There's no next of kin. I thought maybe you could sign the papers since you represent the prison."

The charge nurse handed him a permission form, and Jack signed.

The resident said, "People have been talking about that MRI. Would have been something to get that thing out at surgery."

"What do you mean?"

"The echo hinted at it, but on MRI you can see it plain as day. Nobody's ever described an embryonic tumor like it. It isn't growing in the heart . . . it's leaning against it. And it's not just a tumor. It's a whole little heart growing on its own. It even has what looks like a rudimentary aorta and pulmonary vessels attached."

The anesthesiology resident slid by. "Sorry about that one. We did what we could."

Jack let the others clear away. The body would be sent to the morgue tonight, and he was more certain than ever that Dr. Edelman would assign himself to do the autopsy. And certain routine details such as the potassium level would somehow get lost by the lab.

Jack looked up to see Dan Linh walk into the CCU. "Maybe we can get some answers tonight."

TWENTY-SIX

Jack waited in Dan Linh's office while the autopsy was being performed. He looked at the stacks of journals, his eyes wandering once again across rows of books on the shelves without paying any real attention to what he saw. After a few minutes he got up and walked out into the outer room among the half dozen desks the pathology department secretaries used.

The lights were off but everywhere he turned was a record of death—slides of tissue and tumors that once thrived inside someone, reams of paper with final pathology reports to be put on charts early the next morning, and the occasional dark green folder with an autopsy report like the one that documented his father's death.

Jack couldn't bring himself to watch Dan perform the postmortem exam on Jackson Tillis. Deep down he'd known Dan's advice had been right. The risk he'd taken in learning the details of his father's autopsy was the kind that lived with you, the kind that would raise itself on long solitary nights.

He thought he had prepared himself for the worst and he'd been OK for a while, but when they covered Tillis and rolled him out of the CCU, Jack froze, unable to follow him to the morgue.

Dan had come over to him, somehow ready, as if

he'd been expecting something to break through the wall Jack had so carefully constructed. The next thing Jack knew, he was sitting in Dan's office with some lukewarm coffee so old it stained the Styrofoam.

That was two hours ago, and it had taken that long for him to regain his bearings and a sense of what needed to be done.

Across the room Detective Tarkington flipped a light switch. He was in khaki pants and a blue blazer that looked like he kept it in the trunk of his car. A dark tie was loose around an open collar.

Tarkington stepped closer. "This better be good."

Jack rose. "I don't understand."

The detective checked his watch. "It's almost eleven. Where's Dr. Linh?"

"Doing an autopsy."

"They must do twenty autopsies a day in this city. I want to know what's so damn important to drag me out here tonight."

Jack knew the only clues he had were a gut feeling, the bruise on his father's arm, and the list from his wallet—not enough evidence to convince a friend, much less a cop. "I didn't call you."

"Linh called. Something about a prisoner dying under suspicious circumstances tonight, and some link to the officer that died in the breakout. You ask me, the most obvious link is still you."

Jack took a breath and sat down. He'd known he'd have to approach the police, but this wasn't the right time. He wasn't ready, but time was running out. "You know anything about the investigation into my father's death?"

"Just what I read in the papers."

"Come off it. You're all over me but you haven't even asked around?"

"So I stirred the fire a little. What's your point?"

"Come up with anything?"

"Nothing."

Jack put the list on top of the desk. "This mean anything to you?"

Tarkington looked at the names. "I recognize Burke. Who are the others?"

"Jackson Tillis is the one getting the post in the morgue as we speak. Havard is an inmate I saw in the clinic—he's got a brain tumor. I don't know the first one."

"So what's this got to do with me?"

"The list was found on the back of a receipt in my father's wallet when he died. Hell of a coincidence."

"Coincidences happen."

"I've got another coincidence for you. Hugo Voss. He's in charge of medical operations for all the companies owned by C.W. Richardson. As of this afternoon, he's my new boss. We argued about whether the company that runs Elrice would pay for Jackson Tillis to have a rare tumor removed from his chest. In the end, I told him I'd go along, but I don't think he believed me. And I'll let you in on a little secret. I talked to some people about arranging the surgery on an emergency basis before he could be transferred back to prison tomorrow. Then I found that list, but by the time I could ask Tillis about it, he'd been on the wrong side of a code blue for half an hour."

"What am I supposed to do with this information?"

"Like I said, I didn't call you. I'm just making conversation."

Tarkington stared at him like a bull about to charge. But at that same moment, Dan entered the room and said, "Thank you for coming, Detective."

Jack walked around the desk, with every intention

of leaving, but Dan put his hand out to stop him. "Blood work taken during the code came back. His potassium was eight-point-nine."

Tarkington asked, "What's that mean?"

"His potassium was so high it made his heart stop beating. The level was normal on routine blood work this morning and again at four P.M. today. We suspect someone gave Tillis a lethal bolus."

Tarkington sat on the edge of a desk. "That's a serious accusation. You got some kind of proof?"

"He's on no medications to account for it, his kidney function is fine, and his pH was not abnormal enough. In short, there's nothing that explains the life-threatening level except an exogenous source."

"A what?"

Jack crossed his arms. "It came from outside his body. If things had gone as planned, he'd have been found stiff and cold, and no one would have run any blood work because it would have been too late for a code. His regular nurse didn't show tonight, and the agency nurse that came in her place is nowhere to be found. The cardiac monitors have alarms, but they'd been cut off. Of course, this could all just be another coincidence."

Tarkington pointed a finger in his direction. "You can be a real a smart-ass."

Jack walked past him on his way out. "Yeah, but maybe not smart enough. I'm getting too close to something, but I've got no idea what. I think my father got too close, and they killed him for it. It doesn't take a genius to know who's next."

It was dark, but from his vantage point across the street, Mason could see Burke and two other black men break into a side window of the house. Mason felt a sense of pride at having guessed where the inmate would strike next. His men were stationed in front and in back of the house that Dr. Scalacey had vacated earlier in the week. It wouldn't take Burke long to realize his intended victim wasn't there, so Mason had drilled his men on a quick assault.

Mason gave the word over the secure radio, and his men were inside the house in seconds.

Mason entered the front door just after his men ushered Burke, JT, and Neon to the back bedroom. All the curtains in the house had been drawn shut when Scalacey moved. The lights were on timers, and as planned, one of the men turned off the lights in the front rooms. Others secured the perimeter of the house, and six of them stayed in the bedroom with Mason.

All three hostages were handcuffed with their arms behind their backs, and made to sit in folding chairs. Mason walked over and hit Burke across the face with the back of his hand. Burke bared his teeth but didn't say a word.

"You didn't seriously think you could get away from us, did you?" Mason asked.

Burke looked at his companions. Neon was bigger than anyone else in the room, but he looked scared. JT's eyes were ablaze with hate, and it was directed at Burke.

"We want to know who you've talked to."

Burke looked straight ahead and said nothing.

Mason clinched some brass knuckles and punched him in the face twice. He nodded to one of the men and they fought Burke into a standing position, holding him for a series of blows to the gut.

Burke doubled at the waist, and the men dropped him back into the chair.

Mason brought over a baseball bat and touched it to Burke's left jaw. "You can make this easy, or you can make it hard."

Burke spat at him. "Fuck you."

Mason brought the bat back, then thought better of it. He looked at one of his men, pointed to Neon, and said, "That one first."

Burke looked frantic as the man took a Glock pistol with a silencer, and pressed it hard against Neon's chest.

Neon was near hysteria. "Tell them what they want. Tell them."

"What do you want?" Burke cried out.

Mason's smile was taut. "Who have you talked to?"

"About what?"

"About our deal?"

"Nobody."

Mason nodded, and his man shot Neon in the heart at point-blank range.

Burke was on his feet, but two men restrained him. "Nobody, damn it. I said nobody. I ain't talked to nobody. Not even them."

Neon's mouth was open, his eyes vacant. His body slouched to the side, and the men eased him onto the oriental rug. The hollow-point bullet did its work without exiting the body.

JT tried to run, but the men tackled him. JT bucked and kicked, grimacing in pain from his bad knee. He bit one of the men on the arm before they had him pinned. They beat his head until he quit bucking.

Mason swung the bat at Burke's shin. He fell out of the chair, screaming.

"I know you talked to people. I've got friends inside

the police department who told me about that girl
you assholes raped and killed. It was the bartender's
niece, by the way. He gave you up, and the police are
all over it. So are you going to tell me the truth, or you
want a broken jaw?"

Burke was curled on the floor, his hands still cuffed
behind his back. "I know something you want."

Mason laughed. "You do? Why don't you tell me,
and we can sit around and have tea?"

"I know where she is."

Mason tapped the bat on Burke's jaw, but was taken
aback by the comment.

"What are you talking about?"

"I saw him in the newspaper."

"Who?"

"That guard from Elrice. The one who killed himself."

Mason motioned to his men, and they picked
Burke up and put him in the chair. "Come again?"

"I saw his picture in the paper. It was next to a picture of that doctor I took hostage. That's when I put
it together."

Mason moved closer and pushed the end of the bat
onto Burke's chest. "You better start making some
sense, or your other friend is going to take it in the
head."

Burke squinted in pain. "I know where she is. The
guard that killed himself . . . I was in the infirmary the
night before he died. I heard him talking about the
one you're looking for. I know where she is."

Mason moved the bat away. He motioned for the
men to put JT back in his chair. JT's head bobbed in
semiconsciousness.

Mason said, "Get them some water. There's ice in
the kitchen. Put a bag on Burke's jaw."

Burke said, "You don't get it without a deal."

"You're not in a position to make any deals."

"I know what you want. And I know how bad you want it. This is the deal: I get fixed—you undo what you did to me. And I'll tell you what you want to know."

Mason realized he wasn't bluffing. He knew the truth—his information was too accurate. He moved close to Burke. "If your information is as good as you say, then maybe we can cut a deal."

"You can start by getting me out of these handcuffs."

Mason gave a sign, and one of the men unlocked the cuffs. Another man brought the ice.

Mason said, "Now tell me real slow, and don't leave out anything."

Half an hour later, Mason watched his men stuff Neon's body in the trunk of one of their cars behind the house. His 290 pounds were wrapped in the rug to keep bloodstains out of the car.

They put JT and Burke in the backseat. As far as Burke knew, he was being taken for surgery. And they'd keep that story line as long as they needed him alive. Neon's body would be flown a hundred miles offshore and dropped into the Atlantic tonight. His friends would join him after Mason got what he wanted.

When the car was out of sight, Mason used his cell phone to call Mr. Richardson.

Richardson answered, and Mason said. "I'm switching to line A." Richardson set his phone to unscramble the transmission, and Mason told his boss what Burke had said.

After a moment of silence, Richardson said, "You'll need the chopper. Get in, and get out. And don't leave anyone behind who can trace it back to us."

TWENTY-SEVEN

Jack left Tarkington and Dan in the pathology department. Things were unraveling too fast. He took the stairs to be alone, and to think. In spite of all that had happened, he hadn't uncovered any substantive evidence at the prison to explain his father's tie to the others on the list.

Scalacey and Voss weren't on the list, but Jack was sure that they were somehow involved with the tumors he'd found in the prisoners. Despite what he'd been told about special treatment for some of the inmates, there was nothing in the prison medical records about it. He stopped on a stair landing. He said his last thought out loud, but in a different way. "There was nothing about it in the medical records *at the prison.*"

He suddenly realized the records may not ever have been there. And the answer had been staring him in the face all along.

Jack hurried to the ground floor and found a bank of pay phones in the outpatient clinic of the hospital. No one else was around; there weren't even any lights on. He put money in the phone and called Elrice. As before, he got through to the infirmary by claiming to be another physician at Garity.

A woman's voice answered, but he had to be sure. "This is Dr. Falcon for Geneva Lott."

"Speaking."

"We met earlier over barbecue."

There was a moment's hesitation before she spoke. "Yes, I remember."

"Can you talk?"

"I'm alone."

He found the paper from his pants pocket. "What do you know about an inmate named Elroy Halsey?"

"I don't know him."

"I think you do."

She didn't answer.

"His name was on a list found in my father's wallet the day he died. The other names were Otis Burke, Emmit Havard, and Jackson Tillis. Somebody killed my father because he linked those people. I don't think they stopped with my father. And I think you know why."

"I told you before that I don't want to get involved."

"I don't think they did all the work there."

"How . . . what do you mean?"

She had caught herself, but not before the mistake told him what he needed to know. "I've looked through all the records I could find. Some are missing, but the police say they didn't take them. That means that Scalacey took them out of the prison, or the ones I'm interested in weren't there to begin with."

"I didn't work anywhere but the infirmary."

What she wasn't saying spoke volumes. It was as if she wanted him to realize it. "It doesn't matter if you didn't work at the other place," he said. "You're in danger whether you know it or not."

"Jesus, my Jesus . . ."

"You've got to trust me. Get out of there."

"I can't just leave."

"Listen to me. Anybody asks, you say that the public

health officer called to report that your throat culture has come back positive with a resistant strain of *staph aureus*. It poses a serious threat to the patients and could cause an epidemic among the rest of the inmate population. Tell them you need IV antibiotics."

"I can't leave now."

"Call in one of the PAs or another nurse, but get out of there as soon as you can."

"People will check."

"The operator will verify you got a call from a Dr. Falcon at Garity tonight. It'll be enough."

"We've got inmates in the ward."

"Is there someplace you can go? Someplace you can be safe?"

"My people are all dead. I've got nobody but my husband."

"You can't go home."

"You've got no right . . . no right to talk to me like this. You don't know what you've dug up."

"Someone killed Jackson Tillis in the hospital tonight."

He let her silence hang there before he spoke again. "That leaves you, me, and Emmit Havard. And something tells me he won't die from that brain tumor."

"Havard's here . . . in a coma. They found him unconscious in the shower."

"You get out of there and don't call in for a replacement until you're miles away. And use a pay phone."

"I don't know—"

"I can help. We can meet at the barbecue, but I need a couple of hours."

He waited but she didn't respond.

"If you won't do it for me, do it for my father."

She abruptly hung up on him. But there was something odd about the way it happened, something odd about the sound, or rather the lack of sound—like the line had been cut.

Jack looked around the dark lobby with its rows of chairs in the waiting room. There was no one there. But he knew that if they had gotten to Tillis and Havard, they'd be watching every move he made. His only hope was the possibility that they needed to keep him alive long enough to find out how much he knew. Geneva Lott's only hope was if she listened to his warning.

He had to get into Richardson's research facilities before they took away his security clearance, and before anyone would be around to stop him.

He made his way to the residents' parking lot, trying to be as inconspicuous as possible as he scanned the dark streets for one of Richardson's cars. They were nowhere in sight, but that didn't mean much. He knew they were there.

TWENTY-EIGHT

Richardson's headquarters was illuminated across acres of dark lawn, but Jack remained focused on the car lights that had picked up his trail about two blocks from Garity Hospital. When he turned onto the main compound, the car slowed but didn't follow.

Just beyond the fountain he turned at a sign that marked the route for delivery vehicles. He slowed when he realized there was a guard booth up ahead. It was too late to turn around without looking suspicious. Besides, he'd come too far to turn back. Jack slowed and held up his ID card with his finger covering his name, and to his amazement, the guard waved him through.

Past the booth the road entered a heavily wooded section. He rounded a curve, then pulled over and turned off his headlights. After nearly a minute, no other vehicle had come along. If they were waiting across the road from the compound, it probably meant that a new team would be picking up his trail on the property. He tried to locate the surveillance cameras, but in the dark they remained well hidden among the pine trees.

He continued down the road until it eventually opened onto a well-lit parking lot at the back side of the main building. Off to one side was a large open hangar with a fleet of trucks, mowers, and golf carts. Farther down the hill was the first of the series of windowless white buildings he'd seen from Voss's office.

He was surprised to find nearly a dozen cars and pickups in the lot this hour of the morning. He parked but kept his eyes on a van that was backing up to the loading dock. By the time Jack got onto the platform, a man in a T-shirt and worn jeans was coming out of the back of the van, carrying a stack of boxes that came up to his nose.

Jack beat him to the back door of the building and said, "Let me get that for you."

The man stopped with a concerned look in his eyes. "You work here?"

Producing his ID, Jack said, "First day on the job."

"I've never seen anyone coming in this time of day."

"Just trying to get off to a good start. Thought I'd try to get the lay of the land before someone brought me a stack of paperwork. Find the bathrooms, that sort of thing." He held open one of the double doors.

The man went inside, put the boxes down, then extended his hand. He was missing an upper tooth. "Owens. Ray Owens."

They shook hands. "Jack Harris. I'll be helping Dr. Voss coordinate all the research that goes on here. How about you?"

"I guess you'd say I work the other end. I'm a supervisor. My crew cleans the animal cages, washes down the halls; then we feed the little bastards breakfast. All these damn regulations—these boxes are full of some special soap. Hell, my house isn't as clean as these cages. But, like they say, it's a livin'. Shift's over at seven." He picked up the boxes and the one on top slid off and landed on the floor.

"Let me help you with those."

"I can manage."

Jack picked up the box anyway. In the distance he could hear an occasional cage door closing, but he didn't see any other member of the crew. "Any chance you could help me get my bearings?"

The man hesitated, then said, "Yeah, I guess so. My work's about done. Gotta put these up first."

Jack helped him stack the boxes in a closet, then followed him through a series of doors that led to a long corridor. The floor, walls, and ceiling were white tile. The only areas that weren't brightly lit were where the animals were housed. Each species seemed to have its own hall. There were small cages for rats, larger ones for dogs, and some huge cages for chimpanzees. Theirs were the only ones that opened onto an outdoor play area with a tree and a jungle gym.

The man turned and walked back down the hall. "That's pretty much it."

"What about the rabbits?"

The man looked puzzled.

"The other night, Dr. Voss brought me down from the main building. He showed me a rabbit that had a limb . . ." He stopped in midsentence. "I figured I could find my way around upstairs if I got back to that elevator."

"I don't know about no rabbits." Then he raised his eyebrows. "Maybe they're in the restricted area. You got to have security clearance."

"There was a large double door at the end of the hall. You get in by putting your hand on a scanner."

"That'd be the place. I can take you."

Jack followed the man around a maze of halls that led to the double doors.

"I can't get you in there. Day shift cleans them cages while the researchers watch. One of my fishin' buddies supervises that shift. Some wild stories about that place."

Jack put his entire right hand on the blue scanning plate next to the door. Seconds later the door unlocked and Jack pulled it open.

"What kind of stories?"

"Like they're growing things."

"What do you mean?"

"I think he's full of it. Bullshit stories after he's had a few beers."

"Such as . . ."

"He said he'd seen an ear growing on the side of a pig. Shit like that."

"They're working on a drug to prevent rejection of transplants. I'm sure it's unsettling to see."

"They didn't transplant nothin'. My friend says the pig didn't have no operation. He saw the ear start real tiny. Over a few months it got bigger."

Jack stared back at the man. "This friend, you think he's reliable?"

"Yeah. I guess. But sometimes the Budweiser talks for him."

"They probably transplanted the ear from an embryo. It would be so small your friend might not have noticed."

"That pig ain't the only one that's growed parts. I told him to shut up. Made me sick to hear about it."

Jack looked into the corridor where Voss had been so abrupt with him and Elaine. "I can make my way from here. Thanks for the tour."

"Good luck with the new job."

Jack returned the comment with a wave. As the door closed automatically, he thought to himself that all the luck in the world wouldn't be enough for what he had to do.

He went right to the rabbit cage. It was much larger than the rodent cages he'd just seen, measuring roughly eight by twelve feet. The rabbit was sleeping in the back corner, nestled far enough under some hay to keep Jack from getting another look at that leg. He leaned down and examined the card tied to the gate. Voss had looked at the same card just before he'd told him the date the animal had its transplant. Jack flipped it over, but there were no dates on either side of the card. It did have a series of codes written in a column, including RC-130, the experimental antirejection drug that Voss said they'd given to the animal.

Jack took paper from his pocket and wrote down the codes. He walked the perimeter of the room, and saw that only one other cage was occupied. A chimpanzee awoke when Jack touched the door. He was sure this animal hadn't been here when Voss gave the tour. The chimp sat up, and touched his right wrist repeatedly where an extra paw seemed to be growing.

Jack was startled, but the chimp ambled over, allowing him to see the extra paw up close. The hair on the arm looked to be the same length as that on the left, with no sign of having once been shaved. He wanted to touch the chimp, to befriend him somehow, but there wasn't time.

Jack checked the card on the door, wrote down the numbers, then walked down a side hall. There were three lab rooms with metal doors that had small windows. The doors were locked. On the next hall he found a similar series of doors and was about to give up when he found what he was looking for. The door at the end of the unlit hall had a hand scanner next to it on the wall. Through the small window he could tell the room was no bigger than a closet—just enough space for a built-in desk with a computer.

He checked the corners of the ceiling for a security camera. Seeing none, he put his palm on the scanner, and the door clicked open. He gently closed it behind him before booting up the computer.

The first image was the Richardson Enterprises logo; then the screen changed to a dark blue background with the message *Optical Scanner for Access.*

Jack knew that someone or something would log his activity on the network as soon as the camera mapped his retina. He imagined that ordinarily this kind of information would be lost in a stack of security data on Harold Mason's desk. But this wasn't an ordinary time, and he wasn't an ordinary blip on Mason's radar screen.

He checked his watch, aware that every minute he spent on the network would give Richardson's men the extra time they needed to locate him. He wasn't going to stay here long enough to get caught.

In less than fifteen seconds the computer screen changed to a light blue desktop. There were over thirty folders. He had hoped to find the names that were listed in his father's wallet, but the folders were only labeled with a jumble of letters and numbers. Jack checked the codes he'd just written against the screen and was able to match each one.

He opened file RC-130 first. It held pages of file names. He opened the protocol file and began reading. It was much longer than he could digest easily in one sitting. He looked on the only shelf, but unfortunately there was no printer in the work area, so he skimmed the file as quickly as he could.

The information was the type of thing that might be sent to an institutional review board whose purpose would be to ensure the safety of animals or humans participating in any trial. The contents were quite detailed, but on the whole were very similar to the summary Voss had outlined to him earlier.

Jack closed the file and opened nearly a half dozen others without finding anything of use, so he closed the folder. He then found the folder for each of the other codes he'd gotten from the rabbit cage. The protocol files under each described earlier test phases of the compound used for antirejection of transplanted organs. Other files contained well-organized narrative summaries and multiple data tables followed by interpretation and conclusion statements. He repeated the search with the numbers from the chimp's cage. Every file seemed to have the same format. Everything was in perfect order.

Jack pushed back from the screen, then realized what was bugging him. There wasn't a single reference to the operation that transplanted the extremities onto the two animals in the cages down the hall.

He opened the first folder again, the one for RC-130. Third page. The heading on the fifth paragraph was *Injection Protocol*. He reread it quickly. The first line said *The following is the procedure for injecting the drug RC-130*. But buried in the middle was the statement: *According to protocol the date of injecting the exogenous source would be known as Day 1. Timing is key, since survival of the specific activity of the specimen has been shown to be less than one hour after procurement.*

He closed the folder, and opened the one that corresponded to the second code he'd written down. The paragraph describing the injection protocol was essentially the same. The first sentence described injection of the drug that matched the code letters on the file. But in the middle of the paragraph, the sentence referred to injection of the *exogenous source*. He quickly opened the chimpanzee's file. It had the same statement.

"Shit." He punched the power button on the computer, ran down the hall to the double doors, and put his open hand on the scanner. He could hear the blood surging through his ears as he waited for the door to unlock.

Drugs were produced, not procured. And an exogenous source that had a limited life activity had to be living tissue—serum, blood cells, slurried fragments of an organ, but not a manufactured compound. Either someone had sanitized the file to remove details about the surgical technique of transplanting the extremities, or the surgery had never taken place—regardless of what Voss had told him. That left only one explanation—the organs were *grown* on the host animal.

He ran down the tile hall, but stopped at the double doors that led to the loading dock. Seeing no one, he opened the door just enough to get a glimpse of the platform.

The loading dock was empty except for the van. Jack knew Richardson's men would be watching for his truck—if not now, then as soon as security relayed the message that he'd accessed the computer. He had to assume they were already alerted. In his mind's eye he could almost see the car that had tailed him closing off the entrance to the compound.

If he tried to run for it, he'd be out in the open much too long to go unnoticed. He opened one side of the double doors just wide enough to slip through, then took care that the van shielded him from the parking lot.

He opened the back door of the van, uncertain of what he might do next. A few boxes remained. The floor had traces of dried mud and discarded corrugated strips. He looked for something to cover his body, thinking that he could smuggle his way out when the supervisor left for the day, but there was nothing in the cargo area that would work.

He leaned toward the front seats hoping to find a coat or a tarp. The passenger side held nothing but some junk mail and an empty coffee cup. But then he saw what he needed. The keys were still in the ignition.

Remaining behind the seat, he slowly looked over the parking lot—the pickups and small cars all seemed unmanned. Satisfied, he maneuvered behind the wheel, but hesitated before touching the keys. This was too easy. For hours he'd had a nagging feeling that Richardson's people would take him out rather than let him get close to the truth. The keys in the van could be part of a setup. With a simple turn of the ignition he could be blown into a million pieces. No body to dispose of.

He took his hands off the keys. He scanned each vehicle in the parking lot, and watched for the glint off someone's glasses or any motion behind a windshield. Again, he saw nothing that could betray his follower.

The choices weren't good. Walk, and at the very best he'd be seen by the surveillance cameras. Take the van, and maybe he'd get out. He somehow hoped for another outlet. The side mirror gave only a limited view of the loading dock, but there were no shadows or shifting light—not much, but at least a sliver of evidence that he was still alone. He thought about the shocked look on the supervisor's face when he surprised him on the platform. He was either the best actor in the world, or a legitimate cleaning crew supervisor.

Jack tried to judge the few clues he had. Even if he'd walked into a trap, Voss had no way of knowing what time of day Jack would take the bait. They couldn't just leave a bomb at the back door until he showed up.

He closed his eyes and turned the key.

The engine started. He could hardly keep his arms from shaking as he drove toward the maintenance hangar, then around the perimeter of the lot, hoping to find another way out, but there was none. If they had ID'd him on the loading dock, he'd know soon enough.

He turned down the delivery drive, then sped beyond the dense growth of trees. The gate on the exit road was up and the guard didn't seem to care that he hadn't stopped. As he pulled out of the compound, the street was deserted. The car that had followed him, or at least the one he thought had followed him, was nowhere to be seen. Blocks passed without any sign of being tailed.

He changed lanes and checked each side mirror, but there was no one following. After a few more blocks, he pulled into the right lane and slowed. Several more blocks passed. Still no one.

The tension he'd felt for hours began to abate, but from the depths of memory came a story his father had told him about training for patrol in Vietnam. His words rang their warning: "You're never in greater danger than at the moment you feel you are safe." As he checked the mirrors again, the events of the last hour began to crystallize.

He had assumed that Richardson's men hadn't interfered because they wanted to find out how much he knew. But it bothered him that he'd gotten access so easily. He turned cold with the realization that there was another explanation. Voss had planted the idea of returning to the animal research area, and he'd done just as they'd hoped.

They hadn't interfered because he was right where

they wanted him. Or more specifically, he wasn't where they feared he might go.

He floored the accelerator and the van rattled. He'd warned Geneva Lott, all right. But in doing so, he'd put her right where they wanted her—alone.

TWENTY-NINE

Jack sped across the city, following the route he'd first taken to meet Geneva Lott. He rolled down the window, hoping the air would clarify his mind as he took a shortcut through a residential neighborhood. Dew glistened when his lights crossed a lawn. The predawn moisture felt oddly cool as the wind slipped over his neck.

As he drove farther, the streetlights gave way to the shot-out darkness in the partly abandoned section of town where he'd met her at Rudy's Bar-B-Que. The only sign of life was a homeless man sleeping on the top step of a church whose parishioners had long ago left for safer ground.

The air soon confirmed his fears. He smelled it long before he was sure. Within blocks the night sky flashed with odd shadows, orange and black, formed by the rumbling flames that engulfed the house behind Rudy's.

People from the neighborhood stood in small groups. The house was so far gone that he couldn't understand why the fire trucks weren't yet on the scene. In the front yard, two men were bent over, consoling the crumpled figure of a woman. Her husband straightened into a defensive stance when Jack walked up. The back of his shirt was ripped and blood was dripping from his back like he'd been hit with buck-shot. Jack bent down and wrapped his arm around the nurse.

Geneva's body shivered under his hand, then stopped. The change was abrupt, as if she'd been slapped. She turned, her face full of rage, "Get away from me." She remained on her knees, her arms bracing her chest off the ground. "Lord, what I've done . . ."

Her husband said, "I came out to meet her when she drove up. The house exploded just after I stepped off the front porch. If she'd have opened the door and come inside, we'd both be burning in there."

They turned at the sound of a loud crack and saw the rafters give way and crash into the front room, bringing down what remained of the flaming roof.

Jack started toward her again, but her husband grabbed him around the chest. Jack struggled against the man's massive forearms and shouted to her, "You've got to get out of here."

She beat her palm against the sidewalk, mumbling unintelligibly through her tears.

The man began to move Jack away. "That's enough. Maybe you ought to leave before there's trouble."

But Jack kept his eyes on Geneva Lott. "They won't stop here, and you know it."

Her body changed subtly, and he knew she'd heard him.

"But you can stop them. You can help me."

Her husband's arms tightened around Jack's chest, and lifted him off the ground. "I said that's enough." Before Jack could do anything, the man threw him, smashing his shoulder against the ground.

Geneva glared at him. The reflection of the fire danced on her face. Her eyes were swollen and full of hate, but as her husband was about to kick him in the ribs, she held up her hand, and he stopped.

She shook her head. "It's over."

Jack didn't dare move. "It's not over. I know more than they think. But I need you to fill in the missing pieces."

She stared back with an expression of resignation. He sensed that if ever there was a chance, this was it.

"Why did they kill my father?"

She looked back at her house but didn't respond. Flames were licking at the tall pines in the backyard.

"I know about the injections. The eosinophil count was elevated in Jackson Tillis. That day you brought me the old records of Otis Burke I found some blood work several months old. His eosinophil counts were off the wall, but the values a month before had been normal. They even did a serum protein electrophoresis, but all his values were normal. Nobody orders a test like that on a person with normal protein levels. And then I figured it out. The normal values were a baseline screen before they gave him something. And they checked to make sure he didn't have any early signs of problems with his bone marrow. The eosinophil elevation was a reaction to a foreign substance. Something they had injected in them. Something *you* injected."

Her face jerked back at him, but she didn't say anything.

"Some experimental compound that Richardson's company made. My father figured it out, and they killed him."

She looked down. "It's not about your father."

"The hell it isn't."

"It's about Ed."

The stunning effect of her words changed his indignation into fear. He'd been so sure of his prey, so sure that he was about to unravel the ball of lies and deception that Voss had created to protect Richardson. But now he realized that their tricks had heightened his own sense of being hunted, and he'd fallen for it. It wasn't just Geneva Lott he'd left in the open. He'd left his brother vulnerable—what Voss had wanted all along.

But to stop them, he had to know more. He looked back at the man towering over him, then back at her. "The tumors, and the blast cells—they had to be a reaction to the injections. Something that went wrong."

"There was no reaction, they were grown on purpose."

He thought of the animals in the research pens, then put it together. "Tillis had a cardiac tumor—I saw the echo report. But the MRI said mass wasn't in the heart, like most tumors. It was outside the heart, attached to the great vessels, just like an embryonic heart would develop."

"They aren't tumors. There're new organs."

He thought of the exogenous source mentioned in the animal research protocols. "What did you inject?"

"They had me inject ten cc's of blood. And every one of those men grew some kind of mass in their body. Tillis was growing a new heart, Havard was growing new brain cells. Burke's growing a liver."

He stood up, then helped her to her feet. She couldn't have weighed more than a hundred pounds. "What does this have to do with my brother?"

"I'm not sure. But your father figured out what was going on. He was working those extra night shifts, and he saw me giving the injections. Your father was a smart man—maybe too smart. He noticed the pattern: men getting injected in the early morning hours

turned up dead in less than six months. He confronted Dr. Scalacey, but instead of reporting it, he
began to believe that the research might help Ed.
That they might figure a way to regenerate the damaged part of Ed's brain."

Jack reeled with the absurdity of how little his father
understood. "But why was he killed?"

"I don't know."

He grabbed her arms. "You know, and you're going
to tell me."

Her husband came closer, but Geneva waved him
off. "I'd tell you if I understood it, but I don't. I've
told you what I know."

"You said the two of you talked late at night. Perhaps he said something, anything . . ."

"He was worried about Ed. Kept saying they'd mis-
led him about Ed's chances. Betrayed. That's the
word he used. Betrayed Ed."

"I don't understand." Then it hit him. "Oh God, tell
me you didn't inject my brother."

Her eyes met his. "No, no injections." She shook
her head and couldn't keep eye contact with him.
"Your father brought him one night. It was all
planned. He said it was going to help his son."

"What did you do to him?"

Her voice was pleading. "Dr. Voss and Dr. Scalacey
OK'd it, and your father said it was to help."

Jack grabbed her by the arms again. "What did you
do?"

"I *took* blood from your brother."

Jack felt as if he'd been shoved in the chest.

"Dr. Scalacey took it to Dr. Voss's lab. What they did
with it, I don't know. It came back a week later. I know
it was Ed's because I had to verify the serial numbers
in our records before I injected the prisoners."

"And you kept a separate list for yourself."

"No, but your father did. He saw me writing them down in the logbook."

"The list in his wallet . . ."

"The men on that list all got blood from your brother."

"Blood that had been modified before you rein-jected it."

"I don't know."

"What did Scalacey say about the blood he brought back for you to inject?"

"He didn't say much. He said it was to stimulate something."

"I need you to think hard. What exactly did he say?"

"I hadn't really thought about it, but I think he said it was to stimulate cells to—"

Jack interrupted. "Stem cells."

There was a flicker of recognition in her troubled eyes. "Yes . . . stems. Voss called them stems. I thought it meant stimulation."

"Stem cells have the potential to become any com-ponent of the body. But to produce a single organ Voss would have had to inject individual cell lines to grow a defined organ—lines several generations downstream from pure stem cells. But why inject it into normal inmates? Why not grow them in the lab?"

She wiped her eyes. "One thing for sure, the pris-oners thought they were going to get a commuted sentence in exchange for participating in the study. Some of them talked about how powerful Mr. Richardson was, and about his connections. They knew his company ran the prison. Everyone there was on his payroll. Those prisoners thought they'd be out of Elrice in a few months."

Jack could hear the sirens in the distance. "You said

the first group of prisoners died within six months of the injections. Is it possible that Otis Burke saw what was happening and figured out that they were nothing more than guinea pigs? Is that why he broke out?"

She held herself tightly. "Burke was a dangerous man. He wasn't like the others. I just assumed he was crazy. But maybe you're right."

"What about Henrietta Franklin? The police said she used to work at Elrice . . ."

"I didn't really know her. She didn't work in the infirmary. I think she must have worked with Dr. Scalacey in his special clinic."

"The special clinic—the one the prisoners could use without having to go through the PAs?"

"I heard some talk about it, but I never worked there. I rarely saw the prisoners after I gave them an injection. Maybe she did all the follow-up testing."

"Why would they kill her?"

"I don't know. Maybe she saw something she shouldn't have. Or maybe she tried to blackmail them."

"But someone injected her before they killed her."

She looked suspiciously at him. "Where did you hear that? It wasn't in the papers."

Jack didn't answer, but he wondered if Burke had killed the nurse or if Voss had made it look like that way as a diversion.

Jack looked up at the sound of a wall of her house falling outward, pouring flames onto the wood fence that outlined the backyard of Rudy's.

He looked at her and had to touch her arm before she turned away from what remained of her house. "Who else did you take blood from?"

It took her a moment before she answered. "For a while I took it from prisoners. Then we injected them with their own blood after Dr. Voss brought it back.

But eventually we injected everyone with your brother's blood."

Jack felt his stomach knot. "No one else's?"

"That's right."

"So they thought Ed's blood was special somehow?"

"Evidently. They brought him back two more times."

"What?"

"The day before your father died, they brought your brother in the morning. Your father had been reassigned to supervise some work in the warden's office. Ed was in and out before your father came back to his post in the clinic."

Jack was churning inside. He had to get to Ed before Richardson's men did. "Did you do anything else to my brother?"

She shook her head.

"They're going to try to kill him, you know. They'll try to kill us all."

She looked back at her house. "They'll go for the ones you love. The threat was always there. That's how they kept us quiet. Now look." Her arm limply pointed to the flames.

In the face of that horror, he thought of Elaine. Richardson had seen them together at his gala. "You've got to leave before they come back."

Her arms held her chest tightly, as if a part of her would escape if she didn't grasp it. She didn't say anything, and didn't bother to wipe the tears that fell silently down her face.

He wondered if she'd heard him, or if she was too lost to respond anymore. "Are you sure there's nothing else?"

She finally looked back at him. "There's nothing more. And there's nothing you can do to stop them.

Nobody cares about those prisoners. Nobody cares about some old black nurse. And by the time they finish, nobody will care about you either."

THIRTY

Jack saw the flashing lights and moved quickly to back the van down the street before the fire trucks blocked his exit. The sirens had brought out whatever neighbors hadn't already been awakened by the explosion. He found himself walking against the current of onlookers as he made his way to the pay phone on the corner.

He gripped the receiver tightly and dialed his home number. As it kept ringing, Geneva Lott's warning ran through his mind. *"They'll go for the ones you love."* He listened to the phone as the firemen pulled the entire length of hose from the truck. It must have rung twenty times. As he was about to hang up, a man answered.

"Yes."

Jack didn't recognize the voice, but he was sure he'd dialed the right number. If Richardson's men were with his brother, he might be able to scare them off. "Where's Ed?"

"Who's calling?"

"I want to talk to my brother."

The voice was muffled on the other end as the man spoke to someone in the house. Jack suddenly worried that Richardson's people could pinpoint his location if they held him on the line long enough.

Another voice came on the line. "Is this Mr. Harris? I mean Dr. Harris?"

"Who are you?"

"Officer Travis, Atlanta PD."

"What's wrong? Where's my brother?"

"That's what we want to know. We've been trying to reach you for an hour. I think you better come down here, sir."

Jack scanned the street, half expecting someone to be walking toward him. "Why are you there? Where is Mrs. Logan?"

There was a pause at the other end, then more muffled conversation before the officer came back on. "There's been some trouble. Mrs. Logan was beaten up pretty bad. She was found unconscious on the floor. Paramedics took her to the hospital."

Jack closed his eyes. "Those bastards."

"Come again?"

He leaned against the scarred Plexiglas surrounding the phone. "Could they rouse her?"

"I don't think so. Like I said, it looks pretty bad."

"Where'd they take her?"

"Not sure."

"What about Ed?"

"A witness saw someone—we believe it was your brother—running down the front steps just before Mrs. Logan was discovered."

"What witness?"

"There was a photographer staked out across the street. He says he tried to get pictures of your brother, but it was too dark. It looked suspicious so he went to the door to see if there was something worth getting on film. He saw her lying just inside the front door and called us."

"Did he see the ones who did it?"

The silence spoke volumes.

"You don't think Ed—he's not capable of doing this."

"Your brother is wanted for questioning."

"I'm standing about a hundred yards from a house that's burning to the ground. The place went up in minutes. They say it was a bomb. The same people are trying to get to my brother."

"What makes you say that, sir?"

Jack checked his watch. There wasn't much time. If they'd gotten to Ed, they would likely try to get Elaine. "Let me guess, the photographer's no longer there."

"We have his name and number."

"So this guy watches my house for days, but suddenly decides to leave just when things start to hit the fan?"

"We've got no right to hold him. He said he had a deadline and had to develop the pictures. If he wants to leave, that's his business."

"Which way did this trustworthy witness say my brother went?"

"He could be anywhere. He took the victim's car."

"Look, Officer Travis. You've got no reason to believe me. But do us both a favor and call Detective Tarkington. He's based out of the downtown headquarters. Wake him up at home if you need to, but tell him what happened. Then have him talk to Dr. Daniel Linh at Garity. Dr. Linh can explain what's going on if something happens to me."

"If you're harboring your brother, you'd be considered an accessory, Doctor."

"You spell his name L-I-N-H. And when you get Tarkington on the phone, be sure and tell him one more thing."

"What's that?"

"My brother can't drive."

Jack slammed the receiver in its cradle but held it in

his grip while he tried to decide if it would be safer to call Elaine from another phone. Richardson's influence had few bounds. How could he know that the man he'd just spoken to wasn't working for Richardson? He again wondered if they had been able to trace the call. If they got to him now, there was no hope for Ed.

He dialed Elaine's number and waited. There was no answer.

He redialed and let it ring until he lost count. He felt as if hanging up would somehow guarantee that they'd taken all he'd ever had, that her fate would be sealed the moment her phone stopped ringing.

Down the street, the mob of onlookers let out a collective gasp as another wall crashed into what remained of Geneva Lott's house. Jack could see orange embers surging in the dark high above the trees. He looked at the receiver as if it had some kind of power. He let it dangle, and walked away.

He drove several blocks before he came to a halt in the middle of the deserted street, several yards from the intersection. He wanted to pace—he always could think better when he walked—but no one in his right mind would walk alone in this part of town. He drove on until he got to an area he recognized. He thought about calling Dan Linh, but Dan would just want him to wait for the police. And perhaps that was what he should do. But he was convinced they'd putz around until it was too late to help Ed and Elaine.

Then it hit him. If he couldn't think of where they were, the next best thing was to find someone who could.

It was nearly four-thirty by the time he got there. No lights were on in the one-story house, but still he recognized it. The rest of the neighborhood was still asleep, which was fine by him. Jack followed the concrete walk to the porch. The front door had eight small windowpanes, which made it easy.

He looked around once more, and seeing no one, broke the glass with the back of his fist. He unlocked the door, then rammed his shoulder hard enough to rip the chain lock from the door facing. Adrenaline and raw instinct took over, and he quickly made it to the back of the house. The bedroom door was ajar, and within seconds he was on the bed and had his hands around Dr. Scalacey's neck.

Scalacey's body surged against him with surprising strength, but Jack tightened his grip. Guttural sounds came from the man's neck and his elbows sliced the air, catching Jack in the ribs. The pain was enough to cause Jack to loosen his grip, and as soon as he did, Scalacey brought his legs underneath and flipped Jack onto the floor.

Jack spun around and leaped for the bed, but not before Scalacey got his hand in the nightstand drawer. Jack shoved his body against the drawer, pinning Scalacey's hand inside. Scalacey cried out, but Jack rammed the drawer several times, until Scalacey let go in pain.

Jack pulled the pistol out of the drawer before Scalacey could recover.

The man slid down onto the floor with his wrist bent back at an unnatural angle. Jack clicked the safety off. The sound was unmistakable.

Scalacey became silent, and Jack turned on the lamp.

"Where'd they take my brother?"

Scalacey winced as he laid his wrist against his knee. His long hair was disheveled. "I don't know what you're talking about."

He pointed the gun at Scalacey's head. "You know, and you're going to take me there."

"You're in way over your head."

Jack fired into the mattress a few inches over Scalacey's shoulder. The blood seemed to drain out of Scalacey's face.

"What are they doing with him? What's so important about his blood?"

Scalacey used his good hand to help prop himself up. His eyes focused on the gun. "It will be over soon. You're probably too late."

"For what?"

Scalacey just stared back. Jack held the gun with both hands. "If it's too late, then I don't need you alive." He aimed between the man's eyes.

"Wait."

"What do they want with Ed's blood?"

"They'll kill me. . . . "

Jack kicked the knee that propped his broken wrist and Scalacey screamed in pain. "You might be better off."

Scalacey braced against the bed. He looked like he was about to pass out. Jack feigned a second kick but Scalacey burst out first. "It's Voss."

"Tell me something I don't know."

Scalacey tried to straighten his body, but the pain stopped him. "Voss has perfected a method of growing tissue from stem cells."

"There are dozens of labs doing the same thing."

"In petri dishes and incubators, but there's a big difference between cultivating liver cells and growing an entire liver. Nobody's been able to support an intact organ, but Voss has done it, and can grow it inside a human host."

"Get to the point."

"Replacement organs." Scalacey winced as he worked his good hand under his wrist. "Do you have any idea how much money could be made if you were the first person to perfect the ability to replace people's organs? You have a massive heart attack, you get a new heart. But not just any heart, and not a transplant . . . you grow your own, inside your own body. No antibodies, no rejection."

"That's bullshit."

"People have been killed for less."

Jack felt his grip tighten on the gun. "My father."

Scalacey swallowed, but didn't drop his gaze. "Yes."

"Why?"

"Your father overheard the prisoners . . . they were the guinea pigs, but they didn't know it. We've grown organs, or parts of organs in over a half dozen so far. Of course we had to keep them away from each other, so they wouldn't find out when one of them died.

"No one caught on until Burke. We think he figured it out, and that's why he bolted. The guard he killed was one of our men. He made sure there was absolute privacy for any of our tests. Burke must have figured it was payback time. Didn't have anything to lose. He'd get me, too, if he could find me."

"What about the others . . . how many have you killed?"

"What difference does it make? The rest are too stupid to figure it out. Bunch of schmucks—all death row or lifers. Like they had a prayer of ever getting out. But you get that desperate, I guess you'll believe anything."

"I asked about my father."

"Your father heard enough talk, and somehow put things together. We thought he was going to blackmail us, but all he wanted was to have the technique used to fix your brother's brain."

"Even if this fantasy had a grain of truth, it couldn't help Ed. There's no room in the skull to grow another brain."

"Your father didn't think of that."

Jack knew his father couldn't come close to understanding why they couldn't fix Ed. "Why take Ed's blood?"

"The discovery came by accident. Voss was looking for the perfect medium to support the stem cell growth. He had already discovered how to stimulate individual organ growth, but he couldn't control it. It's a process known as *immortalizing*—once stimulated, the stem cells don't know when to die. The number of cells grow exponentially with successive divisions. And if you know how to make the stem cells differentiate into a particular cell line, you can grow a small organ in a matter of weeks. Unfortunately those organs continued to have uncontrolled growth, like a cancer.

"When your father found out about the experiments, he demanded that Ed be part of the study. Voss had no choice but to lead him to believe your brother could be helped. He took his blood and stimulated the stem cells, just like he'd done in the prisoners. And that's when the real breakthrough came."

Jack checked the time. "Get on with it."

"Voss experimented with injecting stem cells from one person into another. But he tested every combination in the lab first. Every time stem cells were mixed with another person's blood, it produced a mass of cells that showed uncontrolled growth, like a tumor. But when stem cells were mixed with a vial of your brother's blood, the cells would grow to a certain size and then stop.

"Then he mixed your brother's serum with cells whose DNA had been pruned so that it would only express liver genes. The result was a very small liver that maintained itself for a short time. If given proper nutrition and a blood supply, the liver would probably last a normal life span. In short, when added in the right combination, your brother's blood created a *mortal* strain of differentiated stem cells. Voss had only to figure out why."

"And you think he's done that."

"Voss thinks there's some cofactor in your brother's blood that prevents the organs from growing out of control."

"Why not just clone the cofactor?"

Scalacey shook his head. "We don't know what it is."

Jack glanced at the small bruise in the crease of his own arm.

Scalacey snickered. "I see you figured that out. We wondered if the trait ran in the family. We won't know your results for a few more days. It's the only reason you're still alive, but the hot money says you don't have it."

He now understood that the invitation to work at Richardson's headquarters had been a ruse for them to take his blood. And that his father's blood didn't have an abnormal eosinophil count because he didn't get injected like the others. "Someone drew my father's blood before he died."

"I'm certain they would have tested his blood. Your father would have been quite valuable if he was a natural producer of the cofactor." He said the words with no more emotion than he would if talking about the weather.

"My mother . . ."

"There's a million dollars for the first man who finds her."

Jack wanted to unload the gun into the man's chest, but he needed him alive.

Scalacey must have sensed his position. His voice took on a nervous edge. "We don't know what percentage of the population has the qualities of your brother's blood, but so far we've checked several thousand employees, and his is the only one.

"After we discovered that your father didn't have the cofactor, we began to wonder if your brother's uniqueness is somehow related to his brain damage. For example, he may have lost some critical neurologic signal that promotes cell growth. Or perhaps the injured brain actually releases a damaged protein that now acts as a cofactor to stop cell growth. We'd like to test stroke victims, but we haven't figured out how to gain access."

"You're sick."

"Think about it. A damaged brain never shows any attempt to regenerate. Voss postulated that the injured brain cells secrete some signal into the blood—some protein or enzyme that prevents any regeneration. It's purely theoretical, but the truth remains that your brother is much more valuable to us in his current state."

"What happened to my father?"

"He found out that your brother wasn't going to be helped. He was furious. We couldn't take the risk."

"So you killed him."

"Not me."

"Who?"

"I'm afraid you'll have to find that out for yourself."

Jack fired again, putting a hole in the mattress above Scalacey's other shoulder. "Who?"

Scalacey seemed frozen by his fear. His words stuttered. "I don't know. Voss ordered it."

"Who?"

"I don't know. One of Richardson's men. Probably the one who'll kill the two of us."

"Why did they have to *kidnap* my brother? Why not just take some of his blood and be done with it?"

"The process requires a special support medium, and the exchange must be immediate. To grow that first liver they had to bring your brother back to the infirmary to mix his blood with stem cells they'd prepared from one of the prisoners. It won't work if they just draw the blood and transport it to the lab."

"Why now?"

"It's always been about getting him. But there's been one obstacle after another. Voss got your father out of the way, and then you appeared. There was always the possibility that you would play ball, but it was clear from the start you'd be trouble. Killing you without getting your brother wouldn't do Voss any good, so he's obviously decided to take him first."

"He could have done that at any time. Why *now?*"

"I suspect Voss has figured something out about the process. Something he'd been waiting to discover. Something critical that requires access to your brother's blood."

"Where?"

"Right under your nose."

He thought of how Richardson's men were content to follow him all over town without interfering. As long as he didn't go where they didn't want him. "The prison."

"Even Richardson couldn't pull that off."

"I've toured the headquarters, even the secure areas."

"You saw what they wanted you to see. Nothing more."

His mind raced. He thought of the tour he'd gotten, the layout of the grounds he'd seen from Voss's office. The workers walking along the manicured paths. "The buildings down the hill. The farthest one was set off from the others by a thick stand of trees."

Scalacey nodded. "But I suspect you're too late."

Jack motioned to the door with the gun. "They won't kill him if he's the key to their research."

Scalacey stood, holding his wrist. "In order to get enough cofactor to grow an organ large enough to save a grown man, Voss estimates it would take almost half of your brother's blood volume. On the other hand, if he's figured a way to stimulate the cofactor, there's no reason to keep your brother alive much longer. Either way, your brother's good as dead."

Jack shoved him into the hall. "Move."

THIRTY-ONE

Scalacey drove his car, his broken wrist cradled in his lap, while Jack sat in the passenger seat with the gun trained on him. Even in the dark it was easy to tell that the wrist was swollen to twice its normal size and discolored. Scalacey had wanted to ice it down, but Jack refused. It made him easier to control.

They pulled into the long drive to Richardson's headquarters, then took the first right at the fountain, stopping at a fortified gate about a fourth of a mile down the road. Scalacey clicked the remote on the sun visor, then drove on after the gate opened.

It seemed that they were going in a wide circle through the woods. They passed a few metal buildings set back in the trees and finally came to a small unlit parking lot with numbered plates assigning each space. Jack recognized the black Cadillac that had ferried him earlier, but the limo was nowhere to be seen.

They parked, and Jack was careful to keep the gun on Scalacey as they approached the walking trail. In the distance back to their left was the glass headquarters building, and Jack made a mental image of the grounds as he'd seen them laid out from Voss's office. The loading dock would be almost straight ahead through the woods, but the building he was interested in should be quite a downhill hike to their right.

Scalacey started down the gravel path in that direction, passing his first test.

Jack was on edge as they followed the trail into a thick growth of woods. Something in him sensed an ambush. Some rocks shifted under Scalacey's foot and Jack quickly scanned the woods on either side. There was no one there.

Jack watched Scalacey's dark form in front of him. "You said they'll kill you when they find out."

Scalacey slowed, the angle of his shoulders changing, but he didn't turn around. "It's not like I've got a choice."

"You could cut a deal."

Scalacey turned, but kept his distance. He cradled his swollen wrist. "I'm not exactly in what you'd call the mainstream of medicine. I've washed out of a few jobs. They don't give deals to people like me."

"Maybe. Maybe not."

"I'm listening."

"Neither of us trusts each other, but you've got some choices to make. You're either going to help me, or set me up."

Scalacey seemed to be considering his options.

"If I lose, you lose too. If I win, I can help you. You could tell the police what you told me. I could tell them what you did to save my brother and Elaine."

Scalacey just stared at him through the darkness. "And if you get killed?"

Jack didn't know how to answer that. "Keep moving."

They continued down the trail. Jack wasn't sure what to make of Scalacey's response. He kept the gun trained on his back. The path led them by the series of white buildings he'd been waiting for, but Scalacey didn't break stride. Eventually the trail stopped, but they walked on through the woods.

Jack had the feeling he could have been in the middle of rural Georgia. Eventually they came upon a dark green building. Trees grew within ten feet of the structure, and they easily towered above the top of the building. As he got a better look, he could tell that the outside walls had vertical black stripes of varying widths. From the air it would be hard to pick this structure out from the pines. Jack started to walk closer but Scalacey stopped him with his good hand.

"Don't walk out there until you know exactly what you're going to do."

The windowless building had two stories. Jack noticed a security camera at the corner near the roof, and a series of floodlights at each corner, but none of them was on, which made Jack even more suspicious. Either they wanted him to fall completely into the trap, or they were so interested in keeping this place hidden that it was worth the security problems that came with no lighting.

Scalacey turned to him. "I need some assurance."

"I can't give you any other than my word."

"You go down, there's nothing in it for me."

"I don't know what else I can do."

"At least a name."

Jack studied the man's face. He'd probably been involved in more shady deals than some of the prisoners he treated. The gun had gotten them this far, but Jack would be outnumbered the moment he went inside that building. It was apparent that he had to deal with Scalacey if they were going to make it out of here alive.

"Tarkington."

"Who's he?"

"With the police. A detective. Half the time he's crawling up my back. But there are some loose ends in my father's death, and the prison breakout. I've been tying them together. I think he believes me."

"That isn't much."

"Would you rather take your chances with Richardson?"

Scalacey eased closer. His gaze moved slowly across Jack's face, like he was looking for something but couldn't quite see it. He turned back toward the dark building. "They'll be in a large room. It can hold several patients. I don't know how many are there right now."

"What about guards?"

"As a routine there aren't many. But with all this going down, I'd expect the worst."

Jack checked his watch. "We've got another half hour before dawn. You think Voss or Richardson could be in there?"

"Richardson won't be here. He's too smart for that. I don't know about Voss. Depends on what he's discovered. But he won't be far."

In silent agreement they moved toward the building.

The door had a dark awning. As they got close enough, Jack could tell the awning was made of a camouflage pattern of greens and blacks. Scalacey was only two paces ahead. If there was a guard at the door, it would take some quick talking for Scalacey to get the two of them inside.

He imagined where he'd shoot, if Scalacey double-crossed him. He thought about how he'd shoot to incapacitate him without killing him. He'd never thought himself capable of maiming another human being, but that was before. Now he could hardly believe what he was willing to do to get to Ed and Elaine . . . to get his father's killer.

Scalacey hesitated. "We won't have much time. If

he's still alive, he'll be on the first floor. The door is midway down the hall."

Scalacey released his good hand from under his broken wrist and put it on the scanner. "Once we get in, we'll have only a few minutes before Voss knows it." The lock clicked, and Scalacey opened the door.

The hall was sterile white tile, brightly lit. In the middle was a muscular guard on the verge of nodding off in a chair. He woke at the sound of the door closing.

Scalacey quickly moved to the guard, who obviously recognized him. "I've come with some more injections." He nodded toward Jack. "This is my assistant."

The guard was dressed in a dark suit and had an earphone discreetly tucked in one ear. "I've got to make a call before I can clear you."

He reached for a microphone in his pocket, but was a split second too late, as Jack had his gun pointed right at the man's head before he could speak. "Keep your mouth shut, and don't move."

Jack pulled the Colt .45 from the man's shoulder holster. "How many guards in the room?"

The man's smug expression didn't flinch. Jack cocked the gun and pressed the barrel against his forehead.

"Just me."

Jack didn't believe him, but there wasn't enough time to get the truth.

Scalacey moved to the door. He put his hand on the scanner. The light swept under his hand, but the door didn't unlock. "This is new."

Jack pressed the gun harder against the guard's head. "Open it."

The guard had developed fine tremors. "It won't work. I'm not cleared."

Jack shoved his back, and put the gun at the base of

his neck. The man put his hand on the screen, but the lock didn't release.

Scalacey said, "You'll have to blow the lock."

Jack knew an army of Richardson's people would swarm down as soon as they heard the shot, but there wasn't much time. He moved Scalacey aside but kept his body at an angle where he could see the guard while he shot the scanner.

A loud alarm screamed throughout the building. Jack pulled the door open. The room inside looked like a large ICU. Ed was in a bed next to a young man on a ventilator. Elaine was standing between the two beds, hugging herself. She seemed to be turning toward the sound of the gun as Jack caught her eye. She began to move slowly toward him, but Jack held up his hand, intending to give her quick instructions. But what he saw made him lose his concentration.

His mother was on a third bed near the corner. She appeared to be sedated, with a sheet pulled up to her chest. She was pale and had lost weight in the months since he'd last seen her. Even with her eyes closed, her face had a sadness that made him want to wipe away tears that weren't there. Jack sat on the bed and pulled her upright. Her body flopped against his chest like a heavy rag doll.

Scalacey yelled, "We've only got seconds."

Jack looked back at him and then seemed to regain some composure. He gently laid his mother back down and moved to Ed's bed.

He was closer to consciousness than their mother. There was a large-bore IV needle in his arm, but it had been capped off as a heparin lock so it could be used repeatedly to draw blood. He looked exhausted and his skin was a pasty white, but there was motion in his arms and a grimace on his face. There was no telling how much blood they'd taken from him. Jack slapped his face to arouse him.

Ed awoke and slowly sat up on his elbows, but he could hardly keep his eyes open. Jack quickly glanced at the man in the other bed, that was only a foot from his brother's. The young man was jaundiced and had so much edema over his entire body that even his lids couldn't close over his swollen eyes. He had an IV in each arm, and a central-line IV that was hooked up to two unmarked bottles, one of which appeared to be blood. He was clearly unresponsive, and near death. Jack recognized the classic look of end-stage liver and kidney failure.

Scalacey said, "There's no more time. We've got to go."

Jack motioned to the guard. "Get under there."

The man had to work to fit under the dying man's bed. Jack pressed the controls and lowered the bed tight against the guard. "You so much as move, you're dead."

Jack strained to help his brother out of the bed. Scalacey draped Ed's arm around his neck, but Ed withdrew it, and said, "I can walk."

Jack looked at Elaine. "Help me with my mother."

Elaine removed the covers and helped Jack reposition his mother. "How did you find us?"

"There's no time. We'll talk later."

His mother slumped into him. He struggled, finally managing to loop his arms under hers from the back. Jack said, "Let's go. Now."

They could hear heavy footsteps running down stairs at the other end of the hall. Elaine helped Ed, and Jack pulled his mother behind them. They cleared the door with the awning just as two men burst onto the far end of the hall. The guard's hand-gun was in Jack's pocket.

Scalacey said, "We've got to get as deep as possible into the woods."

They were about fifty yards into the trees when the floodlights from the building came on. Ed was able to keep up a good pace, but they would be no match for the guards. Their only advantage was that no one saw which direction they'd taken.

Scalacey was unencumbered and had run ahead, then stopped abruptly.

Reaching him, Jack saw a long, narrow open space in the middle of the pine forest. They were directly across from a small cabin at the edge of the clearing.

Scalacey whispered. "It's an archery range."

"I've been here."

"A few acres beyond the targets is a fence. Beyond it is a deep ravine that takes the rain runoff. It's our best chance of getting out."

Jack could hear men yelling behind them.

Scalacey ran ahead. "We can't stop."

The run had made Ed more alert. "I can run, Jack."

Jack was convinced it was worth a try. "All of you go ahead. I'll bring my mother. Try to meet up once we hit the fence."

Scalacey and Ed ran down the range. Ed was slow, but held his own. Elaine ignored Jack's suggestion and picked up his mother's feet, and said, "You can't make it alone."

He didn't argue. Jack moved backward as quick as he could, but stumbled several times as the terrain dropped abruptly. As they finally passed the thick circular targets, Jack couldn't help noticing that most had holes dead center in the bull's-eye.

Flashlights were strafing the ground in the woods

they had just left. Jack couldn't tell how many men were coming their way, but there were at least two.

Limbs and pine needles slapped his back and arms as they moved deeper into the woods. Some branches broke in their wake, and Jack realized they were leaving a well-marked trail for Richardson's men to follow.

Scalacey slowed alongside Jack. "We've got to split up."

Jack glanced behind them. "Maybe so."

"You've got both guns. If you get hit, we can't defend ourselves."

Jack hesitated, then decided he had to take the chance. He handed him the Colt .45.

Just then they heard what sounded like lawnmowers.

Scalacey started to run again. "They've got four-wheelers. We've got to beat them to the fence."

The lights of the four-wheelers fanned shadows off the pines. They were closing fast. In spite of the plan, they hadn't run far before they could see the chain-link fence. Jack realized they hadn't had enough time to gain any meaningful separation from each other.

Scalacey was the first to reach the fence, and Ed was right behind him. There were no trees on the other side, only a barren ravine that cut down into darkness. Scalacey stuffed the gun in his belt and started an awkward climb with only one good hand before Jack could warn him. The four-wheelers were too close.

Jack dropped his mother and pushed Ed and Elaine down as the red pinpoint light danced on Scalacey's back. Before Jack could open his mouth, bullets ripped Scalacey off the fence. The body fell next to Ed, scaring him more than the threat of the bullets. Jack had to jerk his brother to the ground again to keep him from getting shot.

A searchlight flooded them. Within seconds the four-wheelers pulled up. There were only two guards, but they had rifles, and Jack knew he'd lost.

He faced the guards and slowly raised his hands. One of them took the gun from his hand, then shoved him on the ground. He felt the kick of a boot against his back and then the cold muzzle of the rifle.

Neither of the guards spoke, but they both had earpieces. Jack assumed someone else was giving them orders.

One of the guards motioned with his rifle at Ed and Elaine. She got up first, and helped Ed to his feet. The confused and frightened look in Ed's eyes was almost more than Jack could take.

Jack coughed then said, "It's OK, Ed. Just follow Elaine and do what she says."

The guard over him kicked his ribs. "Shut up."

Jack winced; at least two of his ribs were broken. His only consolation was that they weren't beating anyone else.

The guards both stood quite still, apparently getting instructions through their earpieces. The other guard pushed Ed and Elaine and said, "Start walking."

Jack felt the rifle barrel under his chin. For a second he thought they were going to kill him right there.

The guard barked, "Get up."

Jack stood and tried to look back at Scalacey's body. He hadn't been able to check, but he knew he was dead. One of the guards lifted his mother's limp body onto the four-wheeler.

The guard shoved Jack in the back. "Follow them. You even twitch funny, you'll end up like your friend."

He wanted to hold Elaine, to put his arm around his brother, and let them know how much he loved them, but he could barely even see their dark figures walking through the pines ahead.

The first breaking light of the morning sun was casting gray hues through the trees by the time they reached the archery range. Ed and Elaine had made better time, and were waiting against the wooden shed where Richardson's assistant had changed the targets.

He thought they were at least going to let them be together one last moment, but when he kept walking toward the shack, the guard laid the barrel of the gun across his chest and said, "Wait here."

There was a fine mist of dew on the grass and it seemed to have soaked a thin layer over his entire body. He felt a sick coldness that clarified the fact that he was about to die. The waiting made the feeling worse, but it was giving him the last few minutes to look at Ed and Elaine. The other guard drove his mother back to the building where she'd been held captive.

Voss appeared at the edge of the clearing and walked toward Jack with the poise of a conquering general. He actually smiled as he got close, and for a second it looked as if he might extend his hand, but he didn't.

"I understand you told our chief of security that you were interested in spending some time on the archery range. I hear that he gave you a key to the equipment shed just yesterday. It's a rather dangerous sport, you know."

Jack wanted to spit in his face.

Voss turned and walked to the shack. He put on latex gloves, put a key in the lock, then opened the door. "Too bad about Dr. Scalacey. Word on the street is that he got involved in a drug deal that went bad. He had some priors with college kids who were selling his narcotic prescriptions on the street. Almost cost him his license a few years ago. That's when we first met, of course. He was on probation, and couldn't get a job."

Voss brought out a crossbow and pulled an arrow tight across the bridge. "What was I thinking? I meant the word on the street *tomorrow*. They won't even find his body until then."

Voss stepped away from the shack.

"Scalacey was a troubled man. Not unlike your father." Voss cocked his head ever so slightly. "And of course your mother . . . we found her in a halfway house for the mentally ill in Waycross, Georgia. Mason, our security man, was able to get her tonight. Hasn't been here more than two hours. Sorry about the sedation. She won't even get to say good-bye."

"You bastard."

Voss reared the back of his hand as if he were going to slap it across Jack's face, but he caught himself. "There mustn't be any unusual bruising."

Jack braced his palm against the side of his chest. "How are you going to explain these broken ribs?" He knew he shouldn't have said it the second it came out of his mouth.

Voss smiled. "Why, thank you, Doctor." He moved closer and positioned the crossbow with the arrow against the broken ribs. "These things have a hair trigger. Drop one, and they fire. We'll all be shocked to hear the details. Close-range, accidental, self-inflicted wound. Right through the heart. What a tragedy for us all."

Voss was enjoying this. It was in that moment that Jack was finally certain. "You pulled the trigger on my father, didn't you."

Voss stepped back, seeming to admire what he was about to do. "You want something done right—"

The arrow exploded through the side of Jack's

chest before he realized what had happened. The force spun him to the ground and Voss fell on top of him The pain sliced through him, and he heard a sucking sound with each breath. Jack's face was covered with blood and gritty, hard particles. He was pinned on his back with the bloody arrowhead several inches outside his chest. The base of the arrow pried against the ground, ripping the entry wound on his right side. He tried, but couldn't move a hand to it.

Only then did he realize there'd been a series of shots. He craned his neck to look at the shack, but he couldn't see the others. No one was firing back.

He saw Ed walking toward him. As he got closer, Jack recognized the gun in his hand. It was the Colt .45 he'd given Scalacey.

Jack tried again to move but couldn't. His breathing became short and fast. He was starving for air, drowning above water. He began to cough blood into his mouth. In his panic he thought the blood was obstructing his airway. Forcing one hand free, he frantically began to tear at his own face. In his hand he saw bloody clumps of brain tissue, and bone fragments.

Ed leaned over to pull Voss's body away. An arm flopped against the arrowhead. The searing pain was more than Jack could take. He gasped in vain for air and his vision grayed out as another piece of the bloody skull fell onto his face.

THIRTY-TWO

A wet cloth dabbed at Jack's forehead. His eyes were heavy and he felt like slipping off to sleep again. It was a familiar sensation he'd had many times before. He wasn't really coming awake. It was more of an awareness that he was close to consciousness.

Someone was talking quietly across the room. Then the voices stopped, and he felt a hand on his face.

He tried to turn over, but the pain shot through his chest, and he opened his crusted eyes.

Elaine was at his bedside. Her eyes were red and she had blotches on her neck, but she smiled with a look of relief that brought more tears.

He looked around the hospital room. Ed was sitting in a chair behind Elaine, and Dan Linh was at the foot of the bed. Dan smiled. "Welcome back, man."

A wave of nausea coursed through him and Elaine grabbed the plastic basin in time to catch the streaks of acid from his stomach. She wiped his face with a cold washcloth until it seemed the dry heaves were through.

Under the hospital gown he could feel the pull of the tape and sutures around the chest tube that had been placed inside to reinflate his right lung. As the nausea subsided, he began to slip back into sedation, but he opened his eyes when he felt a firm grip on his ankle.

Detective Tarkington released his grip once he seemed satisfied that Jack was finally awake. "Been waiting a few hours. You think you could answer some questions?"

Jack stared until it seemed that Tarkington came into focus. He couldn't tell how much time had passed since Elaine wiped his face. "I don't know." His eyes closed and he felt the tight grip again. He opened his eyes. "Sorry."

"We've already gotten statements from your brother and Ms. Thomas."

Jack's head was pounding. He looked up to his right. There was an IV of Ringer's lactate solution dripping into a vein in his arm. His mouth was so dry his lips were chapped. Elaine seemed to read his mind and offered him a small spoonful of ice chips.

The ice brought another wave of nausea, but it soon passed, and he could talk. He looked back at Tarkington. "Voss?"

"He's dead. Along with one of security guards that work for Richardson. You want to tell me what happened?"

"Voss was going to kill me."

"Who shot those people, Doctor?"

Jack looked at Elaine. There was pressure behind his eyes that got worse when he turned his head. She touched him and said, "It's OK. We told him everything."

He wanted to fall back to sleep but the pain wouldn't let him. He slowly shifted.

"Where's my mother?"

Elaine said, "She's on the medicine ward. She lost blood, but they say she'll be OK."

Tarkington said, "Your mother is obviously fragile, but she told us that your father hired someone who found her in some kind of psychiatric domiciliary in Waycross. They spoke on the phone, and he made plans to pick her up. Best I can tell, that was the night before he died. She said she'd been waiting for him to show up. Someone finally did come, claiming to be sent by your father. She had no way of knowing that it was Richardson's people."

Jack closed his eyes, trying to fight the rush of emotion.

Tarkington touched him on the leg. "I'd still like to know your side of things."

"I don't know for sure what happened." He wondered if his mother even knew that her husband was dead.

Ed stood. "I fixed them, Jack. Did I do the right thing?"

Jack pressed his eyes, but it didn't relieve the pain. "You saved me, big guy."

Elaine said, "Dr. Scalacey dropped the gun when they shot him on the fence. Ed grabbed it. No one thought to check him."

Ed smiled like a child and hugged Elaine. She put an arm around him and eased him away from the bed. Jack stared at the sight of them together, arms around each other. There was something more there, but his thoughts were interrupted before he could fully understand.

Tarkington moved closer. "I need your statement. I can ask them to leave if I need to."

Jack's attention lingered on Elaine and Ed; then he finally looked at the detective, who was getting impatient.

"What happened?" Tarkington asked.

Jack thought through the last day and slowly filled him in on what Geneva Lott had told him and what he had learned from Dr. Scalacey. The more he talked, the more awake he felt. "Last thing I remember was Voss pressing that crossbow against my chest. He moved back; then the thing pierced me. In a second he was on top of me, and I was flat on the ground. There were gunshots, but that's all I know."

Ed shouted, "I shot him, Jack. Got the guard, too."

"They would have killed all of us if Ed hadn't done it," Elaine said.

Tarkington let the silence hang and didn't drop his gaze. After nearly a minute, he seemed satisfied. "What happens from here is up to the DA, not me."

"Voss said he killed my father."

Tarkington looked at Dan Linh, then back to Jack. "I've recommended that your father's case be reopened. Under the circumstances I don't think they'll press charges against you or your brother, but, like I said, it's not my call."

"Who'll look into my father's case?"

"I've asked for it."

Jack looked at him a moment, then reached his right hand across the rail. Tarkington didn't seem to understand at first, but then grasped the hand.

For the first time Jack knew someone else believed him—more importantly, someone else believed in his father. It seemed to put some issues to rest. "How did I get here?"

Tarkington released his grip. "I got the early wake-up from the patrolman who'd been called to your house. You're lucky I decided to call Dr. Linh instead of cussing that guy and telling him what he could do with the report."

Jack's concentration had begun to wander, but he felt a sudden panic and looked at Dan. "How's Mrs. Logan?"

Dan's expression grew serious. "The paramedics took her to Laxton Hospital. She'd been beaten up pretty bad. She had a broken right arm and a concussion. They also had to drain a subdural hematoma. I've been by twice. She looks rough but she's a tough old lady. May take some rehab but they think she'll make it."

Pain shot through Jack's chest when his arm accidentally hit the chest tube. "There's a nurse, Geneva Lott. She was forced to work with them. I think she'll testify. She needs protection."

Tarkington said, "We're way ahead of you on that one, Doc."

"The Franklin woman had a tourniquet on the ground, just like the guard that Burke killed."

"How'd you know about that?"

"Richardson showed me some photos of the guard tied up in the barn. I don't know how he got them. Probably paid off somebody."

"Burke's fingerprints matched some we found on the tourniquet by her body. But we can't fit the tourniquets into the puzzle."

Jack said, "I think Burke knew he was dying. Geneva Lott told me that a new liver was growing in him. Maybe he thought he was somehow contaminating his victims by injecting some of his blood to give them a taste of what he'd been through. I think the *two* that he carved was a symbol for two organs."

Jack looked at Dan. "That guard didn't bleed to death. The eosinophils and low-platelet count weren't leukemia. It's a reaction from Burke injecting his blood into him."

Dan thought a second, then said, "It would have to be an incredibly fast reaction to an injection. But the blood smears fit a graft-versus-host response. Who knows? They've broken new ground. If an organ can grow in a matter of weeks, perhaps the serum from one of those inmates could induce an immune response faster than we've ever seen before."

No one said anything for a moment. Jack lifted his gown to see the two wounds made by the arrow. "I thought I was dead when that thing ripped through me."

Tarkington looked up from the sight of the wounds. "We figured there were only so many places they could have taken your brother and Ms. Thomas, so we sent patrol cars to the prison, Richardson's mansion, and his headquarters. We were almost too late, but the officers heard the gunfire and got to you pretty quick. The doc said the arrow just missed your heart."

"What about Richardson?"

"He's wanted for questioning."

"What do you mean, *wanted?*"

"We're working on it. We think he's outside the country. If it looks like unlawful flight, the FBI will get involved. Our problem will be finding evidence that directly links him to this whole thing. With Scalacey and Voss dead, there's no one to squeeze."

Jack closed his eyes. "You'll never find him."

"Guy like that can't stop his lifestyle if he had to. It may take a while, but he'll show up."

Jack looked at Elaine and Ed. "Given the right reasons, people will do almost anything, detective."

A nurse entered the room and screwed a syringe into the IV port.

Jack waved his hand. "I don't want any more."

She took her thumb off the plunger but didn't remove the syringe. "Listen, Dr. Harris. I've been working this floor over eight years. You don't know the kind of pain you're going to have from surgery and that fresh chest tube. Besides, it's doctor's orders." She injected the medicine and left before Jack could answer.

No one seemed to know what to do. Jack steadied the chest tube with his hand and coughed, sending blood-tinged bubbles gurgling into the suction bottles on the floor by his bed. The pain was almost as bad as the arrow wound. He realized the nurse was right. "If that's all, I could use some rest."

Everyone started to leave when Jack said, "Elaine, could you stay?"

She glanced to Dan, who nodded. "I'll take Ed to my place. He can stay with me."

Ed seemed to like the idea, so Jack thanked him and waited until they all left.

Elaine stroked his hair slowly. He could smell her skin, and couldn't help thinking of the night she changed the bandage under his chin. It seemed as if a lifetime had passed.

She kissed him lightly on the cheek, then sat back in the chair, tucking one leg under herself. "You get some sleep. I'll be right here."

She looked beautiful despite what she'd been through. He watched her and the silence passed between them without awkwardness, the sign he'd relied upon. The sign that had held his interest. It made the pain that much worse.

He was already feeling the early effects of the injection. His concentration started to wander as he watched her leaf through a magazine. She looked so calm, so relieved. He could keep it to himself, and no one would ever know. Most of him wanted it that way. "Were you ever going to tell me?"

She closed the magazine. "Tell you what?"

"It was the way you had your arm around Ed."

"We've become pretty good friends through all this."

"That time you asked me out to Richardson's gala. In your office . . ."

"Yeah. You were really upset. I almost chickened out."

"There's a picture of you and this guy. You had your arms around each other just like you and Ed did a minute ago."

"Jack, you're tired. Get some rest and we can talk about it tomorrow."

"That nurse, Geneva Lott. She said this one thing that's been nagging me. She told me they got my father reassigned one morning so he wouldn't be there when they brought Ed in a second time to give more blood."

Elaine unfolded her legs. "Jack—"

"The thing is, how did they get Ed down there if my father didn't bring him?"

"I don't know. Richardson has lots of people—"

"Yes, you do. You know, because you brought him."

"You're talking nonsense. Lie back. I'll get the nurse to—"

"I know he looked different with all those tubes and the swelling, but the jaundiced guy in the bed next to Ed . . . he's the same one in the picture you have in your office."

"Jack—"

"They didn't kidnap you at all. You were there to keep Ed calm. And I guess I'm just now realizing that you were there from the very beginning. You helped me get that job, you slept with me, you did whatever it took to keep me in town so Ed would be here."

She sat motionless, seemingly unable to answer.

"Who is he?"

She shook her head slightly, as if she were talking to herself.

"You owe me that, at least."

She finally looked up. There were silent tears down both cheeks. "Richardson's son."

Jack could hardly look at her. "You and Richardson." His mind reeled. He felt like a fool. "All those ex-cons who came through your program. Street people, most with no real name. Nobody would miss them. . . . Did you serve up a few? Richardson got some guinea pigs to help his boy, you got more funding. Nice deal."

"No one in my program took part in this."

"What else did Richardson give you? House in Martinique? A retirement account? A little free time in his bed?"

Her face snapped back. She looked distant and defeated, as if she'd been the only survivor of the most incomprehensible horror. "He's my brother."

"Richardson's son?"

She looked down again. "Yes."

He felt as if he'd been sliced by glass shards. He hated the injection, and wanted more at the same time. Enough to kill the pain forever. He turned his head away.

"I hadn't seen my father in years. He left us with nothing when I was too young to remember him, and I hated him for it. It was long before he made his money, but it didn't make any difference even when he hit the big time. After he left, my mother had little to offer an employer. She cleaned houses, worked at convenience stores. George and I worked after school. She took back her maiden name, the one we grew up with. She drank herself to death."

Jack looked back at her, aware that the medication was slowing his mind, if not his anger. "You expect me to feel sorry? You think this explains things?"

Her face grew taut. "What wouldn't you do to help Ed?"

"You work in a *church*. You went there to set those people up."

"No." There was a flash of anger in her eyes. "I worked there because that's what I do. That's who I am. I was there long before Richardson approached me."

"Maybe you should just quit now. I don't believe anything you've got to say."

"My brother may not be a saint, but he's what I held on to growing up. We survived only because we had each other. You're not the only one in the world who loves his brother just because he's all you've got."

Jack felt the sting of her comment, and just looked at her, wondering how many people she could change into when it suited her.

"My brother is an alcoholic. He's got cirrhosis, bleeding ulcers, bad kidneys. He's dying. He went to Richardson after he got turned down for a liver transplant. My father tracked me down, and had me tested as a possible organ donor."

"But it didn't work."

"I wasn't a good match."

"So you sent them some ex-cons from your little mission."

"No. Not one."

Jack could feel the sedation creeping over him. "But you sent them Ed."

"No, it wasn't like that."

Jack thought back to how the occupational therapist at the hospital had recommended that Ed work at the soup kitchen. He couldn't think of any connection between Richardson and the advice they'd been given, but how could he be sure?

"I worked with Ed like I worked with many others. And I didn't turn him over to my father."

"Then who did?"

Her eyes swelled with tears, but she didn't say a word. She just watched until it seemed that he knew the answer himself. Geneva Lott had told him as much. His own father had pulled Ed into it. "But you brought Ed that time they diverted my father. You knew what you were doing."

"They told me they just needed his blood. Nothing more. It was to help my brother. What could that hurt?"

"Just how many people's death were you willing to accept?"

"It wasn't supposed to be like that. . . . It's not what they told me would happen. . . ."

"You lied to me."

"I tried to make you quit. The morning after we made love . . . I tried to make you mad enough to leave. But you came back anyway. And then I didn't want you to leave anymore."

Jack looked away a moment, then looked back as he struggled to get the words out—words he never dreamed he'd have to say, but words that had to be said. "You've got two hours. Tell Tarkington about your involvement, or I'll tell him myself. Maybe they'll go easier on you if you turn yourself in."

"Jack . . ."

He looked away from her. From her eyes. He couldn't bear to see them cause him any more pain. The list of people who'd been killed ran through his mind. "Two hours."

The view out his window of the interstate began to blur as the pain shot took effect. Sunlight flicked off the cars that sped by, moving faster and faster, the drivers speeding headlong without any way to tell if the one in front would make a bad move that could change their lives forever.

Tears came to his eyes as he heard her close the door.

THIRTY-THREE

Jack watched a seagull dive into the Gulf of Mexico from high in the air, then come up with a fish in its talons. Sheets of red and orange spread in the western sky as the sun began the descent that would be complete in another thirty minutes. He finished the rest of his Corona.

Ed ran past him. "Telephone's for you. I'm going to look for shells."

His brother was on the beach before Jack could say anything. He eased himself out of the cedar Adirondack chair that he had positioned for a perfect view of the sunset. He was still recuperating after his operation—the pain had eased up and his frequent coughing had finally stopped.

The place he'd rented had two bedrooms and a screened-in porch that ran the length of the house, facing the gulf. It was probably built in the early fifties, with no dishwasher, no microwave, and no high-rise next door. As far as he could see, there was nothing except single-family homes on this stretch of the Louisiana coast. The only restaurant was a bar, and there wasn't enough action around here for high school or college kids. It provided a rare taste of solitude, which was just what he needed.

Ed's cat rubbed against his legs as he picked up the portable phone in the kitchen. "Hello."

"How's your lung?" Dan had called every few days since they'd left Atlanta three weeks ago.

"I've been drinking some Mexican painkillers."

"I got some news today."

Jack took the phone out on the porch. "Good or bad?"

"Tarkington wanted you to know that Richardson's security man had a change of heart. This isn't for public consumption yet, but Mason made a plea bargain and testified before a grand jury today about Voss's and Richardson's activities. I don't know how to say this easily, but the guy confirmed that Voss shot your father."

Jack took a breath and let his eyes follow the seagulls as they searched the shallow waves for food. "I guess I ought to feel good. But I don't."

"I know what you mean. I've been putting off this call for two hours, but I knew you'd want to know. And get this—Mason implicated the medical examiner's office. He said that Edelman took money to falsify autopsies on the prisoners who had died in their experiments."

"Is he still working?"

"They picked him up this afternoon. Right from his office, in front of everybody."

"That explains the problems with my father's report."

"I'll be sure that Tarkington knows about that."

"I hired an attorney. My father's life insurance policy wouldn't pay the claim because the police had labeled it a suicide, but that's changed now. It's not a lot of money, but it will keep us going long enough for me to sort things out and decide where I'm going to end up."

"You're not coming back to Atlanta?"

"I honestly don't know what I'm going to do. My mind is sorta scrambled. I've got Mom in a treatment facility about an hour from here. The counselors seem good, and she's so much more at ease there, but I don't know if she'll ever be able to cope on her own."

"There are plenty of good facilities here."

"I know, but she likes Louisiana. Plus, the last few weeks haven't done much for my job prospects in the Atlanta area."

"The news people are going to have a field day when Mason's testimony is made public. They've already labeled you the hero in all this."

"Yeah, but doctors in private practice can be funny about people who get in the news a lot. I can work in a local ER for now; in fact, I start next week. Things will have to die down before I can get the kind of job I want."

"The chief of medicine would write you a recommendation that would have people knocking at your door."

He thought about his residency picture that had somehow made its way into the newspaper. "They owe me one, that's for sure."

"We all do, Jack."

A moment passed; then he asked, "What about Richardson?"

"The FBI is involved, but Tarkington said they don't have any leads. He had a lot of his money in offshore accounts."

Jack saw a shrimp boat trolling about a half mile offshore with its outriggers deployed. "Any new word on Elaine?"

Dan didn't answer right away. "She's still in jail. The DA convinced the judge that Richardson had enough money to make bail meaningless, and since there's still no sign of her father, she's considered a high flight risk."

Jack was thinking about Elaine, and found it hard to concentrate. "Listen, the offer still stands. We've got a pullout sofa with your name on it."

"I may take you up on it for a long weekend if I can get my schedule worked out."

"Thanks for calling. I know it wasn't easy."

He put down the phone and took his binoculars with him to the beach. The sky had an aliveness about it that you couldn't capture on canvas. Far to the west the sunlight reflected off the beach in a silver spray, but where he stood the breeze had begun to cool and the colors around him had a polarized tint that made blues and greens deeper than at any other time of day. But it, like so many things in his life, was somehow distant. Too distant to feel.

The only thing he knew for sure was that he was alone. The news about his father had settled something deep inside, but the whole ordeal had left him with new pain. Deeper pain. And a sense of emptiness that he couldn't express.

Over the last few days he'd become aware of how he'd changed. All his life he'd swept conflict and loss into a neat package to be buried so deep he didn't have to deal with it. But Elaine had opened him. Now her loss was raw, and he couldn't put it away.

In that moment he became aware that it would take some time before he'd return to Atlanta. He'd lived there nearly eight years, but the only memories of that city that mattered right now were of her.

He looked across the water with his binoculars and could just barely pick out three oil derricks several miles away. They weren't the ones he'd worked on, but it didn't matter. Despite all that had happened, they still had a hold on him.

He draped the binoculars around his neck. Ed came up with a handful of shells, and went to wash them with the hose.

Jack stared south, southeast, wondering if Richardson was on one of those tiny islands in the Caribbean. He'd heard that drug smugglers dodged the police for years, running from one isolated island to the next. With his money, there was no telling what kind of privacy he could buy.

He raised the binoculars again and saw the distant image of a yacht moving deeper into the gulf. The longer he looked, the more he wished that he had let Elaine go. She could have been on that very boat. He watched until the white reflection grew faint. In his mind he imagined, as he'd done for several nights, that she was looking back, and that she would miss him.